The Best
AMERICAN SHORT STORIES 2013

GUEST EDITORS OF
THE BEST AMERICAN SHORT STORIES

1978 TED SOLOTAROFF
1979 JOYCE CAROL OATES
1980 STANLEY ELKIN
1981 HORTENSE CALISHER
1982 JOHN GARDNER
1983 ANNE TYLER
1984 JOHN UPDIKE
1985 GAIL GODWIN
1986 RAYMOND CARVER
1987 ANN BEATTIE
1988 MARK HELPRIN
1989 MARGARET ATWOOD
1990 RICHARD FORD
1991 ALICE ADAMS
1992 ROBERT STONE
1993 LOUISE ERDRICH
1994 TOBIAS WOLFF
1995 JANE SMILEY
1996 JOHN EDGAR WIDEMAN
1997 E. ANNIE PROULX
1998 GARRISON KEILLOR
1999 AMY TAN
2000 E. L. DOCTOROW
2001 BARBARA KINGSOLVER
2002 SUE MILLER
2003 WALTER MOSLEY
2004 LORRIE MOORE
2005 MICHAEL CHABON
2006 ANN PATCHETT
2007 STEPHEN KING
2008 SALMAN RUSHDIE
2009 ALICE SEBOLD
2010 RICHARD RUSSO
2011 GERALDINE BROOKS
2012 TOM PERROTTA
2013 ELIZABETH STROUT

The Best AMERICAN SHORT STORIES® 2013

Selected from
U.S. and Canadian Magazines
by Elizabeth Strout
with Heidi Pitlor

With an Introduction by Elizabeth Strout

MARINER BOOKS
HOUGHTON MIFFLIN HARCOURT
BOSTON • NEW YORK 2013

www.hmhbooks.com

ISSN 0067-6233
ISBN 978-0-547-55482-2
ISBN 978-0-547-55483-9 (pbk.)

Printed in the United States of America
DOC 10 9 8 7 6 5 4 3 2 1

Contents

Foreword

OCCASIONALLY SOMETHING HORRIFIC transpires—and in what seems like a minute, this something changes us. It changes us as sentient beings with souls and minds. It changes us as parents and siblings and children, as travelers and citizens and individuals. Certainly as artists and readers, certainly as writers.

After 9/11, writers wondered how or even if it was possible to understand the events that occurred. How and what and why to write now? What to read? Little seemed relevant or urgent enough. Were we as Americans anywhere near as savvy or admired as we had thought? One of our toughest, bravest, proudest cities was revealed to be susceptible. Even baldly vulnerable.

To me, the mass shooting at Sandy Hook Elementary School on December 14, 2012, in Newtown, Connecticut, was similar to 9/11 in its ability to demolish a country's posture, not to mention its values and even aesthetics. As the news broke that day, disbelief rippled throughout the country and the world. No, we thought. Many of us glanced at each other, wondering whether this or that person was thinking the same thing: This cannot be right. THIS cannot have happened. This, here. And then, as confirmations came of all that had occurred in that school, a collective shudder and the impulse to turn away, perhaps inward, to regain our breath. To hold our children and our parents for dear life. And later, the impulse to assign blame (to graft meaning onto the meaningless)—to blame gun makers, the country's health-care system for abandoning its mentally ill, politicians, a culture that glamorizes violence, video games that do the same, and the media for shining its spotlight on mass killers.

Again, the human capacity for violence has proven to be greater than we previously thought. Again, a dark cloud has settled over our country.

This unthinkable event, the sixteenth mass shooting of 2012, occurred toward the end of my reading cycle, just in time for me to freeze up each time I read a story featuring groups of children in harm's way or gun violence or, heaven forbid, a school shooting. Pity the writers who may have still been trying to comprehend the shooting at Columbine High School. This was not the time to publish a short story about such matters.

A few months later, I write this with a still-jumpy heart. The reality and possibility of mass shootings have come to occupy my thoughts many times daily. When I walk my twin children into their kindergarten classrooms in their small elementary school. When I return to their school in order to drop off forgotten sneakers, when I stand beneath the camera that is now mounted beside the school entry in order to identify myself. When I go to any large, enclosed, crowded space. Malls, movie theaters—or not even large spaces. The subway, the train, any place where strangers find themselves in close proximity. There is a heavy stone in my chest during these moments that was not there before the shooting at Newtown.

I am enormously lucky—I have never witnessed or known anyone who was killed in a mass shooting. I do not and have never lived anywhere near where such a thing took place. I can only imagine how different every inch of the world looks to those who did lose a loved one.

In 1946, my predecessor, Martha Foley, wrote, "It is a literary truism that there must be a period of distillation before the real impact of some tremendous event, either historical or personal, can emerge in writing." Now, due to the speed with which we receive our news and the graphic nature of its delivery, I think that the actual distillation time has shrunk, although I'm not certain that this yields writing as rich in perspective or depth of emotion. Before now, the strongest and most timeless stories about a transformative event had been written after a good amount of time elapsed. Now, writers' frequent use of the present tense combined with our widespread exposure to up-to-the-minute news has led to a rise in stories and novels that trace the microscopic jigs and jags of grief itself. In other words, while we are grieving, we are now writing.

We may be sacrificing perspective or depth, but this does not necessarily amount to lesser writing. If anything, there is a new sort of immediacy, a newfound intimacy and urgency in our fiction these days. Witness, in the following pages, Karl Taro Greenfeld's story of one man's clumsy grappling with being let go from his job. Or David Means or Steven Millhauser as they tunnel so deep inside their characters' fears and hopes that at least this reader was rendered nearly breathless. For evidence of technology's increasing impact, see Elizabeth Tallent's magnificent "The Wilderness," which scrolls before us as if on a computer screen.

As I read in 2013, I will listen for a slightly faster heartbeat, one closer to our schools and children, one differently attuned to crowds and violence. And in years beyond, I hope to find a glimmer of meaning and the salve of perspective in some wise story about one of our saddest days.

Elizabeth Strout was a wonderful reader, an author who knows well that the sound of one's writing is just as important as and indivisible from the content. Some years I work closely with guest editors as they read and hone their list. Other years, they prefer to read and select privately. Elizabeth was the latter sort, and delivered to me a terrifically diverse, interesting, and impressive table of contents. There was a bit of back-and-forth, but very little was needed in the end. Here are twenty compellingly told, powerfully felt stories about urgent matters with profound consequences.

The stories chosen for this anthology were originally published between January 2012 and January 2013. The qualifications for selection are (1) original publication in nationally distributed American or Canadian periodicals; (2) publication in English by writers who are American or Canadian, or who have made the United States their home; and (3) original publication as short stories (excerpts of novels are not knowingly considered). A list of magazines consulted for this volume appears at the back of the book. Editors who wish for their short fiction to be considered for next year's edition should send their publication or hard copies of online publications to Heidi Pitlor, Houghton Mifflin Harcourt, 222 Berkeley Street, Boston, Massachusetts 02116.

HEIDI PITLOR

Introduction

THERE WAS A TIME when a telephone was something that hung on the wall or sat on a table, and when it rang you had no idea who was calling. "Hello?" People had different ways of saying this, of course. Those expecting disaster (my grandmother) would say the word with quiet dread. Those who wanted to appear friendly (my mother) would say it with perkiness: "*Hel*-lo!" Or a self-conscious adolescent might mumble "Hullo?" It was a question, more than a greeting. Before answering machines and caller ID, that word asked, *Who's there? What are you calling about? What is it you have to tell me?* Rarely was one more attuned to the sound of voice than in the moment before the answer. Whoever had telephoned had done so for a reason: to deliver bad news or good, to report something overheard in the grocery store, to spread gossip or stop it, or to express concerns about the world. One anticipated the *tone* of the voice as much as the words.

A reader is in the position of saying hello. Tentatively, enthusiastically, or even with trepidation, the reader approaches a piece of writing with the unspoken question *What do you have to say?* And the writer answers, *This. I have this to say, and I want you to listen to my voice, to the tone of my voice, because that will tell you what I have to say.* In fact, in the first story of this collection, the narrator, an out-of-work actor, observes, "I should be clear about something: it is never the words, but how they are spoken that matters."

Quite naturally, we choose to listen to certain voices based on personal taste. And these days, as we glance at our ringing phone, we can make a decision: *No, I don't feel like talking to her right now, she goes on about herself and thinks every detail matters and who cares what her loser of a husband said last night.* Turning away from a solipsistic, unedited voice. Or we think, *Oh, it's him, yay, I always want to listen to him.* "Hello?" we say, with anticipation, because this guy knows when to spring the surprise, how to make us feel that what he says is confidential and important. His voice pulls us toward him. He lets us in.

So if you wonder why I chose the stories I chose, I would say it had a great deal to do with voice. That sound—if it is working well—has authority, probably the most important dimension of voice. We really hope the writer knows what he or she is doing. And we really hope that this sense of authority will be sustained throughout. We look for this the same way we look for authoritative competence in any other trade. We don't want to be lying on a dentist's chair with a wide-open mouth and hear the dentist say, "Oh, *hell.*" We don't want a plumber to gaze at a broken pipe that has flooded the floor and mutter, "Huh, I don't know." And we don't want a writer whose voice wobbles or becomes false. I don't think readers think about this analytically, but instead, they experience it as a feeling about the writer that grows stronger as they read: *I want to be in your company, I want to keep going, I like the way you sound.*

This authoritative voice will differ from one writer to the next, which is how it should be; the writers are different people, and each has a singular way of putting words together, developed in a particular culture, place, and time. The authority that Alice Munro brings to the page has a very different sound than that of George Saunders, which is entirely distinct from the sound of Junot Díaz.

I remember sitting a number of years ago in a diner in a small town in Maine with my mother, my small daughter, and her father, the latter two raised near New York City. In the next booth two middle-aged local women, short-haired and wearing flannel shirts, were speaking in the flat unexpressive tones familiar to me; I had grown up in northern New England among such voices. One woman said to the other laconically, as if telling of a leaky faucet, "Yuh. Well, she killed her husband, didn't she?" And the other woman responded, "Ay-yuh, she did. Shot herself a month later." And they nodded matter-of-factly.

What is notable to me in these voices is the sense of place and culture. What struck my child and her father as surprising—the utter lack of expression—was not surprising to me. Very big news was swapped in very few words. In terms of storytelling technique, much was left to the listener. Had the same story been told in a different part of the country by members of a more outwardly expressive culture, we might have heard all sorts of details exchanged in urgent tones. Through a change in voice, the same story would have been a different story.

In this way, the sound of the story intuitively and naturally merges with what is being said. Listen, for example, to the breathless voice of the narrator in David Means's "The Chair," as his anxiety in watching over his young son unfolds. Or observe how Steven Millhauser's "A Voice in the Night" is exactly that: the almost run-on language and razor-sharp memories that arise when a person lies alone in the hours of darkness—waiting. In "The Provincials," Daniel Alarcón, writing from the point of view of an actor, suddenly switches from prose and presents the spoken words of characters in the form of a script. At that moment in the story the narrator feels as if he is in a scene from a play, and Alarcón writes it as such, which heightens the moment—literally—in a dramatic way.

I did not choose a story primarily based on its subject. This doesn't mean that I paid no attention to subject, but rather that subject matter is part and parcel with voice, and if that doesn't work, the subject is irrelevant. Yet despite this, when we finish a story, it is most often the subject that we remember, or think we remember, and this is the thrill of reading good writing. We are moved by a lingering image or emotion, we can't get the "story" out of our mind. But it has been conveyed to us through sound; it is the sound we trust, the sound that brings us the subject.

Nonetheless, the subjects that are developed in this collection are wonderful, varied, and full of surprises, because good storytellers know how to surprise. The surprise can seem tiny: perhaps a quiet realization, such as the one that comes at the end of Michael Byers's story, "Malaria," or a sudden oddity that feels strikingly believable, as when a madwoman in Prague tells a young bride her future in Charles Baxter's "Bravery." These surprises satisfy readers ("Oh, I didn't expect that!") but work only if the entire piece maintains its authority. This means that the writer makes and keeps this unspoken promise to the reader, *Go ahead and trust me. Whatever surprise I deliver will not be gratuitous, I won't lie to you, and*

I won't show off. I'll tell you something you'll be glad to know; even if it is something painful or discomfiting, you can still trust me. And readers, I think, want to trust. Or at least this desire, this almost childlike attitude, is in the ascendancy. It's a tricky thing to speak of honest writing, but part of us knows it when we hear it, and often when a reader loses interest in a story, and so sets it down, it is because the writer did not sustain authority—honest sentences being a big part of that—and in some fundamental way the reader stops believing. What seems a loss of interest is in fact a failure of trust, of shared intimacy.

Jim Shepard's "The World to Come" is so exquisitely intimate that we feel almost as if we have trespassed upon the purity of a woman whose voice reveals the deep loneliness of upstate New York farming life more than a century ago. It doesn't matter that we don't live that way, or didn't live back then, any more than it matters that we are not made to wear a scarlet letter these days. The story still *takes* us away, brings us to a time and place in which women were isolated by their losses while their husbands worked the unrelenting land.

Isolation, just like storytelling, comes in many forms. In Lorrie Moore's "Referential," set in contemporary times, a mother is kept to a limited life because of loyalty to a son who is ill. The story holds no note of complaint or judgment: life is what it is, people endure what they can, and they turn away from what they can't. In the best stories that sense comes through: it is what it is. The writer brings the news from his or her corner of imagined experience.

So what news is included in these pages? Our excessive worry about status, aging parents who require care, trips to A.A. meetings, job losses and mortgage crises, divorce and its upheaval for the kids, the arrival of computers and cell phones in the classroom, the distance between generations, and between the city and those left behind. Spelled out like this—nothing but thin subject matter—the richness of experience and voice is lost, which is to say the experience of reading the story is lost. Antonya Nelson's "Chapter Two" gives us the A.A. meeting and the variety of ways to tell a story there, as well as the drink had after it and the life lived before it; the naked woman at the door is heartbreakingly believable, and the first-person narrator knows enough to step to the side and let that character make her final bow. In "The Semplica-Girl Diaries," George Saunders, in his inimitable voice, shows us poignantly and satirically the lengths we go to make our children happy, even if it means buying immigrant girls to decorate our front lawns. Junot Díaz leaves us with the image of Miss Lora in her red dress, so real that I expect to bump into her when I walk down the sidewalk. Joan Wickersham's "The Tunnel, or The News from Spain" sets out the irony and confusion that arise when an ill and aging mother simply will not die.

Arguably, authorial voice is more important in a short story than in a longer piece of fiction. The ride is quicker, the reader must be engaged right away, and less space is available to absorb patches of soggy writing or gratuitous detail. Where I came from in northern New England, talking too much was considered incontinent, and respect for a person might lessen considerably if he or she was disposed to chatter. I remember how family members agreed that "Uncle Norris talks just to hear the sound of his own voice." As a result, no one listened to him; I myself cannot remember anything he said, though I recall the thin drone of his voice. In my childhood those who had the power of voice managed it with good timing and economy of detail, just like those two women in the diner. They did not find it necessary to say how the woman had killed her husband, why or where she shot herself, or whether she left children behind. The writer chooses details in accord with the narrative voice most fit to tell the story, sensing how much is needed and what might need to be cut.

In Bret Anthony Johnston's "Encounters with Strange Animals," the details are compact and sharply precise. In only a few pages he delivers the dilemma of a father losing his illusion of control. In "Nemecia," by Kirstin Valdez Quade, the narrator is a Hispanic woman looking back on her life as a young girl, and the child's puzzlement is conveyed through carefully chosen, telling details that bring the reader into that experience.

Just as voice and subject are not separate entities, form does not stand on its own either. Like subject and voice, it is closely tied to a particular historical time and place, and is, necessarily and naturally, always changing—especially now. Certainly for many decades, the American short story typically involved one incident, one narrator, and one point of view. This is no longer true. As our vision becomes more global, our storytelling is stretching in many ways. Stories increasingly change point of view, switch location, and sometimes pack in as much material as a short novel might.

Today stories are being written in the midst of an enormous upheaval in the way we communicate and transfer and receive information. Think of this: the agricultural revolution took three thousand years to unfold, the industrial revolution three hundred. These were slowly unfolding developments compared to what we experience now. People alive today have gone through more changes more quickly than at any other time in history. What is to be made of this? I think we don't know. But we do recognize that the wide world is not as "foreign" as it once was. Faraway places appear in our hands as we hold our cell phones, international crises are texted within seconds, and classes and conferences and family conversations are Skyped across the globe. The American experience is broadening, and so are its stories. They touch down in Boston, South Africa, Peru, and Canada, but even more than variety of location, the spectrum of voices is the strongest indicator of change.

Yet a few stories in this collection look back in time. For an early-twentieth-century character in "Nemecia," a move from New Mexico to California feels as changeful as a move to a different continent might today. Alice Munro's "Train" begins right after a young man returns from World War II, and his transition, years later, from a rural life to the city of Toronto is written with such clarity, we feel this "modern" world crash into us too. But it is "The Wilderness" by Elizabeth Tallent that brings us to where we live right now, with machines—or information devices—occupying us a great deal of the time. And though they threaten to increase our sense of isolation, they likewise offer the hope—whether false or not—of connection; the story heartbreakingly whispers the word *me,* as though it is the self we may be losing.

But it is the self we are always looking for, or always trying to escape, and fiction provides us with both options; they are wrapped together, these flights to and from who we are. We read because we are looking to see what others are thinking, feeling, seeing; how they are acting out their frustrations, their happiness, their addictions; we see what we can learn. How do people manage marriage and loss and illness and sex and parenting? How do they do all this? Often, the emotions that fill our inner lives are too large to make sense of; chaos and irrationality jump around inside us. To enter the form of a story is to calm down, or excite ourselves, within a controlled space.

In a world where telephone calls are made less and less frequently, where a tweet makes e-mail seem a little antiquated, we have more information, yet fewer voices. These changes, I suspect, make us desire the sound of a true voice even more. And we still want that news from the front. Not just the war front, or the economic front, or the navel-gazing front. We want the news that is kept secret, the unsayable things that occur in the dark crevices of the mind on a night when insomnia visits. We want to know, I think, what it is like to be another person, because somehow this helps us position our own self in the world. What are we without this curiosity? Who in the world, and where in the world, and what in the world might we be? So we pay attention to that inner demand, the pressure of that question. Hello? Please—tell me.

ELIZABETH STROUT

The Best AMERICAN SHORT STORIES 2013

DANIEL ALARCÓN

The Provincials

FROM *Granta*

I'D BEEN OUT of the conservatory for about a year when my great-uncle Raúl died. We missed the funeral, but my father asked me to drive down the coast with him a few days later, to attend to some of the postmortem details. The house had to be closed up, signed over to a cousin. There were a few boxes to sift through as well, but no inheritance or anything like that.

I was working at the copy shop in the Old City, trying out for various plays, but my life was such that it wasn't hard to drop everything and go. Rocío wanted to come along, but I thought it'd be nice for me and my old man to travel together. We hadn't done that in a while. We left the following morning, a Thursday. A few hours south of the capital, the painted slums thinned, and our conversation did too, and we took in the desolate landscape with appreciative silence. Everything was dry: the silt-covered road, the dirty white sand dunes, somehow even the ocean. Every few kilometers there rose out of this moonscape a billboard for soda or beer or suntan lotion, its colors faded since the previous summer, edges unglued and flapping in the wind. This was years ago, before the beaches were transformed into private residences for the wealthy, before the ocean was fenced off and the highway pushed back, away from the land's edge. Back then, the coast survived in a state of neglect, and one might pass the occasional fishing village, or a filling station, or a rusting pyramid of oil drums stacked by the side of the road; a hitchhiker, perhaps a laborer, or a woman and her child strolling along the highway with no clear destination. But mostly you passed nothing at all. The monotonous landscape gave you a sense of peace, all the more because it came so soon after the city had ended.

We stopped for lunch at a beach town four hours south of the capital, just a few dozen houses built on either side of the highway, with a single restaurant serving only fried fish and soda. There was nothing remarkable about the place, except that after lunch we happened upon the last act of a public feud; two local men, who might've been brothers or cousins or best of friends, stood outside the restaurant, hands balled in tight fists, shouting at each other in front of a tipped-over moto-taxi. Its front wheel spun slowly but did not stop. It was like a perpetual-motion machine. The passenger cage was covered with heavy orange plastic, and painted on the side was the word *Joselito.*

And I wondered: which of these two men is Joselito?

The name could've fit either of them. The more aggressive of the pair was short and squat, his face rigid with fury. His reddish eyes had narrowed to tiny slits. He threw wild punches and wasted vast amounts of energy, moving like a spinning top around his antagonist. His rival, both taller and wider, started off with a look of bemused wonder, almost embarrassment, but the longer the little one kept at it, the more his expression darkened, so that within minutes they and their moods were equally matched.

A boy of about eighteen stood next to me and my father. With crossed arms, he observed the proceedings as if it were a horse race on which he'd wagered a very small sum. He wore no shoes, and his feet were dusted with sand. Though it wasn't particularly warm, he'd been swimming. I ventured a question.

"Which one is Joselito?" I asked.

He looked at me like I was crazy. "Don't you know?" he said in a low voice. "Joselito's dead."

I nodded, as if I'd known, as if I'd been testing him, but by then the name of the dead man was buzzing around the gathered circle of spectators, whispered from one man to the next, to a child then to his mother: *Joselito, Joselito.*

A chanting; a conjuring.

The two rivals continued, more furiously now, as if the mention of the dead man had animated them, or freed some brutal impulse within them. The smaller one landed a right hook to the bigger man's jaw, and this man staggered but did not fall. The crowd *ooh*ed and *aah*ed, and it was only then that the two fighters realized they were being watched. I mean, they'd known it all along, of course they must have, but when the crowd reached a certain mass, the whispering a certain volume, then everything changed. It could not have been more staged if they'd been fighting in an amphitheater, with an orchestra playing behind them. It was something I'd been working out myself, in my own craft: how the audience affects a performance, how differently we behave when we know we are being watched. True authenticity, I'd decided, required an absolute, nearly spiritual denial of the audience, or even of the possibility of being watched; but here, something true, something real, had quickly morphed into something fake. It happened instantaneously, on a sandy street in this anonymous town: we were no longer accidental observers of an argument, but the primary reason for its existence.

"This is for Joselito!" the little man shouted.

"No! *This* is for Joselito!" responded the other.

And so on.

Soon blood was drawn, lips swollen, eyes blackened. And still the wheel spun. My father and I watched with rising anxiety—someone might die! Why won't that wheel stop?—until, to our relief, a town elder rushed through the crowd and pushed the two men apart. He was frantic. He stood between them, arms spread like wings, a flat palm pressed to each man's chest as they leaned steadily into him.

This too was part of the act.

"Joselito's father," said the barefoot young man. "Just in time."

We left and drove south for another hour before coming to a stretch of luxurious new asphalt, so smooth it felt like the car might be able to pilot itself. The tension washed away, and we were happy again, until we found ourselves trapped amid the thickening swarm of trucks headed to the border. We saw northbound traffic being inspected, drivers being shaken down, small-time smugglers dispossessed of their belongings. The soldiers were adolescent and smug. Everyone paid. We would too, when it was our turn to head back to the city. This was all new, my father said, and he gripped the wheel tightly and watched with mounting concern. Or was it anger? This corruption, the only kind of commerce that had thrived during the war, was also the only kind we could always count on. Why he found it so disconcerting, I couldn't figure. Nothing could have been more ordinary.

By nightfall we'd made it to my father's hometown. My great-uncle's old filling station stood at the top of the hill, under new ownership and doing brisk business now, though the truckers rarely ventured into the town proper. We eased the car onto the main street, a palm-lined boulevard that sloped down to the boardwalk, and left it a few blocks from the sea, walking until we reached the simple public square that overlooked the ocean. A larger palm tree, its trunk inscribed with the names and dates of young love, stood in the middle of this inelegant plaza. Every summer, the tree was optimistically engraved with new names and new dates, and then stood for the entire winter, untouched. I'd probably scratched a few names there myself, years before. On warm nights, when the town filled with families on vacation, the children brought out remote-control cars and guided these droning machines around the plaza, ramming them into each other or into the legs of adults, occasionally tipping them off the edge of the boardwalk and onto the beach below, and celebrating these calamities with cheerful hysteria.

My brother Francisco and I had spent entire summers like this, until the year he'd left for the U.S. These were some of my favorite memories.

But in the off-season, there was no sign of these young families. No children. They'd all gone north, back to the city or further, so of course, the arrival of one of the town's wandering sons was both unexpected and welcome. My father and I moved through the plaza like rock stars, stopping at every bench to pay our respects, and from each of these aged men and women I heard the same thing. First: brief, rote condolences on the death of Raúl (it seemed no one much cared for him); then, a smooth transition to the town's most cherished topic of discussion, the past. The talk was directed at me: *Your old man was so smart, so brilliant . . .*

My father nodded, politely accepting every compliment, not the least bit embarrassed by the attention. He'd carried the town's expectations on his shoulders for so many years, they no longer weighed on him. I'd heard these stories all my life.

"This is my son," he'd say. "You remember Nelson?"

And one by one the old folks asked when I had come back from the United States.

"No, no," I said. "I'm the other son."

Of course they got us confused, or perhaps simply forgot I existed. Their response, offered gently, hopefully: "Oh, yes, the *other* son." Then, leaning forward: "So, when will you be leaving?"

It was late summer, but the vacation season had come to an early close, and already the weather had cooled. In the distance, you could hear the hum of trucks passing along the highway. The bent men and stooped women wore light jackets and shawls and seemed not to notice the sound. It was as if they'd all taken the same cocktail of sedatives, content to cast their eyes toward the sea, the dark night, and stay this way for hours. Now they wanted to know when I'd be leaving.

I wanted to know too.

"Soon," I said.

"Soon," my father repeated.

Even then I had my doubts, but I would keep believing this for another year or so.

"Wonderful," responded the town. "Just great."

My father and I settled in for the night at my great-uncle's house. It had that stuffiness typical of shuttered spaces, of old people who live alone, made more acute by the damp ocean air. The spongy foam mattresses sagged and there were yellowing photographs everywhere—in dust-covered frames, in unruly stacks, or poking out of the books that lined the shelves of the living room. My father grabbed a handful and took them to the kitchen. He set the water to boil, flipping idly through the photographs and calling out names of the relatives in each picture as he passed them along. There was a flatness to his voice, a distance—as if he were testing his recall, as opposed to reliving any cherished childhood memory. You got the sense he barely knew these people.

He handed me a small black-and-white image with a matt finish, printed on heavy card stock with scalloped edges. It was a group shot taken in front of this very house, back when it was surrounded by fallow land, the bare, undeveloped hillside. Perhaps twenty blurred faces.

"Besides a few of the babies," my father said, "everyone else in this photo is dead."

For a while we didn't speak.

A bloom of mold grew wild on the kitchen wall, bursting black and menacing from a crack in the cement. To pass the time, or change the subject, we considered the mold's shape, evocative of something, but we couldn't say what. A baby carriage? A bull?

"Joselito's moto-taxi," my father said.

And this was, in fact, exactly what it resembled.

"May he rest in peace," I added.

My father had been quiet for most of the trip—coming home always did this to him—but he spoke up now. Joselito, he said, must have been a real character. Someone special. He hadn't seen an outpouring of emotion like that in many years, not since he was a boy.

"It was an act," I said, and began to explain my theory.

My old man interrupted me. "But what isn't?"

What he meant was that people perform sorrow for a reason. For example: no one was performing it for Raúl. My great-uncle had been mayor of this town when my father was a boy, had owned the filling station, and sired seven children with five different women, none of whom he bothered to marry. He'd run the town's only radio station for a decade and paid from his own pocket to pave the main boulevard, so he could drive in style. Then in the late 1980s, Raúl lost most of his money and settled into a bitter seclusion. I remembered him only for his bulbous nose and his hatred of foreigners, an expansive category in which he placed anyone who wasn't originally from the town and its surrounding areas. Raúl's distrust of the capital was absolute. I was eleven the last time I saw him, and I don't think he ever eyed me with anything but suspicion.

It was easier to talk about Joselito than about my great-uncle. More pleasant, perhaps. This town brought up bad memories for my father, who was, in those days, entering a pensive late middle age. That was how it seemed to me at the time, but what does a twenty-two-year-old know about a grown man's life and worries? I was too young to recognize what would later seem more than obvious: that I was the greatest source of my old man's concern. That if he were growing old too soon, I was at least partly to blame. This would've been clear, had I been paying attention.

My father shifted the conversation. He brought the tea out and asked me what I planned to do when I got to California. This was typical of the time, a speculative game we were fond of playing. We assumed it was fast approaching, the date of my departure; later, I would think we'd all been pretending.

"I don't know," I said.

I'd spent so much time imagining it—my leaving, my preparations, my victory lap around the city, saying goodbye and good luck to all those who'd be staying behind—but what came after contained few specifics. I'd get off the plane, and then . . . Francisco, I guess, would be there. He'd drive me across the Bay Bridge to Oakland and introduce me to his life there, whatever that might be. From time to time, when curiosity seized me, I searched for this place online and found news items that helped me begin to envision it: shootings mostly, but also minor political scandals involving graft or misused patronage or a city official with liens on his property; occasionally something really exciting, like an oil tanker lost in fog and hitting a bridge, or the firebombing of a liquor store by one street gang or another. There'd even been a minor riot not too long before, with the requisite smashed windows, a dumpster in flames, and a set of multiracial anarchists wearing bandannas across their faces so that all you could see in the photos were their alert and feral eyes; and I'd wondered then how my brother had chosen to live in a city whose ambience so closely mimicked our own. Could it really be an accident of geography? Or was it some latent homing instinct?

What it all had to do with me was never quite clear. Where I would fit in. What I would do with myself once I was there. These were among the many questions that remained. The visa, whenever it came, would not arrive with life instructions. Nor would it obligate me to stay in Oakland, of course, and I had considered other alternatives, though none very seriously, and all based on a whimsical set of readings and the occasional Internet search: Philadelphia, I liked for its history; Miami, for its tropical ennui; Chicago, for its poets; Los Angeles, for its sheer size.

But one can start over in any number of places, right? Any number of times?

"I'll get a job," I told my father. "Isn't that what Americans do?"

"It's what everyone does. In a copy shop?"

"I'm an actor."

"Who makes photocopies."

I frowned. "So I'll make photocopies my entire life. Why not?"

He wanted me to study because that was what he'd wanted for himself so many years before. And for Francisco too. He'd hoped my brother would be a professor by now, an academic, though he was far too proud ever to share this disappointment with me. He had his own issues with me: his unbounded respect for playwrights and artists and writers was completely abstract; on a more concrete level, he wished I'd considered some more reliable way to earn a living. As for my day job, my mother told me once that seeing me work as the attendant at the copy shop made my old man sad. His sadness, in turn, made me angry. His politics affirmed that all work held an inherent dignity. This was what he'd always repeated, but of course no ideology can protect a son from the unwelcome inheritance of his father's ambitions.

"When I was a boy," my old man said, "this town was the middle of nowhere. It still is, I know. But imagine it before they re-routed the highway. We knew there was something else out there—another country to the south, the capital to the north—but it felt very far away."

"It was."

"You're right. It was. We were hours from civilization. Six or seven to the border, if not more. But the roads were awful. And *spiritually*—it was even farther. It required a certain kind of imagination to see it."

I smiled. I thought I was making him laugh, but really, I was just trying to close off the conversation, shut it down before it headed somewhere I didn't want it to go. "I've always been very imaginative," I said.

My old man knew what I was doing, even if I didn't.

"Yes, son. You have. Maybe not imaginative enough, though."

I didn't want to ask him what he meant, so I sat, letting the silence linger until it forced him to answer my unspoken question.

"I'm sorry," my old man said. "I wonder if you've thought much about your future, that's all."

"Sure I have. All the time."

"To the exclusion of thinking about your present?"

"I wouldn't say that."

"What would you say?"

I paused, attempting to strip my voice of any anger before I spoke. "I've thought a great deal about my future, so that my present could seem more livable."

He nodded slowly. We sipped carefully from our steaming cups. For once, I was grateful for my old man's obsession with tea—it allowed us to pause, gather our thoughts. It excused us from having to talk, and the danger of saying things we might not mean.

"You and Rocío seem well."

I never spoke about my relationships with my parents.

"Sure. We're doing fine."

There was something else he wanted to ask me, I could tell, but he didn't. He narrowed his eyes, thinking, and then something changed in his face—a slackness emerged, the edges of his mouth dropped. He'd given up.

"I always hated this house," my old man said after a few minutes. "I can't imagine that anyone would want it. We should bulldoze the thing and be done with it."

It was all the same to me, and I told him so. We could set it on fire, or shatter every last brick with a sledgehammer. I had no attachments to this place, to this town. My father did, but he preferred not to think about them. It was a place to visit with a heavy heart, when an old relative died. Or with your family on holiday, if such a luxury could be afforded. Francisco, it occurred to me, might feel the same way toward the city where we'd been raised.

"I've let you down," my old man said. His voice was timid, hushed, as if he hadn't wanted me to hear.

"Don't say that."

"We should have pushed you harder, sent you away sooner. Now . . ." He didn't finish, but I understood that *now*, in his estimation, was far too late.

"It's fine."

"I know it is. Everyone's fine. I'm fine, you're fine, your mother's fine too. Even Francisco is fine, or so the rumor goes, God bless the U.S.A. Everything is fine. Just ask the mummies sitting on the benches out there. They spend every evening telling the same five stories again and again, but if you ask them, they'll respond with a single voice that everything is *just fine*. What do we have to complain about?"

"I'm not complaining," I said.

"I know you aren't. That's precisely what concerns me."

I slumped, feeling deflated. "I'll leave when the visa comes. I can't leave before that. I can't do anything before that."

My father winced. "But it isn't entirely accurate to say you can't do *anything*, is it?"

"I suppose not."

"Consider this: what if it doesn't come? Or what if it comes at an inconvenient time. Let's say you're in love with Rocío—"

"Let's suppose."

"And she doesn't want to leave. So then you stay. What will you do then?"

He was really asking: *What are you doing right now?*

When I didn't say anything, he pressed further, his voice rising in pitch. "Tell me, son. Are you sure you even want that visa? Are you absolutely certain? Do you know yet what you're going to do with your life?"

We were determined not to shout at each other. Eventually, he went to bed, and I left the house for a walk along the town's desolate streets, where there was not a car to be seen, nor a person. You could hear the occasional truck roaring by in the distance, but fewer at this hour, like a sporadic wind. It looked like an abandoned stage set, and I wondered: who's *absolutely certain* about anything? I found a pay phone not far from the plaza and called Rocío. I wanted her to make me laugh, and I sighed with relief when she answered on the first ring, as if she'd been waiting for my call. Maybe she had. I told her about the drive, about the fight we witnessed, about my great-uncle's dank and oppressive house, filled with pictures of racehorses and marching bands and the various women who'd borne his children and had their hopes and their hearts shattered. I didn't tell her about the conversation with my father.

"I've taken a lover," Rocío said, interrupting.

It was a game we played; I tried to muster the energy to play along. I didn't want to disappoint her. "And what's he like?"

"Handsome, in an ugly sort of way. Crooked nose, giant cock. More than adequate."

"I'm dying of jealousy," I said. "Literally dying. The life seeps from my tired body."

"Did you know that by law, if a man finds his wife sleeping with another man on their marriage bed, he's allowed to murder them both?"

"I hadn't heard that. But what if he finds them on the couch?"

"Then he can't kill them. Legally speaking."

"So did you sleep with him on our bed?"

"Yes," Rocío answered. "Many, many times."

"And was his name Joselito?"

There was quiet. "Yes. That was his name."

"I've already had him killed."

"But I just saw him this morning."

"He's gone, baby. Say goodbye."

"Goodbye," she whispered.

I was satisfied with myself. She asked me about the town, and I told her that everyone confused me with my brother. So many years separated my family from this place that they'd simply lost track of me. There was room in their heads for only one son; was it any surprise they chose Francisco?

"Oh, that's so sad!" Rocío said. She was mocking me.

"I'm not telling you so you'll feel sorry for me."

"Of course not."

"I'm serious."

"I know," she said, drawing out the syllable in a way she probably thought was cute, but which just annoyed me.

"I'm hanging up now." The phone card was running out anyway.

"Goodnight, Joselito," Rocío said, and blew a kiss into the receiver.

We spent a few hours the next morning in my great-uncle's house, sifting through the clutter, in case there was anything we might want to take back with us. There wasn't. My father set some items aside for the soldiers, should it come to that; nothing very expensive, but things he thought might *look* expensive if you were a bored young man with a rifle who'd missed all the action by a few years, and were serving your time standing by the side of a highway, collecting tributes: a silver picture frame; an antique camera in pristine condition; an old but very ornate trophy, which would surely come back to life with a little polish. It didn't make much sense, of course; these young men wanted one of two things, I told my father: cash or electronics. Sex, perhaps, but probably not with us. Anything else was meaningless. My father agreed.

Our unfinished conversation was not mentioned.

After lunch, we headed into town. There was some paperwork to be filed in order to transfer Raúl's property over to a distant cousin of ours, an unmarried woman of fifty who still lived nearby and might have some use for the house. Raúl's children wanted nothing, refused, on principle, to be involved. My father was dreading this transfer, of course, not because he was reluctant to give up the property, but because he was afraid of how many hours this relatively simple bureaucratic chore might require. But he hadn't taken his local celebrity into account, and of course we were received at city records with the same bright and enthusiastic palaver with which we'd been welcomed in the plaza the night before. We were taken around to greet each of the dozen municipal employees, friendly men and women of my father's generation and older who welcomed the interruption because they quite clearly had nothing to do. It was just like evenings in the plaza, I thought, only behind desks and under fluorescent lights. Many of them claimed some vague familial connection to me, especially the older ones, and so I began calling them all *uncle* and *auntie* just to be safe. Again and again I was mistaken for Francisco—When did you get back? Where are you living now?—and I began to respond with increasingly imprecise answers, so that finally, when we'd made it inside the last office, the registrar of properties, I simply gave in to this assumption, and said, when asked: "I live in California."

It felt good to say it. A relief.

The registrar was a small, very round man named Juan, with dark skin and a raspy voice. He'd been my father's best friend in third grade, or so he claimed. My old man didn't bother to contradict him, only smiled in such a way that I understood it to be untrue; or if not untrue exactly, then one of those statements that time had rendered unverifiable, and about which there was no longer any use debating.

The registrar liked my answer. He loosened his tie and clapped his hands. "California! Oh, my! So what do you do there?"

My father gave me a once-over. "Yes," he said now. "Tell my old friend Juan what you do."

I thought back to all those letters my brother had written, all those stories of his I'd read and nearly memorized in my adolescence. It didn't matter, of course; I could have told Juan any number of things: about my work as a ski instructor, or as a baggage handler, or as a bike-repair technician. I could have told him the ins and outs of Wal-Mart, about life in American small towns, about the shifting customs and mores of different regions of the vast United States. The accents, the landscapes, the winters. Anything I said at that moment would've worked just fine. But I went with something simple and current, guessing correctly that Juan wasn't much interested in details. There were a few facts I knew about my brother, in spite of the years and the distance: a man named Hassan had taken him under his wing. They were in business together, selling baby formula and low-priced denim and vegetables that didn't last more than a day. The details were arcane to me, but it was a government program, which, somehow, was making them both very rich.

"I work with an Arab," I said. "We have a store."

The registrar nodded severely, as if processing this critical information. "The Arabs are very able businessmen," he said finally. "You must learn everything you can from this Arab."

"I intend to."

"So you can be rich!"

"That's the idea," I said.

A smile flashed across Juan's face. "And the American girls? Ehhhhh?"

His voice rose with this last drawn-out syllable, so that it sounded like the thrum of a small revving motor.

I told him what he wanted to hear, in exactly the sly tone required. "They're very *affectionate.*"

Juan clapped again. "Wonderful! Wonderful! These young people," he said to my father. "The whole world is right there for them, just ripe for the taking. Tell me, are you happy, young man?"

I had to remind myself he was addressing that version of me that lived in California, that worked with Hassan, the one who was going to be unspeakably wealthy as a result. Not the me who'd never left the country, who wanted to be an actor but was actually a part-time employee in a copy shop run by a depressive.

"Yes," I said. "Yes, I'm very happy."

Juan smiled broadly, and I knew my part in the conversation

was over. He and my father got down to business. The paperwork was prepared, a long stack of forms and obtusely worded declarations, all signed in triplicate, and in a matter of minutes, my great-uncle's house was officially no longer our problem. I stood when my father did. Juan took my hand and shook it vigorously.

"California!" he said again, as if he didn't quite believe it.

Once we were free of Juan and the municipal offices, outside again and breathing the briny, life-giving sea air, I congratulated my old man. I said: "Now we don't have to burn the house down."

He gave me a weary look. "Now we can't, you mean."

We walked toward the plaza. It was late afternoon, still hours of light remaining, but where else could one go in this town? The regulars would be in their habitual spots, waiting for the sunset with steadfast, unflagging patience. It had been barely a day, but already I could understand why my father had fled this place the moment he had the chance. He'd gone first to the provincial capital, a nice enough place that he began to outgrow the moment he arrived. He was young; he wanted more. He moved to the capital itself, where he finished his education, won more prizes, married, and went abroad, fulfilling, if only partially, the expectations of those he'd left behind. They'd wanted him to be a judge, or a diplomat, or an engineer. To build bridges or make law. His actual job—head librarian of the antiquarian books and rare manuscripts section of the National Library—was a wholly inconceivable occupation. It sounded less like work one did for a wage, and more like an inherited title of nobility. But then it was precisely the rarefied nature of his position that gave my father such prestige in these parts.

We hadn't gone far when he said, "Quite the act in there."

I was feeling good and opted not to listen for any trace of sarcasm. Instead I thanked him.

"An Arab?" he said. "A store? How precise!"

"Everything's an act, right? I was improvising. You have to say the lines like you mean them."

"I see your studies at the conservatory have really paid dividends. It was very convincing."

"Your best friend thought so."

"Best friend, indeed," my old man said. "I suppose it's obvious, but I have no memory of him."

I nodded. "I don't think he noticed, if that's what you're worried about."

We still hadn't returned to the discussion of the previous night, and now there seemed no point. Instead we'd come to the plaza, with its view of the sea and its benches filling up one by one. We ducked into a tiny restaurant, hoping to have a quiet meal alone, but everyone recognized my father, and so the basic ritual of our stay in town began anew. We entered the dining room, waving, accepting greetings. A few men called my father's name excitedly—Manuel! Manolito!—and by the way his face shifted, the way his eyes darkened, I could see this prominence beginning to weigh on him. I saw him draw a deep breath, as if preparing for a steep climb. He was bored with it all, though every instinct told him he must bury this cynicism, ignore it. There are no cynics in this town—that is something you learn when you travel. When you live in the capital and become corrupt. One cannot be rude to these people, one cannot make fun of them. They know almost nothing about you anymore, but they love you. And this was the bind my old man was in. The night demanded something, some way to shift its course; and perhaps this was why, when we approached the table that had called us, he threw an arm over my shoulder, squeezed me tightly, and introduced me as his son, Nelson, home from abroad.

"From California," my father said. "Just back for a visit."

His announcement caught me by surprise. I hadn't intended to reprise the role debuted in Juan's office, but now there was no choice. I scarcely had a moment to glance in my old man's direction, to catch sight of his playful smile, before a couple of strangers wrapped me in a welcoming embrace. Everything happened quite quickly. A few narrow wooden tables were pushed together; my father and I pressed into perversely straight-backed chairs. We were surrounded. Everyone wanted to say hello; everyone wanted to get a look at me. I shook a dozen hands, grinning the entire time like a politician. I felt very grateful to my old man for this opportunity. It was—how do I explain this?—the role I'd been preparing for my entire life.

Scene: A dim restaurant off the plaza, in a small town on the southern coast. Santos (fifteen or twenty years older than the others, whom they call Profe) and his protégé, Cochocho, do most of the talking; Erick and Jaime function as a chorus and spend most of their energy drinking. They've been at it all afternoon when an old friend, Manuel, arrives with his son, Nelson. It is perhaps two hours before dark. Manuel lives in the capital, and his son is visiting from the United States. The young man is charming but arrogant, just as they expect all Americans to be. As the night progresses, he begins to grate on them, something evident at first only in small gestures. Bottles of beer are brought to the table, the empties are taken away, a process as fluid and automatic as the waves along the beach. How they are drained so quickly is not entirely clear. It defies any law of physics. The waitress, Elena, is an old friend too, a heavyset woman in her late forties, dressed in sweatpants and a loose-fitting T-shirt; she observes these men with a kind of pity. Over the years, she has slept with all of them. A closely guarded secret; they are men of ordinary vanity, and each of the four locals thinks he is the only one. Elena's brown-haired daughter, Celia, is a little younger than the American boy—he's in his early twenties—and she lingers in the background, trying to catch a glimpse of the foreigner. Her curiosity is palpable. There are dusty soccer trophies above the bar, and a muted television, which no one watches. Occasionally the on-screen image lines up with the dialogue, but the actors are not aware of this.

NELSON: That's right. California. The Golden State.
ERICK: Hollywood. Sunset Boulevard.
COCHOCHO: Many Mexicans, no?
ERICK: Route 66. James Dean.
JAIME: I have a nephew in Las Vegas. Is that California?
COCHOCHO *(after opening a bottle of beer with his teeth):* Don't answer him. He's lying. He doesn't even know where Las Vegas is. He doesn't know where California is. Ignore him. Ignore the both of them. That's what we do.
ERICK: Magic Johnson. The Olympics.
COCHOCHO *(to Erick):* Are you just saying words at random? Do you ever listen to yourself? *(to Nelson)* Forgive him. Forgive us. It's Friday.
NELSON: I understand.
JAIME: Friday is an important day.
ERICK: The day before Saturday.
NELSON: Of course.
JAIME: And after Thursday.
COCHOCHO: As I said, forgive us.

As well as being the oldest of the group, Santos is also the most formal in speech and demeanor. Suit and tie. He's been waiting for the right moment to speak. He imagines everyone else has been waiting for this too, for their opportunity to hear him.

SANTOS: I'm appalled by all this. This . . . What is the phrase? This lack of discipline. We must be kind to our guest. Make a good impression. Is it very loud in here? Perhaps you don't notice it. I'm sure things are different where you live. Orderly. I was your father's history teacher. That is a fact.

Nelson looks to his father for confirmation. A nod from Manuel.

MANUEL: He was. And I remember everything you taught me, Profe.
SANTOS: I doubt that. But it was my class, I believe, that inculcated in your father the desire to go north, to the capital. I take responsibility for this. Each year, my best students leave. I'm retired now and I don't miss it, but I was sad watching them go. Of course they have their reasons. If these others had been paying any attention at all to history as I taught it, they might have understood the logic of migration. It's woven into the story of this nation. I don't consider this something to celebrate, but they might have understood it as a legacy they'd inherited. They might have been a bit more ambitious.
COCHOCHO: Profe, you're being unfair.
SANTOS *(to Nelson, ignoring Cochocho):* Your father was the best student I ever had.
MANUEL *(sheepishly):* Not true, Profe, not true.
SANTOS: Of course it's true. Are you calling me a liar? Not like these clowns. I taught them all. *(nodding toward Erick, who is pouring himself a glass of beer)* This one could barely read. Couldn't sit still. Even now, look at him. Doesn't even know who the president is. *(Television: generic politician, his corruption self-evident, as clear as the red sash across his chest.)* The only news he cares about is the exchange rate.
ERICK: The only news that matters. I have expenses. A son and two daughters.
COCHOCHO *(to Nelson):* And you can marry either of them. Take one of the girls off his hands, please.
SANTOS: Or the boy. That's allowed over there, isn't it?
NELSON: How old are the girls?
COCHOCHO: Old enough.
NELSON: Pretty?
ERICK: Very.
COCHOCHO *(eyebrows raised, skeptical):* A man doesn't look for beauty in a wife. Rather, he doesn't look *only* for beauty. We can discuss the details later. Right, Erick?

Erick nods absent-mindedly. It's as if he's already lost the thread of the conversation.

SANTOS: So, young man. What do you do there in California?
NELSON *(glancing first at his father):* I have my own business. I work with an Arab. Together we have a store. It's a bit complicated, actually.

SANTOS: Complicated. How's that? What could be simpler than buying and selling? What sort of merchandise is it? Weapons? Metals? Orphans?

Television: in quick succession, a handgun, a barrel with a biohazard symbol, a sad-looking child. The child remains on-screen, even after Nelson begins speaking.

NELSON: We began with baby supplies. Milk. Formula. Diapers. That sort of thing. It was a government program. For poor people.
JAIME: Poor Americans?
NELSON: That's right.
COCHOCHO: Don't be so ignorant. There are poor people there too. You think your idiot cousin in Las Vegas is rich?
JAIME: He's my nephew. He wants to be a boxer.
COCHOCHO *(to Nelson):* Go on.
NELSON: This was good for a while, but there is—you may have heard. There have been some problems in California. Budgets, the like.
SANTOS *(drily):* I can assure you these gentlemen have not heard.
NELSON: So we branched out. We rented the space next door, and then the space next door to that. We sell clothes in both. We do well. They come every first and fifteenth and spend their money all at once.
JAIME: You said they were poor.
NELSON: American poor is . . . *different.*
SANTOS: Naturally.
COCHOCHO: Naturally.
NELSON: We drive down to Los Angeles every three weeks to buy the inventory. Garment district. Koreans. Jews. Filipinos. Businessmen.
SANTOS: Very well. An entrepreneur.
MANUEL: He didn't learn this from me.
SANTOS: You speak Arabic now? Korean? Hebrew? Filipino?
NELSON: No. My partner speaks Spanish.
COCHOCHO: And your English?
MANUEL: My son's English is perfect. Shakespearean.
COCHOCHO: Two stores. And they both sell clothes.
NELSON: We have Mexicans, and we have blacks. Unfortunately these groups don't get along very well. The Mexicans ignore the blacks, who ignore the Mexicans. The white people ignore everyone, but they don't shop with us and so we don't worry about them. We have a store for each group.
SANTOS: But they—they all live in the same district?

Television: panning shot of an East Oakland street scene: International Boulevard. Mixed crowds in front of taco trucks, tricked-out cars rolling by very slowly, chrome rims spinning, glinting in the fierce sunlight. Latinas pushing strollers, black boys in long white T-shirts and baggy jeans, which they hold up with one hand gripping the crotch.

NELSON: They do. And we don't choose sides.
COCHOCHO: Of course not. You're there to make money. Why would you choose sides?
JAIME: But you live there too? With the blacks? With the Mexicans?

They look him over, a little disappointed. They'd thought he was more successful. Behind the scene, Elena prepares to bring more beer to the table, but her daughter stops her, takes the bottles, and goes herself.

NELSON: Yes. There are white people too.
CELIA: Excuse me, pardon me.

Celia has inky black eyes and wears a version of her mother's outfit—an old T-shirt, sweatpants, sandals. On her mother, this clothing represents a renunciation of sexual possibility. On Celia, they represent quite the opposite.

NELSON *(eagerly, wanting to prove himself—to the men? to Celia?):* I'd like to buy a round. If I may.
COCHOCHO: I'm afraid that's not possible. *(slips Celia a few bills)* Go on, dear.

Celia lingers for a moment, watching Nelson, until her mother shoos her away. She disappears offstage. Meanwhile the conversation continues.

ERICK: You're the guest. Hospitality is important.
SANTOS: These things matter to us. You think it folkloric, or charming. We're not offended by the way you look at us. We are accustomed to the *anthropological gaze. (this last phrase accompanied by air quotes)* We feel sorry for you because you don't understand. We do things a certain way here. We have traditions. *(to Manuel)* How much does your boy know about us? About our town? Have you taught him our customs?
NELSON: I learned the songs when I was a boy.
MANUEL: But he was raised in the city, of course.
COCHOCHO: What a shame. Last time I went was six years ago, when I ran for Congress. A detestable place. I hope you don't mind my saying that.
MANUEL: Certainly you aren't the only one who holds that opinion.
SANTOS: He wanted very badly to win. He would've happily moved his family there.
JAIME: And your wife, she's from the city?
MANUEL: She is.
COCHOCHO *(to Nelson):* You're lucky to have left. How long have you been in California?

NELSON: Since I was eighteen.
JAIME: It's a terrible place, but still, you must miss home quite a bit.
NELSON *(laughing):* No, I wouldn't say that, exactly.
ERICK: The food?
NELSON: Sure.
JAIME: The family?
NELSON: Yes, of course.
MANUEL: I'm flattered.
JAIME: Your friends?
NELSON *(pausing to think):* Some of them.
ERICK: Times have changed.
SANTOS: No, Erick, times have not changed. The youth are not all that different than before. Take Manuel. Let's ask him. Dear Manuel, pride of this poor, miserable village, tell us: how often do you wake up missing this place where you were born? How often do you think back, and wish you could do it over again, never have left, and stayed here to raise a family?

Manuel is caught off guard, not understanding if the question is serious or not. On the television: a shot of the plaza by night. Quickly recovering, he decides to take the question as a joke.

MANUEL: Every day, Profe.

Everyone but Santos laughs.

SANTOS: I thought as much. Some people like change, they like movement, transition. A man's life is very short and of no consequence. We have a different view of time here. A different way of placing value on things. We find everything you Americans—
NELSON: *We* Americans? But I lived in this country until I was eighteen!
SANTOS *(talking over him):* Everything you Americans say is very funny. Nothing impresses us unless it lasts five hundred years. We can't even begin to discuss the greatness of a thing until it has survived that long. *(It's not clear whom Santos is addressing. Still, there's a murmur of approval. His eyes close. He's a teacher again, in the classroom.)* This town is great. The ocean is great. The desert and the mountains beyond. There are some ruins in the foothills, which you surely know nothing about. They are undoubtedly, indisputably great; as are the men who built them, and their culture. Their blood, which is our blood, and even yours, though unfortunately . . . how shall I put it? *Diluted.* Not great: the highway, the border. The United States. Where do you live? What's that place called?
NELSON: Oakland, California.
SANTOS: How old?

NELSON: A hundred years?
SANTOS: Not great. Do you understand?
NELSON: I'm sure I don't. If I may: those five-hundred-year-old ruins, for example. You'll notice I'm using your word, Profe. *Ruins.* Am I wrong to question whether they've lasted?

Television: the ruins.

SANTOS *(taking his seat again):* You would have failed my class.
NELSON: What a shame. Like these gentlemen?
SANTOS: Nothing to be proud of. Nothing at all.
NELSON *(transparently trying to win them over):* I'd be in good company.
ERICK: Cheers.
JAIME: Cheers.
MANUEL *(reluctantly):* Cheers.
COCHOCHO *(stern, clearing his throat):* I did not fail that class or any class. It's important you know this. I didn't want to mention it, but I am deputy mayor of this town. I once ran for Congress. I could have this bar shut down tomorrow.
ERICK/JAIME *(together, alarmed):* You wouldn't!
COCHOCHO: Of course not! Don't be absurd! *(pause)* But I *could.* I am a prominent member of this community.
ERICK: Don't be fooled by his name.
COCHOCHO: It's a nickname! A term of endearment! These two? Their nicknames are vulgar. Unrepeatable. And your father? What was your nickname, Manuel?
MANUEL: I didn't have one.
COCHOCHO: Because no one bothered to give him a name. He was cold. Distant. Arrogant. He looked down on us even then. We knew he'd leave and never come back.

Manuel shrugs. Cochocho, victorious, smiles arrogantly.

NELSON: Here he is! He's returned!
SANTOS: How lucky we are. Blessed.
COCHOCHO: Your great-uncle's old filling station? It's mine now. Almost. I have a minority stake in it. My boy works there. It'll be his someday.

As if reminded of his relative wealth, Cochocho orders another round. No words, only gestures. Again Celia arrives at the table, bottles in hand, as Elena looks on, resigned. This time all the men, including Nelson's father, ogle the girl. She might be pretty after all. She hovers over the table, leaning in so that Nelson can admire her. He does, without shame. Television: a wood-paneled motel room, a naked couple on the bed. The window is open. They're fucking.

SANTOS *(to Manuel):* Don't take this the wrong way. The primary issue . . . What Cochocho is trying to say, I think, is that some of us . . . We feel abandoned. Disrespected. You left us. Now your son is talking down to us.
NELSON *(amused):* Am I?
MANUEL: Is he?
SANTOS: We don't deserve this, Manuel. You don't remember! *(to the group)* He doesn't remember! *(to Nelson)* Your father was our best student in a generation. The brightest, the most promising. His father—your grandfather, God rest his soul—had very little money, but he was well liked, whereas your great-uncle . . . We tolerated Raúl. For a while he was rich and powerful, but he never gave away a cent. He saw your father had potential, but he wanted him to help run the filling station, to organize his properties, to invest. These were his ambitions. Meanwhile, your father, I believe, wanted to be—
NELSON: A professor of literature. At an American university. We've discussed this.
COCHOCHO: Why not a local one?

Manuel has no response, is slightly ashamed.

SANTOS: Pardon me. It's a very conventional ambition for a bookish young man. Decent. Middle of the road. You had politics?
MANUEL: I did. *(pause)* I still do.
SANTOS: A rabble-rouser. An agitator. He made some people here very angry, and the teachers—and I was leader of this concerned group, if I remember correctly—we collected money among us, to send him away. We didn't want to see his talent wasted. Nothing destroys our promising youth more than politics. Did he tell you he won a scholarship? Of course. That's a simpler story. He made his powerful uncle angry, and Raúl refused to pay for his studies. Your grandfather didn't have the money either. We sent him away for his own good. We thought he'd come back and govern us well. We hoped he might learn something useful. Become an engineer. An architect. A captain of industry. *(sadly)* We expected more. We needed more. There's no work here. Jaime, for example. What do you do?
JAIME: Sir?
SANTOS *(impatiently):* I said, what do you do?
JAIME: I'm unemployed. I was a bricklayer.
SANTOS: Erick?
ERICK: I'm a tailor. *(to Nelson, brightly, with an optimism that does not match the mood of the table)* At your service, young man!
SANTOS: See? He made me this suit. Local cotton. Adequate work.

I'm on a fixed income. Cochocho. He is deputy mayor. You know that now. But did you know this? The money he just spent on our drinks? That is our money. He stole it like he stole the election. He brings his suits from the capital. We don't say anything about it because that would be rude. And he is, in spite of his questionable ethics, our friend.
COCHOCHO *(appalled):* Profe!
SANTOS: What? What did I say? You're not our friend? Is that what you're alleging?

Cochocho, dejected, unable or unwilling to defend himself. Erick and Jaime comfort him. Just then, Elena's daughter reappears, eyes on Nelson. Television: motel room, naked couple in an acrobatic sexual position, a yogic balancing act for two, a scramble of flesh, such that one can't discern whose legs belong to whom, whose arms, how his and her sexual organs are connecting or even if they are.

CELIA: Another round, gentlemen?
MANUEL: I insist—
NELSON: If you'll allow me—
SANTOS *(stopping them both with a wave, glaring at Cochocho):* So, are you our friend or not? Will you spend our money or keep it for yourself? *(to Nelson)* Unfortunately, this too is tradition.
NELSON: Five hundred years?
SANTOS: Much longer than that, boy.
NELSON: Please. I'd consider it an honor to buy a round.
COCHOCHO *(still angry):* Great idea! Let the foreigner spend his dollars!

At this, Nelson stands and steps toward the startled Celia. He kisses her on the mouth, brazenly, and as they kiss, he takes money from his own pocket, counts it without looking, and places it in her hand. She closes her fist around the money, and it vanishes. It's unclear whether he's paying for the drinks or for the kiss itself, but in either case, Celia doesn't question it. The four local men look on, astounded.

SANTOS: Imperialism!
COCHOCHO: Opportunism!
JAIME: Money!
ERICK: Sex!

Manuel stares at his son, but says nothing. Takes a drink. Curtain.

I should be clear about something: it is never the words, but how they are spoken that matters. The intent, the tone. The farcical script quoted above is only an approximation of what actually occurred that evening, after my father challenged me to play Francisco, or a version of him, for this unsuspecting audience. Many other things were said, which I've omitted: oblique insults; charmingly ignorant questions; the occasional reference to one or another invented episode of American history. I improvised, using my brother's letters as a guide, even quoting from them when the situation allowed—the line, for example, about Mexicans ignoring blacks and vice versa. That statement was contained within one of Francisco's early dispatches from Oakland, when he was still eagerly trying to understand the place for himself and not quite able to decipher the many things he saw.

My most significant dramatic choice was not to defend myself all too vigorously. Not to defend Oakland, or the United States. That would have been a violation of character, whereas this role was defined by a basic indifference to what was taking place. They could criticize, impugn, belittle—it was all the same to me, I thought (my character thought). They could say what they wanted to say, and I would applaud them for it; after all, at the end of the day, I (my character) would be heading back to the U.S., and they'd be staying here. I needed to let them know this, without saying it explicitly. That's how Francisco would have done it—never entirely sinking into the moment, always hovering above it. Distant. Untouchable.

Through it all, my old man sat very quietly, deflecting attention even when they began discussing him directly, his choices, the meaning and impact of his long exile. I've hurried through the part where my father's friends expressed, with varying levels of obsequiousness, their admiration, their wonder, their jealousy. I've left it out because it wasn't the truth; it was habit—how you treat the prodigal son when he returns, how you flatter him in order to claim some of his success as your own. But this fades. It is less honest and less interesting than the rest of what took place that night. The surface: Jaime and Erick drank heavily, oblivious and imperturbable to the end, and were for that very reason the most powerful men in the room. I could not say they were any drunker when we left than they were when we arrived. Cochocho, on the other hand, drank and changed dramatically: he became more desperate, less self-possessed, revealing in spite of himself the essential joylessness at the core of his being. His neatly combed hair somehow became wildly messy, his face swollen and adolescent, so that you could intuit, but not see, a grown man's features hidden beneath. No one liked him; more to the point, he did not like himself. And then there was Santos, who was of that generation that catches cold if they leave the house without a well-knotted necktie; who, like all retired small-town teachers, had the gloomy nostalgia of a deposed tyrant. I caught him looking at Celia a few times with hunger—the hunger of an old man remembering better days—and it moved me. We locked eyes, Santos and I, just after one of these glances; he bowed his head, embarrassed, and looked down at his shoes. He began to hate me, I could feel it. He expressed most clearly what the others were unwilling to acknowledge: that the visitors had upset their pride.

We'd reminded them of their provincialism.

Which is why I liked Santos the best. Even though the role I was inhabiting placed us at opposite ends of this divide; in truth, I identified very closely with this wounded vanity. I felt it, would feel it, would come to own this troubling sense of dislocation myself. I knew it intimately: it was how the real Nelson felt in the presence of the real Francisco.

Hurt. Small.

Now the lights in the bar hummed, and the empty beer bottles were magically replaced with new ones, and my father's old history teacher aged before my eyes, the color draining from him until he looked like the people in Raúl's old photographs. Jaime and Erick maintained the equanimity of statues. Cochocho, with his ill humor and red, distended skin, looked like the mold spreading on Raúl's kitchen wall. He'd removed his suit jacket, revealing dark rings of sweat at the armpits of his dress shirt. He asked about my great-uncle's house, and when my father said he'd transferred the property to a cousin of ours, the deputy mayor responded with a look of genuine disappointment.

"You could have left it to your son," he said.

It wasn't what he really meant, of course: Cochocho probably had designs on it himself, some unscrupulous plan that would net him a tidy profit. But I played along, as if this possibility had just occurred to me.

"That's true," I said, facing my old man. "Why didn't you?"

My father chose this moment to be honest. "I didn't want to burden you with it."

And then the night began to turn: my old man frowned as soon as the words had escaped. It was more of a grimace, really, as if he were in pain; and I thought of those faces professional athletes make after an error, when they know the cameras are on them: they mime some injury, some phantom hurt to explain their mistake. It's a shorthand way of acknowledging, and simultaneously deflecting, responsibility. We sat through a few unpleasant moments of this, until my father forced a laugh, which sounded very lonely because no one joined him in it.

"A burden, you say?"

This was Santos, who, excluding a year and a half studying in France, had lived in the town for all of his seventy-seven years.

Just then Celia came to the table with two fresh bottles. "Sit with us," I said. I blurted this out on impulse, for my sake and my father's, just to change the subject. She smiled coquettishly, tilting her head to one side, as if she hadn't heard correctly. Her old T-shirt was stretched and loose, offering the simple line of her thin neck, and the delicate ridge of her collarbone, for our consideration.

"I would love to," Celia said, "but it appears there is no room here for a lady."

She was right: we were six drunken men pressed together in a crowded, unpleasant rectangle. If more than two of us leaned forward, our elbows touched. It was a perfect answer, filling us all with longing, and though we hurried to make room, Celia had already turned on her heel and was headed back to the bar. She expected us to stay for many hours longer, was confident she'd have other opportunities to tease us. Her mother glared at her.

But the men hadn't forgotten my father's insult.

"Explain," said Santos.

My old man shook his head. He wore an expression I recognized: the same distant gaze I'd seen that first night, when we'd sat up, drinking tea and looking through Raúl's old photographs. Who are these people? What do they have to do with me? He wasn't refusing; he simply found the task impossible.

I decided to step in, playing the one card my father and I both had.

"I think I know what my old man is trying to get at," I said. "I believe I do. And I understand it because I feel the same way toward the capital. He meant no offense, but you have to understand what happens, over time, when one leaves."

Santos, Cochocho, and the others gave me skeptical looks. Nor, it should be said, did my father seem all that convinced. I went on anyway.

"Let's take the city, for example. I love that place—I realize that's a controversial statement in this crowd, but I do. Listen. I love its gray skies, its rude people, its disorder, its noise. I love the stories I've lived there, the landmarks, the ocean, which is the same as the ocean here, by the way. But now, in spite of that love, when I have a son, I would not *leave* it to him. I would not say: here, boy, take this. It's your inheritance. It's yours. I would not want him to feel obligated to love it the way I do. Nor would that be possible. Do you understand? Does that make sense? He'll be an American. I have no choice in the matter. That's a question of geography. And like Americans, he should wake into adulthood and feel free."

I sat back, proud of my little speech.

"Ah!" Santos said. It was a guttural sound, a physical complaint, as if I'd injured him. He scowled. "Rank nationalism," he said. "Coarse jingoism of the lowest order. Are you saying we're not free?"

We fell silent.

For a while longer the bottles continued to empty, almost of their own accord, and I felt I was perceiving everything through watery, unfocused eyes. The television had been trying to tell me something all night, but its message was indecipherable. I was fully Francisco now. That's not true—I was an amalgam of the two of us, but I felt as close to my brother then as I had in many years. Most of it was internal and could not have been expressed with any script, with any set of lines. But this audience—I thought back to the two antagonists and Joselito's moto-taxi, the way they became fully invested in the scene the moment they realized they were being watched. I'd taken my brother's story and amplified it. Made it mine, and now theirs, for better or for worse. It was no longer a private argument, but a drama everyone had a stake in. I felt good. Content. Seized by that powerful sense of calm you have when you have understood a character, or rather, when you feel that a character has understood you. I felt very confident, very brash, as I'd imagined my brother had felt all these many years on his journey across North America.

I stood then and confirmed what I'd begun to sense while

seated: I was very drunk. It was comforting in a way, to discover that all that drinking had not been done in vain. It was time to go. Celia and her mother came out from behind the bar to clear off the table, and the other men stood as well. And this was the moment I as Francisco, or perhaps Francisco as me, pulled Celia close and kissed her on the mouth. Perhaps this was what the television had been trying to tell me. She kissed me back. I heard the men call out in surprise, heard Celia's mother as well, shrill and protective, but entirely reasonable. After all, who was this young man? And just what did he think he was doing?

I placed one hand at the small of Celia's back, pulling her to me. The crowd continued to voice its disapproval, scandalized, but also—I felt certain—glad for us. The dance is complete. The virile foreigner has made his mark. The pretty girl has claimed her property. And it was the role of the gathered men to be appalled, or to pretend to be; the role of the mother to wail about her daughter's chastity when she herself had never been chaste. But when it was over, when Celia and I separated, everyone was grinning. The old men, my father, even Elena.

Very late that night I called Rocío. I did not feel any guilt. I just wanted to talk to her, perhaps have her read me the letter I'd already imagined. Be amused by her. Perhaps laugh and discuss her lover's murder. It must have been three or four in the morning, and I could not sleep. I'd begun to have doubts about what had happened, what it meant. A few hours before, it had all seemed triumphant; now it felt abusive. The plaza was empty, of course, just like the previous night; only more so—a kind of emptiness that feels eternal, permanent. I knew I would never come back to this place, and that realization made me a little sad. From where I stood, I could see the sloping streets, the ocean, the unblinking night; and nearer, the listing palm tree scarred with names. I would have written Celia's name on it—a useless, purely romantic gesture, to be sure—but the truth is I never knew her name. I've chosen to call her Celia because it feels disrespectful to address her as *the barwoman's daughter.* So impersonal, so anonymous. A barwoman's daughter tastes of bubblegum and cigarettes, whereas Celia's warm tongue had the flavor of roses.

Santos and Cochocho and Jaime and Erick left us soon after the kiss, and it was just me and my father, still feeling amused by what had happened, what we'd been a part of. We maybe felt a little shame too, but we didn't talk about it because we didn't know how. Grown men with hurt feelings are transparent creatures; grown men who feel dimly they have done something wrong are positively opaque. It would've been much simpler if we'd all just come to blows. Santos and Cochocho wandered off, a bit dazed, as if they'd been swindled. My father and I did a quick circle around the plaza and begged off for the evening. We never ate. Our hunger had vanished. I tried and failed to sleep, spent hours listening to my father's snores echoing through the house. Now I punched in the numbers from the phone card, and let the phone ring for a very long time. I wasn't drunk anymore. I liked the sound because it had no point of origin; I could imagine it ringing in the city, in that apartment I shared with Rocío (where she was asleep and could not hear, or was perhaps out with friends on this weekend night), but this was pure fantasy. I was not hearing that ring at all, of course. The ringing I heard came from inside the line, from somewhere within the wires, within the phone, an echo of something mysterious emerging from an unfixed and floating territory.

I waited for a while, listening, comforted; but in the end, there was no answer.

We left the next morning; locked the house, dropped the key in the neighbor's mail slot, and fled quickly, almost furtively, hoping to escape without having to say goodbye to anyone. I had a pounding headache, and I'd barely slept at all. We made it to the filling station at the top of the hill without attracting notice, and then paused. My father was at the wheel, and I could see this debate flaring up within him—whether to stop and fill the tank or head north, away from this place and what it represented. Even the engine had doubt; it would not settle on an idling speed. We stopped. We had to. There might not be another station for many hours.

It was Cochocho's son tending the pumps. He was a miniature version of his father: the same frown, the same fussy irritation with the world. Everyone believes they deserve better, I suppose, and in this respect, he was no different from me. Still, I disliked him intensely. He had fat adolescent hands and wore clothes that could have been handed down from Celia's mother.

"So you're off, then?" the boy said to my father through the open window.

The words were spoken without a hint of friendliness. His shoulders tensed, his jaw set in an expression of cold distrust. There was so much disdain seeping toward us, so determined and intentional, I almost found it funny. I felt like laughing, though I knew this would only make matters worse. Part of me—a large part—didn't care: my chest was full of that big-city arrogance, false, pretentious, and utterly satisfying. The boy narrowed his eyes at us, but I was thinking to myself:

Goodbye, sucker!

"Long drive," said Cochocho's son.

And I heard my father say, "A full day, more or less."

Then Cochocho's son, to me: "Back to California?"

I paused. Remembered. Felt annoyed. Nodded. A moment prior I'd decided to forget the boy, had dismissed him, disappeared him. I'd cast my eyes instead down the hill, at the town and its homes obscured by a layer of fog.

"That's right," I said, though California felt quite far away—as a theory, as a concept, to say nothing of an actual place where real human beings might live.

"I used to work here, you know," my old man offered.

The boy nodded with sublime disinterest. "I've heard that," he said.

The tank was filled, and an hour later we were emptying our pockets for the bored, greedy soldiers. They were the age of Cochocho's son, and just as friendly. Three hours after that, we were passing through Joselito's hometown, in time to see a funeral procession; his, we supposed. It moved slowly alongside the highway, a somber cloud of gray and black, anchored by the doleful sounds of an out-of-tune brass band. The two men who'd fought over the moto-taxi now stood side by side, holding one end of the casket and quite obviously heartbroken. Whether or not they were acting now, I wouldn't dare to speculate. But I did ease the car almost to a stop; and I did roll my window down and ask my old man to roll down his. And we listened to the band's song, with its impossibly slow melody, like time stretched thin. We stayed there a minute, as they marched away from us, toward the cemetery. It felt like a day. Then we were at the edge of the city; and then we were home, as if nothing had happened at all.

CHARLES BAXTER

Bravery

FROM *Tin House*

AS A TEENAGER, her junior year, her favorite trick involved riding in cars with at least two other girls. You needed a female cluster in there, and you needed to have the plainest one driving. They'd cruise University Avenue in Palo Alto until they spotted some boys together near a street corner. Boys were always ganged up at high-visibility intersections, marking territory and giving off cigarette smoke and musk. At the red light, she'd roll down the window and shout, "Hey, you guys!" The boys would turn toward the car slowly—*very* slowly—trying for cool. Smoke emerged from their faces, from the nose or mouth. "Hey! Do you think we're pretty?" she'd shout. "Do you think we're cute?"

Except for the plain one behind the wheel, the girls she consorted with *were* cute, so the question wasn't really a test. The light would turn green, and they'd speed away before the boys could answer. The pleasure was in seeing them flummoxed. Usually one of the guys, probably the sweetest, or the most eager, would nod and raise his hand to wave. Susan would spy him, the sweet one, through the back window, and she'd smile so that he'd have that smile to hold on to all night. The not-so-sweet good-looking guys just stood there. They were accustomed to being teased, and they always liked it. As for the other boys—well, no one ever cared about them.

Despite what other girls said, all boys were not all alike: you had to make your way through their variables blindly, guessing at hidden qualities, the ones you could live with.

Years later, in college, her roommate said to her, "You always go for the *kind* ones, the *considerate* ones, those types. I mean, where's the fun? I hate those guys. They're so *humane,* and shit like that. Give me a troublemaker any day."

"Yeah, but a troublemaker will give *you* trouble." She was painting her toenails, even though the guys she dated never noticed her toenails. "Trouble comes home. It moves in. It's contagious."

"I can take it. I'm an old-fashioned girl," her roommate said, with her complicated irony.

Susan married one of the sweet ones, the kind of man who waved at you. At a San Francisco art gallery on Van Ness, gazing at a painting of a giant pointed index finger with icicles hanging from it, she had felt her concentration jarred when a guy standing next to her said, "Do you smell something?"

He sniffed and glanced up at the ceiling. Metaphor, irony, a come-on? In fact, she *had* smelled a slightly rotten egg scent, so she nodded. "We should get out of here," he said, gesturing toward the door, past the table with the wineglasses and the sign-in book. "It's a gas leak. Before the explosion."

"But maybe it's the paintings," she said.

"The paintings? Giving off explosive gas? That's an odd theory."

"Could be. Part of the modernist assault on the audience?"

He shrugged. "Well, it's rotten eggs or natural gas, one of the two. I don't like the odds. Let's leave."

On the way out, he introduced himself as Elijah, and she had laughed and spilled some white wine (she had forgotten she was holding a glass of it) onto her dress just above the hemline. He handed her a monogrammed handkerchief that he had pulled out of some pocket or other, and the first letter on it was *E,* so he probably was an Elijah, after all. A monogrammed handkerchief! Maybe he had money. "Here," he said. "Go ahead. Sop it up." He hadn't tried to press his advantage by touching the handkerchief against the dress; he just handed it over, and she pretended to use it to soak up the wine. With the pedestrians passing by and an overhead neon sign audibly humming, he gave off a blue-eyed air of benevolence, but he also looked on guard, hypervigilant, as if he were an ex-Marine. God knows where he had found the benevolence, or where any man ever found it.

"Elijah." She looked at him. In the distance a car honked. The evening sky contained suggestions of rain. His smile persisted: a sturdy street-corner boy turned into a handsome pensive man but very solid-seeming, one thumb inside a belt loop, with a street lamp behind him to give him an incandescent aura. Physically, he had the frame of a gym rat. She had the odd thought that his skin might taste of sugar, his smile was so kind. Kindness had always attracted her. It made her weak in the knees. "Elijah the prophet? Who answers all questions at the end of time? That one? Your parents must have been religious or something."

"Yeah," he said noncommittally, bored by the topic. "'Or something' was exactly what they were. They liked to loiter around in the Old Testament. They trusted it. They were farmers, and they believed in catastrophes. But when you have to explain your own name, you . . . well, this isn't a rewarding conversation, is it?" He had a particularly thoughtful way of speaking that made him sound as if he had thought up his sentences several minutes ago and was only now getting around to saying them.

She coughed. "So what do you do, Elijah?"

"Oh, that comes later," he said. "Occupations come later. First tell me *your* name."

"Susan," she said. "So much for the introductions." She leaned forward, showing off her great smile. "This wine. It's so bad. I'm kind of glad I spilled it. Shall I spill more of it?" She hadn't had more than a sip, but she felt seriously drunk.

"Well, you could spill it here." He reversed his index finger and lifted up his necktie. "Or there." He pointed at the sidewalk.

"But it's white wine. White wine doesn't really stain." She threw the wineglass into the gutter, where it shattered.

Twenty minutes later in a coffee shop down by the Embarcadero she learned that he was a pediatric resident with a particular interest in mitochondrial disorder. Now she understood: out on the street, he had looked at her the way a doctor looks at a child. She herself was a psychiatric social worker, with a job waiting for her at an outpatient clinic in Millbrae. She and Elijah exchanged phone numbers. That night, rattled by their encounter, she couldn't sleep. Three days later, still rattled, she called him and proposed a date, something her mother had advised her never to do with a man. They went to dinner and a movie, and Elijah fell asleep during the previews and didn't wake up for another hour—poor guy, he was so worn out from his work. She didn't bother to explain the plot; he was too tired to care.

He didn't warm up to her convincingly—not as she really hoped he would—for a month, until he heard her sing in a local choir, a program that included the Vaughan Williams Mass in G Minor. She had a solo in the opening measures of the Benedictus, and when Elijah found her at the reception afterward, his face, as he looked at her, was softened for the first time with actual love, the real thing, that yearning, both hungry and quizzical.

"Your voice. Wow. I was undone," he said, taking a sip of the church-basement coffee, his voice thick. *Undone.* He had a collection of unusual adjectives like that. He had a collection of them. *Devoted* was another. And *committed.* He used that adjective all the time. Never before had she ever met a man who was comfortable with that adjective.

A few months after they were married, they took a trip to Prague. The plan was to get pregnant there amid the European bric-a-brac. On the flight over the Atlantic he held her hand when the Airbus hit some turbulence. In the seats next to theirs, another young couple sat together, and as the plane lurched, the woman fanned her face with a magazine while the man read passages aloud from the Psalms. "'A thousand shall fall at thy side, and ten thousand by thy right hand,'" he read. When the plane bucked, passengers laughed nervously. The flight attendants had hastily removed the drink carts and were sitting at the back, doing crossword puzzles. The woman sitting next to Susan excused herself and rushed toward the bathroom, holding her hand in front of her mouth as she hurried down the funhouse-lurching aisle. When she returned, her companion was staring at his Bible. Having traded seats with Susan, Elijah then said some words to the sick woman that Susan couldn't hear, whereupon the woman nodded and seemed to calm down.

How strange it was, his ability to give comfort. He doled it out in every direction. He wasn't just trained as a doctor; he was a doctor all the way down to the root. Looking over at him, at his hair flecked with early gray, she thought uneasily of his generosity and its possible consequences, and then, in almost the same moment, she felt overcome with pride and love.

*

In Prague, the Soviet-era hotel where they stayed smelled of onions, chlorine, and goulash. The lobby had mirrored ceilings. Upstairs, the rooms were small and claustrophobic; the TV didn't work, and all the signs were nonsensical. *Pozor!* for example, which seemed to mean "Beware!" Beware of what? The signs were garbles of consonants. Prague wasn't Kafka's birthplace for nothing. Still, Susan believed the city was the perfect place for them to conceive a child. For the first one, you always needed some sexual magic, and this place had a particular Old World variety of it. As for Elijah, he seemed to be in a mood: early on their second morning in the hotel, he stood in front of the window rubbing his scalp and commenting on Prague's air quality. "Stony, like a castle," he said. Because he always slept naked, he stood before the window naked, with a doctor's offhandedness about the body, surveying the neighborhood. She thought he resembled the pope blessing the multitudes in Vatican square, but no: on second thought, he didn't resemble the pope at all, starting with the nakedness. He loved the body as much as he loved the spirit: he liked getting down on his knees in front of her nakedness to kiss her belly and incite her to soft moans.

"We should go somewhere," she said, thumbing through a guidebook, which he had already read. "I'd like to see the Old Town Square. We'd have to take the tram there. Are you up for that?"

"Hmm. How about the chapels in the Loreto?" he asked. "That's right up here. We could walk to it in ten minutes and then go to the river." He turned around and approached her, sitting next to her on the bed, taking her hand in his. "It's all so close, we could soak it all up, first thing."

"Sure," she said, although she didn't remember anything from the guidebooks about the Loreto chapels and couldn't guess why he wanted to see them. He raised her hand to his mouth and kissed her fingers one by one, which always gave her chills.

"Oh, honey," she said, leaning into him. He was the only man she had ever loved, and she was still trying to get used to it. She had done her best not to be scared by the way she often felt about him. His intelligence, the concern for children, the quiet loving homage he paid to her, the wit, the indifference to sports, the generosity, and then the weird secret toughness—where could you find another guy like that? It didn't even matter that they were staying in a bad hotel. Nothing else mattered. "What's in those chapels?" she asked. "How come we're going there?"

"Babies," he told her. "Hundreds of babies." He gave her a smile. "Our baby is in there."

After dressing in street clothes, they walked down Bělohorská toward the spot on the map where the chapel was supposed to be. In the late-summer morning, Susan detected traceries of autumnal chill, a specifically Czech irony in the air, with high wispy cirrus clouds threading the sky like promissory notes. Elijah took her hand, clasping it very hard, checking both ways as they crossed the tramway tracks, the usual *Pozor!* warnings posted on their side of the platform, telling them to beware of whatever. The number 18 tram lumbered toward them silently from a distance up the hill to the west.

Fifteen minutes later, standing inside one of the chapels, Susan felt herself soften from all the procreative excess on display. Elijah had been right: carved babies took up every available space. Surrounding them on all sides—in the front, at the altar; in the back, near the choir loft, where the carved cherubs played various musical instruments; and on both walls—were plump winged infants in various postures of angelic gladness. She'd never seen so many sculpted babies in one place: cherubs not doing much of anything except engaging in a kind of abstract giggling frolic, freed from both gravity and the earth, the great play of Being inviting worship. What bliss! God was in the babies. But you had to look up, or you wouldn't see them. The angelic orders were always above you. At the front, the small cross on the altar rested at eye level, apparently trivial, unimportant, outnumbered, in this nursery of angels. For once, the famous agony had been trumped by babies, who didn't care about the Crucifixion or hadn't figured it out.

"They loved their children," Susan whispered to Elijah. "They worshiped infants."

"Yeah," Elijah said. She glanced up at him. On his face rested an expression of great calm, as if he were in a kingdom of sorts where he knew the location of everything. He *was* a pediatrician, after all. "Little kids were little ambassadors from God in those days. Look at that one." He pointed. "Kind of a lascivious smile. Kind of *knowing*."

She wiped a smudge off his cheek with her finger. "Are you hungry? Do you want lunch yet?"

He dug into his pocket and pulled out a nickel, holding it out as if he were about to drop it into her hand. Then he took it back. "We just got here. It's not lunchtime. We got out of bed less than two hours ago. I love you," he said matter-of-factly, apropos of nothing. "Did I already tell you this morning? I love you like crazy." His voice rose with an odd conviction. The other tourists in the chapel glanced at them. Was their love that obvious? Outside, the previous day, sitting near a fountain, Susan had seen a young man and a young woman, lovers, steadfastly facing each other and stroking each other's thighs, both of them crazed with desire and, somehow, calm about it.

"Yes," she said, and a cool wind passed through her at that moment, right in through her abdomen and then out the back near her spine. "Yes, you do, and thanks for bringing me here, honey, and I agree that we should go to the Kafka Museum too, but you know what? We need to see if we can get tickets to *The Marriage of Figaro* tonight, and anyway I want to walk around for a while before we go back to that hotel."

He looked down at her. "That's interesting. You didn't say you loved me now." His smile faded. "I said I love you, and you mentioned opera tickets. I hope I'm not being petty, but my love went out to you and was not returned. How come? Did I do something wrong?"

"It was an oversight. No, wait a minute. You're wrong. I did say that. I *did* say I love you. I say it a lot. You just didn't hear me say it this time."

"No, I don't think that's right," he said, shaking his head like a sad horse, back and forth. "You didn't say it."

"Well, I love you now," she said, as a group of German tourists waddled in through the entranceway. "I love you this very minute." She waited. "This is a poor excuse for a quarrel. Let's talk about something else."

"There," he said, pointing to a baby angel. "How about that one? That one will be ours. The doctor says so." The angel he had pointed to had wings, as they all did, but this one's arms were outstretched as if in welcome, and the wings were extended as if the angel were about to take flight.

After leaving the chapel, walking down a side street to the old city, they encountered a madwoman with gray snarled hair and only two visible teeth who was carrying a shopping bag full of scrap cloth. She had caught up to them on the sidewalk, emerging from an alleyway, and she began speaking to them in rapid vehement Czech, poking them both on their shoulders to make her unintelligible points. Everything about her was untranslatable, but given the way she was glaring at them, she seemed to be engaged in prophecy of some kind, and Susan intuited that the old woman was telling them both what their future life together would be like. "You will eventually go back to your bad hotel, you two," she imagined the old woman saying in Czech, "and you will have your wish, and with that good-hearted husband of yours, you will conceive a child, your firstborn, a son, and you will realize that you're pregnant because when you fall asleep on the night of your son's conception, you will dream of a giant raspberry. How do I know all this? Look at me! It's my business to know. I'm out of my mind." Elijah gently nudged the woman away from Susan, taking his wife's hand and crossing the street. When Susan broke free of her husband's grip and looked back, she saw the crone shouting. "You're going to be so terribly jealous of your husband *because of the woman in him!*" the old woman screamed in Czech, or so Susan imagined, but somehow that made no sense, and she was still trying to puzzle it out when she turned around and was gently knocked over by a tram that had slowed for the Malostranské stop.

The following commotion—people surrounding her, Elijah asking her nonsensical diagnostic questions—was all a bit of a blur, but only because everyone except for her husband was speaking Czech or heavily accented English, and before she knew it, she was standing up. She looked at the small crowd assembled around her, tourists and citizens, and in an effort to display good health she saluted them. Only after she had done it, and people were staring, did she think that gestures like that might be inappropriate.

"Good God," Elijah said. "Why'd you do that?"

"I felt like it," she told him.

"Are you okay? Where does it hurt?" he asked, touching her professionally. "Here? Or here?"

"It doesn't hurt anywhere," she said. "I just got jostled. I lost my balance. Can't we go have lunch?" The tram driver was speaking to her in Czech, but she was ignoring him. She glanced down at her jeans. "See? I'm not even scuffed up."

"You almost fell under the wheels," he half groaned.

"Really, Elijah. Please. I'm fine. I've never been finer. Can't we go now?" Strangers were still muttering to her, and someone was translating. When they calmed down and went back to their business after a few minutes, she felt a great sense of relief. She didn't want anyone to think of her as a victim. She was no one's and nothing's victim ever. Or: maybe she was in shock.

"So here we are," Elijah said. "We've already been to a chapel, seen a baby, talked to a crazy person, had an accident, and it's only eleven."

"Well, all right, let's have coffee, if we can't have lunch."

He held her arm as they crossed the street and made their way to a sidewalk café with a green awning and a signboard that seemed to indicate that the café's name had something to do with a sheep. The sun was still shining madly in its touristy way. Ashtrays (theirs was cracked) were placed on all the tables, and a man with a thin wiry white beard and a beret was smoking cigarette after cigarette nearby. He gazed at Susan and Elijah with intense indifference. Susan wanted to say: *Yes, all right, we're stupid American tourists, like the rest of them, but I was just hit by a tram!* The waiter came out and took their order: two espressos.

"You didn't see that thing coming?" Elijah asked, sitting up and looking around. "My God. It missed me by inches."

"I wasn't hit," she said. "I've explained this to you. I was nudged. I was nudged and lost my balance and fell over. The tram was going about two miles an hour. It happens."

"No," he said. "It *doesn't* happen. When has it ever happened?"

"Elijah, it just did. I wasn't thinking. That woman, the one we saw, that woman who was shouting at us . . ."

"She was just a crazy old lady. That's all she was. There are crazy old people everywhere. Even here in Europe. Especially here. They go crazy, history encourages it, and they start shouting, but no one listens."

"No. No. She was shouting at *me*. She had singled me out. That's why I wasn't looking or paying attention. And what's really weird is that I could understand her. I mean, she was speaking in Czech or whatever, but I could understand her."

"Susan," he said. The waiter came with their espressos, daintily placing them on either side of the cracked ashtray. "Please. That's delusional. Don't get me wrong—that's not a criticism. I still love you. You're still beautiful. Man, are you beautiful. It just kills me, how beautiful you are. I can hardly look at you."

"I know." She leaned back. "But listen. Okay, sure, I know it's delusional, I get that, but she said I was going to be jealous of you. That part I didn't get." She thought it was better not to mention that they would have a son.

"Jealous? Jealous of me? For what?"

"She didn't . . . *say.*"

"Well, then."

"She said I'd get pregnant."

"Susan, honey."

"And that I'd dream of a giant raspberry on the night of conception."

"Oh, for Christ's sake. A raspberry. Please stop."

"You're being dismissive. I'm serious. When have I ever said or done anything like this before? Well, all right, maybe a few times. But I *can't* stop."

The man sitting next to them lifted his beret and held it aloft for a moment before putting it back on his head.

"Yeah, that's right. Thank you," Elijah said to the man. He pulled out a bill, one hundred crowns, from his wallet and dropped it on the table. "Susan, we need to get back to the hotel. Okay? Right now. Please?"

"Why? I'm fine. I've never been better."

He gazed at her. He would take her back to the hotel, pretending to want to make love to her, and he *would* make love to her, but the lovemaking would just be a pretext so that he could do a full hands-on medical examination of her, top to bottom. She had seen him pull such stunts before, particularly in moments when the doctor in him, the force of his caretaking, had overpowered his love.

What she saw in her dream wasn't a raspberry. The crone had gotten that part wrong. What she saw was a tree, a white pine, growing in a forest alongside a river, and the tree swayed as the wind pushed at it, setting up a breathy whistling sound.

*

They named their son Raphael, which, like Michael, was an angel's name. Elijah claimed that he had always liked being an Elijah, so they had looked up angel names and prophet names on Google and quickly discarded the ones like Zadkiel and Jerahmeel that were just too strange: exile-on-the-playground names. Susan's mother thought that naming a child after an angel was extreme bad luck, given the name's high visibility, but once the baby took after Susan's side of the family—he kept a stern gaze on objects of his attention, though he laughed easily, as Susan's father did—the in-laws eventually softened and stopped complaining about his being a Raphael. Anyway, Old Testament names were coming back. You didn't have to be the child of a Midwestern farmer to have one. On their block in San Francisco, an Amos was the child of a mixed-race couple; a Sariel belonged to a gay couple; and Gabriel, a bubbly toddler, as curious as a cat, lived next door.

After they brought Raphael home from the hospital, they set up a routine so that if Elijah was home and not at the hospital, he would give Raphael his evening feeding. On a Tuesday night, Susan went upstairs and found Elijah holding the bottle of breast milk in his left hand while their son lay cradled in his right arm. They had painted the room a boy's blue, and sometimes she could still smell the paint. Adhesive stars were affixed to the ceiling.

A small twig snapped inside her. Then another twig snapped. She felt them physically. Looking at her husband and son, she couldn't breathe.

"You're holding him wrong," she said.

"I'm holding him the way I always hold him," Elijah said. Raphael continued to suck milk from the bottle. "It's not a big mystery. I *know* how to hold babies. It's what I do."

She heard the sound of a bicycle bell outside. The thick bass line on an over-amped car radio approached and then receded down the block. She inhaled with great effort.

"He's uncomfortable. You can tell. Look at the way he's curled up."

"Actually, no," Elijah said, moving the baby to his shoulder to burp him. "You can't tell. He's nursing just fine." From his sitting position, he looked up at her. "This is my job."

"There's something I can't stand about this," Susan told him. "Give me a minute. I'm trying to figure it out." She walked into the room and leaned against the changing table. She glanced at the floor, trying to think of how to say to Elijah the strange thought that had an imminent, crushing weight, that she had to say aloud or she would die. "I told you you're not holding him right."

"And I told you that I am."

"Elijah, I don't want you feeding him." There. She had said it. "I don't want you nursing him. I'm the mother here. You're not."

"What? You're kidding. You don't want me nursing him? Now? Or ever?"

"I don't want you feeding Raphael. Period."

"That's ridiculous. What are you talking about?"

"I can't stand it. I'm not sure why. But I can't."

"Susan, listen to yourself, listen to what you're saying. You don't get to decide something like this—we both do. I'm as much a parent here as you are. All I'm doing is holding a baby bottle with your breast milk in it while Raphael sucks on it, and then—well, *now*—I'm holding him on my shoulder while he burps." He had a slightly clinical, almost diagnostic expression on his face, checking her out.

"Actually, no, I don't think you're paying attention to what I'm saying." She fixed him with a sad look, even though what she felt was positive rage. Inwardly, she was resisting the impulse to snatch their baby out of his arms. With one part of her mind, she saw this impulse as animal truth, if not actually unique to her; but with another part, she thought: *Every mother feels this way, every mother has felt this, it's time to stand up*. She was not going to chalk this one up to postpartum depression or hormonal imbalances or feminine moodiness. She had come upon this truth, and she would not let it go. She felt herself lifting off. "You can't be his mother. You can't do this. I won't let you."

"You're in a moment, Susan," he said. "You'll get over it."

"No, I won't get over it." Raphael burped onto Elijah. "I'll never get over it, and you will not fucking tell me that I will."

"Please stop shouting," he said, ostentatiously calm.

"This is not your territory. This is my territory, and you can't have it."

"Are we going to argue about metaphors? Because that's the wrong metaphor."

"We aren't going to argue about anything. Put him down. Put him into the crib."

Elijah stood for a few seconds, and then with painfully executed elaboration he lowered Raphael into the crib and pulled over him the blue blanket that Elijah's mother had made for the baby. He started up the music box and turned around. Both his hands were tightened into fists.

"I'm going out," he said. "I've got to go out right now."

She closed her eyes, and when she opened them, he was gone.

She went downstairs and turned on the TV. On the screen—she kept the sound muted because she didn't really want to get attached to the story—a man with an eagle tattoo on his forearm aimed a gun at a distant figure of indistinct gender. The man fired, whereupon the distant figure fell. The screen cut to a brightly lit room where male authority figures of some kind were jotting down notes and answering landline telephones while they held cups of coffee. Perhaps, she thought, this was an old movie. One woman, probably a cop, heard something on the phone and reacted with alarm. Then she shouted at the others in the room, and their shocked faces were instantly replaced by a soap commercial showing a cartoon rhinoceros in a bubble bath set upon by a trickster monkey, and this commercial was then replaced by another one, with grinning skydivers falling together in a geometrical pattern advertising an insurance company, and then the local newscaster came on with a tease for the ten o'clock news, followed by a commercial for a multinational petroleum operation apparently dedicated to cleaning up the environment and saving baby seals, and Susan scratched her foot, and she was looking at the no-longer-distant figure (a young woman, as it turned out) on an autopsy table as a medical examiner pointed at a bullet hole in the victim's rib-cage area—tantalizingly close to her breasts, which were demurely covered, though the handheld camera seemed eager to see them—and Susan felt her eyes getting heavy, and then another, older woman was hit by a tram in Prague, which was how Susan knew she was dreaming. Sleeping, she wondered when Elijah would return. She wondered, for a moment, where her husband had gone.

When she woke up, Elijah stood before her, bleeding from the side of his mouth, a bruise starting to form just under his left eye. His knuckles were caked and bloody. On his face was an expression of joyful defiance. He was blocking the TV set. It was as if he had come out of it somehow.

She stood up and reached toward him. "You're bleeding."

He brushed her hand away. "Let me bleed."

"What did you say?"

"You heard me. Let me bleed." He was smilingly jubilant. The smile looked like one of the smiles on the faces of the angels in the Loreto chapel.

"What happened to you?" she asked. "You got into a fight. My God. We need to put some ice or something on that." She tried to reach for him again, and again he moved away from her.

"Leave me alone. Listen," he said, straightening up, "you want to know what happened? This is what happened. I was angry at you, and I started walking, and I ended up in Alta Plaza Park. I walked in there, you know, where it was dark? Off those steep stairs on Clay Street? And this is the thing. I wanted to kill somebody. That's kind of a new emotion for me, wanting to kill somebody. I mean, I wasn't looking for someone to kill, but that's what I was *thinking*. I'm just trying to be honest here. So I went up the stairs and found myself at the top, with the view, with the famous view of the city.

"Everybody admires the view, and I looked off into the darkness and thought I heard a scream, somewhere off there in the distance, and so, you know, I went toward it, toward the scream, the way anybody would. So I made my way off into the shadows, and what I saw was this other thing."

"This thing?"

"Yeah, that's right. This other thing. These two guys were beating up this girl, tearing her clothes, and then they had her down, one of them was holding her down, and the other one was, you know, lowering his jeans. No one else was around. So I went in.

"I wasn't even thinking. I went in and grabbed the guy who was holding her down, and I slugged him. The other one, he got up and punched me in the kidneys. The woman, I think *she* stood up. No, I *know* she stood up because she said something in Spanish, and she ran away. I was fighting these guys, and she took off. She didn't stay. I know she ran because when I hit the guy who was behind me with my elbow, I saw her running away, and I saw that she was barefoot."

"This was in Alta Plaza Park?"

"Yeah."

"That's in Pacific Heights. They don't usually have crime over there."

"Well, they did tonight. I was fighting with those guys, and I finally landed a good one, on the first guy, and I broke his jaw. *I heard it break.* That was when they took off. The second guy took off, and the one with the broken jaw was groaning and went after him. No honor among thieves." He smiled. "Goddamn, I feel great."

She lifted his hand and touched the knuckles where scabs were forming. "So you were brave."

"Yes, I was."

"You saved her."

"Anybody would have done it."

"No," she said. "I don't think so."

She led him upstairs and sat him down on the edge of the bathtub. With a washcloth, she dabbed the blood off his hands and face. There was something about his story she didn't believe, and then for a moment she didn't accept a word of it, but she continued to wash him tenderly as if he were the hero he said he was. He groaned quietly when she touched some newly bruised part of him. He would look terrible for a while. How happy that would make him! She could easily get some steak, or hamburger, or whatever you were supposed to apply to a black eye to make the swelling go away, but no, he wouldn't want that. He would want his badge. They all wanted that.

"Should we go to bed, doctor?" she asked.

"Yes."

"I love you," she said. They would postpone the argument about feedings until tomorrow, or next week.

"I love you too."

She took him upstairs and undressed him, just as if he were a child, before lowering him onto the sheets. He sighed loudly. She could hear Raphael's breath coming from the nursery. She was about to go to her son's room to check on him and then thought better of it. Standing in the hallway, she heard a voice asking, "What will you do with another day?" Who had asked that? Elijah was asleep. Anyway, it was a nonsensical question. The air had asked it, or she was hearing voices. She went into the bathroom to brush her teeth. She didn't quite recognize her own face in the mirror, but the reflected swollen tender breasts were still hers, and the smile, when she thought of sweet Elijah bravely fighting someone, somewhere—that was hers too.

MICHAEL BYERS

Malaria

FROM *Bellevue Literary Review*

WHEN I WAS in college in Eugene I had a girlfriend named Nora Vardon. We had fallen together sort of accidentally, I talked to her first at a vending machine where we were both buying coffee, and things progressed in the usual slow ways, we went out one cold night to look at the blurry stars, and that led to some kissing, and from there we started the customary excavation of our families, revealing, not quite competitively, how crazy they both were, she with a raft of depressives and schizophrenics and me with a bunch of drunks, mainly the men on my father's side. She had an open, genial, feline face, with big cheeks and dark eyes, and a big, soft body that was round in parts and that was covered, for three months out of the year, with the big textured bruises left by lacrosse balls. She was very pretty, really, and I counted myself lucky to be around her. I was skinny and out of necessity got cheap haircuts, so I wasn't much to look at, and I tended to be secretive, I suppose you could put it that way, although I had nothing to be secretive about, being only twenty and unadventurous.

But Nora and I hit it off. She was studying botany, for which the college had a sort of reputation, and spent her hours in the long white greenhouses at the edge of campus. The heat affected her well. Her hair, brown and a little wavy, would become affixed to her cheeks, and as she worked at the potting tables her dark eyes would take on a comfortable, meditative languor there amid the odor of the soil and the dense humid air and the metallic smell of water dripping from the galvanized piping. To find Nora there I would have come from the library's back door and out across a section of newly planted pines, which were staked to the earth as though they might otherwise pull up their roots and walk away. The sky in winter was usually sealed with a dense marine overcast, but inside the greenhouses the light was bright, brilliant, and contained. "My ride is here," Nora would say to no one, as I came down the concrete walkway—or, "My Orlando," with the accent purposely wrong, on the last syllable, and her mouth would make its charming little O, and I'd give her a kiss, and it would be enough to make me happy.

Nora and I had friends, most of them Nora's, actually, and we did the usual collegiate things, mostly just drinking, sitting around talking until late: black Emory from Philadelphia, fat Harold the townie, tall flaxen Winnie from Texas, the sad red-haired poet Matt Grange. I worked with Matt three mornings a week in the alumni office, answering phones. Matt would sit at his desk, composing his lines and crumpling them up and throwing them away, and I would sit at my desk across the room from him, doing nothing, and every now and then a perfect peace would come over me, for no reason I could find, and even just sitting and typing under the fluorescent lights—with the rain clouds gathering beyond the tall windows—seemed a civilized and decent thing to do, maybe for the rest of my life. At the time I didn't have much idea of what I wanted, in the larger sense, but it didn't worry me. I thought I might like to work for a newspaper one day, maybe in Eugene, or maybe in Seattle, where I came from, but there was plenty of time, I thought, and plenty of time after that too. I wasn't headed anywhere on any fast track, that was plain even then, and I didn't have any kind of natural flair, but I had Nora, and it felt to me like a fair exchange. I was romantic, in the silly way of young men. The rest of my life, I imagined at the time, would be only a collection of details—addings-on—corollaries—to the central fact of Nora Vardon.

Eventually it came time to visit Nora's parents, Jack and Annette Vardon, who lived a few hundred miles north in Vancouver, British Columbia. Mr. Vardon turned out to have a friendly oblong head and a mustache, and he worked—I was never quite sure about this—as an engineering manager, or a consultant engineer, maybe as a consultant to other engineering managers, at any rate he went off every day in his beige raincoat and came back at night and seemed to make a good living at his business, whatever it was. We didn't see much of him. Mrs. Vardon stayed at home and played tennis in the backyard, and had given Nora her dark eyes and round girlish cheeks. "Orlando," said Annette, on the back porch where we ate, "what an interesting name that is." The day was unusual, almost warm, though it was only the middle of March.

"They wanted me to be different," I said.

"You're not Spanish?"

"No," I said. "German, mostly."

"We named Nora after her Spanish great-grandmother." Nora's mother wore a little white dress that showed her knobby knees. "Believe it or not, my mother always wanted to be Jewish. In fact she always *said* she was Jewish, but everyone knew she wasn't. But she wanted to be."

"Be Jewish?" I asked, for clarity.

"Oh, God knows why. She thought it had some cachet, I suppose. Out of the frying pan and into the fire, if you ask me, in terms of what you have to face in this world."

"Sure."

"Now, I admire the Jews," said Annette.

"Mom."

"I *do*. I guess everyone does these days. If you don't, you're an anti-Semite. But I suppose in admiring them I'm doing something wrong."

"You're making them exotic," said Nora. "You're *othering* them."

"Well, I guess I don't know what you mean. And they *are* exotic. They *are*. To me, they are. I don't know any, really, except Elly Bergman, and she doesn't count, she's not really *anything*. Which not knowing any is a failing on my part. But they're a very healthy people. Doctors. And they're a *sad* people, which I like. I like sad people. It's the way people should be. If everyone was sad, we wouldn't have all these *problems*." She cast her arms wide. "Don't tell me we need all these *problems*."

While visiting her parents Nora and I slept in separate bedrooms: me in her older brother George's room (he was living in an apartment a mile or so away and had taken all his things with him, so the room had a neutral, underinhabited feeling) and Nora in her old childhood bedroom with the posters and so forth. Nora wouldn't sneak in to see me at night, and I didn't exactly want to take the initiative and go next door, but during the long days, with the father gone and the mother off somewhere with friends, we made up for it in George's room. Not in hers, Nora insisted, because that would be too weird. And then afterward we'd laze around naked with the light through the windows, listening to the garbage trucks churn through the neighborhood. "I can't believe she said those things," said Nora. "You know, she's always had a thing about Jewish people. I think she's afraid she's secretly somehow *one* of them. That her mother was right. That wouldn't bother you, would it?"

"Your mom's cute," I said. "She looks like you."

"Like me?" She considered this. "Maybe me on a very bad day."

We were going to be there for about a week, and on the second day, George, the brother, came around to do laundry and to eat. George was thin and dried-out, like a kind of cowboy, and his long fingers fiddled, fiddled, and touched his hair, and pulled his turtleneck sweater up over his chin. Nora loved him and grew sly and contentious with him around. "Mom says you still don't have a decent job," she said.

"Oh, but I do. I'm fully employed, soaking the rich." He rolled his eyes at their parents in the next room. "You know how that goes."

"No," she said, "I'm *working* for my money."

"Sure. You just get the check in the mail. I've got to *manage* the little dollies. Manage, manage, manage. They require," he said, turning to me, "manipulation."

"I like them."

He eyed me appraisingly. "Where'd you get this one?" he said.

"Don't tease him."

"Actually, I'm not teasing," he said gently. "The last one she brought around here was a real bastard."

"Ingraham," she explained, "from high school."

"But I like this new guy."

"I'm likable."

"Hey," George cried agreeably, "me too! Okay, let's play some tennis." He thrust himself out of his chair and clambered around in the closet under the stairs, emerging with a pair of old wooden rackets.

"Well, George," Nora said, "we've got perfectly good regular rackets."

"No." He bowed. "This is the tradition. If you don't mind."

"Okay," I said.

"It is," he pronounced, "more sporting this way."

He was better than I was, I think—I mean, he could hit the ball squarely and very hard and he served fast and accurately, he had grown up with the court in his backyard, after all, whereas I had bonked the ball around only in the neighborhood parks. But he had no stamina, and he wouldn't run for balls he could have got, so I kept it fairly close for a while. He began to get red in the face, and he took off his shirt, which showed his narrow chest, with a fuzzy badge of black hair on his sternum. The sun lit half the court through the pine trees with a stagey, slanty beauty. I wasn't in the best shape either, I began to fade halfway through the set, but I did all right, and finally I beat him, 6–4. He sagged at the back line and I felt a moment's compunction for my having been, as it seemed to me suddenly, impolite, a poor houseguest, but then he joined me at the net, flushed and sweaty. "Nice," he said.

"Thanks. You too."

"Yeah, well, I've got malaria," he said, flicking sweat from his eyebrows, "just for your information."

He wasn't that much older than me: a year, maybe two. It stung him, I thought, to have been beaten at home, with his sister watching, off and on, from the upstairs windows. I said, "Sorry."

"Not your fault. Got it in Ecuador."

"You're better than I am," I said. "Just lost your wind. Plus these rackets."

"Yeah, well, don't go to Ecuador."

"Okay." But as far as I knew, he'd never been to Ecuador.

"Or if you do," he said significantly, "take precautions."

My only real dealing with Mr. Vardon came just after this, while I was in the hall, heading for the shower. "You give the boyo a workout?" he asked.

I said something nice, I don't know what.

"I used to play. That's why we built it. For me. But I fouled up my back. Fixing a flat tire, if you can believe it. So I just get to sit here and look at it. At least it gets some use from somebody. My wife likes it. And you beat George. Good for you. I never could. That lucky bastard."

"Said he's a little sick."

"Sure. Actually he smokes too much and never exercises. He's got the body of a forty-year-old man. Like a little skinny one."

I thought about telling Mr. Vardon what his son had said to me, but I thought both of us would end up looking a little strange. Or he'd look strange and I'd look mean for repeating it. So I just kept my mouth shut, and Nora's father walked off into his bedroom, where, with the door open, he shucked off his white shirt with a brisk, demonstrative flourish. His stomach was still trim, his biceps hefty. Then he reached over and closed the door, and that was really the last I saw of him until several months later, after everything had changed.

Heading home aboard the all-night charter bus, Nora slept on my shoulder and I sat with my head resting against the glass, with the sewery citrus stink of the bathroom catching me now and then. At about three in the morning we passed through Seattle, where all the drunken uncles of my line were sleeping it off. My own parents had managed to construct a safe little life for themselves and for me, but this project had taken up all their effort, as I thought of it then, and while they were proud of me for walking the straight and narrow, and I could admire them for having done the same, we didn't really have a lot to say to one another anymore. (This has remained true until today, in fact.) It was as though none of the three of us quite knew what to do with ourselves if our lives weren't burning down in the way everyone else's were. So I wasn't sad or particularly anything as the bus barreled through the city and south toward Oregon. The bus stopped in Kelso and we all wandered around stunned in the fluorescent lights, smelling the hash browns, and then it was back on the bus for the last hours south into Eugene, which, in the early morning, was a lovely place, pink and yellow, with sheets of pale sunlight falling over the college buildings and fog rising from the fountains, the fast-food franchises just opening up, and the dark gray houses holding within themselves their little secrets, innumerable men and women starting up from their beds, getting on with the day. The joke, when I was in high school—or maybe it was really a joke from *The Breakfast Club,* I don't remember—was that if you didn't actually have a girlfriend, you said you had a Canadian girlfriend, someone who was off somewhere out of sight, immune to judgment. But here I was with the Canadian girlfriend on my shoulder, for real. It was true now, and different from what I thought it would be, easier, less contentious, more like real life than I had imagined.

Nora and I stayed in Eugene that summer, working, and over the weeks that followed Nora got mostly bad news from home. George had gone back to work, then quit again. Then it turned out he'd actually been fired after he started a fire in the grease trap, which closed the restaurant for two days, after which he moved back home, into his old bedroom. Then he stopped coming out of his room. It sounded ominous to me, as though he was seriously off-track, but Nora never thought of it that way until George was arrested naked, in the summer rain, in the middle of the high school athletic fields, turning in circles and talking to himself. After this his parents kept him at home for a while, watching him, and there were long conversations back and forth, which I basically got the gist of, they were obviously worried about his mind, and eventually (after what seemed a long delay) they took him in to see a doctor, and he was medicated, which seemed to help. The Vardon family history had found another occasion to express itself, evidently. I never told Nora about his malaria comment, though I felt uneasy about it—I saw it now for what it seemed to be, an early indication of some delusion.

"He says he's hearing voices," Nora told me. "But *everybody* hears voices. *I* hear voices. Everybody does. I hear my name in the cafeteria, I always think somebody's calling me, it's this *voice,* but it's not—it doesn't have any *qualities*. It's not masculine, it's not feminine, it's just a voice, it's like the *idea* of a voice. It's like telepathy."

I regarded the pretty curve of her shoulders. The easy warmth of an Oregon July filtered around the edges of the window frame. I put my hand on the small of her back. I whispered: *"Nora."*

"Don't." She swatted at me.

"But sweetheart," I said, "you'd know if you were crazy."

"But I probably *wouldn't.* Don't you see? That's sort of the definition of crazy." She fixed me with a hard, calculating stare. She had her own opinions, and I didn't then know how to talk her out of them, or that I was supposed to simply listen to her; I was too young to know what to say or do, I had so little experience with things and with women in particular, and I believed a kind of frictionless amiability was what would serve my interests. So when she said things like this, I mostly just discounted them, thinking that would help. She said, finally, "We're sort of a pathetic couple, when you think about it."

"No, we're not," I said. "You're great, and I'm great."

"Not you and *me*, dummy," she said, "me and *George*."

What I did next was, I took up tennis as seriously as I could. I found I remembered the nice contact the ball made with the strings—a kind of exponential action, with the ball plus the strings multiplying to more force than I could have hoped to exert on my own. It was partly an aesthetic choice, looking back; I suppose I liked the way it felt when I hit a ball well, but I can further see that something else must also have been at work, some unkind fascination with the strangeness of George, with the fact that he had begun to fail in this very obvious fashion while I had, so far, not. With my summer ID card I could use the courts behind the recreation building. I signed up on the bulletin board and ended up playing with a set of people who were variously serious about the game—a doctor from Ghana who wore blinding whites; a janitor who owned the most expensive racket I had ever seen, a Mark-8 Wonder, which produced a faint supernatural whistling noise like a hunting owl; a homeschooled sixteen-year-old boy named Elliott who had no offensive instincts whatsoever but who could return nearly anything I sent his way, so he beat me consistently—and so on. I was not exactly serious about the tennis itself, but about the project of self-definition, as I see it now, because this was something very straightforward that I could be, or at least *do*. Nora's lacrosse friends would not recognize me in the fall, and neither would Matt Grange—or better yet, they would recognize that they had never really seen the true me. And it was not just that I was not failing as George was. I think this summer was also the period when I first struck on the idea of ambition, that I could be something in particular, rather than just myself in general.

Nora went back and forth to Vancouver by herself a few times that summer and fall, but it wasn't until Thanksgiving that I went north with her again. By this time George had been living at home for some months. Mrs. Vardon greeted us at the bus station, wearing a white sweater and a puffy white parka, her black eyes and round cheeks seeming, in the cold morning light, like something arctic, adapted for long darkness. "Orlando," she said, taking my arm. "Now, you know about George. You know he's a little different than when you last saw him."

It was a Saturday, so Mr. Vardon was home too. He was in the dining room, reading a newspaper. "Hello, Orlando," said Mr. Vardon. "Welcome again."

"Hello. Thank you."

Together Nora and I went upstairs. George's white door was closed. No sound came from it. Nora knocked. "Come in," he said.

In some ways her brother looked the same. A smoky, sweaty, outdoor odor had filled the room, not unpleasantly; a window was open, and the room was cool, almost cold. He wore a T-shirt and was skinnier than he was the last time I'd seen him. His expression was different, less fierce, more uncertain. "Hey," he noted, "it's the boyfriend."

"Hi," I said.

Nora said, "You look good, Georgie."

"Yeah, bullshit," he said.

"It's cold in here," said Nora.

"I still get hot," he said. "It's something to do with the pills." Addressing me, he gestured languidly toward the dresser, where five brown plastic bottles stood. "Screws up your thermostat."

She said, "You should comb your hair."

"Sure, but if I started now it'd look suspicious."

"Oh, it would *not*."

"The other thing is," said George, but only to me, "you know how I was hearing voices. Well, it's still happening. But now it's like in the background. Like the radio. But I can't even listen to the radio anymore. It's just too much blabber. Music's okay. But even then, they talk through the music, it's like annoying, it's like they have a plan to talk during the good parts." He shrugged. "Whatever. You know."

Sensing that Nora and George wanted to be alone, I left them and went downstairs into the hallway. Mr. Vardon had gone off somewhere. I could hear Mrs. Vardon knocking around in the kitchen, making breakfast. I didn't know what to do with myself. What could I say to anyone that wouldn't sound hollow and ridiculous? I had had such a featureless life to that point, so free of pain,

I thought, that I had no training in delivering sympathy. I didn't know how to do it. And Nora did, or was quickly figuring it out. I stood alone in the front hall, feeling stupid and useless.

After a few minutes Nora came back down. "I got cold," she said.

"Listen," I said.

"He's better than he *was,*" she said.

"Listen, when we were here in the spring," I said, "George said something to me, and I know it maybe doesn't matter, but I just wanted to tell you. He said he had malaria. After we played tennis. I feel like I should have told someone. Like maybe it was a warning sign."

"Oh," she said, distantly, "don't worry about it."

"But I do." I took her in my new strong arms. "I worry about it."

"Please don't," she insisted.

"Maybe I should have said something earlier."

"But sweetheart," she said, looking up at me, "you realize we couldn't have done anything."

"But I just thought maybe we could have."

"Oh, sweetheart," she sighed, sinking against me in quiet disappointment, "this has nothing to do with you." George had left his door open, and it was becoming cold in the downstairs hallway, and then we were shivering there next to the banister, in our light traveling clothes.

Poor George lived on, and lives on still, as far as I know, sick and probably messed up in the predictable ways. He was important to me in the way such people can be, surprisingly, really out of proportion to their actual size in your life. I remember, for example, thinking about him some years later, one Seattle winter, a long time after Nora and I had gone our separate ways. I had come down with the flu and was deep under the covers at home, my wife off at work and me alone in the bedroom in the strange empty middle of the day. The peculiar quiet that entered my sickroom—the heated stillness—the dense damp packing of my chest—the fluid limpness that had overtaken me—and the individual details of the wallpaper, which my wife and I had newly hung, with its tiny red strawberries, and the imagined vastness of my old city beyond the windows—all the city's long streets and silent windowed towers, and above it a complex geography of clouds and sky—all of it combined in some alchemy of illness so that I seemed, momentarily, to be inhabiting a continent of wildness, of strangeness. In the manner of men getting older I sometimes ended up thinking sort of longingly about the past whenever my current life was slow, or whenever I felt I deserved better, which meant that over the years I had on and off thought of Nora and her air of restrained tragedy, and her poor brother George. But this new fevered condition felt like a different world, one that I occupied for only a few hours, where love meant nothing and where you could see, delirious, through walls—where you knew everything, and where no one would ever ask anything of you. That's not quite it, but it was something like that. I was pretty sick, and it was a terrible afternoon, during which I felt a hideous estrangement from the plain objects of everyday life. The trees and empty cars I could see from my pillow seemed filled with a brooding, unaccommodating presence—a malingering spirit—and a peculiar half-light, like that of an eclipse, seemed to enter the room through the venetian blinds. I shivered because I felt, as I had never felt in my life, alone in the world—not only alone but as though I were the only human left around. But then after a while I returned to my senses. I was only sick, after all, and it was only a passing feeling, and slowly things resolved themselves into their familiar places, and I went on, after a day or so, pretty much the way I had before.

I don't want to say that I ever really gave poor George Vardon a whole lot of serious thought. It's just that once in a while his story, his terrible fate, would secretly animate a day for me as I walked around, and I would wonder what I was supposed to do with what I knew about him—with the whole fact of his sad life as I understood it. It was not the saddest life ever lived, of course, but it was enough so I would wonder: What are we supposed to do with what we know? What is George Vardon to me?

And these days it strikes me that possibly these aren't exactly the questions. Maybe we're not supposed to do anything. Maybe this is just a story of something that happened to me, and not even really to me at all. It's really George's story, that is, but naturally he can't tell it, and neither can I.

JUNOT DÍAZ

Miss Lora

FROM *The New Yorker*

YEARS LATER, YOU would wonder if it hadn't been for your brother, would you have done it? You'd remember how all the other guys had hated on her—how skinny she was, no culo, no titties, como un palito, but your brother didn't care. I'd fuck her.

You'd fuck anything, someone jeered.

And he had given that someone the eye. You make that sound like it's a bad thing.

Your brother. Dead from the cancer, and sometimes you still felt a fulgurating sadness over it, even though he really was a super asshole at the end. He didn't die easy at all. Those last months, he just steady kept trying to run away. He'd be caught trying to hail a cab outside Beth Israel or walking down some Newark street in his greens. Once he conned an ex-girlfriend into driving him to California, but outside of Camden he started having convulsions and she called you in a panic. Was it some atavistic impulse to die alone, out of sight? Or was he just trying to fulfill something that had always been inside him? Why do you keep doing that? you asked, but he just laughed. Doing what?

In those last weeks, when he finally became too feeble to run away, he refused to talk to you or your mother. Didn't utter a single word until he died. Your mother didn't care. She loved him and prayed over him and talked to him like he was still okay. But it wounded you, that stubborn silence. His last fucking days and he wouldn't say a word. You'd ask him something straight up, How are you feeling today, and Rafa would turn his head. Like you all didn't deserve an answer. Like no one did.

You were at the age where you could fall in love with a girl over an expression, a gesture. That's what happened with your girlfriend Paloma—she stooped to pick up her purse, and your heart flew out of you.

That's what happened with Miss Lora too.

It was 1985. You were sixteen years old and you were messed up and alone like a motherfucker. You were also convinced—like totally, utterly convinced—that the world was going to blow itself to pieces. Almost every night you had dreams that made the ones the president was having in *Dreamscape* look like pussy play. In your dreams the bombs were always going off, evaporating you while you walked, while you ate a chicken wing, while you rode the bus to school, while you fucked Paloma. You would wake up biting your own tongue in terror, the blood dribbling down your chin.

Someone should have medicated you.

Paloma thought you were being ridiculous. She didn't want to hear about mutual assured destruction, *The Late Great Planet Earth,* "We begin bombing in five minutes," SALT II, *The Day After, Threads, Red Dawn, WarGames,* Gamma World—any of it. She called you Mr. Depressing. And she didn't need any more depressing than she had already. She lived in a one-bedroom apartment with four younger siblings and a disabled mom, and she was taking care of all of them. That and honors classes. She didn't have time for *anything* and mostly stayed with you, you suspected, because she felt bad about what had happened with your brother. It's not like you ever spent much time together or had sex or anything. Only Puerto Rican girl on the earth who wouldn't give up the ass for any reason. I can't, she said. I can't make *any mistakes.* Why is sex with me a mistake, you demanded, but she just shook her head, pulled your hand out of her pants. Paloma was convinced that if she made *any mistakes* in the next two years, *any mistakes at all,* she would be stuck in that family of hers forever. That was her nightmare. Imagine if I don't get in anywhere, she said. You'd still have me, you tried to reassure her, but Paloma looked at you like the apocalypse would be preferable.

So you talked about the coming apocalypse to whoever would

listen—to your history teacher, who claimed he was building a survival cabin in the Poconos, to your boy who was stationed in Panama (in those days you still wrote letters), to your around-the-corner neighbor, Miss Lora. That was what connected you two at first. She listened. Better still, she had read *Alas, Babylon* and had seen part of *The Day After,* and both had scared her monga.

The Day After wasn't scary, you complained. It was crap. You can't survive an air burst by ducking under a dashboard.

Maybe it was a miracle, she said, playing.

A miracle? That was just dumbness. What you need to see is *Threads.* Now, that is some real shit.

I probably wouldn't be able to stand it, she said. And then she put her hand on your shoulder.

People always touched you. You were used to it. You were an amateur weight lifter, something else you did to keep your mind off the shit of your life. You must have had a mutant gene somewhere in the DNA, because all the lifting had turned you into a goddamn circus freak. Most of the time it didn't bother you, the way girls and sometimes guys felt you up. But with Miss Lora you could tell something was different.

Miss Lora touched you, and you suddenly looked up and noticed how large her eyes were in her thin face, how long her lashes were, how one iris had more bronze in it than the other.

Of course you knew her; she lived in the building behind, taught over at Sayreville H.S. But it was only in the past months that she'd snapped into focus. There were a lot of these middle-aged single types in the neighborhood, shipwrecked by every kind of catastrophe, but she was one of the few who didn't have children, who lived alone, who was still kinda young. Something must have happened, your mother speculated. In her mind, a woman with no child could be explained only by vast untrammeled calamity.

Maybe she just doesn't like children.

Nobody likes children, your mother assured you. That doesn't mean you don't have them.

Miss Lora wasn't anything exciting. There were about a thousand viejas in the neighborhood who were way hotter, like Mrs. del Orbe, whom your brother had fucked silly until her husband found out and moved the whole family away. Miss Lora was too skinny. Had no hips whatsoever. No breasts, either, no ass, even her hair failed to make the grade. She had her eyes, sure, but what she was most famous for in the neighborhood was her muscles. Not that she had huge ones like you—chick was just wiry like a motherfucker, every single fiber standing out in outlandish definition. Bitch made Iggy Pop look chub, and every summer she caused a serious commotion at the pool. Always in a bikini despite her curvelessness, the top stretching over these corded pectorals and the bottom cupping a rippling fan of haunch muscles. Always swimming underwater, the black waves of her hair flowing behind her like a school of eels. Always tanning herself (which none of the other women did) into the deep lacquered walnut of an old shoe. That woman needs to keep her clothes on, the mothers complained. She's like a plastic bag full of worms. But who could take their eyes off her? Not you or your brother. The kids would ask her, Are you a bodybuilder, Miss Lora? and she would shake her head behind her paperback. Sorry, guys, I was just born this way.

After your brother died, she came over to the apartment a couple of times. She and your mother shared a common place, La Vega, where Miss Lora was born and where your mother had recuperated after the Guerra Civil. One full year living just behind the Casa Amarilla had made a vegana out of your mother. I still hear the Río Camú in my dreams, your mother said. Miss Lora nodded. I saw Juan Bosch once on our street when I was very young. They sat and talked about it to death. Every now and then she stopped you in the parking lot. How are you doing? How is your mother? And you never knew what to say. Your tongue was always swollen, raw, from being blown to atoms in your sleep.

Today you come back from a run to find her on the stoop, talking to la doña. Your mother calls you. Say hello to la profesora.

I'm sweaty, you protest.

Your mother flares. Who in carajo do you think you're talking to? Say hello, coño, to la profesora.

Hello, profesora.

Hello, student.

She laughs and turns back to your mother's conversation.

You don't know why you're so furious all of a sudden.

I could curl you, you say to her, flexing your arm.

And Miss Lora looks at you with a ridiculous grin. What in the world are you talking about? I'm the one who could pick *you* up.

She puts her hands on your waist and pretends to make the effort.

Your mother laughs thinly. But you can feel her watching the both of you.

When your mother confronted your brother about Mrs. del Orbe, he didn't deny it. What do you want, Ma? Se metío por mis ojos.

Por mis ojos my ass, she'd said. Tu te metiste por su culo.

That's true, your brother admitted cheerily. Y por su boca.

And then your mother punched him, helpless with shame and fury, which only made him laugh.

It is the first time any girl ever wanted you. And so you sit with it. Let it roll around in the channels of your mind. This is nuts, you say to yourself. And later, absently, to Paloma. She doesn't hear you. You don't know what to do with the knowledge. You ain't your brother, who would have run right over and put a rabo in Miss Lora. Even though you know, you're scared you're wrong. You're scared she'd laugh at you.

So you try to keep your mind off her and the memory of her bikinis. You figure the bombs will fall before you get the chance to do shit. When they don't fall, you bring her up to Paloma in a last-ditch effort, tell her la profesora has been after you. It feels very convincing, that lie.

That old fucking hag? That's *disgusting*.

You're telling me, you say in forlorn tones.

That would be like fucking a stick, she says.

It would be, you confirm.

You better not fuck her, Paloma warns you after a pause.

What are you talking about?

I'm just telling you. Don't fuck her. You know I'll find out. You're a terrible liar.

Don't be a crazy person, you say, glaring. I'm not fucking anyone. Clearly.

That night, you are allowed to touch Paloma's clit with the tip of your tongue, but that's it. She holds your head back with the force of her whole life, and eventually you give up, demoralized.

It tasted, you write your boy in Panama, like beer.

You add an extra run to your workout, hoping it will cool your granos, but it doesn't work. You have a couple of dreams where you are about to touch Miss Lora, but then the bomb blows N.Y.C. to kingdom come, and you watch the shock wave roll up, and then you wake, your tongue clamped firmly between your teeth.

And then you are coming back from Chicken Holiday with a four-piece meal, a drumstick in your mouth, and there she is, walking out of Pathmark, wrestling a pair of plastic bags. You consider bolting, but your brother's law holds you in place. *Never run.* A law that he ultimately abrogated, but which you right now cannot. You ask meekly, You want help with that, Miss Lora?

She shakes her head. It's my exercise for the day. You walk back together in silence, and then she says, When are you going to come by to show me that movie?

What movie?

The one you said is the real one. The nuclear-war movie.

Maybe if you were someone else you would have the discipline to duck the whole thing, but you are your father's son and your brother's brother. Two nights later, you are home and the silence in there is terrible and it seems like the same commercial for fixing tears in your car upholstery is on over and over again. You shower, shave, dress, pick up the tape.

I'll be back.

Your mom is looking at your dress shoes. Where are you going?

Out.

It's ten o'clock, she says, but you're already out the door.

You knock on the door once, twice, and then she opens up. She is wearing sweats and a Howard T-shirt, and she tenses her forehead. Her eyes look like they belong on a giant's face.

You don't bother with the small talk. You just push up and kiss. She reaches around and shuts the door behind you.

Do you have a condom? (You are a worrier like that.)

Nope, she says, and you try to keep control, but you come in her anyway.

I'm really sorry, you say.

It's okay, she whispers, her hands on your back, keeping you from pulling out. Stay.

Her apartment is about the neatest place you've ever seen and, for its lack of Caribbean craziness, could be inhabited by a white person. On her walls she has a lot of pictures of her travels and her siblings, and they all seem incredibly happy and square. So you're the rebel? you ask her, and she laughs. Something like that.

There are also pictures of some guys. A few you recognize from when you were younger, and about them you say nothing.

She is very quiet, very reserved while she fixes you a cheeseburger. Actually, I hate my family, she says, squashing the patty down with a spatula until the grease starts popping.

You wonder if she feels like you do. Like it might be love. You put on *Threads* for her. Get ready for some real shit, you say.

Get ready for me to hide, she responds, but you two only last an hour before she reaches over and takes off your glasses and kisses you.

I can't, you say.

And just before she pops your rabo in her mouth, she says, Really?

You try to think of Paloma, so exhausted that every morning she falls asleep on the ride to school. Paloma, who still found the energy to help you study for your S.A.T.'s. Paloma, who didn't give you any ass because she was terrified that if she got pregnant she wouldn't abort it out of love for you and then her life would be over. You're trying to think of her, but what you're doing is holding Miss Lora's tresses like reins and urging her head to keep its wonderful rhythm.

You really do have an excellent body, you say after you blow your load.

Why, thank you. She motions with her head. You want to go into the bedroom?

Even more photos. None of them will survive the nuclear blast, you are sure. Nor will this bedroom, whose window faces toward New York City. You tell her that. Well, we'll just have to make do, she says. She gets naked like a pro, and once you start she closes her eyes and rolls her head around like it's on a broken hinge. She clasps your shoulders with a nailed grip, and you know that afterward your back is going to look like it's been whipped.

Then she kisses your chin.

Both your father and your brother were sucios. Shit, your father used to take you on his pussy runs, leave you in the car while he ran up into cribs to bone his girlfriends. Your brother was no better, boning girls in the bed next to yours. Sucios of the worst kind, and now it's official: you are one too. You'd hoped the gene had missed you, skipped a generation, but clearly you were kidding yourself. The blood always shows, you say to Paloma on the ride to school the next day. Yunior, she stirs from her doze, I don't have time for your craziness, okay?

You figure you can keep it to a onetime thing. But the next day you go right back. You sit gloomily in her kitchen while she fixes you another cheeseburger.

Are you going to be okay? she asks.

I don't know.

It's just supposed to be fun.

I have a girlfriend.

You told me, remember?

She puts the plate on your lap, regards you critically. You know you look like your brother. I'm sure people tell you that all the time.

Some people.

I couldn't believe how good-looking he was. He knew it too. It was like he never heard of a shirt.

This time you don't even ask about the condom. You just come inside her. You are surprised at how pissed you are. But she kisses your face over and over, and it moves you. No one has ever done that. The girls you've boned were always ashamed afterward. And there was always panic. Someone heard. Fix the bed up. Open the windows. Here there is none of that.

Afterward, she sits up, her chest as unadorned as yours. So what else do you want to eat?

You try to be reasonable. You try to control yourself, to be smooth. But you're at her apartment every fucking night. The one time you try to skip, you recant and end up slipping out of your apartment at three in the morning and knocking furtively on her door until she lets you in. You know I work, right? I know, you say, but I dreamed that something happened to you. It's sweet of you to lie, she sighs, and even though she is falling asleep, she lets you bone her straight in the ass. Fucking amazing, you keep saying for all four seconds it takes you to come. You have to pull my hair while you do it, she confides. That makes me shoot like a rocket.

It should be the greatest thing, so why are your dreams worse? Why is there more blood in the sink in the morning?

You learn a lot about her life. She came up in Santo Domingo with a doctor father who was crazy. Her mother left them for an Italian waiter, fled to Rome, and that was it for Pops. Always threatening to kill himself, and at least once a day she'd had to beg him not to, and that had messed her up but good. In her youth, she'd been a gymnast, and there was even talk of making the Olympic team, but then the coach stole the money and the D.R. had to cancel for that year. I'm not claiming I would have won, she says, but I could have done something. After that bullshit, she put on a foot of height and that was it for gymnastics. Then when she was eleven her father got a job in Ann Arbor, Michigan, and she and her three little siblings went with him. After six months he moved them in with a fat widow, una blanca asquerosa who hated Lora. She had no friends at all in school, and in ninth grade she slept with her history teacher. Ended up living in his house. His ex-wife was also a teacher at the school. You can only imagine what that was like. As soon as she graduated, she ran off with a quiet black boy to an air force base in Germany, but that hadn't worked out either. To this day, I think he was gay, she says. And finally, after trying to make it in Berlin, teaching, of all things, she came back to the States. She moved in with a Michigan girlfriend who had an apartment in the Terrace, dated a few guys, one of her ex's old air force buddies who visited her on his leaves, a moreno with the sweetest disposition. When the girlfriend got married and moved away, Miss Lora kept the apartment and found a teaching job. Made a conscious effort to stop moving. It was an okay life, she says, showing you the pictures. All things considered.

She is always trying to get you to talk about your brother. It will help, she says.

What is there to say? He got cancer, he died.

Well, that's a start.

She brings home college brochures from her school. She gives them to you with half the application filled out. You really need to get out of here.

Where? you ask her.

Go anywhere. Go to Alaska, for all I care.

She sleeps with a mouth guard. And she covers her eyes with a mask.

If you have to leave, wait till I fall asleep, okay?

But after a few weeks it's Please don't go. And finally just: Stay.

And you do. At dawn, you slip out of her apartment and into your basement window. Your mother doesn't have a fucking clue. In the old days, she used to know everything. She had that campesino radar. Now she is somewhere else. Her grief, tending to it, takes all her time.

You are scared stupid at what you are doing, but it is also exciting and makes you feel less lonely in the world. And you are sixteen, and you have a feeling that now the Ass Engine has started, no force on the earth will ever stop it.

Then your abuelo catches something in the D.R., and your mother has to fly home. You'll be fine, la doña says. Miss Lora said she'd look after you.

I can cook, Ma.

No, you can't. And don't bring that Puerto Rican girl in here. Do you understand?

You nod. You bring the Dominican woman in instead.

She squeals with delight when she sees the plastic-covered sofa and the wooden spoons hanging on the wall. You admit to feeling a little bad for your mother.

Of course you end up downstairs in your basement. Where your brother's things are still in evidence. She goes right for his boxing gloves.

Please put those down.

She pushes them into her face, smelling them.

You can't relax. You keep swearing that you hear your mother or Paloma at the door. It makes you stop every five minutes. It's unsettling to wake up in your bed with her. She makes coffee and scrambled eggs and listens not to Radio Wado but to the Morning Zoo and laughs at everything. It's too strange. Paloma calls to see if you are going to school, and Miss Lora is walking around in a T-shirt, her flat skinny rump visible.

Then, your senior year, she gets a job at your high school. To say it is strange is to say nada. You see her in the halls, and your heart goes through you. That's your neighbor? Paloma asks. God, she's fucking looking at you. The old whore. At the school, the Spanish girls are the ones who give her trouble. They make fun of her accent, her clothes, her physique. They call her Miss Pat. She never complains about it—It's a really great job, she says—but you see the nonsense firsthand. That's just the Spanish girls, though. The white girls love her to death. She takes over the gymnastics team. She brings the girls to dance programs for inspiration. And in no time they start winning. One day, outside the school, the gymnasts are egging her on and she does a back handspring that nearly staggers you with its perfection. It is the most beautiful thing you've ever seen. Naturally, Mr. Everson, the science teacher, falls all over her. He's always falling over someone. For a while it was Paloma, until she threatened to report his ass. You see them laughing in the hallway; you see them having lunch in the teachers' room.

Paloma doesn't stop busting. They say Mr. Everson likes to put on dresses. You think she straps it on for him?

You girls are nuts.

She probably does strap it on.

It all makes you very tense. But it makes the sex even better.

A few times you see Mr. Everson's car outside her apartment. Looks like Mr. Everson is in the hood, one of your boys laughs. You suddenly find yourself weak with fury. You think about fucking up his car. You think about knocking on the door. You think a thousand things. But you stay at home, lifting, until he leaves. When she opens the door, you stalk in without saying a word to her. The apartment reeks of cigarettes.

You smell like shit, you say.

You walk into her bedroom, but the bed is made.

Ay mi pobre, she laughs. No seas celoso.

But of course you are.

You graduate in June, and she is there with your mother, clapping. She is wearing a red dress, because you once told her it was your favorite color, and matching underwear underneath. Afterward, she drives you both to Perth Amboy for a Mexican dinner. Paloma can't come along because her mother is sick. But you saw her at graduation.

I did it, Paloma says, cheesing.

I'm proud of you, you say. And then you add, uncharacteristically, You are an extraordinary young woman.

That summer, you and Paloma see each other maybe twice, and there are no more make-out sessions. Paloma's already gone. In August, she leaves for the University of Delaware. You are not surprised when after about a week on campus she writes you a letter with the header "Moving On." You don't even bother finishing it. You think about driving all the way down there to talk to her, but you realize how hopeless that is. As might be expected, she never comes back.

You stay in the neighborhood. You land a job at Raritan River Steel. At first you have to fight the Pennsylvania hillbillies, but eventually you find your footing and they leave you alone. At night, you go to the bars with some of the other idiots who stuck around the neighborhood, get seriously faded, and show up at Miss Lora's door with your dick in your hand. She's still pushing the college thing, offers to pay all the admission fees, but your heart isn't in it and you tell her, Not right now. Occasionally you two meet up in Perth Amboy, where people don't know either of you. You have dinner like normal folks. You look too young for her, and it kills you when she touches you in public, but what can you do? She's always happy to be out with you. You know this ain't going to last, you tell her, and she nods. I just want what's best for you. You try your damnedest to meet other girls, telling yourself they'll help you transition, but you never meet anyone you really like.

Sometimes after you leave her apartment you walk out to the landfill where you and your brother played as children and sit on the swings. This is also the spot where Mr. del Orbe threatened to shoot your brother in the nuts. Go ahead, Rafa said, and then my brother here will shoot you in the pussy. Behind you in the distance hums New York City. The world, you tell yourself, will never end.

It takes a long time to get over it. To get used to a life without a Secret. Even after it's behind you and you've blocked her completely, you're still afraid you'll slip back to it. At Rutgers, where you've finally landed, you date like crazy, and every time it doesn't work out, you're convinced that you have trouble with girls your own age. Because of her.

You certainly never talk about it. Until senior year, when you meet the mujerón of your dreams, the one who leaves her moreno boyfriend to date you, who drives all your little chickies out of the coop. She's the one you finally trust. The one you finally tell.

They should arrest that crazy bitch.

It wasn't like that.

They should arrest her ass today.

Still, it is good to tell someone. In your heart you thought she would hate you—that they would all hate you.

I don't hate you. Tú eres mi hombre, she says proudly.

When you two visit your mother, she brings it up. Doña, es verdad que tu hijo taba rapando una vieja?

Your mother shakes her head in disgust. He's just like his father and his brother.

Dominican men, right, doña?

These three are worse than the rest.

Afterward, she makes you walk past Miss Lora's building. There is a light on.

I'm going to go have a word with her, the mujerón says.

Don't. Please.

I'm going to go.

She bangs on the door.

Negra, please don't.

Answer the door! she yells.

No one does.

You don't speak to the mujerón for a few weeks after that. It's one of your big breakups. But finally you're both at a Tribe Called Quest show and she sees you dancing with another girl and she waves at you and that does it. You go up to where she's seated with all her evil sorority sisters. She has shaved her head again.

Negra, you say.

She pulls you over to a corner. I'm sorry I got carried away. I just wanted to protect you.

You shake your head. She steps into your arms.

Graduation: it's not a surprise to see her there. What surprises you is that you didn't predict it. The instant before you and the mujerón join the procession, you see Miss Lora standing alone in a red dress. She is finally starting to put on weight; it looks good on her. Afterward, you spot her walking alone across the lawn of Old Queens, carrying a mortarboard she picked up. Your mother grabbed one too. Hung it up on her wall.

What happens is that in the end she moves away from London Terrace. Prices are going up. The Banglas and the Pakistanis are moving in. In a few years, your mother moves too, up to the Bergenline.

Later, after you and the mujerón are over, you will type her name into the computer, but she never turns up. On one D.R. trip you drive up to La Vega and put her name out there. You show a picture too, like a private eye. It is of the two of you, the one time you went to the beach. Both of you are smiling. Both of you blinked.

KARL TARO GREENFELD

Horned Men

FROM *ZYZZYVA*

BOB WAS IN THE DARK. He was looking down at his new home through the gap in the ceiling near the edge of the crawlspace, seeking where he could drop a coaxial line into his living room. His jeans and T-shirt were caked in dust, his Nikes were discolored, and he realized, as he squirmed between beams closer to the corner, that he had misjudged the location of the living room wall and was now above his thirteen-year-old daughter's bedroom. He could make out a sliver of her stuff—a red plastic lampshade, a pair of old Converses—through the loose seals around an HVAC duct. There was also a sixteenth-inch hole he found drilled near the smoke alarm. From here, through an imperfect semicircle, as if he were staring through pinpricked cardboard at a solar eclipse, he could discern the area above his daughter's bed where he had put up a wall-mount Ikea shelf. He had imagined that Becca would set out her crystals or KidRobots or some other colorful, youthful collectibles. But Becca hadn't even bothered to unpack her boxes; his wife, Minnie, had been in several arguments with Becca over that subject. If he cocked his head, he could just make out the base of the monolithic pile of books and linen boxes with the moving company's red-and-white logo on them. They stood in the center of her room, a monument to family discord.

What he had initially chosen to interpret as a sign of Becca's inner strength—her indifference to moving to a new city and school even though she was in a phase of early adolescence her pediatrician labeled "the first change o' life"—was actually confirmation of what Bob had silently suspected all along: Becca didn't have any friends. Bob, who didn't have many friends himself but tried to be an optimist, told her she would make plenty of friends at her new school. Becca just nodded and said, "Really? REALLY? That school, just a hundred miles away from my old school, will be so completely and totally different, in terms of people, personalities, demographics, THE WHOLE ECOSYSTEM, that my whole, entire life will be MAGICALLY transformed?"

Bob had smiled and done an exaggerated shrug. Like, who knows? Like this was one of those crazy adventures that will be fun for the whole family.

Now, gazing again through the gap around the HVAC, he saw a flash of movement, the faded brown-blue of old, dirty denim, as Becca entered her room, her recently more protuberant rear end framed perfectly in the gap for an instant. He froze, suddenly ashamed. But this wasn't spying, he assured himself. He tried to silently wiggle back through the attic, his thighs pressing down into old coaxial lines, perhaps staying too low in order to overcompensate for the occasional roofing nails that protruded down from the sloped ceiling, and then he felt something bite into his arm. Dropping his flashlight, he turned his elbow up, craned his neck, and saw two little pinpricks, as if he had backed his arm into the exposed prongs of a staple. Then he noticed, passing through the beam of the fallen light, scurrying away, a brown and orange, half-dollar-sized spider.

He crawled backward, not worrying as much about keeping his butt down, and swung out of the attic, down the ladder, and into the bathroom, where he checked his arm in the mirror to see if it was already swelling.

It was.

Bob would do it himself, goddammit, yes, he would. Prove that the years spent behind a desk, selling Alt-As, 7+1s, 5+1s, 3+1s, liar loans, subprimes, and refis, hadn't rendered him soft and incapable. He may have been a desk jockey, a mortgage broker, but that career had evaporated and now he was going to make the best of what he had left, in terms of money and time.

In the past, he would have hired guys to do all this, the installations and the wiring, the climbing and crawling and drilling, but now he had the time, so why pay the hundreds to have guys no more capable than he was—less capable, probably—do shit that he could do himself. So he bought the dish, mounted it on the shingle roof—that was easy, a matter of finding the beams, aiming the dish, and drilling holes for brackets, and then anchoring the gray metal plate, which sat in its brace like an auction paddle in a bidder's hand—and then ran the coaxial cable down the beam and along the doorframe, and threaded it through a hole he drilled, sleeved, and collared in the TGB paneling by the door. He regarded this little bit of handiwork and compared it to the vast yardage of co-ax that he had found strung over his roof, up and down rain gutters, tossed over attic joists, and hung from nails in crawlspaces, carpet tacked and staple-gunned into beams and over doorframes, and marveled at how crappily it had all been done. We are a nation drowning in coaxial cable, Bob decided, each house on this block suffocating in unused vines of dead co-ax. Phone companies, cable companies, Internet companies, broadband companies, all of them unspooling miles of the stuff and leaving it behind them, a fiber-optic breadcrumb trail leading nowhere. A million such houses, ten million, twenty million; every time a house was sold, remodeled, flipped, foreclosed, that meant more co-ax: badly strung, high-speed tumbleweed. Nobody gave a fuck anymore, and he knew that firsthand, having been one of those well paid for not giving a fuck, for not caring about who made how much and was borrowing how much for how much house. Not that anyone ever asked. They all wanted as much house as possible—and all that co-ax—as he had, at one point, before he walked away from his last house.

When the firm went belly-up, causing an entire Orange County business park to go vacant in just sixty days and stranding Bob in too much house with too much debt, he didn't hesitate to drive away, his wife and daughter in the Caravan and Bob in his Explorer. That's what all the TV news segments vilifying mortgage brokers never mentioned: that the brokers had drunk the Kool-Aid as well, most of them, and were leveraged and ARMED to the teeth, so when the bubble burst, Bob and his fellow brokers had been among the first to bust. He would have been a gentleman and dropped the keys off with whomever held his note, but he couldn't figure out who had taken that over, so he just left the keys inside the front door. He was lucky, he knew, that he had somewhere to go. Left all that damn cable behind.

But here he was, stringing more of it. He would need to drill a hole through part of the chimney brickwork. He set off for the hardware store, thinking a half-inch bit would do it. On the way, he stopped at the post office to inquire about his mail. Since moving in, there'd been nothing addressed to his family, just unforwarded mail for the previous tenant and the sort of shopping fliers and local retail coupons that every house gets. At the post office, the Asian lady who worked there told him that he'd asked for his mail to be forwarded to an address in Montana.

"No, I didn't."

"Someone filled in and signed a change of address for you," she said, looking at a monitor. "Your mail has been going to Jericho, Montana."

She slid him a new form.

When his mother died of emphysema six years earlier, he did a quick and cheap remodel of Gam's old house and rented it out, starting with a one-year lease but after that letting the Wagonsellers go month to month. He should have sold the old place years ago, but he held on, despite his wife's urging, and by the time he was committed to selling there were open houses on either side and across the street, so he figured he would keep the Wagonsellers, who seemed happy in the old place and anyway never bothered him, even with a plumbing system that Bob knew required regular rooting and a kitchen range with old valves that had to be wired shut manually or they'd leak gas. For five years the Wagonsellers had stayed on, the heavyset father with a broad forehead and his plain-looking wife with bangs. They had two homeschooled children, twin boys.

When Bob called them up to tell them he would be needing the place back, the father, Matthew Wagonseller, reacted angrily.

"Just like that?" he had asked. "No notice? Nothing?"

"This is the notice," Bob explained. "I'm giving you ninety days."

"But after all these years?" Wagonseller said. "We had an arrangement."

Bob tried to be patient. "We didn't have a lease. I haven't raised your rent in six years. You never asked for a lease."

Wagonseller didn't believe he needed one. "My wife is going be very upset."

"You can find a house," Bob reasoned. "There must be plenty of houses for rent now."

"We feel at home here," Wagonseller said. "Our church is here. And now we've been betrayed."

Bob felt that was too strong a word for the situation but wasn't interested in any further debate on the subject. "I'm sorry, Matthew, but I need the place for my family."

"What about my family?"

"Well, you're the renter and I'm the owner, so I guess that's that."

"We'll see," said Wagonseller. "Meanwhile, I'll be praying for you."

But in the end, Wagonseller hadn't put up much of a fight. Bob drove up to take possession, finding Mrs. Wagonseller and the twins on their knees in the front yard, eyes closed in a final prayer before they moved on. He waited on the sidewalk until they stood up, dusted off their khakis, and filed past him in silence.

The place was left a shambles, the walls marked up with crayon, the carpets stained, the linoleum buckling, the already-mentioned surplus of co-ax, but that was to be expected from six years of occupancy, and Bob didn't mind all the little projects. While his wife put away the dishes, slid the DVDs into the bookcases, and piled towels into their dressers, Bob found his tools, augmented the modest selection with a few trips to the hardware store and expeditions to Home Depot, and began to get his house in order.

First in the establishment of the American hearth, of course, was the stringing of cable, for that holy consumer trinity of telephone, Internet, and television, and so Bob found himself back in the attic, swollen arm and all, wearing kneepads this time, flashlight in hand, poking around the chimney to see how far out the chimney bricks extended and if he could drill through that to get into the built-in bookcases in the living room. It was no problem running the cable from the dish, into the attic through another collared sleeve, and then along the joists, but how to drop it down? He had purchased a telescoping guide from Home Depot, a nifty device like a car antenna that could lock into place to push cable through a tight fit, but first he needed to find the right place to drill.

He shone the light around him, the yellow beam catching the constellations of motes he'd roused, the darkened space smelling like the hot dust.

He told himself he was going to check whether there was space to slide a cable through. But now Bob crawled back over Becca's room and gazed through the sliver next to the HVAC duct, peeking through the slot into his daughter's room. She was lying on her bed, listening to music through earphones. He could see the top of her, as if she'd been sliced in half horizontally: Becca's blank, round face that was hard to call beautiful—her neck wasn't visible—her chest in a blue T-shirt with some sort of red logo on it, her flabby belly hanging a little to her left. Her legs were just below his sightline. Next to her was the pile of unpacked boxes.

He found his daughter unfathomable. And he hated to admit it, but she had become disappointing to him. Not in a way he could verbalize or explain; it had to do with her getting older, bigger, thicker, less attractive. She wasn't a pretty girl, and he knew it was wrong for a father to hold that against his daughter, so he never mentioned it, never discussed it with Minnie. And he treated Becca, he believed, exactly as he had before, back when he found her to be as cute as a button. He'd never had any sisters, just a brother a decade older and about as mysterious as a picnic bench; Gus had ended up owning a pair of Five Guys franchises in Atlanta before he died of a heart attack at fifty-six. So Bob was left guessing at what Becca might be going through. Minnie seemed to believe that Becca's struggles had to do with her appearance, and had Becca fitted with contact lenses and a kicky new haircut that did little to alter Becca's perpetual doleful frown. She always looked mad about something, Bob reflected, disappointed, as if she woke up every morning already let down.

They'd been close when Becca was a girl, and Bob struggled to recall when, exactly, they had drifted apart. He'd had a few busy years, with the mortgage business booming and commissions pouring in, but he'd always tried to make time for Becca, to take her to Panda Express on Saturdays for the greasy Chinese food she liked, to the store where they sold those plastic robots she collected. But then, probably around the start of junior high school, Becca had turned inward, or at least retreated from Bob. She had lately, troublingly, also turned destructive, making Sharpie squiggles and shapes—she drew pentagrams and the kind of lettering

Bob remembered from heavy metal albums—on the Explorer's leather interior; she jammed wadded, wet paper into the bathtub drain and had burned a bunch of leaves and twigs in the shower stall. Worrying little acts of vandalism that Bob had trouble fitting into any pattern of behavior he could recognize.

Minnie urged patience, describing what Becca was going through as an "ugly duckling phase."

He pulled his eye away from the gap. This wasn't really spying, he reasoned; he was up here working, trying to solve a problem, lay some cable.

He took another look and she was gone.

He backed away, now careful to slide his kneepads slowly so that the roof beams wouldn't creak. This space had never been used for storage, but as he shone the light around the attic, he saw that various cable and phone companies had left their detritus behind: empty router boxes, cable spools, cellophane wrappers, and over in the corner, for some reason, an old delivery pizza box. This fast-food refuse offended him, so he crawled over and grabbed it and Frisbeed it toward the attic door. As he was about to start backing away, his light caught something in the far corner, near where the roof sloped down at a thirty-degree angle to the external wall. He struggled forward again, uncomfortable as the roof drew lower above him, and reached for the object and yanked it from where it was wedged between ceiling boards. He set the light down so that its beam aimed forward, and he held this discovery in both hands. It was a small brown clay bust, still soft, no larger than a golf ball, mounted on a Popsicle stick. It was exquisitely carved: curly hair, horns, androgynous features, villainous grin, a goatee. Some kind of satyr or devil. Written on the stick, in tiny penciled letters: "And shall cut him asunder, and appoint him his portion with the hypocrites: there shall be weeping and gnashing of the teeth."

Bob was suddenly aware of the rushing of air past his ears. The attic felt momentarily strange, as if it were concealing something from him.

He was tempted to crush the little sculpture, but instead he laid it down so that its cheek rested on one of the beams, and he backed away.

Becca once asked her father if he felt guilty about all the people who had lost their homes. She knew what Bob did for a living, and the daily coverage of the foreclosure crisis coincided with her beginning to take an interest in the news, in the larger world around her. She asked this as if she already knew the answer; she was at the age when she was eager to confirm her suspicion that her father was eminently fallible.

Bob had told her no, he didn't feel guilty, not at all. He said he had been making people's dreams come true, but as soon as that platitude came out of his mouth, he regretted it, because he could see by Becca's smug smile and nodding head that he had just incriminated himself.

"We were loaning people money, to buy houses," Bob began again, "and these people wanted to buy the houses, of course they did. And because maybe they hadn't been good with their money in the past, they could only get certain kinds of loans, with certain kinds of payment terms and interest rates—it's a little complicated."

"So you made them repay way more than they were borrowing," Becca said.

"Well, every mortgage requires that you repay more than you borrow. And, well, no, I didn't make them repay anything. I showed them what kind of loan they could get." Bob was finding it difficult to defend himself while also having to oversimplify his argument so that Becca would understand. "And, well, they wanted the houses. And the houses were appreciating in value—going up—so it seemed like, why shouldn't they borrow the money, at whatever terms, because houses only go—"

"But they didn't go up." Becca jumped in. "They didn't. So they all had to leave those houses. And now they're all, like, broke and homeless and living in meth labs."

"Well, I don't think they're living in—"

"Whatever," Becca said. "They lost their homes. Like we did."

"Well, now, who's they?"

"Only *they* didn't have Gam's old house to go live in."

"Well, we're lucky, but—"

"And you guys KNEW they couldn't pay this money back. Because after like a month, the money they had to pay back would go up like a THOUSAND percent."

"Well—"

By then Becca was gone, back to her room.

*

He found himself now standing in Becca's room, next to the pile of unpacked boxes. She was at school; Minnie was at Costco. Even with most of her stuff still packed, the room was a mess of discarded clothes and scraps of partially filled notebook paper. He picked up a sheet, studied where Becca had scribbled some letters and symbols he couldn't make out, and then let it flutter to the floor.

Should he feel guilty about glimpsing his daughter from the crawlspace or spending this time in her room without her? He was already worried at what he might see or find. The parental mind reeled at the possibilities. The small glimpses he'd had of her were already confusing enough.

His elbow had swollen up to the size of a grapefruit and Bob couldn't get over how alien it looked, as if someone else's joint had ended up on his arm. It was sore and the two red fang marks had emanated disconcerting red ripples. Bob worked his arm open and closed and found his movement restricted so that he couldn't even clench his upper arm into a muscle. He iced it and then applied some antihistamine cream, but that wasn't offering much relief.

He didn't remember walking back to the living room, but he discovered that a pile of mail had finally been pushed through the door slot. There were two plain white envelopes with the State of California seal on them, each containing an identical subpoena to appear in court to answer questions regarding his old firm's policy of nondisclosure during the lending process.

He sat down on the sofa, a masonry bit in the fully charged power drill in his hand, and looked outside at the pomegranate tree that was now ripe and bearing an abundance of red fruit. He hadn't told anyone that he could see his daughter's room from up in the attic, or what he had found up there, or the scripture verse. He had his reasons for keeping quiet: he didn't want to creep out his daughter, he didn't want to frighten his family. Minnie seemed busy enough, ferrying Becca to school and trying to fashion a little charm from their limited budget. And Becca, who had returned from her first day of school with a one-word description—SUCKS—she was struggling to adjust.

Bob liked to see his memory as a collection of index cards with names and dates on them, but the names and dates were hazy and growing hazier. But now, as he was trying to settle into Gam's old house, he felt memories seeping in. He had been busy for so many years, selling those loans, that now, now that he had time—the subpoena had also jogged his memory—he was finally able to think back on that period and was uncomfortable with some of the details he recalled. It had been so easy; nobody seemed very concerned about the terms, just worried about the monthlies. As long as the next month's payment was affordable, they signed.

Then he flashed on those Wagonseller kids, the two of them bowed down in prayer right out there beneath that pomegranate tree, blond heads shining in the sunlight, their lips moving silently.

For the first time, he found himself reluctant to head back up to the crawlspace, but the job needed to be done.

He was up there again, drilling into a corner of the chimney brick, the flashlight beam hitting the spot where the bit was kicking up red dust. He bent down and blew into the hole, pushing a finger into the heat caused by the friction, and then resumed drilling. When he had punched through and into the wood, he replaced the masonry bit with a longer wood bit, but before resuming his drilling, he shone the flashlight around the crawlspace, the yellow beam sliding over the orderly descent of the shingles, the reddish brown of their undersides. In the corner where he had found the horned man, the sweeping glow passed over a white pizza box. Confused, he quickly swung his flashlight back to where he had tossed the box yesterday and found it wasn't there—of course it wasn't; he had taken that down to the recycling bin, hadn't he? Was it possible there had been two pizza boxes and he had tossed only one? He crawled over, his swollen arm making his progress slow, and gathered this box and tossed it behind him. There was the horned man, on the side of its face, where he had left it.

He heard Becca shouting from below. "OHMYGOD. What IS THIS?"

Becca had finally begun to unpack her boxes and was putting her clothes away in a closet with slatted doors. There, in the back of the closet, where a six-by-two-foot plank painted white held a half-dozen screw-in clothes hooks, was another horned man, in the same soft clay, mounted on another stick with runic lettering:

"Breach for breach, eye for eye, tooth for tooth: As he has caused a blemish in a man, so shall it be done to him again."

She was pointing at it the way a frightened housewife would point to a mouse. "LOOK AT THAT!"

Bob took the totem by the stick and inspected it. The work of the same hand.

He drove himself to testify at the law firm in Century City. An attorney from the state representatives' office was there, as was an attorney from the firm that had bought out the remnants of his old firm. While Bob was waiting in a brown leather chair with wooden arms, he saw one of his old coworkers departing. They did not acknowledge each other. When Bob's turn came, he spoke honestly, recalled as best he could his former pitch, patter, and close. But when it came to specific loans and terms, he struggled. There had been so many mortgages, and even when he was shown the loan applications, the small print with circumlocutory explanations about adjustments, penalties, resets, and readjustments, the hundreds of pages of forms that clients hurriedly signed on closing day. He flipped through the sheafs of contracts, dutifully read aloud those portions he was told to, and then answered as best he could, rubbing his throbbing elbow as he spoke. There were hundreds, thousands of such agreements in legal-file boxes all around the conference room. All of them homes, probably lost now.

Mostly the lawyers talked among themselves, occasionally asking Bob for clarification of a term or if he recalled anything about a specific loan. He shook his head. He couldn't remember anything, but he was sorry. He repeated that, as if his apology might make it okay.

The doctor agreed to see him for half her usual fee; he had delayed as long as he could since he no longer had health insurance. His muscles and joints in both arms were aching, his range of motion on the bitten arm had decreased to the point where he couldn't cock his elbow at a right angle, and the skin around the swollen area was numb. She asked when it happened, and where, and he explained, remembering, as he did so, that first day he had discovered he could watch his daughter. He didn't tell the doctor about that.

She prescribed steroids and a strong antibiotic; he would have to pay out of pocket for the medications at CVS.

The old house was going to be fine. It was smaller than the mansion they had left behind, but after those first hard weeks of shaking down—all that time in the crawlspace—it had begun to seem like a decent, functional machine for living, all the house they needed.

He had finally succeeded in dropping that cable through to the living room, set it with carpet tacks, backed out of the crawlspace, and then pulled the access panel shut behind him.

His wife had been panicked by the horned men, speculating the house was cursed: Bob immediately mentioned the Wagonsellers. They had been a strange family; the father had even, sort of, implied revenge. Maybe this was a born-again curse, Christian voodoo.

They condemned the Wagonsellers, wondered whether they should call the police, press charges, or file some sort of complaint. What kind of people would do something like this? Bob listened as Minnie unloaded her concerns before pointing out that, really, they couldn't prove anything and was it, technically, illegal to leave little clay carvings behind? He didn't seem as spooked as his wife.

Bob never told Minnie, or Becca, that while he was up there in the attic, he had inadvertently spied on his daughter in her room. He planned to go back up there just once more. He had with him some spackle and a palette knife, and he slithered along the boards, his elbow still sore—it would ache the rest of his days—to the gap above his daughter's room. He told himself he was going to seal the cracks around the HVAC duct and the hole near the fixture, to make it so he could no longer watch his daughter. This would be the final glimpse, he reassured himself.

In hindsight, the tumult of this period, the little change o' life, all the changes in their lives, would seem almost exciting. Bob would wonder how he ever had the energy for all of this, the foreclosing, the moving, the stringing of cable. He would take a job as a loan officer at the local branch of a national bank; Minnie would soon be back at work herself, doing the books part-time for an interior decorating firm. The family would never again have the means that it had during the great mortgage boom, those years of feeling wealthy, of being flush consumers caught in the profligate mainstream, and Bob would wonder at that, at how he might regain that feeling.

In the late evening, he would walk out into the front garden, to the dry, yellowed grass where the Wagonseller twins had been praying the day he moved in, and from that spot reach up—the muscles around his elbow would never again allow his arm to reach full extension—and pluck a pomegranate, which he would split with his bare hands and then bite into its flesh and seed, sucking the red juice out and shaking at its bitterness.

It wasn't a curse, he would tell himself; the Wagonsellers hadn't cursed them. He didn't believe in such things. A little modeling clay, some stylus work—it was as if they bequeathed him the product of an arts-and-crafts project. He kept the little horned men, found a niche in the attic where he could admire them. And he didn't feel cursed, hexed, whatever.

Not at all, he thought, as he went back into the house, to the attic, to the crawlspace above his daughter's room, where he watched her sleep.

GISH JEN

The Third Dumpster

FROM *Granta*

GOODWIN LEE AND his brother, Morehouse, had bought it at auction, for nothing. Even the local housing shark had looked down at his list and frowned and pinched or maybe itched his nose, but then waved his hand to clarify: no bid. The house was a dog. However, it had a bedroom on the first floor and was located in the same town as Goodwin and Morehouse.

They were therefore fixing it up for their parents. Goodwin and Morehouse were good with fixer-uppers, after all; they were, in fact, when they were working, contractors. And their parents were *Chinese, end of story,* as Morehouse liked to say. Meaning that though they had been Americans for fifty years and could no longer belay themselves hand over hand up their apartment stair rail to get to their bedroom, they nonetheless could not go into assisted living because of the food. Western food every day? *Cannot eat,* they said.

Goodwin had brought them to a top-notch facility anyway, just to visit. He had pointed out the smooth smooth paths, so wonderful for walking. He had pointed out the wide wide doorways, so open and inviting. And the elevators! Didn't they make you want to go up? He had pointed out the mah-jong. The karaoke. The six-handed pinochle. The senior tai qi. The lobby was full of plants, fake and alive. Always something in bloom! he said, hopefully.

But, distracted as they could be, his parents had frowned undistractedly and replied, *Lamb chops! Salad!* And that was that. His brother, Morehouse, of course, did not entirely comprehend their refusal to eat salad, believing as he did in raw foods. He began every day with a green shake whirled in a blender with an engine like a lawnmower's; the drink looked like a blended lawn, perfect for cows. But never mind. Morehouse accepted, as Goodwin did not quite, that their parents were fundamentally different; their Chineseness was inalienable. Morehouse and Goodwin, on the other hand, would never be *American, end of story,* which was why their parents had never been at a loss for words in their prime. *You are finally learn how to act! You are finally learn how to talk! You are finally learn how to think!* they had said in their kinder moods. Now, though, setting their children straight had at last given way to keeping their medications straight. They also had their sodium levels to think of. One might not think the maintenance of a low-salt diet could be a contribution to intergenerational peace, but, in truth, Goodwin found it made his parents easier to love—more like the diffuse-focus old people of fairy tales, and less like people who had above all held steadfast against the irresponsible fanning of their children's self-regard.

The house, however, was a challenge. See these walls? Morehouse had said. And he was right. They were like the walls of a refrigerator box that had been left out in the rain. The bathroom was veined a deep penicillin green; its formerly mauve ceiling was purpuric. Which was why Goodwin was out scouting for dumpsters. Because this was what the recession meant in their neck of the woods: old people moving into purpuric ranch homes unless their unemployed children could do something about it. He did not, of course, like the idea of illicit trash disposal; he would have preferred to do this, as all things, in an aboveboard manner. But Morehouse had pushed up his sun visor, flashing a Taoist ba gua tattoo, and then held this position as if in a yoga class.

Tell me, he said patiently. Tell me—what choice do we have? Tell me.

The gist of his patience being: Sure it was illegal to use other people's dumpsters, but it was going to save him and Goodwin eight hundred dollars! Eight hundred dollars they didn't have between them, four hundred they didn't have each. It was about dignity for their parents, said Morehouse. It was about doing what they were able to do. It was about doing what sons were bound to do, which was not to pussyfoot around. Morehouse said he would do the actual dumping. Goodwin just had to figure out where other people were having work done, and whether their dumpsters were nighttime accessible. As for why Goodwin should do the scouting, that was because Morehouse was good with a sledgehammer and could get the demo started. Goodwin was dangerous with a sledgehammer, especially to himself.

Now he scouted carefully, in his old Corolla wagon, eating Oreos. One dumpster was maybe too close, he thought. Might not its change of fill level be linked with their dumpsterless job right around the corner? Another possibility was farther away. That was a small dumpster, though—too small for the job, really. Someone was being cheap. Also, it was close to a number of houses. People might wake up and hear them.

The third dumpster was a little farther away yet. No houses nearby; that was because it was for the repurposing of a bowling alley. Who knew what the alley was being repurposed for, but an enormous bowling-pin-shaped sign lay on the ground, leaning horizontally against the cinder-block building. It looked as if the pin had been knocked down for eternity and would never be reset. The dumpster in front of it, by contrast, was fresh and empty, apparently brand-new. Bright mailbox-blue, it looked so much more like the Platonic ideal of a dumpster than the real-world item itself that Goodwin found it strangely heartening. Not that he would ever have said so to Morehouse, of course. And, in fact, its pristine state posed a kind of problem, as dumping things into an empty dumpster made noise; the truly ideal dumpster was at least one-quarter full. Goodwin had faith, though, that this one would soon attain that condition. The bowling alley was closed; a construction company had put its sign up by the street. There would be trash. It was true that there were streetlights nearby, one of them in working order. That meant Goodwin and Morehouse would not have the cover of darkness. On the other hand, they themselves would be able to see. That was a plus.

At the house, Goodwin found Morehouse out back, receiving black plastic bags full of debris from some workers. The workers lifted them up to him like offerings; he heaved them, in turn, into a truck. Of course, the workers were illegal, as Goodwin well knew. He knew too that Morehouse knew Goodwin to be against the use of illegals, and that Morehouse knew Goodwin knew Morehouse knew that. There was probably no point in even taking him aside. Still, Goodwin took him aside.

Did you really expect me to demo this place all by my friggin' self? asked Morehouse. Anyway, they need the work.

The workers were Guatemalan—open-miened men who nonetheless looked at each other before they said or did anything. Their names were Jose and Ovidio. They shared a water bottle. As Morehouse did not speak Spanish, and the Guatemalans did not speak English, they called him Señor Morehouse and saved their swearing for each other. Goodwin remembered enough from his Vista teaching days to pick up *¡serote!* and *¡hijo de la gran puta!* and *¡que vaina!* Still, the demo was apparently going fine. Goodwin watched as they delivered another half-dozen bags of debris to Morehouse.

And that's not even the end of the asbestos, said Morehouse.

Asbestos? cried Goodwin.

You can't be surprised there's asbestos, said Morehouse.

And indeed, Goodwin was not surprised, when he thought about it. How, though, could Morehouse have asked Jose and Ovidio to remove it? Their lungs! Goodwin objected.

They want to do it, Morehouse shrugged. We paid them extra. They've got it half in the bags already.

But it's illegal!

We have no choice, said Morehouse. And: They have a choice. They don't have to say yes. They can say no.

Are you saying that they are better off than we are? That they have choices where we have none? That is a gross distortion of the situation! argued Goodwin.

Morehouse looked at his watch: time for his seitan burger.

Dumping asbestos is like putting melamine in milk, Goodwin went on. It's like rinsing off IV needles and selling them back to hospitals. It bespeaks the sort of total disregard for public safety that makes one thankful for lawsuits, as Jeannie used to say.

Jeannie was Goodwin's prosecutor ex-wife—a woman of such standards that she'd been through some two or three marriages since theirs. Morehouse smirked with extra zest at the sound of her name.

You seem to think we have no choice, but we absolutely do have a choice, declared Goodwin then. We could, for example, take Mom and Dad in to live with one of us.

For this was the hot truth; it seared him to say it.

Morehouse, though, gave him the look of a man whose wife brought home the bacon now. It was the look of a man who knew what would fly in his house, *end of story*. He lowered his dust mask.

Did you or did you not find a friggin' dumpster? he asked. His mask was not clean, but neither was it caked with dust, like the masks of Jose and Ovidio. What you could see of their faces looked dull and crackled, like ancient earthworks that had started off as mud.

In the end, Goodwin looked the other way as more bags were filled. And though Morehouse had promised to do the dumping, it was Goodwin, finally, who drove the bags to the mailbox-blue dumpster. At least there was, as he predicted, some trash in it now. He did not make much noise as he threw his bags in deep, where they were less likely to be seen by the bowling-alley crew in the morning. The bags were heavy and shifted as if with some low-valence life force. Still, he hurled them as best he could, glad for the working streetlight but a little paranoid that someone would drive by and see him. No one did. He did think he saw, though, a bit of white smoke rise from the dumpster as he drove away. That was not really possible. The asbestos was in bags, after all; the bags were tied up. He was probably seeing some distortion in the lamplight. And didn't other things besides asbestos send up dust? Sheetrock, for example. Sheetrock sent up dust. Still, he thought he saw asbestos rising up on that dump, and on another dump he made before switching to yet another dumpster he had found, behind a Masonic temple. He didn't think there was asbestos in any of the new bags of trash, but who knew? He didn't ask, and Morehouse didn't say.

In a further effort to save money, Goodwin and Morehouse roughed out the walls themselves; and though they didn't have an electrician's license, they took care of the wiring too. They even set a new used cast-iron tub, or tried to. In fact, they got it three inches too high and had to turn once again to Jose and Ovidio for help getting the thing back out. Of course, Jose and Ovidio shook their heads and laughed when they saw what had happened. *¡Que jodida!* they said. Then they spent an entire day grimacing and straining, their faces almost as purple as the ceiling. When the tub finally rested back on a pallet in the hall, Ovidio stared at it a long moment. *¡Tu madre!* he muttered, to which Jose swore back *¡La tuya!,* his arms jerking up and down, his neck twitching with anger. He pulled up his pants, maybe because they were too big; Goodwin made a mental note to bring him a belt, though what Jose and Ovidio probably needed was more food. Would Goodwin have been right to insist, as he wanted to, on finishing the job without them? After they'd already helped with the dirtiest and most grueling parts? He decided to let Morehouse have his way, and had to admit that Jose, at least, looked happy to have the work. Goodwin gave him a belt, which he seemed to appreciate; he slipped both men an extra twenty too. Take it, Goodwin told them. *Por favor.*

Was this why the work went quickly and well? And yet, still, Morehouse and Goodwin kept their parents from the site for as long as possible, knowing that something about the project was bound to spark their disapproval. *House cost nothing, but look how much you spend on renovation,* their mother might say. Or, *How come even you have no job, you hire other people to work?* Morehouse, naturally, was well stocked with rebuttals, starting with, *Don't worry, we barely pay those workers anything.* What difference these could make, though, was unclear.

Finally, though, it couldn't be helped; their parents came for a visit. They looked around stupefied. The house was not much bigger than their apartment, but it was big enough to make them seem smaller; and all new as it was, it made them look older.

Very nice, said their mother finally. She clutched her leather-trim pocketbook as if to ward off attackers; she showed real excitement about the window in the bathroom and the heating ducts. *No radiators!* she exclaimed. Their father looked as much at Jose and Ovidio as at the house. *Spanish guys,* he said. Jose and Ovidio laughed and kept working. Goodwin tried to explain what they were doing. What the house used to look like. What it was going to look like. And how much they, his parents, were going to like it. It was like trying to sell them on the assisted-living place. Everything on one floor! Close to their sons! Right in the same town! His pitch was so good that Morehouse stopped and listened—as if he himself suddenly was touched by what they had wrought. He beamed as if to say, Behold what we've done for you! He leaned toward their shuffling father, as if expecting to hear, What great sons you boys are!

Instead their father tripped over a toolbox and fell as if hit by a sledgehammer. Dad? Dad? He was conscious but open-mouthed and breathing hard; there was some blood, but only, Goodwin was relieved to see, a little. *I fine,* their father insisted, flapping a shaking hand in the vicinity of his hip. Your hip? asked Goodwin. Their father nodded a little, grimacing—his brown age spots growing prominent as his real self, it seemed, paled. Don't move, it's okay, said Goodwin. It's okay. And, to Morehouse: Do you have an ice pack in your lunchbox?

Morehouse called an ambulance. People said the ambulance service was quick around here, or could be; that was reassuring. As he and his family waited, though, Goodwin stared at his father lying on the floor and was shocked at how much like a house that could not be fixed up he seemed. He stared into the air with his milky eyes as if he did not want any of them to be there and, oddly, covered his mouth with his still-trembling hand. It was a thing he did now at funny times, as if he knew how yellow his teeth were; or maybe it was something else. Goodwin's father had always been a mystery. Now he was more manifestly obscured than ever. The few things he said were like ever-darkening peepholes into fathomless depths. *You don't know what old is,* he said sometimes. *Everything take long time. Long, long time.* And once, simply: *No fun.*

His more demonstrative mother cried the whole way to the hospital, saying that his father fell because he didn't want to move into this house, and that she didn't either. It was her way of making herself clear. She didn't care whether or not it was the sort of house a person could live in by herself one day, she said. Chinese people, she said, did not live by themselves.

They were passing the turnoff for Goodwin's house when she said that. Goodwin was glad they were in an ambulance. He smiled reassuringly at his father though his eyes were closed tight; he had an oxygen mask on.

Right now we need to focus on Dad, Goodwin said.

His mother would not take her pocketbook off her lap.

Morehouse, following them in his car so that they would have a car at the hospital, called Goodwin on his cell phone.

If they ask whether Dad needs a translator, tell them to fuck off, he said.

Does he need a translator? asked the admitting nurse.

He's lived here for fifty years, answered Goodwin politely.

The nurse was at least a grownup. The doctor looked like a paperboy.

Does he need a translator? he asked.

Fuck off, said Morehouse, walking in.

How Goodwin wished he had said that! And how much he wished he had ended up like Morehouse instead of like Morehouse turned inside out. For maybe if he had, he would not have sat in the waiting room later, endlessly hearing what his mother wanted him to say—*You guys can come live with me*—much less what she would say if he said it: *You are finally learn how to take care of people. Who knows, maybe next time your wife get divorced, she come back, marry you again.*

Instead his mother was probably going to say, *You know why your wife dump you? She is completely American, that's why. Even she marry you again, she just dump you again. You wait and see.*

Fuck off, he would want to say then, like Morehouse. Fuck off!

But of course, not even Morehouse would say that to their mother anymore. Now, in deference to her advanced and ever-advancing age, even Morehouse would probably nod and agree. Their mother would say, *That's what American people are. Dump people like garbage. That's what they are.*

And Morehouse would answer, *That's what they are, all right, the fuckers.*

Nodding and nodding, even as he went on building.

BRET ANTHONY JOHNSTON

Encounters with Unexpected Animals

FROM *Esquire*

LAMBRIGHT HAD SURPRISED everyone by offering to drive his son's girlfriend home. The girl was three months shy of seventeen, two years older than Robbie. She'd been held back in school. Her driver's license was currently suspended. She had a reputation, a body, and a bar code tattooed on the back of her neck. Lambright sometimes glimpsed it when her green hair was ponytailed. She'd come over for supper this evening, and though she volunteered to help Robbie and his mother with the dishes, Lambright had said he'd best deliver her home, it being a school night. He knew this pleased his wife and Robbie, the notion of him giving the girl another chance.

Driving, Lambright thought the moon looked like a fingerprint of chalk. They headed south on Airline Road. A couple of miles and he'd turn right on Saratoga, then left onto Everhart, and eventually they'd enter Kings Crossing, the subdivision with pools and sprinkler systems. At supper, Robbie and the girl had told, in tandem, a story about playing hide-and-seek on the abandoned country club golf course. Hide-and-seek, Lambright thought, is that what y'all call it now? Then they started talking about wildlife. The girl had once seen a blue-and-gold macaw riding on the headrest of a man's passenger seat, and another time, in a pasture in the Rio Grande Valley, she'd spotted zebras grazing among cattle. Robbie's mother recalled finding goats in the tops of peach trees in her youth. Robbie told the story of visiting the strange neighborhood in San Antonio where the muster of peacocks lived, and it led the girl to confess her desire to get a fan of peacock feathers tattooed on her lower back. She also wanted a tattoo of a busted magnifying glass hovering over the words FIX ME.

Lambright couldn't figure what she saw in his son. Until the girl started visiting, Robbie had superhero posters on his walls and a fleet of model airplanes suspended from the ceiling with fishing wire. Lambright had actually long been skeptical of the boy's room, worrying it looked too childish, worrying it confirmed what might be called "softness" of character. But now the walls were stripped and all that remained of the fighter fleet was the fishing-wire stubble on the ceiling.

Two weeks ago, one of his wife's necklaces disappeared. Last week, a bottle of her nerve pills. Then, over the weekend, he'd caught Robbie and the girl with a flask of whiskey in the backyard. She'd come to supper tonight to make amends.

Traffic was light. When he stopped at the intersection of Airline and Saratoga, the only headlights he saw were far off, like buoys in the bay. The turn signal dinged. He debated, then clicked it off. He accelerated straight across Saratoga.

"We were supposed to turn—"

"Scenic route," he said. "We'll visit a little."

But they didn't. There was only the low hum of the tires on the road, the noise of the truck pushing against the wind. Lambright hadn't contributed anything to the animal discussion earlier, but now he considered mentioning what he'd read a while back, how bald-eagle nests are often girded with cat collars, strung with the little bells and tags of lost pets. He stayed quiet, though. They were out near the horse stables now. The air smelled of alfalfa and manure. The streetlights had fallen away.

The girl said, "I didn't know you could get to Kings Crossing like this."

They crossed the narrow bridge over Oso Creek, then came into a clearing, a swath of clay and patchy brush, gnarled mesquite trees.

He pulled onto the road's shoulder. Caliche pinged against the truck's chassis. He doused his headlights, and the scrub around them silvered, turned to moonscape. They were outside the city limits, miles from where the girl lived. He killed the engine.

"I know you have doubts about me. I know I'm not—"

"Cut him loose," Lambright said.

"Do what?"

"Give it a week, then tell him you've got someone else."

Her eyes scanned the night through the windshield. Maybe she was getting her bearings, calculating how far out they were. Cows lowed somewhere in the darkness. She said, "I love Rob—"

"You're a pretty girl. You've been to the rodeo a few times. You'll do all right. But not with him."

The chalky moon was in and out of clouds. A wind buffeted the truck and kicked up the odor of the brackish creek. The girl was picking at her cuticles, which made her look docile.

"Is there anything I can say here? Is there something you're wanting to hear?"

"You can say you'll quit him," Lambright said. "I'd like to have your word on that subject."

"And if I don't, you'll leave me on the side of the road?"

"We're just talking. We're sorting out a problem."

"Or you'll beat me up and throw me in the creek?"

"You're too much for him. He's overmatched."

"And so if I don't dump him, you'll, what, rape me? Murder me? Bury me in the dunes?"

"Lisa," he said, his tone pleasingly superior. He liked how much he sounded like a father.

Another wind blew, stiff and parched, rustling the trees. To Lambright, they appeared to shiver, like they'd gotten cold. A low cloud unspooled on the horizon. The cows were quiet.

"I see how you look at me, you know," she said, shifting toward him. She unbuckled her seat belt, the noise startlingly loud in the truck. Lambright's eyes went to the rearview mirror: no one around. She scooted an inch closer. Two inches. Three. He smelled lavender, her hair or cool skin. She said, "Everyone sees it. Nobody'll be surprised you drove me out here."

"I'm telling you to stay away from my son."

"In the middle of the night, in the middle of nowhere."

"There's no mystery here," Lambright said.

"Silly," she said.

"Do what?"

"I said you're silly. There's mystery all around us. Goats in trees. Macaws in cars."

Enough, Lambright thought. He cranked the ignition, switched on his headlights.

"A man who drives his son's underage girl into remote areas, that's awfully mysterious."

"Just turn him loose," he said.

"A girl who flees the truck and comes home dirty and crying. What will she tell her parents? Her boyfriend? The man's depressed wife?"

"Just leave him be," he said. "That's the takeaway tonight."

"Will the police be called? Will they match the clay on her shoes to his tires?"

"Lisa—"

"Or will she keep it to herself? Will it be something she and the man always remember when they see each other? When she marries his son, when she bears his grandbabies? These are bona fide mysteries, Mr. Lambright."

"Lisa," he said. "Lisa, let's be clear."

But she was already out of the truck, sprinting toward the creek. She flashed through the brush and descended the bank, and Lambright was shocked by the languid swiftness with which she crossed the earth. Blood was surging in his veins, like he'd swerved to miss something in the road and his truck had just skidded to a stop and he didn't yet know if he was hurt, if the world was changed. The passenger door was open, the interior light burning, pooling. The girl jumped across the creek and bolted alongside it. She cut to and fro. He wanted to see her as an animal he'd managed to avoid, a rare and dangerous creature he'd describe for Robbie when he got home, but really her movement reminded him of a trickle of water tracking through pebbles. It stirred in him a floating sensation, the curious and scattered feeling of being born on waves or air or wings. He was disoriented, short of breath. He knew he was at the beginning of something, though just then he couldn't say exactly what.

SHEILA KOHLER

Magic Man

FROM *Yale Review*

SANDRA HOLDS HER eldest child, S.P., tightly on her lap while she listens to her sister, who is telling her about her husband, a heart surgeon. S.P. is for Sweet Pea or Sweety Pie or maybe it's Simply Perfect, Sandra can't even remember anymore. The child squirms a little, leaning forward as the mother runs her fingers through her fine brown hair. "Of course, his secretary adores him, his nurses adore him, his patients adore him. He's wonderful with post-op care," her sister is going on, talking about her blond, handsome husband, her large blue eyes shining with tears, while Sandra watches her two little ones, who sit facing each other on the slate that surrounds the big blue pool, their bare legs stretched before them.

Her babies are in their identical white swimsuits and their white sun hats, with the lace around the brim and the elastic under their chins. They are pouring water, which they scoop up from the pool in their green buckets, over each other's legs and feet, wiggling their little toes and laughing loudly.

"They are too close to the water," S.P. says, and Sandra laughs at her and says to her sister, "What a worry wart!" and leans back in the chaise longue.

"I'm not a wart!" S.P. says to her aunt, and adds, "And they can't swim yet."

"I'm only joking! You are my Best One! My Angel! My S.P.! who does know how to swim!" Sandra whispers in her ear, talking to her and squeezing her tightly, taking a playful nibble from her ear. The child shifts about on her lap.

"Do sit still, darling," she says.

Sandra's head is throbbing as she surveys the scene, shading her dazzled eyes from the glare. She stares in some disbelief across the vast, empty garden, the cluster of oaks, jacarandas, and royal palm trees, in the distance the brilliant beds of dahlias, strelitzias, and nasturtium, the fishpond, and the green lawns that stretch out before her. None of it seems quite real: the light too bright, the shadows too dark, the sky too blue. Even her sister's blond curls and large blue eyes, which are filling with tears, don't seem quite real.

There are few visitors visible at the hotel at this dead hour of the afternoon. Perhaps the guests are resting in their rooms in the heat of the day. Or perhaps everyone has gone down to the coast for the holidays, she thinks. The waiters stand about idly in their white uniforms, their arms dangling lifelessly, chatting to one another in low voices.

She feels a little sick, and she has the strangest dizzy-making feeling that she doesn't know what she is doing out here on her own with the children. Why has she made this long, arduous airplane trip out to South Africa over the Christmas holidays without her husband? Why has she come back to the place where *she* was a child? She thinks of the almost sleepless night in the hotel room, the baby girl up so frequently, screaming with pain. Jessamyn often has the earache.

She holds on to her eldest child, S.P., who is squirming on her lap, but she has her eye on her youngest, who is, if the truth be told, her Favorite, her Pet, an adorable flaxen-headed baby girl only three years old who is carrying her green bucket on her arm like a handbag and tottering dangerously along the edge of the pool. "Careful, Jez, don't fall in the water!" she calls out to her baby as her sister looks at her watch. She says she should be getting home. Her husband likes her to come home early in the afternoon.

"Don't go yet. Stay and have a cup of tea," Sandra says. She feels there is something else her sister wants to say to her though she is not certain what it is.

"I don't have time for tea," her sister says, but lingers on.

It is hot, and the sun is in S.P.'s eyes. Her mother is in her blue two-piece, so that S.P. can feel her bare sticky stomach pressing against her back. S.P. is already eight years old and, she's aware, far too big to be on her mother's lap. She tries to make a space between herself and her mother's soft body, but her mother pulls her closer and goes on murmuring in her ear.

S.P. knows her mother is in serious trouble of some kind. She can feel it in the way she holds her so tightly and hear it in the over-cheerful tone of her voice, the way she makes jokes about something she doesn't really think is funny, which is how her mother speaks when she is sad.

S.P. would desperately like to fix things for her mother, though she is not quite certain what needs fixing. She understands that her mother finds her life, her tall husband with his little bristly mustache that scratches the child's cheek when he kisses her, her three children too much for her. She disappears into her room as she would to an island, as a refuge from it all, and leaves S.P. alone.

S.P. would like to keep her mother off that island. She believes that she, the eldest girl, the one who is quick, agile, and smart, is the bridge between her mother's island and the mainland, that it is up to her to keep her mother tethered to the mainland, the real world.

But it's too, too hot, and S.P. doesn't like being held so tightly. She doesn't like being called S.P. either, and she likes being called an angel even less, because she knows she isn't Simply Perfect or an Angel, and it makes her feel she has to try harder to be what her mother thinks she is. She has to pretend to be what her mother wants her to be, which is so difficult.

Her mother is going on talking about her to her aunt and stroking her hair. "She's such a whiz with her little sisters. How did you manage to keep them both so quiet for me this morning?" she asks her.

Her mother had woken S.P. before dawn, tucking the youngest girl, who awakened very early, into her bed, and then Alice had climbed up too shortly after.

"I told them a scary story, so you could sleep," she tells her mother.

"You did? Good for you!" her mother says.

Her aunt asks, "And what was the story about, darling?"

"About the Magic Man. He's called Proppy, and he can do anything he wants to," she says, and waves both her hands in the bright air in circles, magic circles—she can see the stars—to show her mother and her aunt all the magic the Magic Man can do and how he can turn you into a toad too, if he wants. She wonders if the Magic Man might just appear out here in this strange country, which seems a little like a fairy tale to her. Even the name of the hotel where they are staying seems like a fairy-tale name: the Sunnyside Hotel, it is called.

"Well, it must be a very good story. You are such a good, good girl!" her mother says. "I don't know what I'd do without her, my Sweet Pea," her mother says to her aunt, giving S.P. a kiss on her cheek.

S.P. wonders, indeed, what her mother would do without her. She knows it is her father who should help her mother get everyone up in the morning, making sure that she and Alice, who is five, are ready for school. Her mother always tells the children that their father has book business in Brussels, which is what takes him away from them so often and gives him that distant look in his eyes, as though he were not really there, when he drives the lawn mower across the grass. S.P. has long ago decided Brussels is not where her father goes, though she doesn't know where it is. Her father is a slim Frenchman who comes and then disappears bewilderingly. He seems to S.P. to be very bored with his duties as a father and husband.

On the weekend and during the holidays, it is S.P. who takes both her sisters out into the garden, keeps them quiet with her stories, as she did this morning, going out into this green and pleasant place and sitting under the trees.

S.P. asks her mother why they don't live out here in the sunshine all the time, with her grandmother and her aunt nearby, but her mother says her father doesn't want to live in the country where S.P.'s mother was born, that he doesn't think it is a good place to bring up children.

"Do you think he's right?" S.P. asks.

"What do you think?" her mother asks her aunt, who says, "I do think he's right. It's a terrible country!" with so much anger in the voice it surprises the child.

Then her aunt leans forward to whisper something to her mother, which S.P. cannot hear, and her mother looks indignant and whispers something back. The aunt says, "Would you go for me?"

And her mother says, "But what good would that do in the end?" Then her aunt says she has to go, she'll see them all later that evening, and she gets up. She is wearing a cream sundress, and as she waves goodbye the sleeves fill with air like little wings, and S.P. notices a purple bruise on her smooth, plump arm.

The sun glints off the water, and the shadows of the leaves shift in a slight breeze. S.P. would so much like to jump down and wander off across the smooth green lawn and find someone her own age to play with, perhaps even a little boy—she is rather tired of girls—but she knows her mother needs the comfort of her body on her lap, her presence beside her.

She would like to explore the big garden with all its sunlight and shadows. She watches a shadow in the trees in the distance. She sees someone moving between the trees and wonders if it's a little boy who might play with her. She wriggles around on her mother's soft, clammy lap, shifting her hips in her new pink two-piece swimsuit, which has little rosebuds where her breasts are supposed, one day, to appear.

Then she has an idea of how she might escape for a moment.

"I need to wee," S.P. says, and the mother lets her get down from her lap. "Can you find your way?" she asks, for the bathrooms are up the bank and in the thatched-roofed changing huts, which are among the trees at some distance from the pool.

"Of course," S.P. predictably says, and the mother lies back with relief on her plastic chaise longue. She feels the child could find her way out of a labyrinth. She smiles proudly at her eldest, who has such an excellent sense of direction and can already read so well. She is the one who holds the directions when they are in the car and tells the mother where to turn. Indeed, the mother feels, the child has a better sense of direction than she does herself.

She watches S.P. wander up the bank, going toward the changing rooms, and she calls out to her loudly, "Be quick, S.P.," and then closes her eyes, just for a moment, on the bright light, the pool, her little ones.

She wonders how on earth they could possibly have gone from there to here. She still thinks of herself and her younger sister as those shy, light schoolgirls—she can see them clearly in their green tunics, the striped ties, the short-sleeved shirts, the lace-ups, the long green socks, and the panama hats on the back of their pale curls, sitting with their arms around their knees, reading their books, propped up against each other's backs under the old oak tree at boarding school, reading poetry, Blake or Keats or Wordsworth, and looking up at the light between the leaves, dreaming of becoming poets.

That slight girl, with her small waist and long, dark eyelashes that shaded big blue eyes that filled with tears at the slightest pretext, the mention of any suffering or sorrow, still seems more familiar to her than this woman in whose heavy body she finds herself now. That girl is much more who she still *is,* surely, with her somewhat confused mind—she was never any good at math, dreamed her way through science, blowing up Bunsen burners and weeping over the dead rabbit they were supposed to eviscerate. She had no idea of geography—"Where was Sri Lanka?"—but starred at English composition—"What imagination!" Mrs. Walker said—and at history. For some reason she remembered in great detail, their exploits marked indelibly, painfully, on her impressionable mind, the lives of Richard III, Peter the Great (using an innocent serf to show off some machine of torture), Catherine of Russia, Louis XVI and his unfortunate queen (appealing to the mothers in the crowd when accused of incest with her own beloved boy), tales of violence, mayhem, and murder.

Though she no longer reads poetry much except for *A Child's Garden of Verses* to the children, surely that slender, pale sixteen-year-old in her school uniform with her tender heart is more *she* than this plump, pink-skinned woman in her late thirties lying staring up at the blue sky in her blue two-piece, her stomach bulging.

Languidly, she lies on her back, blinking with bewilderment at the blue sky, and then turning to speak to the middle child, Alice, who comes over complaining about something the little one has done or said, whining and tugging on her hand. She wants her to come and play with them. She murmurs that Mummy is still so sleepy, that she is still very, very tired, she's been up all night with baby. Laughing, she tells the child that she feels weighted down with stones. She is incapable of dragging her heavy body off the chaise longue.

How *has* her body grown so heavy, the mother thinks, when

the child has resumed her game with her little sister by the pool, so that it is no longer possible from her appearance, her plump stomach, the rounded arms, the swollen ankles, to tell if she is at the beginning stages of pregnancy or recovering from a former one? How *has* she put on so much weight? She was always good at games, a fast swimmer, even on the hockey team—she had played goalie, for goodness sake!—rushing out bravely to stop the hard ball, albeit much of the time in terror and with her eyes shut.

S.P. is walking barefooted across the grass with her eyes shut, her arms out before her. She likes to pretend she can't see and walk a few steps in darkness, feeling her way blindly, her feet in the coarse grass, going up the bank toward the shade of the trees in her new pink bikini. She feels the cool breeze on her bare skin and hears the rustle of the palm fronds above her. She wiggles her hips a little and spreads out her arms and feels she is flying as she does through the trees in her dreams, swooping up and down, not quite in control, like breathing in and out. She is happy to have escaped the burden of her mother, her aunt, and her sisters, to be on her own in the garden, filled with the pure pleasure of being alive in this lovely place.

It is December and yet so strangely hot out here, when it would be freezing and raining in France, where they normally live, in a house in a suburb of Paris. On Christmas Day, they all ate a turkey sitting outside in her grandmother's garden, sweating in the heat, the flame on the Christmas pudding hardly visible in the bright light.

Now the child hears her mother saying something to Alice about feeling tired, but she keeps on walking, though she opens her eyes.

It's at that moment that S.P. is brought back to reality and realizes that it was not a little boy at all in the shadows of the thick oak tree, but a man who is standing there. She is not certain immediately that he's the Magic Man, for he's not the way she had imagined he would be at all, with black hair, a black cloak, and perhaps a star on his high hat. Instead he's wearing, of all things, white shorts, as if he has been playing tennis, and tennis shoes, as her father does in the summertime, and long socks, and he doesn't have a hat. Instead he wears sunglasses, which cover his eyes and bend back at the sides like a mask. As he moves out of the shadows, his blond hair shines so brightly in the sun, S.P. blinks. She sees him only for a second, and then he disappears again behind the trunk of a tree.

How have they both become *wives* rather than the poets they dreamed of being, Sandra thinks, and in her case the wife of a well-known French writer, an intellectual star, someone who has been hailed by the French press as a magician with words, a bright, slim, energetic man who comes and goes fast, and has by this time in the morning and even if it is a Sunday, probably written several obscure chapters—she is not always quite sure she understands his work—of his latest book. How has she become the wife of a man with such thick dark hair, a perfect profile, a strong jaw, and intelligent steel-blue eyes, an athletic man, on top of everything else, a tennis player, a golf player, a runner, with a hard-muscled abdomen and slender hips, a man of enterprise and ambition, who is gone in the morning, often before dawn, scattering pebbles, roaring down the driveway in his green Porsche long before she wakes, and speeds back up the driveway late at night, most of the time long after she has retreated to bed, unable to take another moment with a child climbing all over her or asking for yet another bedtime story.

But the most surprising, the most unbelievable thing is that she is the mother of three children, for God's sake, and all under nine! A gaggle of girls: S.P., Alice, and the baby, named after her mother, Jessamyn—and all of them beautiful! beautiful! beautiful! though none quite as beautiful as her baby, she thinks, looking at the little one who is pouring water over her sister's head now, her baby girl, who looks like a Fra Angelico angel, with her large blue eyes and plump, edible cheeks, her crown of haloed spun-gold hair, a child she thinks of almost as a holy child, the child who has told her she wants to climb up on the sunflowers to reach the Baby Jesus in the sky.

The man comes striding toward her as she had expected the Magic Man would, as though he knows her, of course, and knows she knows all about him. He beckons to her, grins at her, and flicks back his forelock of blond hair. His teeth are small and a little yellow. In some strange way, he seems familiar to her, as though they have already met, which in a way they have, in her stories. She approaches shyly, wondering what he will say. "Proppy?" she says.

"I beg your pardon?" He looks down at her politely, seeming a little puzzled.

"Isn't your name Proppy?" she asks.

He smiles a slow, pleased smile and nods his head. "And how did you guess?" he says, and seems delighted at her knowledge. She holds out her hand politely, as she has been taught, and bobs a little curtsy, as he shakes it with enthusiasm. "And you are S.P.," he says, for he knows her, of course, knows all about her.

Then she remembers a moment when she was quite little, before her sisters were born, or perhaps she has seen a photograph of the moment with her father, who is, unusually, kneeling beside her in the grass in a panama hat and her mother is kneeling behind in her flowered dress. And she remembers how her father had said at that moment, "You are my Special Person, my S.P.," and she realizes that that is what her name means. And she is a Special Person, she thinks, as she shakes the Magic Man's hand, the best in the class at reading, the only one whose little pipe-cleaner man reached the top of the ladder.

"Would you like to come with me to play with my little boy?" the Magic Man asks her in a kind, soft voice.

S.P. hesitates for a moment because she does remember her mother telling her never, never to go off with strange men, but the Magic Man is not a stranger to her, after all, and he has somehow thought of exactly what she would like to do. Of course, the Magic Man knows everything everyone thinks and wishes and can make it all come true, if he wants it to. Still, she says nothing, just looking up at him and then through the trees and down the bank, back across the lawn, where she can still see her mother, who looks rather small and far away, lying beside the pool on the chaise longue. Then she looks back at the Magic Man, who takes off his sunglasses so that she can see he has blue eyes, which glitter like gems, and a rather pointed nose, and thin lips.

He says, "My little boy has no one to play with, and he's very lonely. You are a lucky girl with your two sisters, after all." S.P. nods her head and feels sorry for his little boy, who is all alone when, it is true, she has her two sisters to play with, though there are times like the present moment when she is happy to be rid of them.

"Where is your little boy?" she asks warily, and he waves his hand in the direction of the changing rooms, where the bathrooms are too, which is where she was going anyway.

The mother is thinking of the conversation she had with her own mother, to whom she mistakenly confided in a moment of desperation on Christmas Day. Her mother could not see why she can't just get up and leave her husband, why she goes on having babies with him. Her mother sees things in an entirely practical way.

"What's important here, it seems to me, is money. And you are the one with the means! So just kick the bastard out! Throw his fancy clothes out the window! What purpose does he serve, in the end? You're still young and pretty and . . ." her mother said, but she interrupted.

"But I have three children! And besides, Mother, I'm in love with him, and I know he's really in love with me. He keeps telling me that he feels so awful about it all, so guilty, that this girl—she's only nineteen—feels so guilty too. He says the guilt is giving him an ulcer and that he's just gone one last time to see her, to say goodbye, and then he'll come back to me and the children."

Her mother looked at her with something like pity in her eyes. "At Christmastime! He's gone off to see this girl at Christmas?"

"That's not important to him! He's not interested in *Christmas,*" she said scornfully, which is exactly how and what her husband had said to her when she expressed the same sentiments. She added, as he had too, "Truly, I believe he loves me."

"I don't understand how you can call that love! How can you hurt someone you love!" her mother said impatiently.

"But he doesn't *want* to hurt me. He can't help what has happened. He just fell irresistibly in love with this girl."

"Magically? With the wave of a wand?" her mother asked with a sneer.

"And he's such an extraordinary man. Such a good writer! He's taught me so much about so many things! I've read so many books because of him: Camus, Balzac, and Flaubert—all the wonderful French writers. I see the world in an entirely different way because of him. And he's so charming, so intelligent, such a good listener, so much fun! . . ."

"There's a time to cut your losses. If you miss one bus, jump on the next, I always say," her mother said impatiently, and then got up and poured herself a gin and tonic.

"Come, I will take you to him," the Magic Man says, talking in the flat way people talk in this country. And it seems quite right to her that she would meet the Magic Man out here in this wonderfully sunny place, which is both strange and familiar to her, with all the bright flowers and the brilliant blue sky and the sun. The sun is making her feel a little dizzy, and her head spins, so she lets the Magic Man take her hand, and she follows him through the trees going toward the changing huts, though she wonders why his little boy would have remained in the thatched-roofed changing rooms and is not by his side.

At the thought of it, Sandra decides she'd like something to drink herself and beckons to a waiter who is standing nearby. He comes over to her now, walking fast across the lawn in a starched white uniform, which rustles as he moves. She says she would like a cup of tea, and some cool drinks for her little girls—and perhaps some cake and a few tea sandwiches? "We'll have a little tea party, when S.P. gets back, shall we?" she asks the little ones, who look up at her and nod their heads enthusiastically. What a nice idea! To hell with her diet! And surely it is teatime? She looks at her watch and wonders where S.P. is.

"Tea for three?" the waiter asks.

"No, actually for four," she says. "I'm waiting for my eldest girl." Then she asks the waiter if, by any chance, he has seen her little girl, a barefoot eight-year-old in a pink bikini. She went to the bathroom a while ago, but surely she should be back by now?

The African waiter shakes his head gravely and says he has not seen her. He suggests the mother might want to look for her little girl. He warns her, "A lot of *skelms* around here, madam," using the local word for a bad man.

"Surely not, in this lovely place, this beautiful hotel?" the mother says, alarmed, and lifts her hands in the air, looking up at the waiter, who shakes his head and clucks his tongue doubtfully at her words. She thinks of her sister's bitter words about this country and her surgeon husband, and she does wonder why it is taking S.P. so long to come back. Is it possible that she might, after all, have got lost? She decides to take the waiter's advice. She asks the nice waiter if he would mind watching her baby girl and Alice for a minute while she goes to find her eldest.

"Not at all, madam," he says, and sits down in the grass close beside her little ones.

The Magic Man has her by the hand and is leading her toward one of the changing huts, the one for men. He tells her to wait a moment, and he goes inside first for some reason, perhaps to tell his little boy she is coming. She waits a minute, and then he beckons for her to follow him. Now she hesitates, but he smiles his mysterious, magical smile and raises his eyebrows and flashes his glittering blue eyes in a way that seems to suggest so many good things up ahead. So she goes in and looks around to find the little boy, who will be blond and blue-eyed like the Magic Man, she supposes.

"Can you see him?" the Magic Man says, as if it is a game or perhaps a task, as in the fairy tales, where something has to be accomplished before one wins the prize. She looks carefully at the wooden benches and under the benches, at the whitewashed walls, and even up at the beams that line the conical thatched roof, where the little boy might have flown, after all. Perhaps he's a Magic Boy too. But there is no little boy there, or not one she can see. There is only the quiet of the still, sunlit afternoon and a smell in the changing rooms of damp and wet and the Magic Man, who stands grinning at her.

The mother lumbers up the bank, sweating in the heat, looking around. Where on earth is S.P? The mother can feel the tears coming into her eyes. What has happened to her child?

She had so hoped somehow that returning home, being out here with her mother and her sister, would help her in her unhappiness, but she can see that nothing has changed at all. The mother looks around this beautiful garden and remembers the one where she and her sister had played as little girls with such freedom. She remembers that feeling of something, she realizes, that she has so sadly and dramatically lost: a sense of the infinite possibilities of things, the giddy belief in her own omnipotence.

She lifts her eyes to the beauty of the fine, fernlike leaves of the jacaranda tree and feels terribly alone. This whole trip out here without her husband has been a mistake. She has simply given him the freedom to be with his girl. What was she thinking? And now S.P. has mysteriously disappeared too.

"Where is your little boy?" she asks, and the Magic Man lifts his shoulders and his hands and opens his eyes wide with surprise. "Where on earth has he gone? The naughty boy! Well, let's look in here," he says, taking her by the hand and leading her toward one of the stalls in the bathroom. "But this is the men's bathroom," she says. "I'm not supposed to go in there," S.P. says, drawing back.

"But he must be hiding in there. He's playing hide-and-seek, and he wants you to find him. Do you think you can find him?" the Magic Man whispers, and smiles his mysterious smile again and chuckles. So she enters the stall with Proppy, but there is no little boy there. Could he be an invisible boy?

But when she looks up into the Magic Man's face, she can see now that this is not so. The Magic Man's face has changed. He's looking at her differently, with an expression of expectation. She can see he has been telling her stories, like her mother does about her father going to Brussels. His name is not Proppy at all, and there is no little boy, she realizes, in the same way she realized once that there were not always happy endings in real life as there are in the fairy tales. She remembers saying to her mother, heartsick with disappointment, "But you mean there are not always happy endings like in the fairy tales?" Her heart is thumping so hard now, she feels as if the gray cement floor is shaking beneath her bare feet.

She bites her lip, trying not to cry, and looking at the door to the stall, which the man has not locked.

Instead, he stands with his back to it, leans against it, and folds his arms, which are strong and sunburned. He wears a short-sleeved white shirt, and she can see the line on his skin where the sunburn ends and the shirtsleeve begins, where the skin is white. He has a yellow pencil in his pocket and the sunglasses, which peep out. She looks down at his long white socks, which are turned over at the top, and then back at his face.

He stares at her in a strange yet familiar way, and she understands for the first time that he cannot do any magic at all, that on the contrary, she's the one who has to do some magic for him, that, like her own mother, it is he who needs her to help him.

Indeed, he says quite politely, "You're such a pretty little girl. You have such pretty brown eyes and such pretty brown hair, but I don't like that pink swimsuit. I don't like it at all. I wonder if you would mind very much taking it off for me, please? Or would you like me to help you take it off?"

She considers calling out for her mother, but decides that she would never hear her, and the bathroom is empty and silent. There is no one else nearby. She listens to the silence of the afternoon and tries not to cry, her lips trembling and her breath coming in great gulps of air.

The man says, with some impatience now, "I'm waiting." Then she reaches up behind her back and starts to undo the top of her two-piece, the top with the little roses where her breasts are supposed, one day, to be. He keeps on looking at her, his eyes now very bright, grinning at her. "Good," he says, "go on," and slowly she lets the top drop to the cement floor. Then she takes off the bottom part and slips it down her legs.

Why is her husband not here with her, the mother thinks angrily, and clenches her fists. She would like to hit him, as her sister's husband repeatedly hits her when she has said something that annoys him. She is suddenly and for the first time in a rage with her husband. She thinks of him wearing the broad-brimmed hat that he has taken to wearing to cover his balding head and grinning his wide, self-satisfied grin. She has a big photo of him grinning like that on her piano in the living room.

Years later, she will remember that moment of rage at the man who was once her husband, and she will feel the rage again, but not as much rage as she will feel at herself.

Now she goes into the women's changing rooms, calling her child's name, and then into the area with the toilets. But all the stalls are empty, the pink doors gaping open. There is no one here at this hour of day. All she can hear is the dripping of a tap. Still, she hopes the child is somewhere nearby. "S.P., darling? Where on earth are you?" she calls out into the emptiness, but there is no response, only the echo of her own words. Could the child who reads so well possibly have made a mistake and gone into the men's changing rooms, she wonders, her heart beginning to thud in her ears.

*

Standing naked before the man, S.P. weeps silently, the tears falling down her cheeks, for he looks very serious now and as if he were thinking about something else. He looks absent, like her father does when he mows the lawn. And he is also opening up his tennis shorts and doing something odd to himself down there, moving his hands back and forth. She doesn't want to look at that; it is making her feel very sick, and she is afraid she might vomit on the floor. Instead, she keeps her gaze fixed on the door, the chink of light behind the man, and wonders if she could somehow quickly slip through his legs, as he seems very busy and preoccupied doing whatever it is he is doing now. Through her tears, she glances at the man's face, which is rather red and sweaty, as he strains to do something that seems to be difficult for him.

Then she hears her mother's voice calling to her, wailing in a desperate way. "S.P.! Sweet Pea! Sweety Pie! Angel! Where are you, my most darling child?" The strange names echo in the stall mournfully, louder and louder, coming closer, but even then she knows, smart girl that she is, that her mother will not come and save her, will not throw open the unlocked door, that she will not find her standing there.

Indeed, the man hears the voice too, and he stops doing whatever he was doing before. Now he puts his hands, sticky with some sort of white stuff, around her neck. He says in a whisper, "You must be quiet, very quiet, child, do you understand?"

Years later, when her sister is dead, killed by her husband driving the car off the road, her child will tell her the whole story, about the man with the white shorts and how he put his hands around her neck and told her to be quiet, how he then turned from her and left her to run out weeping onto the lawn. She will see the garden that day and the tears shining in her sister's large blue eyes and remember her unanswered cry for help.

DAVID MEANS

The Chair

FROM *Paris Review*

DAY AFTER DAY I went through the paternal motions, testing my son while he tested me, trying to teach him not only to do what I said, which seems like a given, but also to see and taste the world in certain ways, with an ideal in mind, a purified vision of the best way to live reduced to a rudimentary, five-year-old version: good eye contact with others, a sustained gaze, not just looking but giving an indication of having seen—a head nod—and maintained long enough to show respect and not too much fear. I wanted to be assured that he wouldn't end up painfully shy. (He didn't.) I feared he'd grow into one of those in-the-corner wallflower types, dainty and delicate, brooding, ponderous, sad as a young kid and then sullen when he hit the teenage years and then, as an adult, deeply depressed. (He didn't.) I wanted him to open up to what was before him. So, I suppose, part of me—in the yard that afternoon, as I followed him up the hill—was happy that he was resisting my commands and remained slightly beyond reach. While of course, another part of me was ready to pounce on him as soon as he turned at the top and headed down to the retaining wall again.

You're in the chair little man, right now, get inside quick, the chair is waiting!

I prefer a gentle pushing against my will—I was thinking in the yard that afternoon, as I got near the top of the hill. By the time I got to the top, he had turned and was jogging slowly north toward the Thompsons' Scotch pines—the hiss, the high-up touch of wind in the crowns. Then he made a tight loop, wobbly with his legs in his jeans, with the cuffs rolled up, and his coat flapping (he refused to zip up, but I let that go), and, after glancing back at me, he pumped his arms up and down and screeched.

To my right, the river beyond the wall stretched at least three miles across, with the ebb tide and the flood tide meeting in the center to form a sheen of calm. The autumnal brown and gold leaves on the Westchester side threw long reflections that blended with the sky. Ah, glorious, I thought. Ah, a lovely and perfect fall afternoon. The sublime nature of taking care of my boy on one more bygone day. There was a deep, submerged loneliness in my chest as I stood feeling the wind, which was lifting, growing firmer and stronger from the north, bringing with it the first hints of winter—along with the sound of the birds, who had flown deeper into the Thompsons' trees. Oh, the beauty of knowing that on that day I'd instruct the boy on how to listen carefully and establish proper eye contact, and how to hold his little wee-wee straight when he peed into the bowl, and how to manage his fork and take care with his chewing. Part of the glory of the moment, I think I thought, was in the pristine clarity of the innumerable potential teaching moments—Christ, I still despise that phrase!—that would bloom in the next few hours, as the light waned and the wind continued to lift and the remaining leaves twisted loose from their stems and were brushed away, skittering across the lawn, lying there, waiting to be blown away by the crew who would arrive midmorning on Saturday, four or five men, and lean down into the roar as their earmuffs snuffed them into a different kind of solitude. Evening would fall, and the lights on the bridge and across the river would throw themselves onto the surface of the water, appearing one by one as the sky faded, and then, safely inside the house, I'd look out the window and feel the fantastic unleashing of the pure, frank wistfulness that used to come to me at that time of day, and I'd feel, ahead, the future in one form or another, without which I could not endure the task. At some point in the future we'd be alone in the house and Gunner would be off at college, or married, and days like that would be sucked into a vortex—what other way to think of it?—of retrospect, with just a few memories of day-to-day tending: car-seat buckling, food feeding, punctuated by more pointed memories of trauma: stitches in his brow (lacrosse), asthma attack (holding him through the night, his tiny chest heaving against my palm), his separation problems at the preschool (me in the window watching him clutch hold of the old scratched-up piano bench, his mouth wide open in a scream, his face bright red and shiny). It was only with that sense that I could survive those moments, I think I thought.

Reaching the top of the yard, I became aware—in a kind of intuitive parenthood tracking mode—that I'd already given him one warning and release and another solid warning. It's possible, I think I thought, that in the pleasure of running downhill, he had forgotten my first warning, which he never really let sink in, distracted by the sound of the birds in the trees (because he had turned to look at them), so that the second warning came to him as a first warning of sorts. I jogged behind him and kept the shadow/father distance and gave him space to decide what to do, wondering again if he'd just weave partway down, having absorbed my warning and then my second warning, which in theory nullified the first warning and showed my hypocrisy at not simply drawing the line and taking him inside, but figuring that another chance was warranted because it was possible that in his delight he simply forgot that first warning, but, on the other hand, I think I thought, this time he has at least two warnings echoing in his head, and so I held back on shouting to him again: if you run too close to the wall, it's the chair. Instead, I stayed quiet and thought about how just that morning I had gone down and looked out the window at the river and thought it was strange that in the past two weeks Sharon had come home late each night, arriving after dinner, appearing in the driveway with perfectly fine excuses, saying the train was late, or there was traffic on the bridge. (Did she not know that I could see the bridge and the traffic, and looked at it in a habitual manner most days, glancing over there when I went down to the shore to examine the wall, worrying over the fact that it was crumbling, wondering how much weight the grass and sod and soil made pushing against the structure while, at the same time, worrying over the potential cost of repair, imagining the mason digging it all out, building some kind of temporary support wall, laying new rebar, framing it up, and then somehow getting a cement truck—Concrete, Sharon corrected me when I verbalized my worry one night. Not cement, it's concrete—down into the yard?) Other excuses she gave included irate clients or long-winded partner conferences she had to attend because she was hell-bent on making partner as soon as possible. I'm hugely aware, I said, of the weird feeling I have about you and your work in relation to me and my position here as at-home caregiver, and sometimes I have to admit, I sit at the window and follow you to work in my imagination. Now don't get me wrong, I cherish this time with Gunner and I'm happy to be doing this, but still, I feel strange about it at times, I said, while she pursed her lips and fixed me with her gaze, which included really fine, deep, dark, big eyes in a face that was smooth with lean cheekbones and a fine, fine nose. A fucking Helen of Troy face, I used to think. The kind of face that would start a war if you let it. And it did, eventually. I'd like to start a war, I used to think, seeing her face. I want to start something big and historic in her name. I want a monument to be built in honor of the torment her face creates in my fellow men. (I think I sensed—those mornings of window gazing—that she was being sucked into Manhattan. The pull of it was apparent to me in the jaunt, the sway of her hips as she skipped out to the car each morning. It appeared in the way she held her chin softly in her fingers, playing them out in a thoughtful manner as she listened to me describe my day while a slight—albeit graceful—incomprehension filled her eyes. All that beauty gave her a density that was prone to the pull of the city, I thought, I think.) Those mornings, with Gunner upstairs asleep—the soft sea-hiss snooze of his breath coming through the baby monitor—I sometimes had that deep, sensual foreboding that came when I thought too much about the short term and the way Gunner's days, still fresh and new, his life just starting, stood logarithmically in relation to my own thirty years. A day was one small fragment of my life, and a day for him was a much larger piece of the pie. One day now is a big hunk of his five years on earth, I used to think, I think.

On those mornings, with my cheek against the glass, I imagined the soft rub of her attaché against her leg as she waited on the station platform, filled with a communal sensation of being in on a secret—a united sense of waiting to head to a common destination, and then on the train, with the attaché at her feet, the prim way she'd hold the paper, while over her shoulder old boat yards—bright blue tarps—and track detritus roared past and the river itself stayed calm and passive, blue on one day, gray on another. At the window, I anticipated the solitude of the upcoming day with Gunner for company, maybe some playtime with another kid and his mother, who would stand awkwardly as the erotic charge failed to form between us, and because of that fact we'd feel even more awkward, aware that it should form, if not a spark then at least a slight vibration of some sort as we watched and, on occasion, shouted instructive bits of information: Be careful now, not so hard, be nice, share, be good, Gunner, let her play with that. Annie, come over here and let me tie your shoe, not so hard. Or larger, more philosophical comments that covered the gamut from sharing to being kind to each other to the way the trees look against the sky, always pointing things out as a way to teach looking, to make sure they were seeing, and then, other times, encouraging them to find deeply imaginative modes—this happened mostly with a mother named Grace, who would instruct the kids to imagine elaborate pizza parlors, saying, Why don't you cook some pizzas for me and Mr. Allison (Call me Bob, I'd say, please call me Bob) . . .

. . . again, at the window those mornings I felt the power of the city—all that culture and commerce compacted, hemmed in on all sides by water, held in to create a force powerful enough to radiate out all the way to our house, to the plot of land and the town itself, which, I imagined, was just at the edge of the force field, catching the last bits of energy before it was absorbed by the parkland to the north, the heavy stone Palisades and trees on my side of the river, and on the other side, the wide-open land and dirt roads and split-rail fences and horse stables and large estates in northern Westchester. (The field slides farther up on that side of the river, I thought at the window. There are fewer obstructions to dull its power over on that side.) At the window, I imagined Sharon entering her firm's building near Forty-second Street, the glossy lobby with the security man up front, watching as she swiped her card. The glass partition zipped neatly open and she felt a grandness that came from her ability to pass through, while behind her messengers and visitors waited to sign in at the desk, looking somewhat distracted, holding on their faces the placid perplexity of the scrutinized, some part of them worrying the idea that a day might come when suddenly, on a big delivery or an important appointment, they'd be denied entry.

During those morning window sessions, I imagined Sharon as she entered a loaded elevator with her colleagues and felt that New York elevator pride that comes with squeezing close without annoyance, moving up into a moneymaking venture of some sort, lifted into the coffee smell of the office space, the brief hello at the reception desk . . . I imagined . . . the lovely entanglement in a web of selfsame need, risk, and obligation. Behind me in the kitchen the coffeemaker burbled and coughed.

We're riding on an apex, I thought, standing in the yard that day, I think. We're on a pivot. On one side is her career and her lively step out the door, while on the other is this deep solitude, with the birds still chirping madly, startling one another into a frenzy of noise, each one simply responding to the others and the others responding in kind. The afternoon light was starting to wane slightly over the water, catching riffles far out, as the smooth, wide, glossy patch near the center began to swirl itself away and waves worked themselves in, lapping the retaining wall. Then the birds seized up for a second, turned themselves into a fury of flapping, papery in nature, like long skeins of tissue being shaken out. I noticed all that as I turned to look at Gunner again. It's not that I feel sorry for myself in any way, because I cherish these moments with my boy, delight in being with him. I relish the line I have to walk between being loving and soft and coddling one second, and the next, having to reestablish my command, or better yet, my guidance—a towering figure in his little mind—over his development at that particular point in time, I was thinking, I think. Love isn't in the actual grab and heft of body when he comes out of school and runs into my arms, crying with glee. No. Love is the moment just as he comes out of the schoolhouse door, standing amid his friends, and searches for my eyes. Love is in the second he sees me, and I see him, dressed in one of his outrageous outfits, bright startling coats, weird hats, drooping strange pants (because we took delight in taking advantage of the fact that at that stage he had no idea what he was wearing, no sense of having to fit in, and we could get him dolled up—Sharon's words—as cute as a button). That's what love is, I thought each time I went to the school to pick him up. Then, as I lifted him and felt his weight, the purity of the moment vanished, and I would smell the stale, tart odor under his collar while he smelled, I suppose, the smoke and coffee on my breath and something else that later, at some point, perhaps even in memory, he would recognize as the first hints of decay.

The birds flew over the water and got about a quarter of the way across the river and then, suddenly, swooped in a wide arc back around toward the Thompsons' trees again, catching up with one another in a teardrop, diverting me from Gunner, who, when he caught my attention again, was striking straight for the wall and the water. His tiny shrill cries mixed with the wind. In the compressed intensity of the moment, the birds were gone. The tide had shifted, heading down toward the city.

You're getting the chair, I said, stop. No more warnings, I yelled as I charged down the hill. He was way ahead of me, of course, and in a moment he'd be at the wall and starting—naturally—his tiptoe tightrope walk along the structure, testing his own sense of balance and fear as it relates to the drop and the water below. (In the summer I'd lower him down to the beach, feeling his shoulder and joints and tiny chest at the tip of my fingers. Then we'd sit on an old pickle bucket and fish.) In a moment he'd be looking back at me, I was thinking, the wind in my hair, feeling, as I moved, a good, manly sense of dominion over everything. This is mine, I was thinking, I think. This is my chance at glory of a sort, perhaps I was thinking. I don't remember. But he was at the wall, wobbling along, and then he tumbled backward, throwing his arms up in the air.

That's it, I said. That's it, Gunner. No more warnings. (Half thinking that perhaps this was actually my fourth warning, and that he'd long forgotten the first one, a few hours ago, before we went to preschool.) Across the river on the Westchester side, a train charged up the tracks like a sliver of glass, and when the wind died I heard not only Gunner's giggles, as he swayed, but also the deep rumble of the diesel express that would go past Ossining, past Croton, and all the way up to Poughkeepsie, and I felt, hearing it, a sorrow that came not only of my inability to get to him on time but also something much deeper—I'd later think—that had to do with the fact that as he fell over the wall, he fell back with his eyes wide, terrorized by the way his balance had defied him.

Then I got to the wall and looked down and saw that the tide was still coming in and he was lying on his side in a few inches of water, with a shawl of wet, black sand around his collar, and his socks muddy, and his eyes guilty but also comic, looking up at me, establishing a long, sustained moment of good eye contact. Keep looking, I thought. Don't ever stop. Continue to look at me like that for the rest of time, I think I thought. Then the fear that had began to form when I was halfway down the yard caught up, pure, sharp, and eternal in form, and struck me under the ribs. I was weeping softly as I lowered myself down to help him, lifting my palms and supporting his feet so he could clamber over the wall.

Then he stood atop it and looked down at me, his old man, as I wiped my eyes. He was looking down at a bright red face, bewhiskered and ruddy. A mouth moving on that face was saying, That's it. You're in the chair. It's the chair for you, little man. No snack. Just the chair. I mean it. I gave you three, at least, maybe four warnings, the mouth kept saying. You're damn lucky the tide wasn't all the way up. Meanwhile, the day had folded into itself and combined with the terror to become vivid and pristine and perfect. Across the river the train was gone.

Then, as the wind roared along the Palisades at Hook Mountain and took on a northerly bite, as night began to descend upon the water and the tidal flow established itself in a southerly direction, working firmly past the bridge pylons, churning up white Vs, my son leaned and offered his hands to help me over the wall, and the air between us, before we actually touched, filled with an astonishingly pure love. It was there for a few seconds, and then it vanished, and I took him into the house to the chair, where I told him to sit until Sharon came home.

He resisted, squirming from the chair, but I insisted, saying, Sit there and wait until your mother gets home. Your time's not up. Your time's not even close to being up.

STEVEN MILLHAUSER

A Voice in the Night

FROM *The New Yorker*

I

THE BOY SAMUEL wakes in the dark. Something's not right. Most commentators agree that the incident takes place inside the temple, rather than in a tent outside the temple doors, under the stars. Less certain is whether Samuel's bed is in the sanctuary itself, where the Ark of the Covenant stands before a seven-branched oil lamp that is kept burning through the night, or in an adjoining chamber. Let's say that he is lying in an inner chamber, close to the sanctuary, perhaps adjacent to it. A curtained doorway leads to the chamber of Eli, the high priest of the temple of Shiloh. We like such details, but they do not matter. What matters is that Samuel wakes suddenly in the night. He is twelve years old, according to Flavius Josephus, or he may be a year or two younger. Something has startled him awake. He hears it again, clearly this time: "Samuel!" Eli is calling his name. What's wrong? Eli never calls his name in the middle of the night. Did Samuel forget to close the temple doors at sunset, did he allow one of the seven flames of the lamp to go out? But he remembers it well: pushing shut the heavy doors of cedar, visiting the sanctuary and replenishing the seven gold branches with consecrated olive oil so that the flames will burn brightly all night long. "Samuel!" He flings aside his goat's-hair blanket and hurries, almost runs, through the dark. He pushes through the curtain and enters Eli's chamber. The old man is lying on his back. Because he is the high priest of the temple of Shiloh, his mattress on the wooden platform is stuffed with wool, not straw. Eli's head rests on a pillow of goat's hair and his long-fingered hands lie crossed on his chest, beneath his white beard. His eyes are closed. "You called me," Samuel says, or perhaps his words are "Here am I; for thou calledst me." Eli opens his eyes. He seems a little confused, like a man roused from sleep. "I didn't call you," he answers. Or perhaps, with a touch of gruffness, since he doesn't like being awakened in the night: "I called not; lie down again." Samuel turns obediently away. He walks back to his chamber, where he lies down but doesn't close his eyes. In his years of attending Eli he's come to understand a great deal about the temple and its rules, and he tries to understand this night as well. Is it possible that Eli called his name without knowing it? The priest is old, sometimes he makes noises with his lips in his sleep, or mutters strange words. But never once has he called Samuel in the night. Has Samuel had a dream, in which a voice called out his name? Only recently he dreamed that he was walking alone through the parted waters of the Red Sea. Shimmering cliffs of water towered up on both sides, and as the watery walls began to plunge down on him he woke with a cry. From outside the walls of the temple he hears the high-pitched wail of a young sheep. Slowly Samuel closes his eyes.

II

It's a summer night in Stratford, Connecticut, 1950. The boy, seven years old, lies awake in his bed on the second floor, under the two screened windows that look down on his backyard. Through the windows he can hear the sound of summer: the *chk chk chk* of crickets from the vacant lot on the other side of the backyard hedge. For donkeys it's hee-haw, for roosters it's cock-a-doodle-doo, but for crickets you have to make up your own sound. Sometimes a car passes on the street alongside the yard, throwing two rectangles of light across the dark ceiling. The boy thinks the rectangles are the shapes of the open windows under the partially raised blinds, but he isn't sure. He's listening: hard. That afternoon in his Sunday school class at the Jewish Community Center, Mrs. Kraus read the story of the boy Samuel. In the middle of the night a voice called out his name: "Samuel! Samuel!" He was an attendant of the high priest and lived in the temple of Shiloh, without his parents. When he heard his name, Samuel thought the high priest was calling him. Three times in the night he heard his name, three times he went to the bedside of Eli. But it was the voice of the Lord calling him. The boy in Stratford is listening for his name in the night. The story of Samuel has made him nervous, tense as a cat. The slightest sound stiffens his whole body. He never thinks about the old man with a beard on the front of his *Child's Illustrated Old Testament,* but now he's wondering. What would his voice be like? His father says God is a story that people made up to explain things they don't understand. When his father speaks about God to company at dinner, his eyes grow angry and gleeful behind his glasses. But the voice in the night is as scary as witches. The voice in the night knows you're there, even though you're hidden in the dark. If the voice calls your name, you have to answer. The boy imagines the voice calling his name. It comes from the ceiling, it comes from the walls. It's like a terrible touch, all over his body. He doesn't want to hear the voice, but if he hears it he'll have to answer. You can't get out of it. He pulls the covers up to his chin and thinks of the walls of water crashing down on the Egyptians, on their chariots and horses. Through the window screens the crickets seem to be growing louder.

III

The Author is sixty-eight years old, in good health, most of his teeth, half his hair, not dead yet, though lately he hasn't been sleeping well. He's always been a light sleeper, the slightest sound jostles him awake, but this is different: he falls asleep with a book on his chest, then wakes up for no damn reason and strains his neck to look at the green glow of his digital clock, where it's always some soul-crushing time like 2:16 or 3:04 in the miserable morning. Hell time, abyss time, the hour of no return. He wonders whether he should turn on his bedside lamp, try to read a little, relax, but he knows the act of switching on the light will wake him up even more, and besides, there's the problem of what to read when you wake up at two or three in the godforsaken morning. If he reads something that interests him he'll excite his mind and ruin his chance for sleep, but if he reads something that bores him he'll become impatient, restless, and incapable of sleep. Better to lie there and curse his fate, like a man with a broken leg lying in a ditch. He listens to the sounds of the dark: *hsssh* of a passing car, *mmmm* of a neighbor's air conditioner, *skriiik* of a floorboard in the attic—a resident ghost. Things drift through your mind at doom-time in the morning, and as he listens he thinks of the boy in the house in Stratford, the bed by the two windows, the voice in the night. He thinks of the boy a lot these days, sometimes with irritation, sometimes with a fierce love that feels like sorrow. The boy tense, whipped up, listening for a voice in the night. He feels like shouting at the boy, driving some sense into that head of his. Oil your baseball glove! Jump on your bike! Do chin-ups on the swing set! Make yourself strong! But why yell at the boy? What'd he ever do to you? Better to imagine the voice calling right here, right now: Hello, old atheist, have I got news for you. Sorry, pal. Don't waste your time. You should've made your pitch when I was seven. Had the boy really expected to hear his name in the night? So long ago: Bobby Benson and the B-Bar-B Riders on the radio, his father at dinner attacking McCarthy. War in Korea, the push to Pusan. Those old stories got to you: Joseph in the pit, the parting of the Red Sea, David soothing the soul of Saul with his harp. In Catholic working-class Stratford, he was the only boy who didn't make the sign of the cross when they passed Holy Name Church on the way to school. Girls with smudges of ash on their foreheads. His God-scorning father driving him to Sunday school but taking him home when the others went to Hebrew class. No bar mitzvah for him. His father mocking his own rabbi for making boys jabber words they didn't understand. "Pure gibberish." A new word: gibberish. He liked it: gibberish. Still: Sunday school, "Rock of Ages," the story of Samuel, why is this night different from all other nights. The boy lying there listening, wanting his name to be called. Had he wanted his name to be called? Through the window the Author hears the sound of a distant car, the cry of the crickets. Sixty years later, upstate New York, and still the cry of the crickets in the summer in Stratford. Time to sleep, old man.

I

Samuel wakes again. This time he's sure: Eli has called his name. The voice stands out sharply, like a name written on a wall. "Samuel!" He throws off the goat's-hair blanket and steps onto the straw mat on the floor by his bed. He has lived with Eli in the temple of Shiloh for as long as he can remember. Once a year his mother and father visit him, when they come up from Ramah to offer the annual sacrifice. When he was born, his mother gave him to the Lord. She had asked the Lord for a son, and that's why his name is Asked-of-the-Lord. That's why he wears a linen ephod, that's why his hair flows down below his shoulders: no razor shall ever come upon his head. Samuel: Asked of the Lord. He enters Eli's chamber, where he expects to find Eli sitting up in bed, waiting impatiently for him. Instead, Eli is lying on his back with his eyes closed, like a man asleep. Should he wake Eli? Did Eli call Samuel's name and then fall back to sleep? Samuel hesitates to wake a man who's old and filled with worries. Though Eli is the high priest of the temple, his sons are wicked. They are priests who do not obey. When flesh is offered for sacrifice, they take the best part for themselves. They practice iniquities with women who come to the doors of the temple. "Here am I!" Samuel says, in a voice a little louder than he intended. Eli stirs and opens his eyes. "For thou didst call me," Samuel says, more softly. The old priest raises his head with difficulty. "I called not, my son; lie down again." Samuel doesn't protest, but lowers his eyes and turns away with the uneasy sense of having disturbed an old man's sleep. As he enters his own chamber, he tries to understand. Why has Eli called his name twice in the night? He called out in a loud, clear voice, a voice that could not be mistaken for some other sound. But Eli, who speaks only truth, has denied it. Samuel lies down on his bed and pulls the blanket up to his shoulders. Eli is very old. Does he call out Samuel's name and then, when Samuel appears beside him, forget that he has called? Old men are forgetful. The other day, when Eli spoke to Samuel of his own childhood, he could not remember a name he was searching for and grew troubled. Samuel has seen an old man at the temple whose body trembles like well water in a goatskin bucket. His eyes are unlit lamps. Eli is old, his eyesight is growing dim, but his body doesn't tremble and his voice is still strong. On the shoulders of his purple-and-scarlet ephod are two onyx stones, each engraved with the names of six tribes of Israel. When he stands in sunlight, the stones shine like fire. Slowly Samuel drifts into sleep.

II

It's the next night, and the boy in Stratford again lies awake, listening. He doesn't really believe he'll hear his name, but he wants to be awake in case it happens. He doesn't like to miss things. If he knows something important is coming, like a trip to the merry-go-round and the Whip at Pleasure Beach, he'll wait for it minute by minute, day after day, as if by taking his attention away from it for even a second he might cause it not to happen. But this is different. He doesn't know it's going to happen. It probably won't happen, how could it happen, but there's a chance, who knows. What he really needs to figure out is how to answer, if his name is called. In the story, Samuel was told to answer "Speak, Lord; for thy servant heareth." He tries to imagine it: "Speak, Lord; for thy servant heareth." It sounds like a boy in a play. Better to say "Yes?," which is what he'd say if his father called his name. But the Lord is not his father. The Lord is more powerful than his powerful father. He's more like the policeman in front of the school on Barnum Avenue, with his dangerous stick hanging from his belt. Better to say "Yes, sir," as he'd say if the policeman called his name. If he hears his name, that's what he'll say: "Yes, sir." Don't shout it: say it. Yes, sir. A voice in the dark, calling his name. The thought stirs him up again. He's too old to be scared of the dark, but the fear still comes on him sometimes. He likes to play a scare-game with his sister, the way they did when he was four and she was two. She lies in her dark room pretending to be asleep and he whispers, "Booooo haunt moan. Booooo haunt moan." Then they both burst into wild, scared laughter. But a voice in the night is not funny. He's through with witches, ghosts, monsters, isn't he, they're not real, so why is he scaring himself with the story of Samuel? It's only a story. His father has explained it to him: the Bible is stories. Like *Tootle* or *The Story of Dr. Dolittle.* Trains don't leave the tracks to chase butterflies, the pushmi-pullyu with a head at each end isn't an animal you'll ever find in the zoo, and the Lord doesn't call your name in the night. Stories are about things that don't happen. They could happen, but they don't. But they could. What if his name was called? He would want to be there. He'd want to know what comes next. What did the Lord say to Samuel? He can't remember. The most important part, and he can't remember. That's one thing about him: he can't remember the important things. He can remember the prince climbing the hair to the top of the tower but he can't remember the capital of Connecticut. Is it Bridgeport? The library in Bridgeport has long stone steps and high pillars. It's what he first thought of when he heard that Samuel was serving the Lord in the temple of Shiloh. A temple is different from a church. Jews go to temple and Christians go to church. But Catholics go to Catholic church. And everybody goes to the library. He's getting tired. At the backyard hedge, Billy turned to him and said, "Do you believe in Jesus?" His eyes were hard. There're two answers to that question. One is "No." The other's what his father said to him: "Jesus was a great teacher." But he was a coward and looked down. A door opens and he hears footsteps in the hall. Do his parents know he's lying awake, listening for his name? He hears the door to the bathroom open and close. Sometimes his father is up in the night. If he opens his door and waits for his father? Tell me about Samuel. Tell me. Tell me about the voice in the night. If you heard that voice, nothing would ever be the same. He pushes the thought away. Tomorrow they're going to drive out past the Sikorsky plant to Short Beach, where he can wade out to the sandbar.

III

One-fifty-four in the morning. The gods are out to get him. Sleep for an hour, wake for no reason, stare like a madman, waiting for sleep. Dragging himself through the day like a stepped-on snail. Won't take a pill, they leave him groggy. Sloggy and boggy. That all you've got? Draggy and saggy. Baggy and shaggy. Like a hag, haggy. Now he's alert, full of useless energy. In the old days he'd recite fistfuls of sonnets. My mistress' eyes are nothing like the sun. Three things there be that prosper up apace. Now all he can do is lie there thinking about things, far-off things, high school, grade school, the boy in the room in Stratford, listening for the voice in the night. Did it really happen that way, or is he embellishing? Habit of the trade. But no, he lay there waiting for his name. The two windows, the two bookcases his father had made from orange crates, the bed against the other wall for his sister to sleep in when one of the grandmothers came to stay. One grandma from West 110th Street, one from Washington Heights. Father's mother, mother's mother, first one, then the other, never together. Waiting for the train at the Bridgeport station, with long dark benches and the row of hand-cranked picture machines. The something-scopes. Turning the handles, making the pictures move. The grandmother with crooked fingers who brought packs of playing cards and dyed her hair orange and wore lots of rattly bracelets, the grandmother with the accent who made cold red soup with sour cream. Mutoscopes. Two women born in the nineteenth century, who can grasp it, one in New York, one in Minsk, before skyscrapers, before horseless carriages, before the extinction of the dinosaurs. His own mother growing up with Russian Jewish parents on the Lower East Side. Her father escaping the tsar, embracing America, naming his first son Abraham, middle name Lincoln. Moving them to a new apartment every few months, skipping out on the rent. She said he sat reading Dostoyevsky in Russian while his sons waited on customers in the store. The Stratford boy's own early childhood in Brooklyn, all there in the photo albums: pretty mother with flower in her hair on a bench in Prospect Park, pretty mother in wide-brimmed hat standing with little son in sailor suit on the Coney Island boardwalk. The two of them riding the trolley. Trolley tracks in the street, wires in the sky, the grooved wheel at the top of the trolley pole: a forgotten world. His invisible father holding up the light meter, adjusting the f-number, staring down into the ground-glass screen of the twin-lens reflex. Then Stratford, working-class neighborhood, where else can a professor afford to live. Milk delivered in glass bottles to the back porch each morning. Italians and Eastern Europeans, Zielski and Stoccatore and Saksa and Mancini. Riccio's drugstore. Ciccarelli's lot. Ralph Politano. Tommy Pavluvcik. Mario Recupido. What is a Jew? A Jew is someone who doesn't cross himself in front of Holy Name Church. A Jew is someone who stays indoors practicing the piano on bright summer mornings while everyone else is outside playing baseball. His mother playing Chopin nocturnes and waltzes, DEE dah-dah-dah, DEE dah-dah-dah, teaching him scales, reading on the couch with her legs tucked under her. The mahogany bookcase by the staircase, the wall bookcase by the fireplace. His father driving them home one night: "Did you see that? Not a book in the house!" What is a Jew? A Jew is someone who has books in the house. His father demolishing an argument for the existence of God, his lips twisted in scorn. Jewish Community Center but no bar mitzvah. A tree every Christmas, a menorah once or twice. No baby Jesuses, no Marys or mangers. A package of matzo once a year: like big saltines. The strange word: unleavened. Dyeing Easter eggs, walking under the roof of cornstalks and branches at Sukkoth, biting into hollow crumbly chocolate bunnies, lighting the yahrzeit candle for the grandmother from Minsk. What is a Jew? A Jew is someone who thinks of Easter as a holiday celebrating rabbits. His mother a first-grade teacher, his father a teacher at the university. The grandmother with crooked fingers, once a piano teacher. The whole family teaching up a storm. A tutor who tooted the flute. Tried to tutor two tooters to toot. What is a Jew? A Jew is someone who comes from people who teach. Erleen, from the project in Bridgeport, watching gently over him each day when he came home from school. The rhyme in the street: Eenie meenie miney mo, catch a nigger by the toe. His father serious, quiet-voiced, his mouth tight: "People use that word, but not in this house. It is disgusting." Negro: a word of respect. Respect people. His all-Jewish Cub Scout troop. "You don't look for trouble," the scoutmaster said. "But you don't let anyone call you a kike." Not in this house. A new word: kike. He tried to imagine it: kike. Hey, kike! Hit him, kill him. Did he really lie awake night after night, listening for his name? The child Samuel. All about obedience. Saul's flaw: disobedience. Samuel thrusting his sword into the belly of the king of the Amalekites. That's what happens when your name is called in the night. The righteous life, the life of moral ferocity. His father and Samuel, two of a kind. Samuel: "Thou art wicked." His father: "You are ignorant." A special sect: the Jewish atheist. The thirteenth tribe. And you? Who are you? I am the one whose name was not called in the night.

I

The voice calls again. This time Samuel doesn't hesitate. He swings his legs out of bed and rushes through the dark to Eli's side. "Here am I," he cries, impatient now, "for thou didst call me." Eli is lying on his back, his eyes closed, his hands crossed on his chest. All at once he's leaning up on an elbow, searching Samuel's face.

Samuel feels aggrieved, anxious, expectant. What is happening? Something is happening. He doesn't know what. The long hand of the priest rests on Samuel's arm. Samuel suddenly understands two things: Eli did not call his name, and Eli knows who did. Does Samuel know? He almost knows. He knows and doesn't dare to know. But Eli is speaking, Eli is telling him who it is that has called his name. It is the Lord. "Go, lie down: and it shall be, if he call thee, that thou shalt say, Speak, Lord; for thy servant heareth." The searching look, the hand on his arm: Samuel understands that he must ask no more questions. He returns to his bed and lies down on his back with his eyes open. He wants to hear with both ears. One hand is pressed against his chest. His heart is like a fist beating against the inside of the bone. What if his name isn't called again? Eli said, "If he call thee." Three times, and he failed to answer. Should he have known? He knew, he almost knew, he was about to know. Now he knows. What he doesn't know is whether he will hear the voice again. If his name is not called, he will never forgive himself. And if his name is called? Then what? What should he say? Oh, don't you remember? Speak, Lord; for thy servant heareth. Speak, Lord; for thy servant heareth. He remembers the first time he saw Eli, the high priest of the temple. A powerful man, with shining gems on the shoulders of his ephod. His legs were like tall columns of stone. His hands the size of oil jars. Now Eli's beard is white, he mutters in his sleep. Difficult sons, wicked sons he cannot restrain. Calm yourself. Stop trembling. Listen.

II

The third night, and the boy in his bed in Stratford still hasn't heard his name. He's not really listening, is he? He thought he heard it once, a distant call, fooling him for a second, that cat cry or whatever it was. He no longer expects to hear anything, so why's he still waiting? By now there's a spirit of stubbornness in it: he's waited this long, might as well wait some more. But that isn't it. What's *it* is, he doesn't believe the voice in the night will come, but his unbelief upsets him as much as belief would, if he believed. If the voice doesn't come, it means he hasn't been chosen. He likes being chosen. He was chosen to represent his class in the school spelling bee. It's easy to spell, he doesn't know how to spell words wrong, but it still feels good to be chosen. He's not so good on the playground, can't kick the ball as hard as most of them, lucky if he gets to first. He wants the voice to call him in the night, even though it won't happen. He doesn't believe those old stories, doesn't believe the prince climbing the hair or the thorns growing up and covering the castle, so why should he believe the story of the voice in the night? His father doesn't believe those stories. His father doesn't believe in God. But when the boy asked, his father didn't get the angry look, he got the serious quiet look. He said you have to think about it yourself and make up your mind when you're older. The boy wonders how old is older. When is when? If he hears the voice now, he'll know. But he already knows. He knows he won't hear the voice. Why should he be chosen? He's no Samuel. He's a good speller. He plays the piano with two hands, he can write a poem about George Washington and draw a picture of a kingfisher or a red-winged blackbird. But Samuel opens the doors to the temple when the sun comes up, Samuel fills the lamp with oil so that it burns all night. Down below he hears a car going by. It's passing his yard and the vacant lot, the two bars of light sliding across the ceiling, now it's passing the bakery down by the stream, he loves the bakery, smell of hot rye, the gingerbread men and the muffins with raisins, now it's climbing the hill, sound of tires like the waterfall in the park earlier this summer, over the hill toward Bridgeport. He feels old, very old, older than Eli, he wishes he were young again, a child. He wishes he'd never heard that stupid story. Sh-h-h. Sleep now.

III

Another night, another waking. Not a good sign. Death by insomnia at sixty-eight. All Samuel's fault, keeping everybody up when they ought to be snoring away. The boy in Stratford battling it out at the age of seven. By high school, no tolerance for the once-a-week churchgoers. Priest or atheist: choose one. The move to Fairfield, the beach, Protestant churches galore. Presbyterian, First Congregational, Episcopalian. Roper. Warren. Kane. No Jews allowed in the beach club. Who'd want to join a beach club? Reading the five arguments for the existence of God and their rebuttals. The ontological argument. The teleological argument. Walking along the beach at night, the deserted lifeguard stands, the lights of Long Island. Challenge to a friend: Why do you go to church? Why only on Sunday? He knew what he knew: always or never. If the voice calls your name, your other life is over. No going back. Short of that, sorry, please pass the ketchup. By the age of fifteen, done with religion, like the baseball books of his childhood. No regrets. Girls in tight skirts reaching up into lockers, girls in tight blouses hugging books to their chests as they hip-swing down the halls. Let me touch! Let me see! The house for sale on his friend's street out near the junior high. "They'll never sell to Jews." "Why not?" "You know how those people are." "How are they?" "They take over the neighborhood." "You're talking to one." "Oh, you're not *that* kind of Jew." At age eleven, the talk with his father: "We don't do anything in Sunday school. Just play games and fool around. I don't want to go anymore." His father taking his pipe out of his mouth, looking at him gravely: "You don't have to go." He'd expected resistance, a look of reproach. Might as well blame it all on Jehovah. Could have called his name in the night. The boy in Stratford, listening. Something extreme in his temperament, even then. Shy and extreme. Stubborn. You don't call my name, I won't call yours. Even Steven. Dr. Dolittle and Pecos Bill instead of Samuel and King Saul. Don't have to go. The neighborhood goes to church, the family stays home and reads. In high school, asking his father whether he liked teaching. His father's pause, his grave look, his utter attention: "If I were a millionaire, I would pay for the privilege of teaching." The son knows he's heard something important. He is moved, he is proud of his father, he's envious. He thinks, I want to say that someday. They call it a calling. Samuel's call in the night. His father's calling. Lying awake remembering these things. Walking in his bathing suit, towel around his neck, to the beach in Fairfield with his parents' friends from the city. Janey with her long black hair and tight white one-piece, waving her arm at the street of ranch houses: "Suburbia." Her voice mocking, disdainful. New York judging Connecticut. Jews moving out of New York: abandoning the tribe. Always the connection to the city. The four years in Brooklyn, corner of Clinton and Joralemon, the grandmother on West 110th Street and the grandmother in Washington Heights, mother growing up on the Lower East Side, father on the Upper West Side. Childhood trips to the city, the stone bridges of the Merritt Parkway. The Museum of Natural History with dinosaur skeletons like gigantic fishbones, lunch at the Automat: the sandwiches behind the little glass windows. Horn & Hardart. Early admission to Oberlin, but he chooses Columbia. Walking along the eighth floor of John Jay Hall, the thrilling sound of violins and cellos behind closed doors: the good Jewish boys practicing their instruments. Weinstein, or was it Marinoff: "What kind of Jew are you?" A Jew from suburbia. A nothing Jew, a secular Jew, an unjewish Jew. A Jew without a bar mitzvah, a Jew without a bump in his nose. Later he develops the idea of the Negative Jew. A Negative Jew is a Jew about whom another Jew says, "You don't *look* Jewish." A Negative Jew is a Jew who says to another Jew, "Judaism is a superstition that I reject," and to an anti-Semite, "I have Jewish blood." A Negative Jew is a Jew who says, "I don't believe in Judaism," while being herded into a cattle car. Hitler, the great clarifier. His father's German Jewish colleague, Dr. What's-Her-Name, one of the first women admitted to a German university, her passion for Kant, for all things German. Stayed put till 1939. Blamed it all on the Polish Jews. "They gave us a bad name." The boy in Stratford, lying awake at night. Hard to remember how it was. A game, was it? Scare yourself with witches, scare yourself with Jehovah. A shudder of delight. All those old stories, wonderful and terrible: the voice in the night, the parting of the Red Sea, Hansel in the cage, the children following the piper into the mountain. *Hamlet* and *Oedipus Rex* as pale reflections of the nightmare tales of childhood. Everything connected: David playing the harp for Saul, the boy in Stratford practicing the piano, the cellos and violins behind the closed doors. The boy listening for his name, the man waiting for the rush of inspiration. Where do you get your ideas? A voice in the night. When did you decide to become a writer? Three thousand years ago, in the temple of Shiloh.

I

And the Lord came, and stood, and called as at other times, Samuel, Samuel. Commentators disagree about the meaning of the word "stood." Some say that the Lord assumes a bodily presence before Samuel. Others argue that the Lord never takes on a bodily form and that therefore the voice has drawn closer to Samuel, so that the effect is of a person drawing closer in the dark. In one version of this argument, the boy hears the voice and imagines a form standing beside him. All this, the Author thinks, can be left to the interpreters. What matters to us is that the voice of the Lord calls Samuel's name. After all, Eli had said, "If he call thee." For it was not inevitable that the voice, which had called three times and not received an answer, would call again. Now the boy Samuel has heard the voice a fourth time and knows who is calling him. He doesn't yet know why the Lord is calling him, but he knows how to answer, for Eli has told him exactly what to say: "Speak, Lord; for thy servant heareth." Samuel resists, the words refuse to come, then he says it aloud: "Speak; for thy servant heareth." He hears his words clearly in the dark: "Speak; for thy servant heareth." There is no doubt: he has said "Speak" and not "Speak, Lord," as he was instructed to do. Was he so frightened of uttering the sacred name? He feels a rush of self-reproach, before commanding himself to be still and listen. He lies motionless, alert all over his body, fiercely calm. He has served in the temple of Shiloh ever since early childhood, but nothing has prepared him for this moment. He does not try to imagine what the Lord will tell him, but he readies himself to remember every word, in the order of speaking. Eli is awake, waiting in the next chamber. Eli will ask him what the Lord has said. Though the voice of the Lord is strong, Samuel knows it cannot be heard by Eli, and not because Eli is too far away to hear. The voice is for him alone. He knows this without arrogance. And he will remember. He has a good memory, he's proud of his memory, though he watches over his pride so that it doesn't become vanity. Words read to him or heard by him remain unchanged inside him. It has always been that way. Now the Lord speaks, and Samuel listens. There is nothing in the world but these words. The words are harsh. The house of Eli will be judged for its iniquity. The sons of Eli are wicked and Eli has not restrained them. Therefore the Lord will perform against Eli all things which he has spoken concerning his house. The sons of Eli will die on the same day. The House of Eli will come to an end. When the Lord departs, it is like the silence after thunder. Samuel lies awake in the dark. It seems to him that the dark has become darker, a dark so dark that it is like the darkness upon the face of the deep, before the Lord moved upon the face of the waters. The words have shaken him like a wind. He can feel Eli lying awake in his chamber, waiting for Samuel to tell him what the Lord has said. But Samuel cannot bring himself to leave his bed and go to Eli's chamber. If Eli asks him, and Eli will certainly ask him, he will speak the truth, but he does not want to speak the truth unbidden. Samuel lies in the dark a long time, listening for the Lord, listening for Eli, but all is silent. Has the darkness become less dark? Can darkness be less dark and still be dark? The darkness is growing lighter. Soon it will be time to open the temple doors. Eli will ask what the Lord has said, and Samuel will repeat the terrible words. Samuel understands that nothing will ever be the same. But now, as the darkness is fading, without yet losing its quality of darkness, he wants to lie in his bed as if he could be a child forever, he wants to lie there as if his name had not been called in the night.

II

It's the fourth night, and by now the boy in Stratford knows he'll never hear his name. Still, he's awake, and in case he's wrong he's still listening, no harm in that, though at the same time he makes fun of himself for lying there, waiting, and for what? His name? It's only a story in a book. You might as well lie awake waiting for a genie to rise up out of a lamp. And even if it isn't only a story, why would the Lord call his name? Samuel was an attendant of the high priest of the temple, Samuel was already favored by the Lord. The boy in Stratford goes to the Jewish Community Center on Sunday for two hours and skips Hebrew lessons. He doesn't make the sign of the cross in front of Holy Name Church, but he looks forward to Christmas as if it's the greatest day of winter. No crosses or angels on his tree, no lit-up statues of Mary blinking on the front lawn, but still, stockings, colored tree lights, glittery tinsel, presents piled high. Christmas: a holiday celebrating the end of the year. Rosh Hashanah: a holiday he can't pronounce, celebrating something he can't remember. The Lord, if he's even up there, shouldn't call his name. And that's fine with him. He doesn't want his name to be called. If your name is called, everything changes. It would be like going to Sunday school all week long. He likes the way things are: catching fly balls and grounders in the backyard, walking in the hot sand at Short Beach, firecrackers on the Fourth of July, sitting in front of the fireplace in winter reading a book while his father grades papers at one end of the couch and his mother reads at the other end, birthday parties, reading *The 500 Hats of Bartholomew Cubbins* to his sister, playing double solitaire with Grandma Lena, watching the black-and-white pictures rise into the white paper in the developing tray in his father's darkroom, riding slowly in the boat through the Old Mill at Pleasure Beach. He doesn't want to leave his family, doesn't want to leave his room with the two windows looking down at the backyard, the big record player in the living room, where he and his sister listen to *Peter and the Wolf.* His mother looking at him one day, touching him, her eyes shining: "Oh, my firstborn." His father answering all his questions with that serious look, as if nothing is more important than those questions. What happens when you die? What is God? What is the most important thing in the world? He doesn't want to leave it all for the temple of Shiloh. School starts in a few weeks, he's still got lots of summer left, picnics by the river, drives into Bridgeport, the smell of hot roasted nuts in Morrow's Nut House, the elevator operators in their maroon jackets and white gloves in Read's department store, the wooden ships with rigging in the window of Blinn's. He's done with Samuel, done with the voice in the night, but now, as he feels sleep coming on, he gives a final listen, just in case, straining his ears, holding his breath, listening for the voice that came to Samuel in that old story that's only a story but one he knows he'll never forget, no matter how hard he tries.

III

Again. Enough already. But hey, look on the bright side: four in the morning, three hours of sleep instead of one. The long walk after dinner, more than an hour, hoping to outwit insomnia. Walk for one hour, wake up at four. Walk for two hours, wake up at five. Walk for three hours, wake up at six. Walk for four hours, drop dead of a heart attack. His flab-armed father's muscular calves. Walked all over Manhattan in his City College days, late nineteen-twenties, Harlem to the Battery. A safe city. The boy in Stratford walking up Canaan Road to the White Walk Market, walking to school along Franklin Avenue and Collins Street and the street that led past Holy Name. Calves skinny as forearms. His father walking a mile to the bus stop each morning to catch the bus to Bridgeport, no car till the boy is in second grade: city people don't drive. No television till fifth grade: TV is for people who don't read. Last in the neighborhood. Back from Manhattan with a ten-inch box, an Air King, set up on a table next to the piano. The feverish pleasure of black-and-white cartoons. Czerny exercises and Farmer Al Falfa. Mozart and Mighty Mouse. His mother playing Schumann and laughing with him at *The Merry Mailman.* His grave father bent over the Scrooge McDuck comic, praising the diving board in the money bin. Reading *Tootle* to him, telling him how good the first sentence is. "Far, far to the west of everywhere is the village of Lower Trainswitch." Far, far to the west of everywhere. His father said, "There are three great opening sentences in all of literature. The first is 'In the beginning God created the heaven and the earth.' The second is 'Call me Ishmael.' The third is 'Far, far to the west of everywhere is the village of Lower Trainswitch.'" A father who's serious and funny: you have to watch his face carefully. The book about the whale: he knows where it is on the shelf, he's held it in his hands, thinking, When I'm older. The whale, God: when he's older. Books, always books. Ten years old: his father lashing out at Eisenhower. "He doesn't open a book!" The trip to Spain after Columbia, one-way ticket, two pieces of luggage: one for clothes, one for books. The boy in Stratford lying awake at night because of a story in a book. What's a story? A demon in the night. He wants to protect the boy, warn him before it's too late. Don't listen to stories! They'll keep you awake at night, suck out your blood, leave teeth marks in your skin. Let him sleep! Let him live! His New York Jew parents in working-class Stratford, with their books and their piano. The professor who doesn't do work with his hands. Joey's father a machinist at the helicopter plant, Mike's father a carpenter who builds his own house in the vacant lot on the other side of the hedge. Joey turning to him with a fighting look: "Can your father make a wheel?" The old sun-browned Italian men working in their gardens. The grapevines growing all over Jimmy Stoccatore's high fence, the bunches of purple grapes, heavy in the hand. Old man Ciccarelli chasing kids out of his lot. Eenie meenie miney mo, catch a tiger by the toe. Not in this house. The Jewish Boy Scout troop, where he learned to tie a sheepshank but never could identify poison sumac. His refusal to be Jesus in the Sunday school play. Mrs. Kraus's shocked surprise.

"But why?" "Because Jesus betrayed the Jews." Her confusion, fear. "I never taught you that!" His father: "Jesus was a great teacher." Sixty years later, awake at night, at the mercy of memory. Rapunzel! Rapunzel! Let down your hair! And the Lord came, and stood, and called as at other times, Samuel, Samuel. The boy in Stratford, listening. Thank you, Old Man of the Sky, for not calling his name. Better for all concerned. He can't really have believed it, can he? Working himself up into a temporary blaze of half-belief, a possibility: a ghost in the dark. Better for him to stay out of the temple of Shiloh, better to go play in the green backyards of Stratford, grow up in a world of family excursions and shelves of books until the writing fever seized him and claimed him for life. A calling. Not Samuel's call but another. Not that way but this way. Samuel ministering unto the Lord, his teacher-father ministering unto the generations. And the son? What about him? Far, far to the west of everywhere, ministering unto the Muse. Thanks, Old Sea-Parter, for leaving me be. Tired now. Soon we'll all sleep.

LORRIE MOORE

Referential

FROM *The New Yorker*

FOR THE THIRD TIME in three years, they talked about what would be a suitable birthday present for her deranged son. There was so little they were actually allowed to bring: almost everything could be transformed into a weapon, and so most items had to be left at the front desk and then, if requested, brought in later by a big blond aide, who would look the objects over beforehand for their wounding possibilities. Pete had brought a basket of jams, but they were in glass jars and so not permitted. "I forgot about that," he said. The jars were arranged by color, from the brightest marmalade to cloudberry to fig, as if they contained the urine tests of an increasingly ill person. Just as well they'll be confiscated, she thought. They would find something else to bring.

By the time her son was twelve and had begun his dazed and quiet muttering, had given up brushing his teeth, Pete had been in their lives for six years, and now four more years had passed. The love they had for Pete was long and winding, with hidden turns but no real halts. Her son thought of him as a kind of stepfather. She and Pete had got old together, though it showed more on her, with her black shirtdresses worn for slimming and her now graying hair undyed and often pinned up with strands hanging down like Spanish moss. Once her son had been stripped and gowned and placed in the facility, she too had removed her necklaces, earrings, scarves—all her prosthetic devices, she said to Pete, trying to amuse—and put them in a latched accordion file under her bed. She was not allowed to wear them when visiting, so she would no longer wear them at all, a kind of solidarity with her child, a new widowhood on top of the widowhood she already possessed. Unlike other women her age (who tended to try too hard, with lurid lingerie and flashing jewelry), she now felt that that sort of effort was ludicrous, and she went out into the world like an Amish woman, or perhaps, even worse, when the unforgiving light of spring hit her face, an Amish man. If she was going to be old, let her be a full-fledged citizen of the old country! "To me, you always look so beautiful," Pete no longer said.

Pete had lost his job in the recent economic downturn. At one point, he had been poised to live with her, but her child's deepening troubles had caused him to pull back. He said that he loved her but could not find the space he needed for himself in her life or in her house. (He did not blame her son—or did he?) He eyed with somewhat visible covetousness and sour remarks the front room, which her son, when home, lived in with large blankets and empty ice-cream pints, an Xbox, and DVDs.

She no longer knew where Pete went, sometimes for weeks at a time. She thought it an act of vigilance and attachment that she did not ask, tried not to care. She once grew so hungry for touch that she went to the Stressed Tress salon around the corner just to have her hair washed. The few times she had flown to Buffalo to see her brother and his family, at airport security she had chosen the pat-downs and the wandings rather than the scanning machine.

"Where is Pete?" her son cried out during visits she made alone, his face scarlet with acne, swollen and wide with the effects of medications that had been changed, then changed again, and she said that Pete was busy today, but soon, soon, maybe next week, he would come. A maternal vertigo beset her, the room circled, and the thin scars on her son's arms sometimes seemed to spell out Pete's name, the loss of fathers etched primitively in an algebra of skin. In the carousel spin of the room, those white webbed lines resembled coarse campground graffiti, as when young people used to stiffly carve the words "PEACE" and "FUCK" into picnic tables and trees, the "C" three-quarters of a square. Mutilation was a language. And vice versa. The cutting endeared her boy to the girls, many of whom were cutters themselves and seldom saw a boy who was one, and so in the group sessions he became popular, which he neither minded nor perhaps really noticed. When no one was looking, he sometimes cut the bottoms of his feet—with crisp paper from crafts hour. In group, he pretended to read the girls' soles like palms, announcing the arrival of strangers and the progress toward romance—"toemances," he called them—and sometimes seeing his own fate in what they had cut there.

Now she and Pete went to see her son without the jams but with a soft deckle-edged book about Daniel Boone, pulled from her own bookcase, which was allowed, even though her son would believe that it contained messages for him, believe that, although it was a story about a long-ago person, it was also the story of his own sorrow and heroism in the face of every manner of wilderness, defeat, and abduction, that his own life could be draped over the book, which was simply a noble armature for the revelation of tales of *him*. There would be clues in the words on pages with numbers that added up to his age: 97, 88, 466. There would be other veiled references to his existence. There always were.

They sat at the visitors' table together, and her son set the book aside and did try to smile at both of them. There was still sweetness in his eyes, the sweetness he'd been born with, even if fury could dart in a scattershot fashion across them. Someone had cut his tawny hair—or, at least, had tried. Perhaps the staff person hadn't wanted the scissors to stay near him for a prolonged period and had snipped quickly, then leaped away, approached again, grabbed and snipped, then jumped back. That's what it looked like. Her son had wavy hair that had to be cut carefully. Now it no longer cascaded down but was close to his head, springing out at angles that would likely matter to no one but a mother.

"So where have you been?" her son asked Pete.

"Good question," Pete said, as if praising the thing would make it go away. How could people be mentally well in such a world?

"Do you miss us?" the boy asked.

Pete did not answer.

"Do you think of me when you look at the black capillaries of the trees at night?"

"I suppose I do." Pete stared back at him, so as not to shift in his seat. "I am always hoping that you are okay and that they treat you well here."

"Do you think of my mom when you stare up at the clouds and all they hold?"

Pete fell silent again.

"That's enough," she said to her son, who turned to her with a change of expression.

"There's supposed to be cake this afternoon for someone's birthday," he said.

"That will be nice!" she said, smiling back.

"No candles, of course. Or forks. We'll just have to grab the frosting and mash it into our eyes for blinding. Do you ever think about how, at that moment of the candles, time stands still, even as the moments carry away the smoke? It's like the fire of burning love. Do you ever wonder why so many people have things they don't deserve but how absurd all those things are to begin with? Do you really think a wish can come true if you never ever ever ever ever ever tell it to anyone?"

On the ride home, she and Pete did not exchange a word, and every time she looked at his aging hands, arthritically clasping the steering wheel, the familiar thumbs slung low in their slightly simian way, she understood anew the desperate place they both were in, though their desperations were separate, not shared, and her eyes then felt the stabbing pressure of tears.

The last time her son had tried to do it, his method had been, in the doctor's words, morbidly ingenious. He might have succeeded, but a fellow patient, a girl from group, had stopped him at the last minute. There had been blood to be mopped. For a time, her son had wanted only a distracting pain, but eventually he had wanted to tear a hole in himself and flee through it. Life, for him, was full of spies and preoccupying espionage. Yet sometimes the spies would flee as well, and someone might have to go after them, over the rolling fields of dream, into the early-morning mountains of dawning signification, in order, paradoxically, to escape them altogether.

There was a storm looming, and lightning did its quick, purposeful zigzag among the clouds. She did not need such stark illustration that horizons could be shattered, filled with messages and broken codes, yet there it was. A spring snow began to fall with the lightning still cracking, and Pete put the windshield wipers on so that they could peer through the cleared semicircles at the darkening road before them. She knew that the world had not been created to speak just to her, and yet, as for her son, sometimes things did. The fruit trees had bloomed early, for instance—the orchards they passed were pink—but the premature warmth precluded bees, and there would be little fruit. Most of the dangling blossoms would fall in this very storm.

When they arrived at her house and went in, Pete glanced at himself in the hallway mirror. Perhaps he needed assurance that he was still alive and not the ghost he seemed.

"Would you like a drink?" she asked, hoping he would stay. "I have some good vodka. I could make you a nice white Russian!"

"Just vodka," he said reluctantly. "Straight."

She opened the freezer to find the vodka, and when she closed it again she stood there for a moment, looking at the photo magnets she'd stuck to the refrigerator door. As a baby, her son had seemed happier than most babies. As a six-year-old, he was still smiling and hamming it up, his arms and legs shooting out like starbursts, his perfectly gapped teeth flashing, his hair in honeyed coils. At ten, he had a vaguely brooding and fearful expression, though there was light in his eyes, and his lovely cousins beside him. There he was, a plumpish teenager, his arm around Pete. And there, in the corner, he was an infant again, held by his dignified, handsome father, whom he did not recall, because he had died so long ago. All this had to be accepted. Living did not mean one joy piled upon another. It was merely the hope for less pain, hope played like a playing card upon another hope, a wish for kindnesses and mercies to emerge like kings and queens in an unexpected twist in the game. One could hold the cards oneself or not: they would land the same way, regardless. Tenderness did not enter into it, except in a damaged way.

"You don't want ice?"

"No," Pete said. "No, thank you."

She placed two glasses of vodka on the kitchen table. She sank into the chair across from him.

"Perhaps this will help you sleep," she said.

"Don't know if anything can do that," he said, taking a swig. Insomnia plagued him.

"I am going to bring him home this week," she said. "He needs his home back, his house, his room. He is no danger to anyone."

Pete drank some more, sipping noisily. She could see that he wanted no part of this, but she felt that she had no choice but to proceed. "Perhaps you could help. He looks up to you."

"Help how?" Pete asked with a flash of anger. There was the clink of his glass on the table.

"We could each spend part of the night near him," she said carefully.

The telephone rang. The Radio Shack wall phone brought almost nothing but bad news, and so the sound of it ringing, especially in the evening, always startled her. She repressed a shudder but still her shoulders hunched, as if she were anticipating a blow. She stood.

"Hello?" she said, answering it on the third ring, her heart pounding. But the person on the other end hung up. She sat back down. "I guess it was a wrong number," she said, adding, "Perhaps you would like more vodka."

"Only a little. Then I should go."

She poured him some more. She'd said what she needed to say and did not want to have to persuade him. She would wait for him to step forward with the right words. Unlike some of her meaner friends, who kept warning her, she believed that there was a deep good side of Pete and she was always patient for it. What else could she be?

The phone rang again.

"Probably telemarketers," he said.

"I hate them," she said. "Hello?" she said more loudly into the receiver.

This time when the caller hung up she glanced at the lit panel on the phone, which was supposed to reveal the number of the person who was calling.

She sat back down and poured herself more vodka. "Someone is phoning here from your apartment," she said.

He threw back the rest of his drink. "I should go," he said, and got up. She followed him. At the door, she watched him grasp the knob and twist it firmly. He opened it wide, blocking the mirror.

"Good night," he said. His expression had already forwarded itself to someplace far away.

She threw her arms around him to kiss him, but he turned his head abruptly so that her mouth landed on his ear. She remembered that he had made this evasive move ten years ago, when they had first met, and he was in a condition of romantic overlap.

"Thank you for coming with me," she said.

"You're welcome," he replied, then hurried down the steps to his car, which was parked at the curb out front. She did not attempt to walk him to it. She closed the front door and locked it as the telephone began to ring again.

She went into the kitchen. She had not actually been able to read the caller ID without her glasses, and had invented the part about its being Pete's number, but he had made it the truth anyway, which was the black magic of lies and good guesses, nimble bluffs. Now she braced herself. She planted her feet.

"Hello?" she said, answering on the fifth ring. The plastic panel where the number should appear was clouded as if by a scrim, a page of onionskin over the onion—or rather, a picture of an onion. One depiction on top of another.

"Good evening," she said loudly. What would burst forth? A monkey's paw. A lady. A tiger.

But there was nothing at all.

ALICE MUNRO

Train

FROM *Harper's Magazine*

THIS IS A SLOW TRAIN anyway, and it has slowed some more for the curve. Jackson is the only passenger left, and the next stop is about twenty miles ahead. Then the stop at Ripley, then Kincardine and the lake. He is in luck and it's not to be wasted. Already he has taken his ticket stub out of its overhead notch.

He heaves his bag and sees it land just nicely, in between the rails. No choice now—the train's not going to get any slower.

He takes his chance. A young man in good shape, agile as he'll ever be. But the leap, the landing, disappoints him. He's stiffer than he'd thought, the stillness pitches him forward, his palms come down hard on the gravel between the ties, he's scraped the skin. Nerves.

The train is out of sight; he hears it putting on a bit of speed, clear of the curve. He spits on his hurting hands, getting the gravel out. Then picks up his bag and starts walking back in the direction he has just covered on the train. If he followed the train, he would show up at the station there well after dark. He'd still be able to complain that he'd fallen asleep and wakened all mixed up, thinking he'd slept through his stop when he hadn't, jumped off all confused.

He would have been believed. Coming home from so far away, from Germany and the war, he could have got mixed up in his head. It's not too late, he would be where he was supposed to be before midnight. But all the time he's thinking this, he's walking in the opposite direction. He doesn't know many names of trees. Maples, that everybody knows. Pines. He'd thought that where he jumped was in some woods, but it wasn't. The trees are just along the track, thick on the embankment, but he can see the flash of fields behind them. Fields green or rusty or yellow. Pasture, crops, stubble. He knows just that much. It's still August.

And once the noise of the train has been swallowed up, he realizes there isn't the perfect quiet around that he would have expected. Plenty of disturbance here and there, a shaking of the dry August leaves that wasn't wind, a racket of unknown, unseen birds chastising him.

People he'd met in the past few years seemed to think that if you weren't from a city, you were from the country. And that was not true. Jackson himself was the son of a plumber. He had never been in a stable in his life or herded cows or stoked grain. Or found himself as now stumping along a railway track that seemed to have reverted from its normal purpose of carrying people and freight to become a province of wild apple trees and thorny berry bushes and trailing grapevines and crows scolding from perches you could not see. And right now a garter snake slithering between the rails, perfectly confident he won't be quick enough to tramp on and murder it. He does know enough to figure that it's harmless, but its confidence riles him.

The little jersey, whose name was Margaret Rose, could usually be counted on to show up at the stable door for milking twice a day, morning and evening. Belle didn't often have to call her. But this morning she was too interested in something down by the dip of the pasture field, or in the trees that hid the railway tracks on the other side of the fence. She heard Belle's whistle and then her call, and started out reluctantly. But then decided to go back for another look.

Belle set the pail and stool down and started tramping through the morning-wet grass.

"So-boss. So-boss."

She was half coaxing, half scolding.

Something moved in the trees. A man's voice called out that it was all right.

Well, of course it was all right. Did he think she was afraid of him attacking Margaret Rose, who had her horns still on?

Climbing over the rail fence, he waved in what he might have considered a reassuring way.

That was too much for Margaret Rose; she had to put on a display. Jump one way, then another. Toss of the wicked little horns. Nothing much, but jerseys can always surprise you with their speed and spurts of temper. Belle called out, to scold her and reassure him.

"She won't hurt you. Just don't move. It's her nerves."

Now she noticed the bag he had hold of. That was what had caused the trouble. She had thought he was just out walking the tracks, but he was going somewhere.

"That's what the trouble is. She's upset with your bag. If you could just lay it down for a moment. I have to get her back toward the barn to milk her."

He did as she asked, and then stood watching, not wanting to move an inch.

She got Margaret Rose headed back to where the pail was, and the stool, on this side of the barn.

"You can pick it up now," she said. "As long as you don't wave it around at her. You're a soldier, aren't you? If you wait till I get her milked, I can get you some breakfast. Good night, I've got out of breath. That's a stupid name when you have to holler at her. Margaret Rose."

She was a short, sturdy woman with straight hair, gray mixed in with what was fair, and childish bangs.

"I'm the one responsible for it," she said, as she got herself settled. "I'm a royalist. Or I used to be. I have porridge made, on the back of the stove. It won't take me long to milk. If you wouldn't mind going round the barn and waiting where she can't see you. It's too bad I can't offer you an egg. We used to keep hens, but the foxes kept getting them and we just got fed up."

We. We used to keep hens. That meant she had a man around somewhere.

"Porridge is good. I'll be glad to pay you."

"No need. Just get out of the way for a bit. She's got herself too interested to let her milk down."

He took himself off around the barn. It was in bad shape. He peered between the boards to see what kind of a car she had, but all he could make out in there was an old buggy and some other wrecks of machinery.

The white paint on the house was peeling and going gray. A window with boards nailed across it, where there must have been broken glass. The dilapidated henhouse where she had mentioned the foxes getting the hens. Shingles in a pile.

If there was a man on the place, he must have been an invalid, else paralyzed with laziness.

There was a road running by. A small fenced field in front of the house, a dirt road. And in the field a dappled, peaceable-looking horse. A cow he could see reasons for keeping, but a horse? Even before the war people on farms were getting rid of them, tractors were the coming thing. And she hadn't looked like the sort to trot round on horseback just for the fun of it. Then it struck him. The buggy in the barn. It was no relic, it was all she had.

For a while now he'd been hearing a peculiar sound. The road rose up a hill, and from over that hill came a clip-clop, clip-clop. Along with the clip-clop some little tinkle or whistling.

Now then. Over the hill came a box on wheels, being pulled by two quite small horses. Smaller than the ones in the field but no end livelier. And in the box sat a half dozen or so little men. All dressed in black, with proper black hats on their heads.

The sound was coming from them. It was singing. Discrete high-pitched little voices, as sweet as could be. They never looked at him as they went by.

It chilled him. The buggy in the barn and the horse in the field were nothing in comparison.

He was still standing there, looking one way and another, when he heard her call, "All finished." She was standing by the house.

"This is where to go in and out," she said of the back door. "The front is stuck since last winter, and it just refuses to open, you'd think it was still frozen."

They walked on planks laid over an uneven dirt floor, in a darkness provided by the boarded-up window. It was as chilly there as it had been in the hollow where he'd slept. He had wakened again and again, trying to scrunch himself into a position where he could stay warm. The woman didn't shiver here—she gave off a smell of frank healthy exertion and what was likely the cow's hide.

She poured the fresh milk into a basin and covered it with a piece of cheesecloth she kept by, then led him into the main part of the house. The windows there had no curtains, so the light was coming in. Also the woodstove had been in use. There was a sink with a hand pump, a table with oilcloth on it, worn in some places to shreds, and a couch covered with a patchy old quilt.

Also a pillow that had shed some feathers.

So far, not so bad, though old and shabby. There was a use for everything you could see. But raise your eyes, and up there on shelves was pile on pile of newspapers or magazines or just some kind of papers, up to the ceiling.

He had to ask her, was she not afraid of fire? A woodstove too.

"Oh, I'm always here. I mean, I sleep here and everything. There isn't any place else I can keep the drafts out. I'm watchful. I haven't had a chimney fire even. A couple of times it got too hot and I just threw some baking powder on it. Nothing to it.

"My mother had to be here anyway," she said. "There was no place else for her to be comfortable. I had her cot in here. I kept an eye on everything. I did think of moving all the papers into the front room, but it's really too damp in there, they would all be ruined. She died in May. Just when the weather got decent. She lived to hear about the end of the war on the radio. She understood perfectly. She lost her speech a long time ago but she could understand. I'm so used to her not speaking that sometimes I think she's here, but she's not."

Jackson felt it was up to him to say he was sorry.

"Oh well. It was coming. Just lucky it wasn't in the winter."

She served him oatmeal porridge and tea.

"Not too strong? The tea?"

Mouth full, he shook his head.

"I never economize on tea. If it comes to that, why not drink hot water? We did run out when the weather got so bad last winter. The hydro gave out and the radio gave out and the sea gave out. I had a rope round the back door to hang on to when I went out to milk. I was going to get Margaret Rose into the back kitchen, but I figured she'd get too upset with the storm and I couldn't hold her. Anyway she survived. We all survived."

Finding a place in the conversation, he asked were there any dwarfs in the neighborhood?

"Not that I've noticed."

"In a cart?"

"Oh. Were they sitting? It must have been the little Mennonite boys. They drive their cart to church and they sing all the way. The girls have to go in the buggy, but they let the boys ride in the cart."

"They never looked at me."

"They wouldn't. I used to say to Mother that we lived on the right road because we were just like the Mennonites. The horse and buggy and we drink our milk unpasteurized but the only thing is, neither one of us can sing.

"When Mother died, they brought so much food I was eating it for weeks. They must have thought there'd be a wake or something. I'm lucky to have them there.

"But they are lucky too, because they are supposed to practice charity and here I am practically on their doorstep and an occasion for charity if you ever saw one."

He offered to pay her when he'd finished but she batted her hand at his money.

But there was one thing, she said. If before he went he could manage to fix the horse trough.

What this involved was actually making a new horse trough, and in order to do that he had to hunt around for any materials and tools he could find. It took him all day, and she served him pancakes and Mennonite maple syrup for supper. She said that if he'd only come a week later, she might have fed him fresh jam. She picked the wild berries growing along the railway track.

They sat on kitchen chairs outside the back door until after the sun went down. She was telling him something about how she came to be here and he was listening, but not paying full attention because he was looking around and thinking how this place was on its last legs but not absolutely hopeless, if somebody wanted to settle down and fix things up. A certain investment of money was needed, but a greater investment of time and energy. It could be a challenge. He could almost bring himself to regret that he was moving on.

Her father—she called him her daddy—had bought this place just for the summers, she said, and then he decided that they might as well live here all year round. He could work anywhere, because he made his living with a column for the Toronto *Telegram.* (Jackson just for a second embarrassingly pictured this as a real column holding or helping to hold up a building.) The mailman took what was written and it was sent off on the train. He wrote about all sorts of things that happened, mentioning Belle's mother occasionally but calling her Princess Casamassima, out of some book. Her mother might have been the reason they stayed year round. She had caught the terrible flu of 1918 in which so many people died, and when she came out of it she was a mute. Not really, because she could make sounds all right, but she seemed to have lost words. Or they had lost her. She had to learn all over again to feed herself and go to the bathroom, but one thing she never learned was to keep her clothes on in the hot weather. So you wouldn't want her just wandering around and being a laughingstock, on some city street. Belle was away at a school in the winters. It took him a little effort to realize that what she referred to as Bishop Strawn was a school. It was in Toronto and she was surprised he hadn't heard of it. It was full of rich girls but also had girls like herself who got special money from relations or wills to go there. It taught her to be rather snooty, she said. And it didn't give her any idea of what she would do for a living.

But that was all settled for her by the accident. Walking along the railway track, as he often liked to do on a summer evening, her father was hit by a train. She and her mother had already gone to bed when it happened and Belle thought it must be a farm animal loose on the tracks, but her mother was moaning dreadfully and seemed to know first thing.

Sometimes a girl she had been friends with at school would write to ask her what on earth she could find to do up there, but little did they know. There was milking and cooking and taking care of her mother and she had the hens at that time as well. She learned how to cut up potatoes so each part has an eye, and plant them and dig them up the next summer. She had not learned to drive, and when the war came she sold her daddy's car. The Mennonites let her have a horse that was not good for farmwork anymore, and one of them taught her how to harness and drive it.

One of the old friends came up to visit her and thought the way she was living was a hoot. She wanted her to go back to Toronto, but what about her mother? Her mother was a lot quieter now and kept her clothes on, also enjoyed listening to the radio, the opera on Saturday afternoons. Of course she could do that in Toronto, but Belle didn't like to uproot her. Or maybe it was herself she was talking about, who was scared of uproot.

The first thing he had to do was to make some rooms other than the kitchen fit to sleep in, come the cold weather. He had some mice to get rid of and even some rats, now coming in from the cooling weather. He asked her why she'd never invested in a cat and heard a piece of her peculiar logic. She said it would always be killing things and dragging them for her to look at, which she didn't want to do. He kept a sharp ear open for the snap of the traps and got rid of them before she knew what had happened. Then he lectured about the papers filling up the kitchen, the fire-trap problem, and she agreed to move them, if the front room could be got free of damp. That became his main job. He invested in a heater and repaired the walls and persuaded her to spend the better part of a month climbing down and getting the papers, rereading and reorganizing them and fitting them on the shelves he had made.

She told him then that the papers contained her father's book. Sometimes she called it a novel. He did not think to ask anything about it, but one day she told him it was about two people named Matilda and Stephen. A historical novel.

"You remember your history?" He had finished five years of high school with respectable marks and a very good showing in trigonometry and geography but did not remember much history. In his final year, anyway, all you could think about was that you were going to the war.

He said, "Not altogether."

"You'd remember altogether if you went to Bishop Strawn. You'd have had it rammed down your throat. English history, anyway."

She said that Stephen had been a hero. A man of honor, far too good for his times. He was that rare person who wasn't all out for himself or looking to break his word the moment it was convenient to do so. Consequently and finally he was not a success.

And then Matilda. She was a straight descendant of William the Conqueror and as cruel and haughty as you might expect. Though there might be people stupid enough to defend her because she was a woman.

"If he could have finished, it would have been a very fine novel."

Jackson of course wasn't stupid. He knew that books existed because people sat down and wrote them. They didn't just appear out of the blue. But why, was the question. There were books already in existence, plenty of them. Two of which he had to read at school. *A Tale of Two Cities* and *Huckleberry Finn*, each of them with language that wore you down, though in different ways. And that was understandable. They were written in the past. What puzzled him, though he didn't intend to let on, was why anybody would want to sit down and do another one, in the present. Now.

A tragedy, said Belle briskly, and Jackson didn't know if it was her father she was talking about or the people in the book that had not been finished. Anyway, now that this room was livable, his mind was on the roof. No use to fix up a room and have the state of the roof render it unlivable again in a year or two. He had managed to patch the roof so that it would do her a couple more winters, but he could not guarantee more than that. And he still planned to be on his way by Christmas.

The Mennonite families on the next farm ran to older girls and the younger boys he had seen, not strong enough yet to take on heavier chores. Jackson had been able to hire himself out to them during the fall harvest. He had been brought in to eat with the others and to his surprise found that the girls behaved giddily as they served him; they were not at all mute, as he had expected. The mothers kept an eye on them, he noticed, and the fathers kept an eye on him. All safe.

And of course with Belle not a thing had to be spoken of. She was—he had found this out—sixteen years older than he was. To mention it, even to joke about it, would spoil everything. She was a certain kind of woman, he a certain kind of man.

The town where they shopped, when they needed to, was called Oriole. It was in the opposite direction from the town where he had grown up. He tied up the horse in the United Church shed there, since there were of course no hitching posts left on the main street. At first he was leery of the hardware store and the barbershop. But soon he realized something about small towns that he should have realized just from growing up in one. They did not have much to do with each other, unless it was for games run off in the ballpark or the hockey arena, where all was a fervent made-up sort of hostility. When people needed to shop for something their own stores could not supply, they went to a city. The same when they wanted to consult a doctor other than the ones their own town could offer. He didn't run into anybody familiar, and nobody showed a curiosity about him, though they might look twice at the horse. In the winter months, not even that, because the back roads were not plowed and people taking their milk to the creamery or eggs to the grocery had to make do with horses.

Belle always stopped to see what movie was on though she had no intention of going to see any of them. Her knowledge of movies and movie stars was extensive but came from some years back. For instance she could tell you whom Clark Gable was married to in real life before he became Rhett Butler.

Soon Jackson was going to get his hair cut when he needed to and buying his tobacco when he ran out. He smoked now like a farmer, rolling his own and never lighting up indoors.

Secondhand cars didn't become available for a while, but when they did, with the new models finally on the scene and farmers who'd made money in the way ready to turn in the old ones, he had a talk with Belle. The horse Freckles was God knows how old and stubborn on any sort of hill.

He found that the car dealer had been taking notice of him, though not counting on a visit.

"I always thought you and your sister was Mennonites but ones that wore a different kind of outfit," the dealer said.

That shook Jackson up a little but at least it was better than husband and wife. It made him realize how he must have aged and changed over the years, and how the person who had jumped off the train, that skinny nerve-racked soldier, would not be so recognizable in the man he was now. Whereas Belle, so far as he could see, was stopped at some point in life where she remained a grown-up child. And her talk reinforced this impression, jumping back and forth, into the past and out again, so that it seemed she made no difference between their last trip to town and the last movie she had seen with her mother and father, or the comical occasion when Margaret Rose—now dead—had tipped her horns at a worried Jackson.

It was the second car they had owned that took them to Toronto in the summer of 1962. This was a trip they had not anticipated and it came at an awkward time for Jackson. For one thing, he was building a new horse barn for the Mennonites, who were busy with the crops, and for another, he had his own harvest of vegetables coming on, which he planned to sell to the grocery store in Oriole. But Belle had a lump that she had finally been persuaded to pay attention to, and she was booked now for an operation in Toronto.

What a change, Belle kept saying. Are you so sure we are still in Canada?

This was before they got past Kitchener. Once they got on the new highway, she was truly alarmed, imploring him to find a side road or else turn around and go home. He found himself speaking sharply to her—the traffic was surprising him too. She stayed quiet all the way after that, and he had no way of knowing whether she had her eyes closed, had given up, or was praying. He had never known her to pray.

Even this morning she had tried to get him to change his mind about going. She said the lump was getting smaller, not larger. Since the health insurance for everybody had come in, she said, nobody did anything but run to the doctor and make their lives into one long drama of hospitals and operations, which did nothing but prolong the period of being a nuisance at the end of life.

She calmed down and cheered up once they got to their turnoff and were actually in the city. They found themselves on Avenue Road, and in spite of exclamations about how everything had changed, she seemed to be able on every block to recognize something she knew. There was the apartment building where one of the teachers from Bishop Strawn had lived (that was only the pronunciation, the name was spelled Strachan, as she had told him a while ago). In the basement there was a shop where you could buy milk and cigarettes and the newspaper. Wouldn't it be strange, she said, if you could go in there and still find the *Telegram,* where there would be not only her father's name but his smudgy picture, taken when he still had all his hair?

Then a little cry, and down a side street she had seen the very church—she could swear it was the very church—in which her parents had been married. They had taken her there to show her, though it wasn't a church they were members of. They did not go to any church, far from it. Her father said they had been married in the basement, but her mother said the vestry.

Her mother could talk then, that was when she could talk. Perhaps there was a law at the time, to make you get married in a church or it wasn't legal.

At Eglinton she saw the subway sign.

"Just think, I have never been on a subway train."

She said this with some sort of mixed pain and pride.
"Imagine remaining so ignorant."

At the hospital they were ready for her. She continued to be lively, telling them about her horrors in the traffic and about the changes, wondering if there was still such a show put on at Christmas by Eaton's store. And did anybody remember the *Telegram*?

"You should have driven in through Chinatown," one of the nurses said. "Now that's something."

"I'll look forward to seeing it on my way home." She laughed, and said, "If I get to go home."

"Now don't be silly."

Another nurse was talking to Jackson about where he'd parked the car and telling him where to move it so he wouldn't get a ticket. Also making sure that he knew about the accommodations for out-of-town relations, much cheaper than you'd have to pay at a hotel.

Belle would be put to bed now, they said. A doctor would come to have a look at her, and Jackson could come back later to say good night. He might find her a little dopey by that time, they said.

She overheard and said that she was dopey all the time, so he wouldn't be surprised, and there was a little laugh all round.

The nurse took him to sign something before he left. He hesitated where it asked for what relation. Then he wrote "friend."

When he came back in the evening he did see a change, though he would not have described Belle then as dopey. They had put her into some kind of green cloth sack that left her neck and most of her arms quite bare. He had seldom seen her so bare or noticed the raw-looking cords that stretched between her collarbone and her chin.

She was angry that her mouth was dry.

"They won't let me have anything but the meanest little sip of water."

She wanted him to go and get her a Coke, something that she never drank in her life as far as he knew.

"There's a machine down the hall—there must be. I see people going by with a bottle in their hands and it makes me so thirsty."

He said he couldn't go against orders.

Tears came into her eyes and she turned pettishly away.

"I want to go home."

"Soon you will."

"You could help me find my clothes."

"No, I couldn't."

"If you won't I'll do it myself. I'll get myself to the train station myself."

"There isn't any passenger train that goes up our way anymore."

Abruptly then, she seemed to give up on her plans for escape.

In a few moments she started to recall the house and all the improvements that they—or mostly he—had made on it. The white paint shining on the outside and even the back kitchen whitewashed and furnished with a plank floor. The roof reshingled and the windows restored to their plain old style, and most of all glories, the plumbing that was such a joy in the wintertime.

"If you hadn't shown up, I'd have soon been living in absolute squalor."

He didn't voice his opinion that she already had been.

"When I come out of this, I am going to make a will," she said. "All yours. You won't have wasted your labors."

He had of course thought about this, and you would have expected that the prospects of ownership would have brought a sober satisfaction to him, though he would have expressed a truthful and companionable hope that nothing would happen too soon. But no. It all seemed quite to have little to do with him, to be quite far away.

She returned to her fret.

"Oh, I wish I was there and not here."

"You'll feel a lot better when you wake up after the operation."

Though from everything that he had heard, that was a whopping lie. Suddenly he felt so tired.

He had spoken closer to the truth than he could have guessed. Two days after the lump's removal, Belle was sitting up in a different room, eager to greet him and not at all disturbed by the moans coming from a woman behind the curtain in the next bed. That was more or less what she—Belle—had sounded like yesterday, when he never got her to open her eyes or notice him at all.

"Don't pay any attention to her," said Belle. "She's completely out of it. Probably doesn't feel a thing. She'll come round tomorrow bright as a dollar. Or maybe she won't."

A somewhat satisfied, institutional authority was showing, a veteran's callousness. She was sitting up in bed and swallowing some kind of bright orange drink through a conveniently bent straw. She looked a lot younger than the woman he had brought to the hospital such a short time before.

She wanted to know if he was getting enough sleep, if he'd found some place where he liked to eat, if the weather had not been too warm for walking, if he had found time to visit the Royal Ontario Museum, as she thought she had advised.

But she could not concentrate on his replies. She seemed to be in an inner state of amazement. Controlled amazement.

"Oh, I do have to tell you," she said, breaking right into his explanation of why he had not got to the museum. "Oh, don't look so alarmed. You'll make me laugh with that face on, it'll hurt my stitches. Why on earth should I be thinking of laughing anyway? It's a dreadfully sad thing really, it's a tragedy. You know about my father, what I've told you about my father—"

The thing he noticed was that she said "father" instead of "daddy."

"My father and my mother—"

She seemed to have to search around and get started again.

"The house was in better shape then than when you first got to see it. Well, it would be. We used that room at the top of the stairs for our bathroom. Of course we had to carry the water up and down. Only later, when you came, I was using the downstairs. With the shelves in it, you know, that had been a pantry?"

How could she not remember that he had taken out the shelves and put in the bathroom? He was the one who had done it.

"Oh well, what does it matter?" she said, as if she followed his thoughts. "So I had heated the water and I carried it upstairs to have my sponge bath. And I took off my clothes. Well, I would. There was a big mirror over the sink, you see it had a sink like a real bathroom only you had to pull out the plug and let the water back into the pail when you were finished. The toilet was elsewhere. You get the picture. So I proceeded to wash myself and I was bare naked, naturally. It must have been around nine o'clock at night so there was plenty of light. It was summer, did I say? That little room facing west?

"Then I heard steps and of course it was Daddy. My father.

He must have been finished putting Mother to bed. I heard the steps coming up the stairs and I did notice they sounded heavy. Somewhat not like usual. Very deliberate. Or maybe that was just my impression afterwards. You are apt to dramatize things afterwards. The steps stopped right outside the bathroom door and if I thought anything I thought, Oh, he must be tired. I didn't have any bolt across the door because of course there wasn't one. You just assumed somebody was in there if the door was closed.

"So he was standing outside the door and I didn't think anything of it and then he opened the door and he just stood and looked at me. And I have to say what I mean. Looking at all of me, not just my face. My face looking into the mirror and him looking at me in the mirror and also what was behind me and I couldn't see. It wasn't in any sense a normal look.

"I'll tell you what I thought. I thought, He's walking in his sleep. I didn't know what to do, because you are not supposed to startle anybody that is sleepwalking.

"But then he said, 'Excuse me,' and I knew he was not asleep. But he spoke in a funny kind of voice, I mean it was a strange voice. Very much as if he was disgusted with me. Or mad at me, I didn't know. Then he left the door open and just went away down the hall. I dried myself and got into my nightgown and went to bed and went to sleep right away. When I got up in the morning, there was the water I had drained and I didn't want to go near it but I did.

"But everything seemed normal and he was up already, typing away. He just yelled good morning and then he asked me how to spell some word. The way he often did, because I was a better speller. So I did and then I said he should learn how to spell if he thought he was a writer, he was hopeless. But then sometime later in the day when I was washing some dishes, he came up right behind me and I froze. He just said, 'Belle, I'm sorry.' And I thought, Oh, I wish he had not said that. It scared me. I knew it was true he was sorry, but he was putting it out in the open in a way I could not ignore. I just said, 'That's okay,' but I couldn't make myself say it in an easy voice or as if it really was okay.

"I couldn't. I had to let him know he had changed us. I went to throw out the dishwater and then I went back to whatever else I was doing and not another word. Later I got Mother up from her nap and I had supper ready and I called him but he didn't come. I said to Mother that he must have gone for a walk. He often did when he got stuck in his writing. I helped Mother cut up her food.

"I didn't know where he could have gone. I got Mother ready for bed, though that was his job. Then I heard the train coming and all at once the commotion and the screeching, which was the train brakes, and I must have known what had happened though I don't know exactly when I knew.

"I told you before. I told you he got run over by the train.

"But I'm not telling you this, I am not telling you just to be harrowing. At first I couldn't stand it and for the longest time I was actually making myself think that he was walking along the tracks with his mind on his work and never heard the train. That was the story all right. I was not going to think it was about me or even what it primarily was about. Sex.

"It seems to me just now I have got a real understanding of it and that it was nobody's fault. It was the fault of human sex in a tragic situation. Me growing up there and Mother the way she was and Daddy, naturally, the way he would be. Not my fault nor his fault.

"There should be acknowledgment, that's all I mean, places where people can go if they are in a situation. And not be all ashamed and guilty about it. If you think I mean brothels, you are right. If you think prostitutes, right again. Do you understand?"

Jackson, looking over her head, said yes.

"I feel so released. It's not that I don't feel the tragedy, but I have in a way got outside the tragedy, is what I mean. It is just the mistakes of humanity that are tragic, if you see what I mean. You mustn't think because I'm smiling that I don't have compassion. I have serious compassion. But I have to say I am relieved. At the same time. I have to say I somehow feel happy. You are not embarrassed by listening to all this?"

"No."

"You realize I am in a slightly abnormal state. I know I am. There is this abnormal clarity. I mean in everything. Everything so clear. I am so grateful for it."

The woman on the bed had not let up on her rhythmical groaning all through this. Jackson felt as if that refrain had entered into his head.

He heard the nurse's squishy shoes in the hall and hoped they would enter this room. They did.

The nurse said that she had to give Belle her sleepy-time pill. He was afraid she would tell him to kiss her good night. He had noticed that a lot of kissing went on in the hospital. He was glad when he stood up that there was no mention of it.

"See you tomorrow."

He woke up early and decided to take a walk before breakfast. He had slept all right but told himself he ought to take a break from the hospital air. It wasn't that he was worried so much by the change in Belle. He thought it was possible or even probable that she would get back to normal, either today or in a couple more days. She might not even remember the story she had told him. Which would be a blessing.

The sun was well up, as you could expect at this time of year, and the buses and streetcars were already pretty full. He walked south for a bit, then turned west onto Dundas Street, and after a while found himself in the Chinatown he had heard about. Loads of recognizable and many not-so-recognizable vegetables were being trundled into shops, and small, skinned, apparently edible animals were already hanging up for sale. The streets were full of illegally parked trucks and noisy, desperate-sounding Chinese. All the high-pitched clamor sounded like they had a war going on, but probably to them it was just everyday. Nevertheless he felt like getting out of the way, and he went into a restaurant run by Chinese but advertising an ordinary breakfast of eggs and bacon. When he came out of there, he intended to turn around and retrace his steps.

But instead he found himself heading south again. He had got onto a residential street lined with tall and fairly narrow brick houses. They must have been built before people in the area felt any need for driveways or possibly before they even had cars. Before there were such things as cars. He walked until he saw a sign for Queen Street, which he had heard of. He turned west again and after a few blocks he came to an obstacle. In front of a doughnut shop he ran into a small crowd of people. They were stopped by an ambulance, backed right up on the sidewalk so you could not get by. Some of them were complaining about the delay and asking loudly if it was even legal to park an ambulance on the sidewalk, and others were looking peaceful enough while they chatted about what the trouble might be. Death was mentioned, some of the onlookers speaking of various candidates and others saying that was the only legal excuse for the vehicle being where it was.

The man who was finally carried out, bound to the stretcher, was surely not dead or they'd have had his face covered. He was not being carried out through the doughnut shop, as some had jokingly predicted—that was some sort of dig at the quality of the doughnuts—but through the main door of the building. It was a decent enough brick apartment building five stories high, housing a Laundromat as well as the doughnut shop on its main floor. The name carved over its main door suggested pride as well as some foolishness in its past.

Bonnie Dundee.

A man not in ambulance uniform came out last. He stood there looking with exasperation at the crowd that was now thinking of breaking up. The only thing to wait for now was the grand wail of the ambulance as it found its way onto the street and tore away.

Jackson was one of those who didn't bother to walk away. He wouldn't have said he was curious about any of this, more that he was just waiting for the inevitable turn he had been expecting, to take him back to where he'd come from. The man who had come out of the building walked over and asked if he was in a hurry.

No. Not specially.

This man was the owner of the building. The man taken away in the ambulance was the caretaker and superintendent.

"I've got to get to the hospital and see what's the trouble with him. Right as rain yesterday. Never complained. Nobody close that I can call on, so far as I know. The worst, I can't find the keys. Not on him and not usually where he keeps them. So I got to go home and get my spares and I just wondered, could you keep a watch on things meanwhile? I got to go home and I got to go to the hospital too. I could ask some of the tenants, but I'd just rather not, if you know what I mean. Natural curiosity or something."

He asked again if Jackson was sure he would not mind and Jackson said no, fine.

"Just keep an eye for anybody going in, out, ask to see their keys. Tell them it's an emergency, won't be long."

He was leaving, then turned around.

"You might as well sit down."

There was a chair Jackson had not noticed. Folded and pushed out of the way so the ambulance could park. It was just one of those canvas chairs but comfortable enough and sturdy. Jackson set it down with thanks in a spot where it would not interfere with passersby or apartment dwellers. No notice was taken of him. He had been about to mention the hospital and the fact that he himself had to get back there before too long. But the man had been in a hurry, and he already had enough on his mind, and he had already made the point that he would be as quick as he could.

Jackson realized, once he got sitting down, just how long he'd been on his feet walking here or there.

The man had told him to get a coffee or something to eat from the doughnut shop if he felt the need.

"Just tell them my name."

But that Jackson did not even know.

When the owner came back he apologized for being late. The fact was that the man who had been taken away in the ambulance had died. Arrangements had to be made. A new set of keys had become necessary. Here they were. There'd be some sort of funeral involving those in the building who had been around a long time. Notice in the paper might bring in a few more. A troublesome spell, till this was sorted out.

It would solve the problem. If Jackson could. Temporarily. It only had to be temporarily.

Yes, all right with him, Jackson said.

If he wanted to take a little time, that could be managed. Right after the funeral and some disposal of goods. A few days he could have then, to get his affairs together and do the proper moving in.

That would not be necessary, Jackson said. His affairs were together and his possessions were on his back.

Naturally this roused a little suspicion. Jackson was not surprised a couple of days later to hear that this new employer had made a visit to the police. But all was well, apparently. He had emerged as just one of those loners who may have got themselves in too deep some way or another but have not been guilty of breaking any law.

It looked as if there was no search party under way.

*

As a rule, Jackson liked to have older people in the building. And as a rule, single people. Not zombies. People with interests. Talent. The sort of talent that had been noticed once, made some kind of a living once, though not enough to hang on to all through a life. An announcer whose voice had been familiar on the radio during the war but whose vocal cords were shot to pieces now. Most people probably believed he was dead. But here he was in his bachelor suite, keeping up with the news and subscribing to the *Globe and Mail,* which he passed on to Jackson in case there was anything of interest to him in it.

Once there was.

Marjorie Isabella Treece, daughter of Willard Treece, longtime columnist for the Toronto *Telegram,* and his wife Helena (née Abbott) Treece, has passed away after a courageous battle with cancer. Oriole paper please copy. July 18, 1965.

No mention of where she had been living. Probably in Toronto. She had lasted maybe longer than he had expected. He didn't spend a moment's time picturing the rooms of work he'd done on her place. He didn't have to—such things were often recalled in dreams, and his feeling then was more of exasperation than of longing, as if he had to get to work on something that had not been finished.

In the building of Bonnie Dundee, there had to be consideration of human beings, as he tackled the upkeep of their surroundings and of what the women might call their nests. (The men were usually uneasy about any improvement meaning a raise in the rent.) He talked them round, with good respectful manners and good fiscal sense, and the place became one with a waiting list. "We could fill it all up without a loony in the place," said the owner. But Jackson pointed out that the loonies, as he called them, were generally tidier than average, besides which they were a minority. There was a woman who had once played in the Toronto Symphony and an inventor who had truly just missed out on a fortune for one of his inventions and had not given up yet, though he was over eighty. And a Hungarian refugee actor whose accent was not in demand but who still had a commercial running somewhere in the world. They were all well behaved, even those who went out to the Epicure Bar every day at noon and stayed till closing. Also they had friends among the truly famous who might show up once in a blue moon for a visit. Nor should it be sneezed at that the Bonnie Dundee had an in-house preacher, on shaky terms with whatever his church might be, but always able to officiate when called upon.

People did often stay until his office was necessary.

An exception was the young couple named Candace and Quincy who never settled their rent and skipped out in the middle of the night. The owner happened to have been in charge when they came looking for a room, and he excused himself for his bad choice by saying that a fresh face was needed around the place. Candace's. Not the boyfriend's. The boyfriend was a crude sort of jerk.

On a hot summer day Jackson had the double back doors, the delivery doors, open, to let in what air he could while he worked at varnishing a table. It was a pretty table he'd got for nothing because its polish was all worn away. He thought it would look nice to put the mail on, in the entryway.

He was able to be out of the office because the owner was in there checking some rents.

There was a light touch on the front doorbell. Jackson was ready to haul himself up, cleaning his brush, because he thought the owner in the midst of figures might not care to be disturbed. But it was all right, he heard the door being opened, a woman's voice. A voice on the edge of exhaustion, yet able to maintain something of its charm, its absolute assurance that whatever it said would win over anybody who came within listening range.

She would probably have got that from her father the preacher. He remembered thinking this before.

This was the last address she had, she said, for her daughter. She was looking for her daughter. Candace her daughter. She had come here from British Columbia. From Kelowna where she and the girl's father lived.

Ileane. That woman was Ileane.

He heard her ask if it was possible for her to sit down. Then the owner pulling out his—Jackson's—chair.

Toronto so much hotter than she had expected, though she knew Ontario, had grown up there.

She wondered if she could possibly beg for a glass of water.

She must have put her head down in her hands as her voice grew muffled. The owner came out into the hall and dropped some change into the machine to get a 7-Up. He might have thought that more ladylike than a Coke.

Around the corner he saw Jackson listening, and he made a gesture that he, Jackson, should take over, being perhaps more used to distraught tenants. But Jackson shook his head violently. No.

She did not stay distraught long.

She begged the owner's pardon and he said the heat could play those tricks today.

Now about Candace. They had left within a month, it could be three weeks ago. No forwarding address.

"In such cases there usually isn't—"

She got the hint.

"Oh, of course I can settle—"

There was some muttering and rustling while this was done. Then, "I don't suppose you could let me see where they were living—"

"The tenant isn't in now. But even if he was, I don't think he'd agree to it."

"Of course. That's silly."

"Was there anything else you were particularly interested in?"

"Oh no. No. You've been kind. I've taken your time."

She had got up now, and they were moving. Out of the office, down the couple of steps to the front door. Then the door was opened and street noises swallowed up her farewells if there were any.

However she had been defeated, she would get herself out with a good grace.

Jackson came out of hiding as the owner returned to the office.

"Surprise," was all the owner said. "We got our money."

He was a man who was basically incurious, at least about personal matters. A thing that Jackson valued in him.

Of course he would like to have seen her. He hadn't got much of an impression of the daughter. Her hair was blond but very likely dyed. No more than twenty, though it was sometimes hard to tell nowadays. Very much under the thumb of the boyfriend. Run away from home, run away from your bills, break your parents' hearts, for a sulky piece of goods, a boyfriend.

Where was Kelowna? In the west somewhere. British Columbia. A long way to come looking. Of course she was a persistent woman. An optimist. Probably that was true of her still. She had married. Unless the girl was out of wedlock and that struck him as very unlikely. She'd be sure, sure of herself the next time, she wouldn't be one for tragedy. The girl wouldn't be, either. She'd come home when she'd had enough. She might bring along a baby, but that was all the style nowadays.

Shortly before Christmas in the year 1940 there had been an uproar in the high school. It had even reached the third floor where the clamor of typewriters and adding machines usually kept all the downstairs noises at bay. The oldest girls in the school were up there—girls who last year had been learning Latin and biology and European history and were now learning to type.

One of these was Ileane Bishop, a minister's daughter, although there were no bishops in her father's United Church. Ileane had arrived with her family when she was in grade nine and for five years, because of the custom of alphabetical seating, she had sat behind Jackson Adams. By that time Jackson's phenomenal shyness and silence had been accepted by everybody else in the class, but it was new to her, and during the next five years, by not acknowledging it, she had produced a thaw. She borrowed erasers and pen nibs and geometry tools from him, not so much to break the ice as because she was naturally scatterbrained. They exchanged answers to problems and marked each other's tests. When they met on the street, they said hello, and to her his hello was actually more than a mumble—it had two syllables and an emphasis to it. Nothing much was presumed beyond that except that they had certain jokes. Ileane was not a shy girl, but she was clever and aloof and not particularly popular, and that seemed to suit him.

From her position on the stairs, when all these older girls came out to see the ruckus, Ileane along with all the others was surprised to see that one of the two boys causing it was Jackson. The other was Bill Watts. Boys who only a year ago had sat hunched over books and shuffled dutifully between one classroom and another. Now in army uniforms they looked twice the size they had been, their powerful boots making a ferocious noise as they galloped around. They were shouting out that school was canceled for the day because everybody had to join the army. They were distributing cigarettes everywhere, even tossing them on the floor where they could be picked up by boys who didn't even shave.

Careless warriors, whooping invaders. Drunk up to their eyeballs.

"I'm no piker," they were yelling.

The principal was trying to order them out. But because this was still early in the war and there was as yet some awe and veneration concerning the boys who had signed up, wrapping themselves so to speak in the costume of death, he was not able to show the ruthlessness he would have called upon a year later.

"Now, now," he said.

"I'm no piker," Billy Watts told him.

Jackson had his mouth open probably to say the same, but at that moment his eyes met the eyes of Ileane Bishop and a certain piece of knowledge passed between them.

Ileane Bishop understood, it seemed, that Jackson was truly drunk but that the effect of this was to enable him to play drunk, therefore the drunkenness displayed could be managed. (Billy Watts was just drunk, through and through.) With this understanding Ileane walked down the stairs, smiling, and accepted a cigarette, which she held unlit between her fingers. She linked arms with both heroes and marched them out of the school.

Once outside they lit up their cigarettes.

There was a conflict of opinion about this later, in Ileane's father's congregation. Some said Ileane had not actually smoked hers, just pretended to pacify the boys, while others said she certainly had. Smoked.

Billy did put his arms around Ileane and tried to kiss her, but he stumbled and sat down on the school steps and crowed like a rooster. Within two years he would be dead.

Meanwhile he had to be got home, and Jackson pulled him so that they could get his arms over their shoulders and drag him along. Fortunately his house was not far from the school. They left him there, passed out on the front steps, and entered into a conversation.

Jackson did not want to go home. Why not? Because his stepmother was there, he said. He hated his stepmother. Why? No reason.

Ileane knew that his mother had died in a car accident when he was very small—this was sometimes taken to account for his shyness. She thought that the drink was probably making him exaggerate, but she didn't try to make him talk about it any further.

"Okay," she said. "You can stay at my place."

It just happened that Ileane's mother herself was away, looking after Ileane's sick grandmother. Ileane was at the time keeping house in a haphazard way for her father and her two young brothers. This was fortunate. Not that her mother would have made a fuss, but she would have wanted to know the ins and outs and who was this boy? At the very least she would have made Ileane go to school as usual.

A soldier and a girl, so suddenly close. Where there had been nothing all this time but logarithms and declensions.

Ileane's father didn't pay attention to them. He was more interested in the war than some of his parishioners thought a minister should be, and this made him proud to have a soldier in the house. Also, he was unhappy not to be able to send his daughter to college, on his minister's salary, because he had to put something by to send her brothers someday. That made him lenient.

Jackson and Ileane didn't go to the movies. They didn't go to the dance hall. They went for walks, in any weather and often after dark. Sometimes they went into a restaurant and drank coffee but did not try to be friendly to anybody. What was the matter with them? Were they falling in love?

Ileane went by herself to Jackson's house to collect his bag. His stepmother raised her skinny eyebrows and showed her bright false teeth and tried to look as if she was ready for some fun.

She asked what they were up to.

"You better watch that stuff," she said, with a big laugh. She had a reputation for being a loudmouth, but people said she didn't mean any harm. Ileane was especially ladylike, partly to annoy her.

She told Jackson what had been said and made it funny, but he didn't laugh.

She apologized.

"I guess you get too much in the habit of caricaturing people, living in a parsonage," she said.

He said it was okay.

That time at the parsonage turned out to be Jackson's last leave. They wrote to each other. Ileane wrote about finishing her typing and shorthand and getting a job in the office of the town clerk. In spite of what she had said about caricatures, she was determinedly satirical about everything, more than she had been in school. Maybe she thought that someone at war needed joking.

When hurry-up marriages had to be arranged through the clerk's office, she would refer to the "virgin bride."

And when she mentioned some stodgy minister visiting the parsonage and sleeping in the spare room, she wondered if the mattress would induce naughty dreams.

He wrote about the crowds on the *Île de France* and the ducking around to avoid U-boats. When he got to England, he bought a bicycle and he told her about places he had biked around to see if they were not out of bounds.

Then about being picked to take a map course, which meant he would work behind the lines if there was ever such a need (he meant of course after D-day).

These letters though more prosaic than hers were always signed with love. When D-day did come, there was what she called an agonizing silence, but she understood the reason for it, and when he wrote again, all was well, though details impossible.

In this letter he spoke as she had been doing, about marriage.

And at last V-E Day and the voyage home. He mentioned showers of summer stars overhead.

Ileane had learned to sew. She was making a new summer dress in honor of his homecoming, a dress of lime-green rayon silk with a full skirt and cap sleeves, worn with a narrow belt of gold imitation leather. She meant to wind a ribbon of the same green material around the crown of her summer straw hat.

"All this is being described to you so you will notice me and know it's me and not go running off with some other beautiful woman who happens to be at the train station."

He mailed his letter to her from Halifax, telling her that he would be on the evening train on Saturday. He said that he remembered her very well, and there was no danger of getting her mixed up with another woman even if the train station happened to be swarming with them that evening.

On their last evening they had sat up late in the parsonage kitchen where there was the picture of King George VI you saw everywhere that year. And the words beneath it.

> I said to the man who stood at the gate of the year, "Give me a light that I may tread safely into the unknown."
>
> And he replied, "Go out into the darkness and put your hand into the hand of God. That shall be to you better than light and safer than a known way."

Then they went upstairs very quietly and he went to bed in the spare room. Her coming to him must have been by mutual agreement because he was not surprised.

It was a disaster. But by the way she behaved, she didn't seem to know. The more disaster, the more frantic became her stifled displays of passion. There was no way he could stop her trying, or explain. Was it possible a girl could know so little? They parted finally as if all had gone well. And the next morning said goodbye in the presence of her father and brothers. In a short while the letters began, loving as could be. He got drunk and tried once more, in Southampton. But the woman said, "That's enough, sonny boy, you're down and out."

A thing he didn't like was women or girls dressing up. Gloves, hats, swishy skirts, all some demand and bother about it. But how could she know that? Lime green, he wasn't sure he knew the color. It sounded like acid.

Then it came to him quite easily, that a person could just not be there.

Would she tell herself or tell anybody else that she must have mistaken the date? He'd told himself that she would make up some lie, surely—she was resourceful, after all.

Now that she was gone, Jackson felt a wish to see her. Her voice even in distress had been marvelously unchanged. Drawing all importance to itself, musical levels. He could never ask the owner what she looked like, whether her hair was still dark, or gray, and she herself skinny or gone stout. He had not paid much attention to the daughter, except on the matter of disliking the boyfriend.

She had married. Unless she'd had the child by herself and that wasn't likely. She would have a prosperous husband, other children. This the one to break her heart.

That kind of girl would come back. She'd be too spoiled to stay away. She'd come back when necessary. Even the mother—Ileane—hadn't she had some spoiled air about her, some way of arranging the world and the truth to suit herself, as if nothing could foil her for long?

The next day whatever ease he had about the woman passing from his life was gone. She knew this place; she might come back. She might settle herself in for a while, walking up and down these streets, trying to find where the trail was warm. Humbly but not really humbly making inquiries of people, in that spoiled cajoling voice. It was possible he would run into her right outside this door.

Things could be locked up; it only took some determination. When he was as young as six or seven, he locked up his stepmother's fooling, what she called her fooling or her teasing when she gave him a bath. He ran out on the street after dark, and she got him in but she saw there'd be some real running away if she didn't stop, so she stopped. She said he was no fun because she could never say that anybody hated her. But she knew he hated her even if she couldn't account for it and she stopped.

He spent three more nights in the building called Bonnie Dundee. He wrote an account for the owner of every apartment and when and what upkeep was due. He said that he had been called away, without indicating why or where to. He emptied his bank account and packed the few things belonging to him. In the evening, late in the evening, he got on the train. He slept off and on during the night and in one of those snatches he saw the little Mennonite boys go by in their cart. He heard their small sweet voices singing.

This had happened before in his dreams.

In the morning he got off in Kapuskasing. He could smell the mills and was encouraged by the cooler air.

ANTONYA NELSON

Chapter Two

FROM *The New Yorker*

TIRED OF TELLING her own story at A.A., Hil was trying to tell the story of her neighbor. It had been a peculiar week. "So she comes to my house a few nights ago," Hil began, "like around nine, *bing-bong,* drunk as a skunk, as usual, right in the middle of this show my roommate and I are watching. I go to the door and there she is, fifty-something, a totally naked lady standing under the porch light." At the time, it had seemed designed to charm, her coy drunken neighbor sporting a plaid porkpie hat and holding a toothbrush like a flag or a flower or a torch. Choreographed, at least, and embarrassing to behold. Bergeron Love, grande dame in her own mind and all around the block.

"Looks like somebody's not getting enough attention," Hil had murmured as she unlocked the door. The night was soggy, Houston autumn, frogs like squeezeboxes wheezing in and out. Her neighbor's nakedness seemed sad and enervated, breasts flat on her chest, a kind of melted look to her flesh, ankles thick on splayed bare feet. Southern belle in decline, a dismal After picture.

What had Before looked like?

"You gonna invite me in?" Bergeron demanded, raising her eyebrows flirtatiously in an attempt to rally her own outlandishness. She was known in the neighborhood for being a character—some composite of Miss Havisham, Norma Desmond, and Scarlett O'Hara—her ancient family manse, with its aspect of ruined wedding cake, fenced off as if to contain inmates, its fetid kidney-shaped pool, by which her multiple orange cats congregated.

Sometimes Bergeron's antics were whimsical—crashing a dinner or a cocktail party, for example, or hiring someone in a gorilla suit to deliver balloons—and sometimes they were a serious pain in the ass: reporting overgrown lawns or loose dogs or long-term parked cars.

"You can't exactly say no to a naked lady on your doorstep, can you?" Hil asked rhetorically at the meeting. She glanced at the smiling older man holding the leash of his helper animal. There ought always to be a blind man grinning encouragingly, receptively, at meetings, she thought. The dog lay panting at his feet, its head held a little unnaturally high by the leash. The man's genial countenance was generic—through every story, no matter how unpleasant, he smiled benignly beneath his lovely hair, wavy and white like meringue. He had, Hil thought, become like a dog himself, unable to judge.

"My roommate had never met my neighbor before, so I introduced them." How strange to see a clothed person shake hands with a naked one; it was like the meeting of two utterly different tribes. *Bergeron Love, this is Janine.*

"Nice to meet you," Janine said, averting her eyes.

"Janine is getting her degree at the U.," Hil offered. "In social work," she added, since Janine was shy.

"Ha!" Bergeron Love said, raising her toothbrush. "You can consider this visit a piece of immersion homework! What the hell is that?" she asked, aiming the brush at the paused image on the television.

"A bullet puncturing somebody's heart in slow motion," Janine said. On the screen, a few perfect circles: bullet, organ, splatter. "Not *actually,*" she added.

"Well, obviously not actually," Bergeron said. "One of those true-crime shows? I love those, but my boyfriend, Boyd, can't take it. He literally can't watch gore. Isn't that just typical?" Boyfriend Boyd was a mousy man who hid behind a pair of giant square glasses and a push-broom mustache. Every school day morning he donned an orange vest and stood blowing into a whistle on the corner of Westheimer and Taft, waving his arms to help the children across. Only with that vivid vest and shrill whistle did he seem to have much confidence. Then, or after a few stiff drinks.

"You want a robe, Bergeron?" Hil asked. The woman was going

to either sit or fall down, and the nearest chair was the one Hil's fifteen-year-old son usually used.

"Why would I want a robe?" Bergeron demanded. "You got a problem with the human body? You're watching that shit on TV and you can't look at *me*?"

"I just didn't want her naked butt on the chair where my son liked to sit," Hil explained to the A.A. meeting. "But she kind of collapses in his chair anyway and starts to ramble on about her fucked-up life. Sorry, Jim," Hil added. The blind man had flinched; his single admission, in all the time that he'd occupied his position as accepting group focal point, was that the word *fuck* hurt his feelings. He nodded now, recovered, absolving.

"Friday night," Bergeron Love had said. "I'm walking buck fucking naked up and down the street, and I can't even get arrested!"

"That's partly your fault, you know, Berge," Hil said, explaining to Janine that Bergeron, years earlier, had been almost solely responsible for rousting a homeless shelter and the homeless who lived there from the neighborhood. "Remember all those drunk bums?" Hil said.

"Pissing in our yards," Bergeron recalled. "Leaving all their Sudafed trash in the park. You don't know the half of what I kept off this street. And then they wanted to turn that flophouse into an AIDS clinic. No, ma'am, said I."

Civic duty had once been a Love family hallmark; there were bridges and schools and state parks commemorating the name. But the more recent generations had had to spend their money on lawyers instead: fighting class-action suits over working conditions at their oil refineries or covering up the scandalous dalliances of other Loves.

"But, Berge, if those homeless guys were still around, there'd have been more action out there tonight. They would have been ecstatic to see you coming," Hil said. And Bergeron laughed appreciatively, conceding the point, then wondered aloud what a person had to do to get a drink around here. "I had an open container until just a little bit ago," she explained. "There might be some broken glass out on your walkway—sorry about that."

Janine jumped at the chance to leave the room to make drinks.

"*That* is a *big* old gal," Bergeron Love whispered.

Hil couldn't disagree; Janine was three times her own size, a woman who must have had to eat most of the day to maintain her weight, and yet Hil had never seen her do it. Janine had her own shelves in the fridge and cupboards, plastic grocery bags came and went, and still Hil had never shared a meal with her.

"You're lucky *she's* not the nudie here," Bergeron said, then added, in her normal voice, "Where's your son? Out on a date? Raising some high school hell?"

"He's here," Hil said. Had he heard Bergeron's arrival, from his bedroom? Declined to enter the fray? No doubt he was just listening to music on headphones, reading a philosophy book, texting with his school-hours-only girlfriend. Jeremy led a quiet, self-contained life; his peers seemed to frighten him a little. He wasn't ready, quite yet, to go unguarded into the night. It was he who every evening checked the locks and switched off the lights. After Hil went to bed, he and Janine would play complex and violent video games into the wee hours, speaking a fascinating coded language together while adroitly operating their controllers, never taking their eyes from the divided screen. For this and other reasons, Janine was an excellent roommate to both Hil and Jeremy, her own social life nearly nonexistent. Like Hil, she went to meetings to discuss her defining, overwhelming weakness; in the kitchen now she was no doubt devouring a frozen chocolate bar in addition to mixing gin and tonics. She insisted on keeping the chocolate frozen, despite the crown she'd broken just last week. Addicts, Hil marveled: so dedicated!

At another A.A. meeting, earlier in the week, Hil had started the story of her longtime neighbor Bergeron Love at a different point. "My neighbor the busybody once reported another of our neighbors to the Child Protective Services. She said he was abusing his daughters." This meeting was for women only; there was no friendly blind man upon whom to settle her eyes in this group. In fact, the women were a tougher audience, overall, than the mixed meetings. Less likely to forgive rambling or giggling during shares, readier to call bullshit on somebody's tears. "She'd heard him through the bathroom window with the girls—'Don't, Daddy, don't! It hurts! Please, Daddy!'—and assumed the worst. But after my neighbor reported this guy, this huge tattooed Hispanic guy, he started stalking her son."

Bergeron's then ten-year-old boy, Allistair. Allistair the fair and pale and earnest and brave, who'd later walked Jeremy around on Halloween, utterly unembarrassed at being seen holding a five-year-old's hand. Reporting the alleged abuse had been a lesson in minding your own business, Hil thought. The gentle and awkward Allistair had had to be moved to another school, separated from his familiar friends. Restraining orders had been required. Bergeron Love's front yard was egged, her car graffitied, her most beautiful live oak killed by mysterious means. She never knew what to expect when she opened her front door in the morning.

Bergeron had gone from one house to another, pleading her case, her car with its windshield covered in red spray paint parked at the curb for all to see. "Racist wore!" it said. "I know it's him because he didn't spray the *car!* He cares so much about cars, he couldn't spray the metal!" It was true that the man loved his vehicles; the house and yard were shabby, but his classic sedan and truck sat sparkling and cherry in the drive. That man still lived in the neighborhood. Neither his daughters nor his wife, to this day, had said a word against him.

"Nobody else ever heard or saw anything," Hil explained. "And Bergeron was always saying outrageous stuff. For all we knew, the kid was overreacting to soap in her eyes—'Stop! It hurts!' It just seemed so unfair that her boy was suffering because of her," Hil went on to the roomful of women, most of them mothers. Little Allistair Love, studious, dutiful, always standing alongside Bergeron at the polling stations on Election Day, shirt clattering with campaign buttons. "I don't know exactly what I'm trying to say, I guess, but she came to my house the other night, *bing-bong,* most likely lonely for her boy, I'm thinking. He's all grown up now, living over in Austin. I mean, I can imagine how it'd be, having your son move away."

Occasionally, on a bad night in the past, she'd heard the teenage Allistair trying to negotiate with his mother and Boyd when they took their drunken disagreements to the street. With a few drinks in him, Boyd could take on a certain defensive bravado, like a person in the woods encountering a wild animal. Their issues were forgettable, at least to them, tomorrow's amnesia—blame and counterblame, outrage shouted upon outrage, insult upon insult—but Allistair couldn't forget them. His entreaties were always the same: *Come inside! Please get out of the street.* Heartbreaking, that pleading adenoidal voice.

"Every time she came to my door, it was, you know, 'What fresh hell is this?' I usually saw her when she was drunk, but I know she had some kind of wits about her because she got shit done in our neighborhood. And she seemed to bring up a pretty great kid, mostly by herself." Bergeron the pitiful, whose only marriage, it was rumored, had not lasted more than a summer, that gold-digging, sperm-donor ex-husband who'd left her pregnant and poorer by half. Also, Bergeron the bully, who'd driven off the homeless and kept out the AIDS patients. Bergeron the hypocrite, who'd fought many a zoning battle from the confines of her own sagging antebellum monstrosity, in need of paint and roofing and porch repair, not to mention its proliferating cat population, inbred and unhealthy. And Bergeron the legend, débutante, socialite, donor, scion of the noble Love family, some sort of mysterious yet commanding black sheep.

At the women's meeting, Hil didn't mention what had happened that very morning: the ambulance and fire truck that had roused the block at daybreak, pulling into place on either side of Bergeron's front walk, half a dozen uniformed people leaping into action, neighbors stepping out in their sweatpants and bathrobes and mussed hair, arms crossed over their chests, curious as to what the mercurial Bergeron Love had set in motion now.

On that earlier naked night, after Janine came back from the kitchen, Hil had excused herself briefly. In the hall, she was grateful for her son's resolutely closed door. She dialed her neighbor's number, making her way to the study, the window of which looked out toward the Love house, where Hil could see, through the tall front window, the shape of Boyd watching television. He didn't answer the phone on the first call. "Oh, hell no," Hil murmured, dialing the number again. She could almost hear it ringing over there. Could almost hear Boyd's reluctant sigh as he rose, this time, and picked up. "Hello?" he said hopefully, as if he hadn't already seen who it was on caller ID. As if he had no idea what he was going to be told. He was a chinless man who routinely let himself be bossed around, made small. Bergeron wouldn't marry him ("Fool me once, shame on you," she'd said on the subject of marriage. "Fool me twice? No, ma'am"), wouldn't let him be anything other than her aging, laughably labeled *boyfriend.* "You maybe want to come retrieve Bergeron?" Hil said to him.

"She told me she was setting out to get arrested."

"That hasn't come to pass just yet. I guess I could call the cops, if you really think she needs all that drama." Thanks to her family, Bergeron rarely feared authority. "But it takes so long when there are uniforms involved. The paperwork."

Five minutes later, Boyd stood wearily at the door, fully clothed, Hil was grateful to see. But instead of taking Bergeron home, Boyd sat down in the second of the blue chairs. "Want a drink?" Janine asked him, probably hoping to sneak another chocolate bar.

Now that there seemed to be a party going on, it was no longer possible for Jeremy to ignore the sounds coming from the living room. He greeted Boyd first, Boyd who'd ferried him many a time across the busy lanes of traffic to his elementary school, whistle shrieking, a protective hand on his back. Then Jeremy spotted Bergeron Love, naked in his favorite chair. He immediately turned away, blushing, a gesture Bergeron pounced upon.

"You can't be shocked!" she declared. "Give me a break! I betcha you've been all over the Internet looking at porn!"

Boyd provided Jeremy with a grimacing shrug; Bergeron Love, in her hat, on the chair, was nothing like Internet porn.

"What are you, on drugs?" Bergeron demanded when Jeremy was silent. "Are you high?"

"No, ma'am," Jeremy said, now directing at her his sober, scornful glare. Telling her, in his way, that he was fully aware that he was the only unintoxicated person in the room. He next fixed his eyes on the television screen, where the bullet through the heart remained, like a new piece of art on the wall, a mesmerizing solar system of bloody mayhem.

"Oh, don't get all saintly," Bergeron said, smiling suddenly at Jeremy's indignation. "Be patient with your elders. Cut us some slack. You're just like Allistair," she added fondly. "All serious and all. You remember my son, Allistair?"

Jeremy said that he did.

"He didn't like to be put on the spot, either, didn't like a direct question, didn't like a big to-do. Played things pretty close to the vest. He was embarrassed by his mom too."

"He's not embarrassed by me," Hil said. Jeremy glanced at her with what she hoped was agreement. After all, Hil wasn't the one who routinely got drunk and was then driven to getting things off her chest to anybody who'd listen. Hil had not, tonight, decided to parade around naked in public. Jeremy went to Al-Anon meetings because his father had made it a condition of their custody arrangement. "They're okay," he'd reported to his mother of those meetings. "Lots of hugging. A little too much God talk, for me. I don't say I'm an atheist anymore, though."

"That's a good lesson, wherever you learn it," she'd said.

"Allistair was embarrassed, but he loved me," Bergeron went on. "He'd have done anything for me. Not like Boyd here. Boyd doesn't love me. The people who love me are all gone, except Allistair. Mother and Daddy, my brother George Jr., but not that son of a bitch Allistair, my brother Allistair—that's Allistair the first. Everybody dead and gone, except Allistair the second."

"I love you," Boyd put in.

"But," Bergeron said, taking a few breaths, "sometimes? Sometimes, it's like Allistair might as well be dead, for as often as I see him. For as often as he seems to think of me."

Janine cleared her throat quietly.

"He thinks of you," Jeremy said.

"Bless your heart," Bergeron told him, "but how in the world would you know?" She then turned to Boyd. "And as for you, Boyd, *you* just learned how to say the *words* 'I love you.' I taught you those three words, and how I wish I hadn't. I might as well live with a parrot, for all they mean to *you*. Hey, where's your dad, anyway?" Bergeron asked Jeremy. "What ever happened to him? How'd you end up with this big gal in your house instead?"

"Hey, now," Hil said. "No need to be bitchy, Bergeron. You can be naked, and you can interrupt our TV program, but no getting flat-out rude."

Poor Jeremy. What would he tell those hugging teenagers at the next Al-Anon meeting?

Jeremy took a seat next to Janine on the couch, loyal to his late-night gaming buddy. As for Janine, she was studying the coffee table, the part in her hair a bright, humiliated red. Like many an obese woman, she tended to her hair and makeup fastidiously. Hil tried to remember if this was the same coffee table that she and Jeremy's father had brought with them when they moved into the house, twenty years ago. Was it the same one on which Bergeron Love had stood during her first visit to them, to deliver her city council campaign speech? Perhaps.

"Do you remember when you were running for city council?" Hil asked.

"Which time?" Boyd said. "She's run more than once. And lost," he added quietly, somehow vindicated.

"A real reformer is never popular!" Bergeron declared.

"Nineteen-ninety or so," Hil said. "You guys were canvassing the street. Bergeron was stumping for herself on the Democratic ticket, and you, Boyd, were signing up Republicans. You got up on this very table to give your speech, Berge." Boyd had stood aside with his clipboard, as if he knew that Bergeron was a perfect argument for the opposition.

Jeremy and Janine laughed.

"Oh, make fun," Bergeron said. "Go ahead, Bergeron Love's a crackpot and a nuisance." She struggled out of the blue chair now, glass of ice in one hand, toothbrush in the other. "Nobody was ever grateful for anything I did, nobody—not you homeowners or your kids, not you, Boyd, you damn cringing mynah bird, not even my own son, Allistair, not even *Allistair!* Everybody's a fucking ingrate. Why run for office? Why give a shit? Why have children?" she demanded of Jeremy, who blinked at the force of her fervor.

"Well," he said, taking a moment to put it politely, "it's not exactly like he asked you to do it."

At the meeting that was mostly men, mostly professional men in the medical district, the story of the naked social call had got some laughs. The men had appreciated the ludicrous image, the backstory details of previous drunken escapades featuring that wild card Bergeron Love. They had even admired Jeremy's visit-ending remark. That innocent teenage observation had defused poor Bergeron Love, and Boyd had then been able to rise from the chair he'd been occupying so ineffectually and guide her limply out the front door.

"Wow," Janine had said. "Talk about true crime."

"Yeah," Jeremy said. He seemed to be studying the paused image on the television screen.

At the front door, Hil had hugged Bergeron Love, taken into her arms that molten clammy body. She'd never held a naked woman before.

"Don't tell Allistair, will you?" Bergeron had said into Hil's ear, no longer angry, no longer an incendiary force, no longer anything but tired. "Don't tell my boy."

After Hil had finished her story and acknowledged the A.A. members' applause, that mild smile still on the blind man's face, she and her friend Joe went, as usual, to their favorite Mexican restaurant to debrief.

Joe said, "You didn't share the part about Bergeron Love being dead now."

"Yeah, well, that part would kind of ruin the fun, wouldn't it? Everybody would get all ashamed when they found out they were laughing about a dead person, right? Five days after the naked visit she was dead."

"Short shelf life for a crazy story."

"Exactly." Joe didn't care that Hil ordered a beer at Chuy's. It was his opinion that beer didn't actually count, since it took so much of it to provide a buzz. He hadn't had a drink in five years, but it had been only two hours since he'd downed a Xanax. He was checking his watch to see when he could have another.

"You could tell the dead part next time, like it just happened. A follow-up on the first story. Chapter Two."

"Could do. You know, if it weren't for you and blind Jim, I'd quit this meeting."

Hil had first chosen the meeting because it was near the medical center and coincided with happy hour. She'd thought she might meet a doctor. Instead, she'd found Joe, a guy she'd known in high school, gay, also looking for a doctor. "I wanted to meet doctors because my dad was a doctor, and I like the fact that these guys are just like him, and yet also, hello, they're no better than me."

"A syllogism," Hil had supplied. "It makes perfect sense."

"Sort of. And maybe you can tell me why I've chosen to live with a porno addict?" he then said.

"Same reason I live with a morbidly obese woman? It's good to have somebody else's bad habits around to put your own in perspective?"

"Agreed. Also to compare and contrast. To get a little clarity."

"I should have known doctors wouldn't think of A.A. as a dating opportunity. In fact, the opposite."

"Live and learn," Joe said. "Or live and don't."

It had been an unusually clear Wednesday when the emergency

vehicles had screamed into the early-morning quiet, halting at the gates of Bergeron Love's beautiful ruin. Boyd the boyfriend had come out to unlock three generations of fence: the faded white picket one that matched the house, the black iron one with its spiky tips, and the hideous yet effective chain-link with concertina wire, the enclosure of most recent vintage. Bergeron Love had been wheeled out on a gurney, feet first, just as she might have predicted she'd exit that formerly lovely home, the place where she'd been born, raised, loved, and abandoned. Suicide, Hil had guessed at the time—Bergeron Love's last jaunt had been a kind of farewell tour of the neighborhood, exposing herself, putting herself at risk because she no longer cared what happened.

Also watching the action was the man who'd been reported for abuse, the man who might simply have been bathing his child. What was going through his head? Hil wondered. *Good riddance, racist wore.*

Hil lied at A.A. meetings. There she led a life of sobriety; there she had not had a drink for eleven months now. Soon she would reach her fictitious one-year mark. When she told Bergeron's story, she was at least telling the truth. But was it a story? Twenty years' worth of half-known information, neighborhood gossip. She'd told it at two different meetings, starting at different places: the naked visitation, the phone call to Child Protective Services. She could also have told a version that began with Bergeron campaigning for city council, using Hil's coffee table as a soapbox, she and her husband both horrified and amused by their new neighbor, still newlyweds themselves, their moving boxes barely unpacked, their son a few years in the future. Or she could have begun with the homeless man who'd been discovered lying beside Bergeron's kidney-shaped swimming pool one night, the man who'd somehow breached the various fences, empty bottle of isopropyl alcohol in hand, and who would have died, had Bergeron not summoned an ambulance, had she not moved with surprising speed to get him aid. Or Hil could have begun with the cocktail party that Bergeron had once interrupted, pushing into Hil's house in an ivory evening gown and trying to seduce her husband. "He's flirting with me!" she'd gaily shrieked, laying her head on Hil's husband's chest. "Look out, Boyd, you've got competition! Careful, Hil! You'll lose him!" Hil and her husband had laughed about it later in bed. As if he would be attracted to the likes of Bergeron

Love! Or to *anybody* else, he'd declared then tenderly to Hil, holding her close and naked, romantic, affectionate, still hers.

It was not a suicide, the neighborhood learned from Boyd after the vehicles had driven soundlessly away, their emergency lights extinguished. A heart attack, very sudden, there in bed. She'd grabbed his earlobe, he told one neighbor, illustrating by grabbing it himself, his face a shocked white, mousier than ever. She couldn't speak, Boyd said. That neighbor told the rest of them, and that was the end. Everybody went back inside.

Allistair would come home, Hil thought. He'd have to. It would be up to him to decide what to do with the Love estate, the squalid monument in which he'd been raised, the mosquito-ridden pool, those many cats, the lingering boyfriend.

Meanwhile, Hil had found a new meeting to go to, one so close to her house she could walk there. Handily, there was a pub situated on the route home. Maybe at this meeting she'd start the story of her eccentric neighbor by talking about the son as a teenager, Allistair trying to keep his mother from trouble at two or three or four in the morning, calling to her uselessly, "Please come back inside, Mom! *Please* get out of the street!"

KIRSTIN VALDEZ QUADE

Nemecia

FROM *Narrative Magazine*

THERE IS A PICTURE of me standing with my cousin Nemecia in the bean field. On the back is penciled in my mother's hand, *Nemecia and Maria, Tajique, 1929*. Nemecia is thirteen; I am six. She is wearing a rayon dress that falls to her knees, glass beads, and real silk stockings, gifts from her mother in California. She wears a close-fitting hat, like a helmet, and her smiling lips are pursed. She holds tight to my hand. Even in my white dress I look like a boy; my hair, which I have cut myself, is short and jagged. Nemecia's head is tilted; she looks out from under her eyelashes at the camera. My expression is sullen, guilty. I don't remember the occasion for the photograph, or why we were dressed up in the middle of the dusty field. All I remember of the day is that Nemecia's shoes had heels, and she had to walk tipped forward on her toes to prevent them from sinking into the dirt.

Nemecia was the daughter of my mother's sister. She came to live with my parents before I was born because my Aunt Benigna couldn't care for her. Later, when Aunt Benigna recovered and moved to Los Angeles, Nemecia had already lived with us for so long that she stayed. This was not unusual in our New Mexico town in those years between the wars; if someone died, or came upon hard times, or simply had too many children, there were always aunts or sisters or grandmothers with room for an extra child.

The day after I was born my great-aunt Paulita led Nemecia into my mother's bedroom to meet me. Nemecia was carrying the porcelain baby doll that had once belonged to Aunt Benigna. When they moved the blanket from my face so that she could see me, she smashed her doll against the plank floor. The pieces were all found; my father glued them together, wiping the surface with his handkerchief to remove what oozed between the cracks. The glue dried brown, or maybe it dried white and only turned brown with age. The doll sat on the bureau in our bedroom, its face round and placidly smiling behind its net of brown cracks, hands folded primly across white lace, a strange and terrifying mix of young and old.

Nemecia had an air of tragedy about her, which she cultivated. She blackened her eyes with a kohl pencil. She spent her allowance on magazines and pinned the photographs of actors from silent films around the mirror on our dresser. I don't think she ever saw a film—not, at least, until after she left us, since the nearest theater was all the way in Albuquerque, and my parents would not in any case have thought movies suitable for a young girl. Still, Nemecia modeled the upward glances and pouts of Mary Pickford and Greta Garbo in our small bedroom mirror.

When I think of Nemecia as she was then, I think of her eating. My cousin was ravenous. She needed things, and she needed food. She took small bites, swallowed everything as neatly as a cat. She was never full and the food never showed on her figure.

She told jokes as she served herself helping after helping, so that we were distracted and did not notice how many tortillas or how many bowls of green-chili stew she had eaten. If my father or little brothers teased her at the table for her appetite, she burned red. My mother would shush my father and say she was a growing girl.

At night she stole food from the pantry, handfuls of prunes, beef jerky, pieces of ham. Her stealth was unnecessary; my mother would gladly have fed her until she was full. Still, in the mornings everything was in its place, the wax paper folded neatly around the cheese, the lids tight on the jars. She was adept at slicing and spooning, so her thefts weren't noticeable. I would wake to her kneeling on my bed, a tortilla spread with honey against my lips. "Here," she'd whisper, and even if I was still full from dinner and not awake, I would take a bite, because she needed me to participate in her crime.

Watching her eat made me hate food. The quick efficient bites, the movement of her jaw, the way the food slid down her throat—it made me sick to think of her body permitting such quantities. Her exquisite manners and the ladylike dip of her head as she accepted each mouthful somehow made it worse. But if I was a small eater, if I resented my dependency on food, it didn't matter, because Nemecia would eat my portion, and nothing was ever wasted.

I was afraid of Nemecia because I knew her greatest secret: when she was five, she put her mother in a coma and killed our grandfather.

I knew this because she told me late one Sunday as we lay awake in our beds. The whole family had eaten together at our house, as we did every week, and I could hear the adults in the front room, still talking.

"I killed them," Nemecia said into the darkness. She spoke as if reciting, and I didn't at first know if she was talking to me. "My mother was dead. Almost a month she was dead, killed by me. Then she came back, like Christ, except it was a bigger miracle because she was dead longer, not just three days." Her voice was matter-of-fact.

"Why did you kill our grandpa?" I whispered.

"I don't remember," she said. "I must have been angry."

I stared hard at the darkness, then blinked. Eyes open or shut, the darkness was the same. Unsettling. I couldn't hear Nemecia breathe, just the distant voices of the adults. I had the feeling I was alone in the room.

Then Nemecia spoke. "I can't remember how I did it, though."

"Did you kill your father too?" I asked. For the first time I became aware of a mantle of safety around me that I'd never noticed before, and it was dissolving.

"Oh, no," Nemecia told me. Her voice was decided again. "I didn't need to, because he ran away on his own."

Her only mistake, she said, was that she didn't kill the miracle child. The miracle child was her brother, my cousin Patrick, three years older than me. He was a miracle because even as my Aunt Benigna slept, dead to the world for those weeks, his cells multiplied and his features emerged. I thought of him growing strong on sugar water and my aunt's wasting body, his soul glowing steadily inside her. I thought of him turning flips in the liquid quiet.

"I was so close," Nemecia said, almost wistfully.

A photograph of Patrick as a toddler stood in a frame on the piano. He was seated between my Aunt Benigna, whom I had never met, and her new husband, all of them living in California. The Patrick in the photograph was fat cheeked and unsmiling. He seemed content there, between a mother and a father. He did not seem aware of the sister who lived with us in another house nine hundred miles away. Certainly he didn't miss her.

"You better not tell anyone," my cousin said.

"I won't," I said, fear and loyalty swelling in me. I reached my hand into the dark space between our beds.

The next day, the world looked different; every adult I encountered was diminished now, made frail by Nemecia's secret.

That afternoon I went to the store and stood quietly at my mother's side as she worked at the messy rolltop desk behind the counter. She was balancing the accounts, tapping her lower lip with the end of her pencil.

My heart pounded and my throat was tight. "What happened to Aunt Benigna? What happened to your dad?"

My mother turned to look at me. She put down the pencil, was still for a moment, and then shook her head and made a gesture like she was pushing it all away from her.

"The important thing is we got our miracle. Miracles. Benigna lived, and that baby lived." Her voice was hard. "God at least granted us that. I'll always thank him for that." She didn't look thankful.

"But what happened?" My question was less forceful now.

My mother shook her head again. "It's best forgotten, hijita. I don't want to think about it."

I believed that what Nemecia told me was true. What confused me was that no one ever treated Nemecia like a murderer. If anything, they were especially nice to her. I wondered if they knew what she'd done. I wondered if they were afraid of what she might do to them. Perhaps the whole town was terrified of my cousin, watching her, and I watched Nemecia too as she talked with the teacher on the school steps, as she helped my mother before dinner. But she never slipped, and though sometimes I thought I caught glimmers of caution in the faces of the adults, I couldn't be sure.

The whole town seemed to have agreed to keep me in the dark, but I thought if anyone would be vocal about her disapproval—and surely she disapproved of murder—it would be my great-aunt Paulita. I asked her about it one afternoon at her house as we made tortillas, careful not to betray Nemecia's secret. "What happened to my grandfather?" I pinched off a ball of dough and handed it to her.

"It was beyond imagining," Paulita said. She rolled the dough in fierce, sharp thrusts. I thought she'd go on, but she only said again, "Beyond imagining."

Except that I *could* imagine Nemecia killing someone. Hell, demons, flames—these were the horrors that I couldn't picture. Nemecia's fury, though—that was completely plausible.

"But what *happened?*"

Paulita flipped the disk of dough, rolled it again, slapped it on the hot iron top of the stove, where it blistered. She pointed at me with the rolling pin. "You're lucky, Maria, to have been born after that day. You're untouched. The rest of us will never forget it, but you, mi hijita, and the twins, are untouched." She opened the front door of her stove with an iron hook and worried the fire inside.

No one would talk about what had happened when Nemecia was five. And soon I stopped asking. Before bed I would wait for Nemecia to say something more about her crime, but she never mentioned it again.

At night I stayed awake as long as I could, waiting for Nemecia to come after me in the dark.

Any new thing I got, Nemecia ruined, not enough that it was unusable, or even very noticeable, but just a little: a scrape with her fingernail in the wood of a pencil, a tear on the inside hem of a dress, a crease in the page of a book. I complained once, when Nemecia knocked my new wind-up jumping frog against the stone step. I thrust the frog at my mother, demanding she look at the scratch in the tin. My mother folded the toy back into my palm and shook her head, disappointed. "Think of other children," she said. She meant children I knew, children from Tajique. "So many children don't have such beautiful new things."

I was often put in my cousin's care. My mother was glad of Nemecia's help; she was busy with the store and with my three-year-old brothers. I don't think she ever imagined that my cousin wished me harm. My mother was hawkish about her children's safety—later, when I was fifteen, she refused to serve a neighbor's aging farmhand in the store for a year because he whistled at me—but she trusted Nemecia. Nemecia was my mother's niece, almost an orphan, my mother's first child.

My cousin was fierce with her love and with her hate, and sometimes I couldn't tell the difference. I seemed to provoke her anger without meaning to. At her angriest, she would lash out with slaps and pinches that turned my skin red and blue. Her anger would sometimes last weeks, aggression that would fade into long silences. I knew I was forgiven when she would begin to tell me stories, ghost stories about La Llorona, who haunted arroyos and wailed like the wind at approaching death, stories about bandits and the terrible things they would do to young girls, and, worse, stories about our family. Then she would hold and kiss me and tell me that though it was all true, every word, and though I was bad and didn't deserve it, she loved me still.

Not all her stories scared me. Some were wonderful—elaborate sagas that unfurled over weeks, adventures of girls like us who ran away. And all her stories belonged to us alone. She braided my hair at night, snapped back if a boy teased me, showed me how to walk so that I looked taller. "I'm here to take care of you," she told me. "That's why I'm here."

After her fourteenth birthday, Nemecia's skin turned red and oily and swollen with pustules. It looked tender. She began to laugh at me for my thick eyebrows and crooked teeth, things I hadn't noticed about myself until then.

One night she came into our bedroom and looked at herself in the mirror for a long time. When she moved away, she crossed to where I sat on the bed and dug her nail into my right cheek. I yelped, jerked my head. "Shh," she said kindly. With one hand she smoothed my hair, and I felt myself soften under her hands as she worked her nail through my skin. It hurt only a little bit, and what did I, at seven years old, care about beauty? As I sat snug between Nemecia's knees, my face in her hands, her attention swept over me the way I imagined a wave would, warm and slow and salty.

Night after night I sat between her knees while she opened and reopened the wound. One day she'd make a game of it, tell me that I looked like a pirate; another day she'd say it was her duty to mark me because I had sinned. Daily she and my mother worked against each other, my mother spreading salve on the scab each morning, Nemecia easing it open each night with her nails. "Why don't you heal, hijita?" my mother wondered as she fed me cloves of raw garlic. Why didn't I tell her? I don't know exactly, but I suppose I needed to be drawn into Nemecia's story.

By the time Nemecia finally lost interest and let my cheek heal, the scar reached from the side of my nose to my lip. It made me look dissatisfied, and it turned purple in the winter.

When Nemecia turned sixteen, she left me alone. It was normal, my mother said, for her to spend more time by herself or with older girls. At dinner my cousin was still funny with my parents, chatty with the aunts and uncles. But those strange secret fits of rage and adoration—all the attention she'd once focused on me—ended completely. She had turned away from me, but instead of relief I felt emptiness.

I tried to force Nemecia back into our old closeness. I bought her caramels, nudged her in church as though we shared some secret joke. Once at school I ran up to where she stood with some older girls. "Nemecia!" I exclaimed, as though I'd been looking everywhere for her, and grabbed her hand. She didn't push me away or snap at me, just smiled distantly and turned back to her friends.

We still shared our room, but she went to bed late. She no longer told stories, no longer brushed my hair, no longer walked with me to school. Nemecia stopped seeing me, and, without her gaze, I became indistinct to myself. I'd lie in bed waiting for her, holding myself still until I could no longer feel the sheets on my skin, until I was bodiless in the dark. Eventually, Nemecia would come in, and when she did, I would be unable to speak.

My skin lost its color, my body its mass, until one morning in May, when, as I gazed out the classroom window, I saw old Mrs. Romero walking down the street, her shawl billowing around her like wings. My teacher called my name sharply, and I was surprised to find myself in my body, sitting solid at my desk. Suddenly I decided: I would lead the Corpus Christi procession. I would wear the wings and everyone would look at me.

Corpus Christi had been my mother's favorite feast day since she was a child, when each summer she walked with the other girls through the dirt streets, flinging rose petals. Every year my mother made Nemecia and me new white dresses and wound our braids with ribbons in coronets around our heads. I'd always loved the ceremony: the solemnity of the procession, the blessed sacrament in its gold box held high by the priest under the gold-tasseled canopy, the prayers at the altars along the way. Now I could think only of leading that procession.

My mother's altar was her pride. Each year she set up the card table on the street in front of the house. The Sacred Heart stood in the center of the crocheted lace cloth, flanked by candles and flowers in Mason jars.

Everyone took part in the procession, and the girls of the town led it all with baskets of petals to cast before the Body of Christ. On that day we were transformed from dusty, scraggle-haired children into angels. But it was the girl at the head of the procession who really was an angel, because she wore the wings that were stored between sheets of tissue paper in a box on top of my mother's wardrobe. Those wings were beautiful, gauze and wire, and tied with white ribbon onto the upper arms.

A girl had to have been confirmed to lead the procession, and was chosen based on her recitation of a psalm. I was ten now, and this was the first year I qualified. In the days leading up to the recitation I surveyed the competition. Most of the girls were from ranches outside town. Even if they did have a sister or parent who could read well enough to help them with their memorization, I knew they wouldn't pronounce the words right. Only my cousin Antonia was a real threat; she had led the procession the year before, and was always beautifully behaved, but she would recite an easy psalm. Nemecia was too old and had never shown interest anyway.

I settled on Psalm 37, which I chose from my mother's cardboard-covered *Manna* for its impressive length and difficult words.

I practiced fervently, in the bathtub, walking to school, in bed at night. The way I imagined it, I would give my recitation in front of the entire town. Father Garcia would hold up his hand at the end of Mass, before people could shift and cough and gather their hats, and he would say, "Wait. There is one thing more you need to hear." One or two girls would go before me, stumble through their psalms (short ones, unremarkable ones). Then I would stand, walk with grace to the front of the church, and there, before the altar, I'd speak with eloquence that people afterward would describe as *unearthly.* I'd offer my psalm as a gift to my mother. I'd watch her watch me from the pew, her eyes full of tears and pride.

Instead, our recitations took place in Sunday school before Mass. One by one we stood before our classmates as our teacher, Mrs. Reyes, followed our words from her Bible. Antonia recited the same psalm she had recited the year before. When it was my turn, I stumbled over the sentence "For my iniquities are gone over my head: and as a heavy burden are become heavy upon me." When I sat down with the other children, tears gathered behind my eyes and I told myself that none of it mattered.

A week before the procession, my mother met me outside school. During the day she rarely left the store or my little brothers, so I knew it was important.

"Mrs. Reyes came by the store today, Maria," my mother said. I could not tell from her face if the news had been good or bad, or about me at all. She put her hand on my shoulder and led me home.

I walked stiffly under her hand, waiting, eyes on the dusty toes of my shoes.

Finally my mother turned to me and hugged me. "You did it, Maria."

That night we celebrated. My mother brought bottles of ginger ale from the store, and we shared them, passing them around the table. My father raised his and drank to me. Nemecia grabbed my hand and squeezed it.

Before we had finished dinner, my mother stood and beckoned me to follow her down the hall. In her bedroom she took down the box from her wardrobe and lifted out the wings. "Here," she said, "let's try them on." She tied the ribbons around my arms over my checked dress, and led me back to where my family sat waiting.

The wings were light, and they scraped against the doorway. They moved ever so slightly as I walked, the way I imagined real angel wings might.

"Turn around," my father said. My brothers slid off their chairs and came at me. My mother caught them by the arms. "Don't go get your greasy hands on those wings." I twirled and spun for my family, and my brothers clapped. Nemecia smiled and served herself seconds.

That night Nemecia went up to bed when I did. As we pulled on our nightgowns, she said, "They had to pick you, you know."

I turned to her, surprised. "That's not true," I said.

"It is," she said simply. "Think about it. Antonia was last year, Christina Garcia the year before. It's always the daughters of the Altar Society."

It hadn't occurred to me before, but of course she was right. I would have liked to argue, but instead I began to cry. I hated myself for crying in front of her, and I hated Nemecia. I got into bed, turned away, and fell asleep.

Sometime later I woke up to darkness. Nemecia was beside me in bed, her breath hot on my face. She patted my head and whispered, "I'm sorry, I'm sorry, I'm sorry." Her strokes became harder. Her breath was hot and hissing. "I am the miracle child. They never knew. *I* am the miracle because *I* lived."

I lay still. Her arms were tight around my head, my face pressed against her hard sternum. I couldn't hear some of the things she said to me, and the air I breathed tasted like Nemecia. It was only from the shudders that passed through her thin chest into my skull that I finally realized she was crying. After a while she released me and set me back on my pillow like a doll. "There now," she said, and arranged my arms over the covers. "Go to sleep." I shut my eyes and tried to obey.

I spent the afternoon before Corpus Christi watching my brothers play in the garden while my mother worked on her altar. They were digging a hole. Any other time I would have helped them, but tomorrow was Corpus Christi. It was hot and windy and my eyes were dry. I hoped the wind would settle overnight. I didn't want dust on my wings.

I saw Nemecia step out onto the porch. She shaded her eyes and stood still for a moment. When she caught sight of us crouched in the corner of the garden she came over, her strides long and adult.

"Maria. I'm going to walk with you tomorrow in the procession. I'm going to help you."

"I don't need any help," I said.

Nemecia smiled as though it was out of her hands. "Well." She shrugged.

"But I'm leading it," I said. "Mrs. Reyes chose me."

"Your mother told me I had to help you, and that *maybe* I would get to wear the wings."

I stood. Even standing, I came only to her shoulder. I heard the screen door slam, and my mother was on the porch. She came over to us, steps quick, face worried.

"Mama, I don't *need* help. Tell her Mrs. Reyes chose *me*."

"I only thought that there will be other years for you." My mother's tone was imploring. "Nemecia will be too old next year."

"But I may never memorize anything so well ever!" My voice rose. "This may be my only chance."

My mother's face brightened. "Maria, of course you'll memorize something. It's only a year. You'll get picked again, I promise."

I couldn't say anything. I saw what had happened: Nemecia had decided she would wear the wings, and my mother had decided to let her. Nemecia would lead the town, tall in her white dress, the wings framing her. And following would be me, small and angry and ugly. I wouldn't want it next year, after Nemecia. I wouldn't want it ever again.

Nemecia put her hand on my shoulder. "It's about the blessed sacrament, Maria. It's not about you." She spoke gently. "Besides, you'll still be leading it. I'll just be there with you. To help."

"Hijita, listen—"

"I don't want your help," I said. I was as dark and savage as an animal.

"Maria—"

Nemecia shook her head and smiled sadly. "That's why I am here," she said. "I lived so I could help you." Her face was calm, and a kind of holiness settled into it.

Hate flooded me. "I wish you hadn't," I said. "I wish you hadn't lived. This isn't your home. You're a killer." I turned to my mother. I was crying hard now, my words choked and furious. "She's trying to kill us all. Don't you know? Everyone around her ends up dead. Why don't you ever punish her?"

My mother's face turned gray, and suddenly I was afraid. Nemecia was still for a moment, and then her face clenched and she ran into the house.

After that, everything happened very quickly. My mother didn't shout, didn't say a word. She came into my room carrying the carpetbag she used when she had to stay at the home of a sick relative. I made my face more sullen than I felt. Her silence was frightening. She opened my bureau drawer and began to pack things into the bag, three dresses, all my drawers and undershirts. She put my Sunday shoes in too, my hairbrush, the book that lay beside my bed, enough things for a very long absence.

My father came in and sat beside me on the bed. He was in his work clothes, pants dusty from the field.

"You're just going to stay with Paulita for a while," he said.

I knew what I'd said was terrible, but I never guessed that they would get rid of me. I didn't cry, though, not even when my mother folded up the small quilt that had been mine since I was born and set it into the top of the carpetbag. She buckled it all shut.

My mother's head was bent over the bag, and for a moment I thought I'd made her cry, but when I ventured to look at her face, I couldn't tell.

"It won't be long," my father said. "It's just to Paulita's. So close it's almost the same house." He examined his hands for a long time, and I too looked at the crescents of soil under his nails. "Your cousin has had a hard life," he said finally. "You have to understand."

"Come on, Maria," my mother said gently.

Nemecia was sitting in the parlor, her hands folded and still on her lap. I wished she would stick out her tongue or glare, but she only watched me pass. My mother held open the door and then closed it behind us. She took my hand, and we walked together down the street to Paulita's house with its garden of dusty hollyhocks.

My mother knocked on the door, and then went in, telling me to run along to the kitchen. I heard her whispering. Paulita came in for a moment to pour me milk and set out some cookies for me, and then she left again.

I didn't eat. I tried to listen, but couldn't make out any words. I heard Paulita click her tongue, the way she clicked it when someone had behaved shamefully, like when it was discovered that Charlie Padilla had been stealing from his grandmother.

My mother came into the kitchen. She patted my wrist. "It's not for long, Maria." She kissed the top of my head.

I heard Paulita's front door shut, heard her slow steps come toward the kitchen. She sat opposite me and took a cookie.

"It's good you came for a visit. I never see enough of you."

The next day I didn't go to Mass. I said I was sick, and Paulita touched my forehead but didn't contradict me. I stayed in bed, my eyes closed and dry. I could hear the bells and the intonations as the town passed outside the house. Antonia led the procession, and Nemecia walked with the adults; I know this because I asked Paulita days later. I wondered if Nemecia had chosen not to lead or if she had not been allowed, but I couldn't bring myself to ask.

I stayed with Paulita for three months. She spoiled me, fed me sweets, kept me up late with her. Each night she put her feet on the arm of the couch to stop the swelling, balanced her jigger of whiskey on her stomach, and stroked the stiff gray hair on her chin while she told stories: about Tajique when she was a girl, about the time she sneaked out to the fiestas after she was supposed to be asleep. I loved Paulita and enjoyed her attention, but my anger at my parents simmered, even when I was laughing.

My mother stopped by, tried to talk to me, but in her presence the easy atmosphere of Paulita's house became stale. Over and over she urged me to visit her in the store, and I did once, but I was silent, wanting so much to be drawn out, disdaining her attempts.

"Hijita," she said, and pushed candy at me across the counter.

I stood stiff in her embrace and left the candy. My mother had sent me away, and my father had done nothing to stop her. They'd picked Nemecia, picked Nemecia over their real daughter.

Nemecia and I saw each other at school, but we didn't speak. Our teacher seemed aware of the changes in our household and kept us apart. People were kind to me during this time, a strange, pitying kindness. I thought they knew how angry I was, knew there was no hope left for me. I too would be kind, I thought, if I met myself on the road.

The family gathered on Sundays, as always, at my mother's house for dinner. That was how I had begun to think of it during those months: my mother's house. My mother hugged me, and my father kissed me, and I sat in my old place, but at the end of dinner, I always left with Paulita. Nemecia seemed more at home than ever. She laughed and told stories, and swallowed bite after neat bite. She seemed to have grown older, more graceful. She neither spoke to nor looked at me. Everyone talked and laughed, and it seemed only I remembered that we were eating with a murderer.

"Nemecia looks well," Paulita said one night as we walked home.

I didn't answer, and she didn't speak again until she had shut the door behind us.

"One day you'll be friends again, Maria. You two are sisters." Her hand trembled as she lit the lamp.

I couldn't stand it anymore. "No," I said. "We won't. We'll never be friends. We *aren't* sisters. She's the killer, and *I'm* the one who was sent away. Do you even *know* who killed your brother?" I demanded. "Nemecia. And she tried to kill her own mother too. Why doesn't anyone *know* this?"

"Sit down," Paulita said to me sternly. She'd never spoken to me in this tone. "First of all, you were not sent away. You could shout to your mother from this house. And, my God, Nemecia is not a killer. I don't know where you picked up such lies."

Paulita lowered herself into a chair. When she spoke again, her voice was even, her old eyes pale brown and watery. "Your grandfather decided he would give your mother and Benigna each fifty acres of land." Paulita put her hand to her forehead and exhaled slowly. "My God, this was so long ago. So your grandfather stopped by one morning to see Benigna about the deed. He was still on the road, he hadn't even made it to the door, when he heard the shouting. Benigna's cries were that loud. Her husband was beating her." Paulita paused. She pressed the pads of her fingers against the table.

I thought of the sound of fist on flesh. I could almost hear it. The flame of the lamp wavered and the light wobbled along the scrubbed wide planks of Paulita's kitchen floor.

"This wasn't the first time it had happened, just the first time your grandfather walked in on it. So he pushed open the door, angry, ready to kill Benigna's husband. There must have been a fight, but Benigna's husband was drunk and your grandfather wasn't young anymore. Benigna's husband must have been closer to the stove and to the iron poker. When they were discovered—" Paulita's voice remained flat. "When they were discovered, your grandfather was already dead. Benigna was unconscious on the floor. And they found Nemecia behind the wood box. She'd seen the whole thing. She was five."

I wondered who had walked in first on that brutality? Surely someone I knew, someone I passed at church or outside the post office. Maybe someone in my family. Maybe Paulita. "What about Nemecia's father?"

"He was there on his knees, crying over Benigna. 'I love you, I love you, I love you,' he kept saying."

How had it never occurred to me that, at five years old, Nemecia would have been too small to attack a grown man and woman all at once? How could I have been so stupid?

At school I watched for signs of what Paulita had told me, but Nemecia was the same: graceful, laughing, distant. I felt humiliated for believing her, and I resented the demands she made on my sympathy. Pity and hatred and guilt nearly choked me. If anything, I hated my cousin more, she who had once been a terrified child, she who could call that tragedy her own. Nemecia would always have the best of everything.

Nemecia left for California three months after Corpus Christi. In Los Angeles, my Aunt Benigna bought secondhand furniture and turned the small sewing room into a bedroom. She introduced Nemecia to her husband and to the miracle child. There was a palm tree in the front yard and a pink-painted gravel walkway. I know this from a letter my cousin sent my mother, signed with a flourish, *Norma.*

I moved back to my mother's house and to the room that was all mine. My mother stood in the middle of the floor as I unpacked my things into the now-empty bureau. She looked lost.

"We missed you," she said, looking out the window. And then, "It's not right for a child to be away from her parents. It's not right that you left us."

I wanted to tell her that *I* had not left, that I had been *left,* led away and dropped at Paulita's door.

"Listen." Then she stopped and shook her head. "Ah, well," she said, with an intake of breath.

I placed my camisoles in the drawer, one on top of the other. I didn't look at my mother. The reconciliation, the tears and embraces that I'd dreamt about, didn't come, and so I hardened myself against her.

Our family quickly grew over the space Nemecia left, so quickly that I often wondered if she'd meant anything to us at all.

Nemecia's life became glamorous in my mind—beautiful, tragic, the story of an orphan. I imagined that I could take that life, have it for myself. Night after night I told myself the story: a prettier me, swept away to California, and the boy who would find me and save me from my unhappiness. The town slept among the vast, whispering grasses, coyotes called in the distance, and Nemecia's story set my body alight.

We attended Nemecia's wedding, my family and I. We took the long trip across New Mexico and Arizona to Los Angeles, me in the backseat between my brothers. For years I'd pictured Nemecia living a magazine shoot, running on the beach, stretched on a chaise longue beside a flat, blue pool, and it was a fantasy that had sustained me. As we crossed the Mojave Desert, though, I began to get nervous—that I wouldn't recognize her, that she'd have forgotten me. I found myself hoping that her life wasn't as beautiful as I'd imagined it, that she'd finally been punished.

When we drove up to the little house, Nemecia ran outside in bare feet and hugged each of us as we unfolded ourselves from the car.

"Maria!" she cried, smiling, and kissed both my cheeks, and I fell into a shyness I couldn't shake all that week.

"Nemecia, cariña," my mother said. She stepped back and looked at my cousin happily.

"Norma," my cousin said. "My name is Norma."

It was remarkable how completely she'd changed. Her hair was blond now, her skin tanned dark and even.

My mother nodded slowly and repeated it, "Norma."

The wedding was the most beautiful thing I'd ever seen, and I was wrung with jealousy. I must have understood then that I wouldn't have a wedding of my own. Like everything else in Los Angeles, the church was large and modern. The pews were pale and sleek, and the empty crucifix shone. Nemecia confessed to me that she didn't know the priest here, that she rarely even went to church anymore. In a few years, I too would stop going to church, but it shocked me then to hear my cousin say it.

They didn't speak Spanish in my aunt's house. When my mother or father said something in Spanish, my aunt or cousins answered resolutely in English. I was embarrassed by my parents that week, the way their awkward English made them seem confused and childish.

The day before the wedding, Nemecia invited me to the beach with her girlfriend. I said I couldn't go—I was fifteen, younger than they were, and I didn't have a swimming suit.

"Of course you'll come. You're my little sister." Nemecia opened a messy drawer and tossed me a tangled blue suit. I remember I changed in her bedroom, turned in the full-length mirror, stretched across her pink satin bed, and posed like a pinup. I felt older, sensual. There, in Nemecia's bedroom, I liked the image of myself in that swimming suit, but on the beach my courage left me. Someone took our picture, standing with a tanned, smiling man. I still have the picture. Nemecia and her friend look easy in their suits, arms draped around the man's neck. The man—who is he? How did he come to be in the photograph?—has his arm around Nemecia's small waist. I am beside her, my hand on her shoulder, but standing as though I'm afraid to touch her. She leans into the man and away from me, her smile broad and white. My scar shows as a gray smear on my cheek. I smile with my lips closed, and my other arm is folded in front of my chest.

Until she died, my mother kept Nemecia's wedding portrait beside her bed: Nemecia and her husband in front of a photographer's arboreal backdrop with their hands clasped, smiling into each other's faces. The photograph my cousin gave me has the same airless studio quality but is of Nemecia alone, standing on some steps, her train arranged around her. She is half-turned, unsmiling, wearing an expression I can't interpret. Neither thoughtful nor stony nor proud. Her expression isn't unhappy, just almost, but not quite, vacant.

When she left for Los Angeles, Nemecia didn't take the doll that sat on the bureau. The doll came with us when we moved to Albuquerque; we saved it, I suppose, for Nemecia's children, though we never said so out loud. Later, after my mother died in 1981, I brought it from her house, where for years my mother had kept it on her bureau. For five days it lay on the table in my apartment before I called Nemecia and asked if she wanted it back.

"I don't know what you're talking about," she said. "I never had a doll."

"The cracked one, remember?" My voice went high with disbelief. It seemed impossible that she could have forgotten. It had sat in our room for years, facing us in our beds each night as we fell asleep. A flare of anger ignited—she was lying, she had to be lying—then died.

I touched the yellowed hem of the doll's dress, while Nemecia told me about the cruise she and her husband were taking through the Panama Canal. "Ten days," she said, "and then we're going to stay for three days in Puerto Rico. It's a new boat, with casinos and pools and ballrooms. I hear they treat you royally." While she talked, I ran my finger along the ridges of the cracks in the doll's head. From the sound of her voice, I could almost imagine she'd never aged, and it seemed to me I'd spent my whole life listening to Nemecia's stories.

"So what about the doll?" I asked when it was almost time to hang up. "Do you want me to send it?"

"I can't even picture it," she said, and laughed. "Do whatever you want. I don't need old things lying around the house."

I was tempted to take offense, to think it was me she was rejecting, our whole shared past in Tajique. I was tempted to slip back into that same old envy, for how easily Nemecia had let those years drop away from her, leaving me to remember her stories. But by then I was old enough to know that she wasn't thinking about me at all.

Nemecia spent the rest of her life in Los Angeles. I visited her once when I had some vacation time saved, in the low house surrounded by bougainvillea. She collected Dolls of the World and Waterford crystal, which she displayed in glass cases. She sat me at the dining room table and took the dolls out one by one. "Holland," she said and set it before me. "Italy. Greece." I tried to see some evidence in her face of what she had witnessed as a child, but there was nothing.

Nemecia held a wineglass up to the window and turned it. "See how clear?" Shards of light moved across her face.

SUZANNE RIVECCA

Philanthropy

FROM *Granta*

DAYS BEFORE SHE MET the novelist, Cora went to the library and brought home a stack of plastic-sleeved hardcovers with one-word titles like *Heirloom* and *Ruffian* and *Seductress.* Her favorite was an early effort with an unusually loquacious title: *The Illegitimate Prince's Child.* At first it was unclear who was illegitimate, the prince or his child. It turned out to be both. During the Hep C Support Group at the drop-in, Cora read aloud sentences like "Evelina knew Rolf would never marry her if she revealed her true station, but having been a bastard himself, how could he inflict the same fate on the unborn child inside her?" She regaled the needle-exchange staff with passages from *Ruffian,* substituting clients' names for the well-endowed hero's. She knew she was being inappropriate but she couldn't stop. She studied Yvonne Borneo's soft-focus author photos and imagined the hilarious incongruity of her vaunted good works—scattering gold pieces to hookers as she was borne down Mission Street on a litter, that sort of thing—and now that the appointed time had arrived for them to meet, she wanted Yvonne Borneo to deliver. She wanted a white mink hat and coat, a thick tread of diamonds across the collarbones, peacock-blue eyeshadow and sharp swipes of blush and impossibly glossy lips: the rigidly contoured, calculatedly baroque opulence of an eighties soap star auditioning for the role of tsarina. And Yvonne Borneo disappointed her by showing up at Capp Street Women's Services in a plain taupe skirt and suit jacket. Her sole concession to decadence was a mulberry cashmere scarf, soft as a runaway's peach fuzz, held in place with a metal pin shaped like a Scottie dog's silhouette.

"Well, you're just a tiny little mite" was the first thing she said to Cora. Her voice was butterfat-rich but filmy, like an old bar of dark chocolate that had taken on a gray cast.

The novelist/philanthropist was more vigorous than her wax-figure photographs, and at the same time much frailer. She thrust her shoulders back with a martial bearing when she laughed, which was often, but Cora noticed her hands trembling slightly when they weren't clasped in front of her. Her hair was beginning to thin. She was grandly imperious in a merrily half-ironic way. When Cora offered her a slice of red velvet cake, which she'd read was the novelist's favorite, Yvonne said, "Bikini season's upon us. I daren't indulge!" Yet she didn't flinch at the posted Rules of Conduct, scrolled in silver marker on black paper, hung above the TV in the main lounge, and frequently amended for circumstance. In the past few months, necessity had compelled Cora to add NO SHOWING GENITALIA, FLUSH THE TOILET AFTER YOU SHIT, and DON'T JERK OFF IN THE BATHROOM. This last rule was intended for the pre-op MTFs.

Yvonne read the rules from top to bottom, and when she was done she ruffled herself slightly, as though shaking off a light drizzle. Then she smiled brightly at Cora.

"Well," she said. "Girls will be girls."

Cora reminded herself that Yvonne Borneo was not easily shocked. How could she be? Her only child, a girl named Angelica, had stepped in front of a bullet train at twenty, after years of struggling with schizophrenia and—it was rumored—heroin addiction and sex work, although Yvonne had never confirmed this. She focused on the schizophrenia, referring to her late daughter as having "lost a battle with a significant and debilitating mental illness." The foundation she established after Angelica's death, the Angel Trust, gave money to provide mental health care for young women who had "lost their way" and were at risk of suicide.

Angelica had been the same age as Cora. As teenagers in the same Utah behavior modification program for troubled youth, they had known each other slightly. Cora was waiting for the right moment to tell Yvonne this. She tried to engineer an interval of quiet, seated intimacy, lowered voices, eye contact. But Yvonne moved too fast and talked too quickly, asking about city contracts and capital campaigns and annual reports, and Cora needed her money—the money from airport book sales and Hallmark Hall of Fame movie rights and the pocket change of millions of frustrated housewives—so badly she could hardly keep the desperation out of her voice. The city cuts had been devastating.

The Department of Public Health's deputy director, who had set up this meeting, warned her to cover her tattoos.

"Even the ones on my face?" Cora had said.

"I forgot about those. Okay, just don't say anything about her daughter being a dope fiend."

In Cora's tiny office, Yvonne lingered a few moments before the Dead Wall, which featured photographs of kids who had overdosed or killed themselves or been stabbed. None of these photos were appropriately elegiac, since the bereaved families usually couldn't be counted on to give Cora a cute school picture or a Polaroid of the deceased with a puppy. Most of the dead were memorialized in the act of flipping off the camera or smoking a bowl.

Yvonne put a hand to her chin. "It's so sad," she said. "Such a waste."

"Yes," Cora said.

"Well," Yvonne said. She sat down, crossing her legs. "What do you envision the Angel Trust being able to do for you?"

She asked this without real curiosity, her tone silky, keen, and as expertly measured as a game-show host's. Cora began to sweat.

"Well, first of all, I wouldn't have to lay off any more outreach staff," she said. Without realizing it, she was counting on her fingers. "And there are basic expenses like rent and utilities. And I'd love to increase Sonia's hours—she's the psychiatrist—because we're seeing a lot more girls with serious mental illness out there right now."

Yvonne frowned. "Well, the psychiatrist's hours, yes, I can get behind that. But as for the layoffs—it's always our preference that my funds not be used as a stopgap for deficits in government funding. My board prefers not to dispense bail-out money."

And this, Cora told herself, was why she hated philanthropists. Their dainty aversion to real emergency and distress, their careful gauging and hedging of risks, their preference, so politely and euphemistically stated, for supporting programs that didn't really *need* help to stay open, but sure could use a shiny new foyer, complete with naming opportunity. This was what she hated about rich people: their discomfort with their own unsettling power to salvage and save, the fear of besiegement that comes with filling an ugly basic need, their distaste for the unavoidably vertical dynamic of dispensing money to people who have none. The way they prided themselves on never giving cash to homeless people on the street, preferring a suited, solvent, 501c3-certified middleman, who knew better. For Cora, the hardest part of running the drop-in was not the necrotized arm wounds, the ubiquity of urine and rot, the occasional OD in the bathroom, the collect calls from prison. It was the eternal quest for money, the need to justify, to immerse herself in the fuzzy, lateral terminology of philanthropy. Over the past ten years Cora had learned that donors don't give a program dollars to save it from extinction; they "build a relationship" with the program. They want "partners," not charity cases. And deep down, they believe in their hearts that people in real, urgent need—the kind of person Cora once was, and the kind she still felt like much of the time—make bad partners.

Cora cleared her throat. "Well," she said, "increasing Sonia's hours won't do much good if we don't have a roof for her to work under, or a way of bringing clients to her."

She thought she saw Yvonne stiffen. Cora knew she was terrible at diplomacy. When she got angry, she preferred to yell; and if she were in front of the board of supervisors or the mayor's staff instead of Yvonne Borneo, she would have. But this woman, this sleek, self-made authoress—that word, with its anachronistic, feline hiss of implied dilettantism, seemed made for her—had to be handled differently. She had no civic obligation to stem disease; she helped at her whim. It had to be some little thing that reeled her in, some ridiculous coincidence, some accident of fate. And Cora remembered her trump card.

There was no time to wait for a transition. She opened her mouth and prepared to blurt something out, something inappropriate and apropos of nothing—*I knew your daughter when she was a dope fiend,* maybe—when a pounding on the gate stopped her. Then a wailing. Someone was wailing her name.

Yvonne Borneo perked up so markedly her neck seemed to lengthen an inch. "Do you need to see to that?" she said.

Cora excused herself and went to the back gate. It was DJ, a regular client who had come to the door and screamed for her plenty of times before, but never when anyone important was present.

Cora had once lanced a six-inch-long abscess on DJ's arm—she'd measured it—and when the clinic doctor pared away the necrotized tissue, bone showed through. DJ had started coming to the women's center at nineteen, freshly emancipated from foster care, clearly bipolar, and Cora had been trying to get her to see Sonia for seven years. She was twenty-six now and looked at least forty.

Today she looked worse than usual, in army pants held together with safety pins and a filthy tank top that revealed the caverns of scar tissue on her arms, the bulging sternum that seemed to twang fiercely under her skin like outraged tuning forks. When she saw Cora, DJ thrust both arms through the bars of the gate, like a prisoner in stocks, and wept.

"You came to see me when no one else did," she sobbed.

"Okay, DJ," Cora said. "Okay."

DJ did this a lot: went back and forth in time. She was talking about when she'd been stabbed by a john two years before and Cora had been the only one to stay with her at SF General, eventually securing her a semiprivate room and making the nurse give her painkillers. "Yeah, she's an addict," she had snapped at the young woman on duty. "It still hurts when she gets stabbed."

Sometimes DJ would recount an unknown past assault, or several, quietly sitting in the corner of the needle exchange and saying, "He raped me, Cora," while peering through the twisted vines of her hair. "I know, hon," Cora would say. "I'd cut his balls off if I could." This always seemed to calm DJ down.

After Cora's sister had a baby and the baby got older and began to speak in lucid sentences, its vocal patterns and flattened sense of chronology reminded Cora of DJ: that tendency to recount, repetitively, in the balanced and slightly bemused tones of a person under hypnosis, past events as though they had just happened. No "I remember this," just "Mama dropped a plate and it broke," meditatively, with an air of troubled, grieving reflection. It seemed to her that DJ, like the baby, was stuck in some cognitive cul-de-sac and, unlike the baby, would never develop a perspective layered and three-dimensional enough to find her way out.

Now Cora looked into her wet face and said, "DJ, I've got someone in there. Someone I'm having a meeting with. If you come back in an hour, when I open the exchange, we'll talk. Okay?"

DJ gazed at her. "An hour?" she said hollowly.

"Yeah."

The girl's face began to twist and shift like there was something behind it, trying to get out. She slumped forward, forearms still resting on the bars of the gate, and moaned. Cora smelled alcohol and urine.

"DJ, please. One hour. I've got someone who might give us money in there, and I can't just leave her sitting in my office."

DJ slumped on the concrete, fingers still poking through the grates, and muttered, "Okay, okay, okay."

When Cora returned and apologized to Yvonne, the novelist said, "Everything all right?" Before Cora could answer, the screaming started again. DJ was now banging her head against the metal bars of the gate and howling, "I'm sorry, I know there's a rich lady in there, but I need to come in!"

Cora grabbed her ring of keys and hurried down the hall. It was starting to get dark outside, but she could see a wet patch of blood on DJ's lip from the banging. When she unlocked the gate, DJ fell against her, almost gracefully. Cora staggered under the weight and struggled to dig her hands into the girl's armpits, hoisting her up to standing. She lost her grip, and they collapsed together on the concrete floor. The crotch of DJ's pants was soaked through. "It's just so cold," the girl slurred. "It's just so cold out there. I keep peeing myself, Cora."

Cora took DJ's chin in her hands and looked into her eyes. They were unfocused and dilated, but not fixed. She was just very drunk.

"I can't be out there right now."

She pressed against Cora. They were entangled now on the floor of the hall, and Cora felt a hot dribble of urine slowly trickle across the floor underneath their bodies. "It hurts," DJ said.

"I think you might have a UTI again, hon," Cora said. "Remember when we talked about pissing right after you fuck?"

"She's fancy," DJ said.

At first Cora thought DJ was going back in time again, but then realized she was referring to Yvonne Borneo, who stood in the middle of the hallway in her gray suit, arms at her sides, projecting the deliberate, neutral composure of a wartime nurse—one of her own heroines, perhaps, kindly but remote and weighted with an incurable private grief.

"Is there anything I can do?" she said.

And so Yvonne Borneo helped Cora haul DJ into the bathroom.

It was Yvonne who picked through the clothes bin and found clean pants and a sweatshirt, who went and bought three black coffees at the diner down the block while Cora helped DJ shower. And later, it was Yvonne who sat in the needle exchange with Lew, the volunteer, while the on-site nurse gave DJ a dose of antibiotics and Cora spent an hour trying to find her a shelter bed for the night. It was fruitless. There was nothing.

"What if we book a decent hotel room for her and you take her there in a cab, make sure she checks in?" Yvonne suggested.

Cora shook her head. "If she's going overnight somewhere, it needs to be a place where people know what they're doing." She looked down at her lap. "The only option is to 5150 her."

Yvonne didn't ask what a 5150 was. She said, "Well, if the alternative is to be on the streets . . ." Her words trailed off. From the exam room came the sound of DJ alternately screaming and sobbing. The sounds were a kind of last gasp, witless and terrifying as the *crunch* before a piece of machinery breaks down for good. Cora stood up and shut the door to her office.

She made the call. Half an hour later, when the paramedics burst in the front door of the drop-in, four big burly men, louder and stompier than necessary in the way paramedics always are—the way anyone is, for that matter, who comes in the guise of eleventh-hour rescuer—and strapped DJ to a gurney, Cora ran alongside the stretcher and told the girl that things would be okay. But she knew this was unlikely, just as she knew her chances with Yvonne Borneo were blown, because the woman had borne witness to Cora's greatest failure, a failure multiplied by the scores of clients just like DJ: girls who could not change. The part of them that knew how to accept help, whatever that part was called—hope? imagination? foresight?—had been destroyed. And what Cora and her staff did for such girls, day after day, felt more and more like hospice care: an attempt to minimize the worst of their pain until death.

Cora stood in the alley after the ambulance took off. It was Friday night and all the barkeeps along Mission and Valencia were dumping empty bottles into recycling bins. The sound of breaking glass seemed gratuitously destructive, nihilistic. She watched a woman walking down Capp Street in a short swingy coat and heels. A car pulled up alongside her and idled. Some idiot from Marin, thought Cora. The woman and the man in the car conferred for a moment, and the woman drew herself up and hurried down the sidewalk, shaking her head, outraged, as the vehicle pulled away.

When Cora came back into the exchange, Lew was alone.

"Where's Yvonne Borneo?" she said.

"You mean that lady? That narc-looking lady?"

"Yes," Cora sighed. "She left, didn't she?"

Lew shrugged. "She left when the paramedics got here. She looked freaked."

'Did she say anything?'

"Nope. Maybe *toodaloo* or something." He flapped his wrist.

Cora sat down. "She did not fucking say *toodaloo*."

"No," Lew admitted. "She did not."

The first time Cora saw Yvonne's daughter was in Ravenswood's recreation room. They were both fifteen. She remembered Angelica as tall and big-framed and slumped, with choppy bangs and sidelong, slippery eyes, seemingly beyond nervousness and fear, reduced to the passive, grim spectatorship of an inured captive. There was sympathy in the look she gave Cora, but it was neutered, the retroactive ghost of sympathy you have for your own past, stupid self.

One of the other girls asked how long Cora would be staying.

"Not long," Cora said, scared. Straining for flippancy. "Two weeks probably."

Angelica laughed.

"That's what we all thought," she said. She spoke in Cora's direction but didn't look at her. Cora tried to snag her gaze but it kept floating away, elusive and directionless. Then Angelica turned to leave the room and that's when she said the chilling thing, head down, so quiet and unassuming she could have been saying it to herself. "Honey," she said, "you are *never* getting out of here."

That night, her first at Ravenswood, Cora cried and sweated in her bed. Every fifteen minutes an aide came in and shone a flashlight on her. She wasn't allowed to talk to her dad on the phone. "Can't be a daddy's girl forever," one of the staff told her cheerfully. A dry-skinned, freckled woman wearing a sweatshirt with a grainy Georgia O'Keeffe flower scanned on the front. "You have a vagina on your shirt," Cora told her. The woman's mouth twisted into a tight, hurt smirk. "You need to grow up," she said. "I won't tell anyone what you said this time, but you need to start growing up."

At night, Cora would watch the snow from the tiny window in the Chill Out Room. She'd discovered that if she said things like *vagina* and *penis* and *fuck* enough, she'd get sent to the Chill Out Room and could be alone and not have to talk to anyone or pretend to be listening. There was no toilet in there, so she tried to limit her beverage intake. The hours stretched on. Cora would sit on the floor, scowling at the aide who came by every half-hour to ensure that she hadn't found an inventive way to hang herself. All the staff on the girls' ward were women, soft and easily hurt but inflexible, vicious in a hand-wringing, motherly way. Turned-down mouths and sad, round faces. If you called one of these women a fucking twat, her eyes would fill up and her voice quaver with genuine injured dignity. Then she would tell you she was very sorry, but you couldn't shower or change your underwear or socks until you apologized and admitted you were wrong. And the terrible thing was, she'd actually *seem* sorry. They were all perpetually cowed by their own brutality, quivering and defeated by the measures they were forced to enact. If Cora was nice to them, they were worse: unpardonably brisk and springy and relieved, presumptuous in their patting and hugging, insufferable in their tentative optimism. Their nonviolent and vaguely cutesy demands—that she sing show tunes in the bathroom to prove she wasn't shooting up or purging, that she do three jumping jacks for every swear word uttered, that she participate in a sock-puppet revue dramatizing what she wanted her life to be like in five years—made her want to kill, and she envied the boys, who, it was rumored, merely got hog-tied and placed in restrictive holds.

When Cora got home after her meeting with Yvonne, she sat on the floor of her living room and did sudoku puzzles for two hours. Then she tried to sleep but couldn't. The apartment was too quiet and she missed her cat, Melly, who had been dead for two weeks. Melly was a soothing, watchful, totemic presence, like a Buddha statue. She had a charming trait of standing on her two back feet for hours at a time, as if this was a restful position, her front legs hanging straight down from her chest, exposing the fur on her stomach, which was wavier and coarser than the rest. Cora and her friends had gathered round and laughed and marveled and taken pictures on their cell phones and praised Melly for being so cute and novel, until the day the vet informed Cora that Melly had advanced bone cancer and the reason she stood on her back feet was that it was the only position that alleviated her excruciating pain. Melly was put to sleep while Cora held her, whispering apologies, and she wanted to get another cat but was afraid of misinterpreting another signal, unwittingly laughing at another decline.

Melly's food and water bowls were still in the kitchen, half full, the water filmed over with bits of fur on the rim, the corners of each room still hoarding tumbleweeds of cat hair. Cora wiped the rim of the water bowl with her thumb. She kept remembering Yvonne Borneo in the bathroom of the drop-in, kneeling on the floor in her taupe skirt, pulling off DJ's army pants with grim, sharpened concentration. In those moments she seemed to have stepped into a transparent sleeve like the plastic sheaths on her novels, an invisible barrier that kept her from getting dirty. Not shying away from the wetness on DJ's pants. Not wincing at the smell. But not registering it, either. At one point, she leaned over DJ, blotting at the girl's bloody lip, and her Scottie-dog pin dinged against DJ's nose. DJ blinked, started, stared at Yvonne as if she hadn't seen her before.

"You're taking my clothes off," she murmured.

"Yes," Yvonne said. "So you can clean up."

"Oh, God," DJ moaned. "Oh, God." Then she squirmed to one side and planted her hands flat on the floor and vomited, not all at once but like a cat with a hairball, a series of back-arching, rippling convulsions.

"Get it all out," Yvonne had said.

The phone rang. A man's voice, clipped and high-pitched.

"Is this Cora Hennessey? Of Capp Street Women's Services?"

"Yes," Cora said.

Someone's dead, she thought. *DJ's dead.*

"My name is Josiah Lambeaux. I'm the personal assistant to Yvonne Borneo."

"Okay," Cora said.

It was raining. The ride to Yvonne Borneo's house felt needlessly meandering, up and down hills and around curves in the dense foggy dark, the car's lights occasionally isolating a frozen, fleeting image—a hooded man in a crosswalk, head bowed; a shivering sheaf of bougainvillea clinging to a stone wall; peeling layers of movie posters and LOST CAT signs and sublet notices trailing wet numbered tabs, plastered across the windows of vacant storefronts. Josiah drove his dove-gray sedan with the decorous effacement of a dad trying not to embarrass his teenage daughter, and she sat in the back and watched his thin neck tensing, his hands modestly manipulating the wheel with a pointed lack of gestural flair as they entered Seacliff, a hazy Land of the Lotus Eaters perched on the edge of the Presidio's red-roofed orderliness: a mirage of wide, silent streets and giant lawns and strangely permeable-looking mansions, many of them white and turreted and vaporous in the dark, whose banks of windows turned a blind slate toward the bay and its light-spangled bridge. As they turned onto the mile-long, cypress-lined lane leading to Yvonne Borneo's estate, Cora stuck her face an inch from the backseat window and imagined how hard it would be to run away from this place. Did Angelica break out under cover of night and run the entire mile from the front door to the road? What intricate alarm systems did she have to disassemble before she even crossed the threshold? And once she was free, adrift in this silent, echoing no-man's-land of ghost-houses and yawning boulevards, how did she keep going? Having known nothing but this eerie greensward with its self-contradictory air of utter desertion and hyper-preservation, how did she know where to go, or even how to leave? Cora's own leave-taking, at fourteen, was comparatively easy. She waited until the house was silent and sneaked out her bedroom window and climbed the backyard chain-link fence, to the road where her twenty-year-old boyfriend, Sammy, waited in his car. Her father barreled out the back door after her, chased her across the yard, grabbed the belt loop of her jeans, and pulled as she threw herself against the springy fence. She'd been shocked by how easily the fence swayed and shuddered as she clung to it. The change she'd filled her pockets with—pennies mostly—poured out, spattering on the ground and hitting her father in the face and arms. As he clutched her ankle, his eyes were screwed shut against the shower of coins and so he didn't see the foot of her free leg swinging toward him with all the lethal agility of the gymnast she'd once aspired to be, and he could only reel back, shocked, as the heel of her boot stomped down on his face.

She broke his nose. Her poor father who was only trying to protect his little girl from statutory rape at the hands of the druggie boy she adored. The weird sexual territoriality of fathers, some ancient holdover from the days of dowries and bloody marital sheets. Even then, she knew it was about his ego, *his* deflowered honor, not hers. When Sammy overdosed and she came crawling back home, strung out and incoherent, her father wouldn't let her in the house or even talk to her. He sent her to Utah, where Angelica was.

During the moral inventory phase of the twelve steps, she called her father and apologized.

"I'm sorry I broke your nose and put you through all that worry and mess," she said.

He seemed dumbfounded. "I don't even like to think about that," he said. "As far as I'm concerned, it never happened. You are what you are now, and that's who my daughter is. You. Not that other person."

"But I have to make amends, Dad," she said.

He said, "You can't make amends for something that never happened."

As the sedan reached the end of the lane and the house reared up before them, Cora forced herself to take deep breaths. Josiah parked and opened the passenger door for her, and she followed him past a row of topiaries and rose bushes, the heads of the flowers bowed by the rain. The house was a giant whitewashed box of sparkling stone, vaguely French Regency, wrought-iron balconies jutting from huge, blue-shuttered casement windows. As she and Josiah walked to the front door, a series of motion-sensor floodlights clicked on, one after the other, dogging their steps.

Yvonne Borneo was waiting for them in the vestibule.

"Cora!" she exclaimed. "You made it!"

Then she hugged Cora. She wore silk lounge pants and a gauzy tunic, and Cora, chin pressed against the novelist's dry, soft neck, smelled lily of the valley and starch.

"Thank you for having me," Cora said. During their embrace, Josiah had vaporized; they were alone in a high-ceilinged foyer of slate and marble.

"You are *such* a tiny thing," Yvonne said, sorrowfully looking Cora up and down.

Dinner was dished out by Josiah: skirt steak and buttered carrots and parsley potatoes on ceramic serving platters. When he produced a bottle of red wine and plucked Cora's glass by its stem, she held up her hand.

"No," she said. "No, thank you."

"It's an excellent wine," he said.

"I don't drink."

She'd been saying this for fifteen years, and the reaction was always the same: a wide-eyed, almost abject solicitude as the implications of the statement were processed. Then an abashed hush. Josiah poured her a glass of water.

As soon as Josiah left the room, Yvonne leaned forward slightly and looked at Cora. A centerpiece of bare black branches sat between them. She gently pushed it aside.

"I wanted to have you over to apologize to you, in person," she said, "for leaving so abruptly last night."

"Oh, no," Cora said. "No, I understand. I figured you had to get going."

Yvonne kept gazing at her. "It was hard for me," she said slowly, "to see someone in that condition."

"Of course," Cora said.

"How is DJ?"

"Well, they've got her on a forty-eight-hour hold. So . . ." Cora shrugged. "I guess at least she's detoxing right now. And maybe she'll have a shelter bed by the time she's out."

Yvonne looked down. "I don't know how you do it," she murmured. "Every single day. How you don't lose hope."

Cora surprised herself by saying, "Oh, I do. I just pretend that I don't."

Yvonne looked up, staring at her sharply, and Cora had a peculiar sensation of loosening, uncurling, and pushing off with a fortifying heedlessness that was liberating and bleak. If she still drank, she would have taken a gulp of wine at that moment. In her mind she saw money, coins and coins of it, running through her fingers.

"May I ask you a question?" Yvonne said.

Cora nodded.

"Why did you leave home?"

Cora had told the story of her downward spiral in front of countless donors. After years of twelve-step testimony she could easily slide into the instructive, talking-points tone this spiel seemed to demand. She always began with a disclaimer: *My parents weren't abusive. Which makes me different from most runaways.* Measured, wide-eyed, absolving everyone of everything. *I made a choice.* And she opened her mouth to say it again and found that she couldn't.

What she heard herself saying instead was "I was in love with an older guy, and I wanted to have sex with him."

Yvonne's fingers closed around the stem of her wineglass. She frowned.

"And that's why you left home?"

"Pretty much," Cora said. "My parents didn't let me date. They were really, really afraid I'd turn into a slut. I mean, *preoccupied* with the possibility I'd turn into a slut. As in, every rule they made revolved around protecting me from that fate. And, um, I wanted to have sex. So."

Yvonne looked grave and slightly stricken.

Cora kept going. "And this guy got me into drugs, and then he overdosed and I just went crazy. I kind of wanted to die with him. And I think it was mourning, the whole time I was on the street like that. I could say to you that I was a bad, bad girl and experimenting and rebelling, or whatever, but I really do think it was my way of mourning. And I could say there was one big, defining experience that changed me and made it okay, but there wasn't. It's still not okay. It'll never be okay. I just eventually stopped mourning."

Yvonne said, "But you got off the drugs. You made a life for yourself."

"The other thing was a life too."

Yvonne looked dismayed. "But what kind of life? Strung out, on the streets? Addicted to drugs?" Her voice trailed off, and she toyed with her fork.

Cora laughed, meanly. She was suddenly very angry. She had been waiting, she realized, for this chance since the moment they had met. Since before.

"Believe me," she said. Her voice was deliberate and low, feeling its way. "No one would do drugs if they weren't fun. The drugs are what I miss the most."

She laughed again, this time with disbelief at having said it out loud. But it was true.

Yvonne gracefully nudged her glass aside and cradled her chin in one long-fingered hand.

"I wouldn't really know," she said evenly.

Cora blurted out, "I was with your daughter at Ravenswood."

Yvonne stared.

"I don't know how long she was there. I was only there for a month. That's the way it worked, you know, if your parents couldn't afford to keep paying, they'd get told you were cured. And if your parents were rich enough, you were never cured."

In the dimness Yvonne's face seemed to tighten into facets, like a diamond, each outraged angle giving off light. And Cora kept going. She couldn't stop.

"That place was, excuse me, a mind fuck. They made up a diagnosis and made you try to fit it. Which may have been what they did to Angelica. Who I only saw once or twice, because I was stuck in a tiny padded room, alone, most of the time."

Her voice was unrecognizable to her ears: ragged, lashing, corrosive. Almost breaking. When she yelled at City Hall, it was mostly a put-on: she was angry, but she also knew she had to seem sane, galvanizing, in the right. Now she was simply ranting. Ranting at the millionaire who had invited her to dinner. And she couldn't stop.

"I was a junkie when I went in there," she said. "Like your daughter. And as soon as I got out, I couldn't *wait* to go do some drugs. I felt *lucky* to be out of that place and doing drugs again."

She was out of breath. For years she had counseled parents, engineered reconciliations, built bridges for girls to reconnect with their estranged families. Even if those families had made terrible mistakes, like sending their daughters to offshore boot camps, beating them, disowning them for getting raped or pregnant. No matter how awful the parents had been, they clung to Cora; they called her and told her how much they loved their daughters. They said things like, "You don't have to tell me where she is; just tell her that I love her." They cried. They listened to her with the chastened raptness of converts. They did what she suggested. And if their daughters came back or pulled themselves clear and forgave their parents, Cora thanked God she'd been patient, bitten her tongue, refused to say the very things she was now saying to Yvonne Borneo.

Yvonne picked up her napkin.

"Let me stop you right there, please, Cora," she said. Her voice was calm.

"I still—"

"Please," Yvonne said. "Please."

She waited until Cora became uncomfortable enough with the silence to sit back, with poor grace, and say, "All right."

"I think," Yvonne said, "I wanted to meet you because I knew something about your past. I knew you were a runaway. And on some level I wanted to see you and find out about you. I wanted to find out why you survived and my daughter didn't."

She folded her hands and cleared her throat, and when she resumed speaking her voice slackened, sagging with the dead weight of futile certainty. "It's because she was schizophrenic, that's what you'd tell me. And maybe you'd be right. But let me ask you this. If the situations were reversed, if you had been the one to die, and if Angelica were sitting in front of your parents right now and saying how awful Ravenswood was, what a mistake they made, what would your parents tell her?"

Cora's mouth was parched. The bitten shreds of her lips stuck together when she tried to separate them.

"I don't know," she said.

Yvonne's mouth stretched into a desolate smile.

"I'll tell you," she said. "They'd say exactly what I'm about to. They'd say, 'My daughter was an ocean underneath an ocean.' And it would be true. I see these girls on the streets, girls like DJ, the girls in your drop-in, and I know every single one of them is someone's daughter. And to their own parents, every single one of them is an ocean underneath an ocean." She tapped her index finger on the table in rhythm with the words. "Fathoms and fathoms deep. A complete mystery. My daughter is completely unfathomable to me. And certainly, if I may say so, to you."

Cora balled her fists under the table. She knew she should be mollified—if this were a TV show, she would be cowed before the unassailable authority of maternal privilege—but she was furious, burning, convinced that nothing had ever made her angrier than this: this artful abdication of responsibility, this consigning of every lost daughter to a communal slag heap of pretty Persephones. She remembered her father's voice on the phone, telling her, "You can't make amends for something that never happened." How matter-of-factly he had absolved her of everything. How she wished she could accept his words as a gift and pretend they didn't feel like a swift and brutal erasure of her entire adolescence as though it were some wartime atrocity, a stack of bodies to be buried and sprinkled with lime. He had excised a part of her and left it on the cutting-room floor. And when he reminisced about her growing up, as he occasionally did on her birthday and when he'd been drinking late at night and watching sentimental films on American Movie Classics, he selectively focused on those childhood behaviors that predicted and explained Cora's choice of career. How she'd always had a charitable bent. Defended smaller children from bullies. Brought home injured baby birds. Cried when starving Ethiopians were on the news. A Florence Nightingale whitewash, obscuring the simple fact that she cared about homeless junkie underage prostitutes because she used to be one. She knew what it was like to be Angelica in a way Yvonne Borneo could never know.

"My parents," she said, "would never say that. Because I am not the same person as your daughter. I don't look at what happened to Angelica and think *there but for the grace of God go I.* We're all different. We're all different people!"

She was sputtering now, losing her eloquence, letting herself go in a way she never had before, and in her mind she saw the drop-in shuttered, saw herself somewhere else, working in an art store, maybe, or walking the streets of a strange city, or telling an entirely new subset of people what she used to be and what it meant, giving it a new spin, all the dead and dying girls of the Mission as distant and abstract to her as Bosnian war orphans, as famine victims, far away and someone else's problem, and she remembered how, at the moment the phone rang in her apartment the night before, there was a panicked, nonsensical moment in which she thought, she *knew,* it was Angelica. It was Angelica, calling to tell her something about her mother. To say be gentle with her, because she's in pain. Every moment of the day she's in pain. And Cora lifted her eyes from her plate and said, "You're not going to give me any money, are you?" When her voice shook, she didn't know if it was with despair or relief.

Honey, you are never *getting out of here.*

She was dimly aware of the thin and careful form of Yvonne Borneo getting up from her chair and walking around the table. Then there was a hand on her shoulder—experimental, inquisitive, in the manner of a cat testing its balance on some unfamiliar surface.

Cora peered through her fingers. The novelist's face was inches from her own. Her brown eyes were very still and steady. Cora knew she was being shown something, that Yvonne was allowing some skimmed-away sediment to settle and collect in her dark eyes, in the grooves of her face, in the curves of her mouth. The look she gave Cora conveyed neither reproach nor remorse. What did it convey? Cora would never really know. She could only register something old and muddied and orphaned between them, a helpless moat of transference, brimming with the run-off of two people whose primary identities were, in the eyes of each other, not that of philanthropist and beneficiary, or writer and caregiver, but of someone else's mother and someone else's child. And it was this—this ancient ooze of crossed signals, this morass of things unsaid—that made Cora lower her forehead to Yvonne's shoulder and whisper, "She loved you. I could *tell* that she loved you," as the novelist stroked her hair the way Cora once imagined her stroking the head of a fox stole, automatically, with the phantom tenderness of a hand toward an object that is not the right thing at all, but is soft at least, and warm.

GEORGE SAUNDERS

The Semplica-Girl Diaries

FROM *The New Yorker*

September 3rd

HAVING JUST TURNED forty, have resolved to embark on grand project of writing every day in this new black book just got at OfficeMax. Exciting to think how in one year, at rate of one page/day, will have written three hundred and sixty-five pages, and what a picture of life and times then available for kids & grandkids, even great-grandkids, whoever, all are welcome (!) to see how life really was/is now. Because what do we know of other times really? How clothes smelled and carriages sounded? Will future people know, for example, about sound of airplanes going over at night, since airplanes by that time passé? Will future people know sometimes cats fought in night? Because by that time some chemical invented to make cats not fight? Last night dreamed of two demons having sex and found it was only two cats fighting outside window. Will future people be aware of concept of "demons"? Will they find our belief in "demons" quaint? Will "windows" even exist? Interesting to future generations that even sophisticated college grad like me sometimes woke in cold sweat, thinking of demons, believing one possibly under bed? Anyway, what the heck, am not planning on writing encyclopedia, if any future person is reading this, if you want to know what a "demon" was, go look it up, in something called an encyclopedia, if you even still have those!

Am getting off track, due to tired, due to those fighting cats.

Hereby resolve to write in this book at least twenty minutes a night, no matter how tired. (If discouraged, just think how much will have been recorded for posterity after one mere year!)

September 5th

Oops. Missed a day. Things hectic. Will summarize yesterday. Yesterday a bit rough. While picking kids up at school, bumper fell off Park Avenue. Note to future generations: Park Avenue = type of car. Ours not new. Ours oldish. Bit rusty. Kids got in, Eva (middle child) asked what was meaning of "junkorama." At that moment, bumper fell off. Mr. Renn, history teacher, quite helpful, retrieved bumper (note: write letter of commendation to principal), saying he too once had car whose bumper fell off, when poor, in college. Eva assured me it was all right bumper had fallen off. I replied of course it was all right, why wouldn't it be all right, it was just something that had happened, I certainly hadn't caused. Image that stays in mind is of three sweet kids in backseat, chastened expressions on little faces, timidly holding bumper across laps. One end of bumper had to hang out Eva's window and today she has sniffles, plus small cut on hand from place where bumper was sharp.

Lilly (oldest, nearly thirteen!), as always, put all in perspective, by saying, Who cares about stupid bumper, we're going to get a new car soon anyway, when rich, right?

Upon arriving home, put bumper in garage. In garage, found dead large mouse or small squirrel crawling with maggots. Used shovel to transfer majority of squirrel/mouse to Hefty bag. Smudge of squirrel/mouse still on garage floor, like oil stain w/embedded fur tufts.

Stood looking up at house, sad. Thought: Why sad? Don't be sad. If sad, will make everyone sad. Went in happy, not mentioning bumper, squirrel/mouse smudge, maggots, then gave Eva extra ice cream, due to I had spoken harshly to her.

Have to do better! Be kinder. Start now. Soon they will be grown and how sad, if only memory of you is testy, stressed guy in bad car.

When will I have sufficient leisure/wealth to sit on hay bale watching moon rise, while in luxurious mansion family sleeps? At that time, will have chance to reflect deeply on meaning of life, etc., etc. Have a feeling and have always had a feeling that this and other good things will happen for us!

September 6th

Very depressing birthday party today at home of Lilly's friend Leslie Torrini.

House is mansion where Lafayette once stayed. Torrinis showed us Lafayette's room: now their "Fun Den." Plasma TV, pinball game, foot massager. Thirty acres, six garages (they call them "outbuildings"): one for Ferraris (three), one for Porsches (two, plus one he is rebuilding), one for historical merry-go-round they are restoring as family (!). Across trout-stocked stream, red Oriental bridge flown in from China. Showed us hoofmark from some dynasty. In front room, near Steinway, plaster cast of hoofmark from even earlier dynasty, in wood of different bridge. Picasso autograph, Disney autograph, dress Greta Garbo once wore, all displayed in massive mahogany cabinet.

Vegetable garden tended by guy named Karl.

Lilly: Wow, this garden is like ten times bigger than our whole yard.

Flower garden tended by separate guy, weirdly also named Karl.

Lilly: Wouldn't you love to live here?

Me: Lilly, ha-ha, don't ah . . .

Pam (my wife, very sweet, love of life!): What, what is she saying wrong? Wouldn't you? Wouldn't you love to live here? I know *I* would.

In front of house, on sweeping lawn, largest SG arrangement ever seen, all in white, white smocks blowing in breeze, and Lilly says, Can we go closer?

Leslie Torrini: We can but we don't, usually.

Leslie's mother, dressed in Indonesian sarong: We don't, as we already have, many times, dear, but you perhaps would like to? Perhaps this is all very new and exciting to you?

Lilly, shyly: It is, yes.

Leslie's mom: Please, go, enjoy.

Lilly races away.

Leslie's mom, to Eva: And you, dear?

Eva stands timidly against my leg, shakes head no.

Just then father (Emmett) appears, says time for dinner, hopes we like sailfish flown in fresh from Guatemala, prepared with a rare spice found only in one tiny region of Burma, which had to be bribed out.

The kids can eat later, in the tree house, Leslie's mom says.

She indicates the tree house, which is painted Victorian and has a gabled roof and a telescope sticking out and what looks like a small solar panel.

Thomas: Wow, that tree house is like twice the size of our actual house.

(Thomas, as usual, exaggerating: tree house is more like one-third size of our house. Still, yes: big tree house.)

Our gift not the very worst. Although possibly the least expensive—someone brought a mini DVD player; someone brought a lock of hair from an actual mummy (!)—it was, in my opinion, the most heartfelt. Because Leslie (who appeared disappointed by the lock of mummy hair, and said so, because she already had one (!)) was, it seemed to me, touched by the simplicity of our paper-doll set. And although we did not view it as kitsch at the time we bought it, when Leslie's mom said, Les, check it out, kitsch or what, don't you love it?, I thought, Yes, well, maybe it is kitsch, maybe we did intend. In any event, this eased the blow when the next gift was a ticket to the Preakness (!), as Leslie has recently become interested in horses, and has begun getting up early to feed their nine horses, whereas previously she had categorically refused to feed the six llamas.

Leslie's mom: So guess who ended up feeding the llamas?

Leslie, sharply: Mom, don't you remember back then I always had yoga?

Leslie's mom: Although actually, honestly? It was a blessing, a chance for me to rediscover what terrific animals they are, after school, on days on which Les had yoga.

Leslie: Like every day, yoga?

Leslie's mom: I guess you just have to trust your kids, trust that their innate interest in life will win out in the end, don't you think? Which is what is happening now, with Les and horses. God, she loves them.

Pam: Our kids, we can't even get them to pick up what Ferber does in the front yard.

Leslie's mom: And Ferber is?

Me: Dog.

Leslie's mom: Ha-ha, yes, well, everything poops, isn't that just *it?*

After dinner, strolled grounds with Emmett, who is surgeon, does something two days a week with brain inserts, small electronic devices? Or possibly biotronic? They are very small. Hundreds can fit on head of pin? Or dime? Did not totally follow. He asked about my work, I told. He said, Well, huh, amazing the strange, arcane things our culture requires some of us to do, degrading things, things that offer no tangible benefit to anyone, how do they expect people to continue to even hold their heads up?

Could not think of response. Note to self: Think of response, send on card, thus striking up friendship with Emmett?

Returned to Torrinis' house, sat on special star-watching platform as stars came out. Our kids sat watching stars, fascinated. What, I said, no stars in our neighborhood? No response. From anyone. Actually, stars there did seem brighter. On star platform, had too much to drink, and suddenly everything I thought of seemed stupid. So just went quiet, like in stupor.

Pam drove home. I sat sullen and drunk in passenger seat of Park Avenue. Kids babbling about what a great party it was, Lilly especially. Thomas spouting all these boring llama facts, per Emmett.

Lilly: I can't wait till my party. My party is in two weeks, right?

Pam: What do you want to do for your party, sweetie?

Long silence in car.

Lilly, finally, sadly: Oh, I don't know. Nothing, I guess.

Pulled up to house. Another silence as we regarded blank, empty yard. That is, mostly crabgrass and no red Oriental bridge w/ancient hoofprints and no outbuildings and not a single SG, but only Ferber, who we'd kind of forgotten about, and who, as usual, had circled round and round the tree until nearly strangling to death on his gradually shortening leash and was looking up at us with begging eyes in which desperation was combined with a sort of low-boiling anger.

Let him off leash, he shot me hostile look, took dump extremely close to porch.

Watched to see if kids would take initiative and pick up. But no. Kids only slumped past and stood exhausted by front door. Knew I should take initiative and pick up. But was tired and had to come in and write in this stupid book.

Do not really like rich people, as they make us poor people feel dopey and inadequate. Not that we are poor. I would say we are middle. We are very, very lucky. I know that. But still, it is not right that rich people make us middle people feel dopey and inadequate.

Am writing this still drunk and it is getting late and tomorrow is Monday, which means work.

Work, work, work. Stupid work. Am so tired of work.

Good night.

September 7th

Just reread that last entry and should clarify.

Am not tired of work. It is a privilege to work. I do not hate the rich. I aspire to be rich myself. And when we finally do get our own bridge, trout, tree house, SGs, etc., at least will know we really earned them, unlike, say, the Torrinis, who, I feel, must have family money.

Last night, after party, found Eva sad in her room. Asked why. She said no reason. But in sketch pad: crayon pic of row of sad SGs. Could tell were meant to be sad, due to frowns went down off faces like Fu Manchus and tears were dropping in arcs, flowers springing up where tears hit ground. Note to self: Talk to her, explain that it does not hurt, they are not sad but actually happy, given what their prior conditions were like: they chose, are glad, etc.

Very moving piece on NPR re Bangladeshi SG sending money home: hence her parents able to build small shack. (Note to self: Find online, download, play for Eva. First fix computer. Computer super slow. Possibly delete "CircusLoser"? Acrobats run all jerky, due to low memory + elephants do not hop = no fun.)

September 12th

Nine days to Lilly's b-day. Kind of dread this. Too much pressure. Do not want to have bad party.

Had asked Lilly for list of b-day gift ideas. Today came home to envelope labeled POSSIBLE GIFT LIST. Inside, clippings from some catalogue: *"Resting Fierceness." A pair of fierce porcelain jungle cats are tamed (at least for now!) on highly detailed ornamental pillows, but their wildness is not to be underestimated. Left-facing cheetah: $350. Right-facing tiger: $325.* Then, on Post-it: DAD, SECOND CHOICE. *"Girl Reading to Little Sister" figurine: This childhood study by Nevada artist Dani will recall in porcelain the joys of "story time" and the tender moments shared by all. Girl and little girl reading on polished rock: $280.*

Discouraging, I felt. Because (1) why does young girl of thirteen want such old-lady gift, and (2) where does girl of thirteen get idea that $300 = appropriate amount for b-day gift? When I was kid, it was one shirt, one shirt I didn't want, usually homemade.

However, do not want to break Lilly's heart or harshly remind her of our limitations. God knows, she is already reminded often enough. For "My Yard" project at school, Leslie Torrini brought in pics of Oriental bridge, plus background info on SGs (age, place of origin, etc.), as did "every other kid in class," whereas Lilly brought in nineteen-forties condom box found last year during aborted attempt to start vegetable garden. Perhaps was bad call re letting her bring condom box? Thought, being historical, it would be good, plus perhaps kids would not notice it was condom box. But teacher noticed, pointed out, kids had big hoot, teacher used opportunity to discuss safe sex, which was good for class but maybe not so good for Lilly.

As for party, Lilly said she would rather not have one. I asked, Why not, sweetie? She said, Oh, no reason. I said, Is it because of our yard, our house? Is it because you are afraid that, given our small house and bare yard, party might be boring or embarrassing?

At which she burst into tears and said, Oh, Daddy.

Actually, one figurine might not be excessive. Or, rather, might be excess worth indulging in, due to sad look on her face when she came in on "My Yard" day and dropped condom box on table with sigh.

Maybe "Girl Reading to Little Sister," as that is cheapest? Although maybe giving cheapest sends bad signal? Signals frugality even in midst of attempt to be generous? Maybe best to go big? Go for "Resting Fierceness"? Put cheetah on Visa, hope she is happily surprised?

September 14th

Observed Mel Redden at work today. He did fine. I did fine. He committed minor errors, I caught them all. He made one Recycling Error: threw Tab can in wrong bucket. When throwing Tab in wrong bucket, made Ergonomic Error, by throwing from far away, missing, having to get up and rethrow. Then made second Ergonomic Error: did not squat when picking up Tab to rethrow, but bent at waist, thereby increasing risk of back injury. Mel signed off on my Observations, then asked me to re-Observe. Very smart. During re-Observation, Mel made no errors. Threw no cans in bucket, just sat very still at desk. So was able to append that to his Record. Parted friends, etc., etc.

One week until L's birthday.

Note to self: Order cheetah.

However, not that simple. Some recent problems with Visa. Full. Past full. Found out at YourItalianKitchen, when Visa declined. Left Pam and kids there, walked rapidly out with big fake smile, drove to ATM. Then scary moment as ATM card also declined. Nearby wino said ATM was broken, directed me to different ATM. Thanked wino with friendly wave as I drove past. Wino gave me finger. Second ATM, thank God, not broken, did not decline. Arrived, winded, back at YourItalianKitchen to find Pam on third cup of coffee and kids falling off chairs and tapping aquarium with dimes, wait staff looking peeved. Paid cash, w/big apologetic tip. Considered collecting dimes from kids (!). Still, overall nice night. Really fun. Kids showed good manners, until aquarium bit.

But problem remains: Visa full. Also AmEx full and Discover nearly full. Called Discover: $200 avail. If we transfer $200 from checking (once paycheck comes in), would then have $400 avail. on Discover, could get cheetah. Although timing problematic. Currently, checking at zero. Paycheck must come, must put paycheck in checking pronto, hope paycheck clears quickly. And then, when doing bills, pick bills totaling $200 to not pay. To defer paying.

Stretched a bit thin these days.

Note to future generations: In our time are such things as

credit cards. Company loans money, you pay back at high interest rate. Is nice for when you do not actually have money to do thing you want to do (for example, buy extravagant cheetah). You may say, safe in your future time, Wouldn't it be better to simply not do thing you can't afford to do? Easy for you to say! You are not here, in our world, with kids, kids you love, while other people are doing good things for their kids, such as a Heritage Journey to Nice, if you are the Mancinis, or three weeks wreck-diving off the Bahamas, if you are Gary Gold and his tan, sleek son, Byron.

There is so much I want to do and experience and give to kids. Time going by so quickly, kids growing up so fast. If not now, when? When will we give them largesse and sense of generosity? Have never been to Hawaii or parasailed or eaten lunch at café by ocean, wearing floppy straw hats just purchased on whim. So I worry: Growing up in paucity, won't they become too cautious? Not that they are growing up in paucity. Still, there are things we want but cannot have. If kids raised too cautious, due to paucity, will not world chew them up and spit out?

Still, must fight good fight! Think of Dad. When Mom left Dad, Dad kept going to job. When laid off from job, got paper route. When laid off from paper route, got lesser paper route. In time, got better route back. By time Dad died, had job almost as good as original job. And had paid off most debt incurred after demotion to lesser route.

Note to self: Visit Dad's grave. Bring flowers. Have talk with Dad re certain things said by me at time of paper routes, due to, could not afford rental tux for prom but had to wear Dad's old tux, which did not fit. Still, no need to be rude. Was not Dad's fault he was good foot taller than me and therefore pant legs dragged, hiding Dad's borrowed shoes, which pinched, because Dad, though tall, had tiny feet.

September 15th

Damn it. Plan will not work. Cannot get check to Discover in time. Needs time to clear.

So no cheetah.

Must think of something else to give to Lilly at small family-only party in kitchen. Or may have to do what Mom sometimes did, which was, when thing not available, wrap picture of thing with note promising thing. However, note to self: Do not do other thing Mom did, which was, when child tries to redeem, roll eyes, act exasperated, ask if child thinks money grows on trees.

Note to self: Find ad with pic of cheetah, for I.O.U. coupon. Was on desk but not anymore. Possibly used to record phone message on? Possibly used to pick up little thing cat threw up?

Poor Lilly. Her sweet hopeful face when toddler, wearing Burger King crown, and now this? She did not know she was destined to be not princess but poor girl. Poorish girl. Girl not-the-richest.

No party, no present. Possibly no pic of cheetah in I.O.U. Could draw cheetah but Lilly might then think she was getting camel. Or not getting camel, rather. Am not best drawer. Ha-ha! Must keep spirits up. Laughter best medicine, etc., etc.

Someday, I'm sure, dreams will come true. But when? Why not now? Why not?

September 20th

Sorry for silence but wow!

Was too happy/busy to write!

Friday most incredible day ever! Do not need to even write down, as will never forget this awesome day! But will record for future generations. Nice for them to know that good luck and happiness real and possible! In America of my time, want them to know, anything possible!

Wow wow wow is all I can say! Remember how I always buy lunchtime Scratch-Off ticket? Have I said? Maybe did not say? Well, every Friday, to reward self for good week, I stop at store near home, treat self to Butterfinger, plus Scratch-Off ticket. Sometimes, if hard week, two Butterfingers. Sometimes, if very hard week, three Butterfingers. But, if three Butterfingers, no Scratch-Off. But Friday won TEN GRAND!! On Scratch-Off! Dropped both Butterfingers, stood there holding dime used to scratch, mouth hanging open. Kind of reeled into magazine rack. Guy at register took ticket, read ticket, said, Winner! Guy righted magazine rack, shook my hand.

Then said we would get check, check for TEN GRAND, within week.

Raced home on foot, forgetting car. Raced back for car. Halfway back, thought, What the heck, raced home on foot. Pam raced out, said, Where is car? Showed her Scratch-Off ticket. She stood stunned in yard.

Are we rich now? Thomas said, racing out, dragging Ferber by collar.

Not rich, Pam said.

Richer, I said.

Richer, Pam said. Damn.

All began dancing around yard, Ferber looking witless at sudden dancing, then doing dance of own, by chasing own tail.

Then, of course, had to decide how to use. That night in bed, Pam said, Partially pay off credit cards? My feeling was yes, okay, could. But did not seem exciting to me and also did not seem all that exciting to her.

Pam: It would be nice to do something special for Lilly's birthday.

Me: Me too, exactly, yes!

Pam: She could use something. She has really been down.

Me: You know what? Let's do it.

Because Lilly our oldest, we have soft spot for her, soft spot that is also like worry spot.

So we hatched up scheme, then did.

Which was: Went to Greenway Landscaping, had them do total new yard design, incl. ten rosebushes + cedar pathway + pond + small hot tub + four-SG arrangement! Big fun part was, how soon could it be done? Plus, could it be done in secret? Greenway said, for price, could do in one day, while kids at school. (Note to self: Write letter praising Melanie, Greenway gal—super facilitator.)

Step two was: send out secret invites to surprise party to be held on evening of day of yard completion, i.e., tomorrow, i.e., that is why so silent in terms of this book for last week. Sorry, sorry, have just been super busy!

Pam and I worked so well together, like in old days, so nice and close, total agreement. That night, when arrangements all made, went to bed early (!!) (masseuse scenario—do not ask!).

Sorry if corny.

Am just happy.

Note to future generations: Happiness possible. And happy so much better than opposite, i.e., sad. Hopefully you know! I knew, but forgot. Got used to being slightly sad! Slightly sad, due to stress, due to worry vis-à-vis limitations. But now, wow, no: happy!

September 21st! Lilly B-Day(!)

There are days so perfect you feel: This is what life about. When old, will feel whole life worth it, because I got to experience this perfect day.

Today that kind of day.

In morning, kids go off to school per usual. Greenway comes at ten. Yard done by two (!). Roses in, fountain in, pathway in. SG truck arrives at three. SGs exit truck, stand shyly near fence while rack installed. Rack nice. Opted for "Lexington" (midrange in terms of price): bronze uprights w/ Colonial caps, EzyReleese levers.

SGs already in white smocks. Microline strung through. SGs holding microline slack in hands, like mountain climbers holding rope. Only no mountain (!). One squatting, others standing polite/nervous, one sniffing new roses. She gives timid wave. Other says something to her, like, Hey, not supposed to wave. But I wave back, like, In this household, is okay to wave.

Doctor monitors installation by law. So young! Looks like should be working at Wendy's. Says we can watch hoist or not. Gives me meaningful look, cuts eyes at Pam, as in, Wife squeamish? Pam somewhat squeamish. Sometimes does not like to handle raw chicken. I say, Let's go inside, put candles on cake.

Soon, knock on door: doctor says hoist all done.

Me: So can we have a look?

Him: Totally.

We step out. SGs up now, approx. three feet off ground, smiling, swaying in slight breeze. Order, left to right: Tami (Laos), Gwen (Moldova), Lisa (Somalia), Betty (Philippines). Effect amazing. Having so often seen similar configuration in yards of others more affluent makes own yard seem suddenly affluent, you feel different about self, as if at last in step with peers and time in which living.

Pond great. Roses great. Path, hot tub great.

Everything set.

Could not believe we had pulled this off.

Picked kids up at school. Lilly all hangdog because her b-day and no one said Happy B-day at breakfast, and no party and no gifts so far.

Meanwhile, at home: Pam scrambling to decorate. Food delivered (BBQ from Snakey's). Friends arrive. So when Lilly gets out of car what does she see but whole new yard full of friends from school sitting at new picnic table near new hot tub, and new line of four SGs, and Lilly literally bursts into tears of happiness!

Then more tears as shiny pink packages unwrapped, "Resting Fierceness" plus "Girl Reading to Little Sister" revealed. Lilly touched I remembered exact figurines. Plus "Summer Daze" (hobo-clown fishing ($380)), which she hadn't even requested (just to prove largesse). Several more waves of happy tears, hugs, right in front of friends, as if gratitude/affection for us greater than fear of rebuke from friends.

Party guests played usual games, Crack the Whip, etc., etc., in beautiful new yard. Kids joyful, thanked us for inviting. Several said they loved yard. Several parents lingered after, saying they loved yard.

And, my God, the look on Lilly's face as all left!

Know she will always remember today.

Only one slight negative: After party, during cleanup, Eva stomps away, picks up cat too roughly, the way she sometimes does when mad. Cat scratches her, runs over to Ferber, claws Ferber. Ferber dashes away, stumbles into table, roses bought for Lilly crash down on Ferber.

We find Eva in closet.

Pam: Sweetie, sweetie, what is it?

Eva: I don't like it. It's not nice.

Thomas (rushing over with cat to show he is master of cat): They want to, Eva. They like applied for it.

Pam: Where they're from, the opportunities are not so good.

Me: It helps them take care of the people they love.

Eva facing wall, lower lip out in her pre-crying way.

Then I get idea: Go to kitchen, page through Personal Statements. Yikes. Worse than I thought: Laotian (Tami) applied due to two sisters already in brothels. Moldovan (Gwen) has cousin who thought she was becoming window-washer in Germany, but no: sex slave in Kuwait (!). Somali (Lisa) watched father + little sister die of AIDS, same tiny thatch hut, same year. Filipina (Betty) has little brother "very skilled for computer," parents cannot afford high school, have lived in tiny lean-to with three other families since their own tiny lean-to slid down hillside in earthquake.

I opt for "Betty," go back to closet, read "Betty" aloud.

Me: Does that help? Do you understand now? Can you kind of imagine her little brother in a good school, because of her, because of us?

Eva: If we want to help them, why can't we just give them the money?

Me: Oh, sweetie.

Pam: Let's go look. Let's see do they look sad.

(Do not look sad. Are in fact quietly chatting in moonlight.)

At window, Eva quiet. Deep well. So sensitive. Even when tiny, Eva sensitive. Kindest kid. Biggest heart. Once, when little, found dead bird in yard and placed on swing-set slide, so it could "see him fambly." Cried when we threw out old rocking chair, claiming it told her it wanted to live out rest of life in basement.

But I worry, Pam worries: if kid too sensitive, kid goes out in world, world rips kid's guts out, i.e., some toughness req'd?

Lilly, on other hand, wrote all thank-you notes tonight in one sitting, mopped kitchen without being asked, then was out in yard w/flashlight, picking up Ferber area with new poop-scoop she apparently rode on bike to buy w/own money at Fas Mart (!).

September 22nd

Happy period continues.

Everyone at work curious re Scratch-Off win. Brought pics of yard into work, posted in cubicle, folks came by, admired. Steve Z. asked could he drop by house sometime, see yard in person. This a first: Steve Z. has never previously given me time of day. Even asked my advice: where did I buy winning Scratch-Off, how many Scratch-Offs do I typically buy, Greenway = reputable company?

Embarrassed to admit how happy this made me.

At lunch, went to mall, bought four new shirts. Running joke in department vis-à-vis I have only two shirts. Not so. But have three similar blue shirts and two identical yellow shirts. Hence confusion. Do not generally buy new clothes for self. Have always felt it more important for kids to have new clothes, i.e., do not want other kids saying my kids have only two shirts etc., etc. As for Pam,

Pam very beautiful, raised w/money. Do not want former wealthy beauty wearing same clothes over and over, feeling, When young, had so many clothes, but now, due to him (i.e., me), badly dressed.

Correction: Pam not raised wealthy. Pam's father = farmer in small town. Had biggest farm on edge of small town. So, relative to girls on smaller farms, Pam = rich girl. If same farm near bigger town, farm only average, but no: town so small, modest farm = estate.

Anyway, Pam deserves best.

Came home, took detour around side of house to peek at yard: fish hovering near lily pads, bees buzzing around roses, SGs in fresh white smocks, shaft of sun falling across lawn, dust motes rising up w/sleepy late-summer feeling, LifeStyleServices team (i.e., Greenway folks who come by 3x/day to give SGs meals/water, take SGs to SmallJon in back of van, deal with feminine issues, etc., etc.) hard at work.

Inside, found Leslie Torrini over (!). This = huge. Leslie never over solo before. Says she likes the way our SGs hang close to pond, are thus reflected in pond. Calls home, demands pond. Leslie's mother calls Leslie spoiled brat, says no pond. This = big score for Lilly. Not that we are glad when someone else not glad. But Leslie so often glad when Lilly not glad, maybe is okay if, just once, Leslie = little bit sad while Lilly = riding high?

Girls go into yard, stay in yard for long time. Pam and I peek out. Girls getting along? Girls have heads together in shade of trees, exchanging girlish intimacies, cementing Lilly's status as pal of Leslie?

Leslie's mother arrives (in BMW). Leslie, Leslie's mother bicker briefly re pond.

Leslie's mom: But, Les, love, you already have three streams.

Leslie (caustic): Is a stream a pond, *Maman?*

Lilly gives me grateful peck on cheek, runs upstairs singing happy tune.

Note to self: Try to extend positive feelings associated with Scratch-Off win into all areas of life. Be bigger presence at work. Race up ladder (joyfully, w/smile on face), get raise. Get in best shape of life, start dressing nicer. Learn guitar? Make point of noticing beauty of world? Why not educate self re birds, flowers, trees, constellations, become true citizen of natural world, walk around neighborhood w/kids, patiently teaching kids names of birds, flowers, etc., etc.? Why not take kids to Europe? Kids have never been. Have never, in Alps, had hot chocolate in mountain café, served by kindly white-haired innkeeper, who finds them so sophisticated/friendly relative to usual snotty/rich American kids (who always ignore his pretty but crippled daughter w/braids) that he shows them secret hiking path to incredible glade, kids frolic in glade, sit with crippled pretty girl on grass, later say it was most beautiful day of their lives, keep in touch with crippled girl via e-mail, we arrange surgery for her here, surgeon so touched he agrees to do for free, she is on front page of our paper, we are on front page of their paper in Alps?

Ha-ha.

(Actually have never been to Europe myself. Dad felt portions there too small. Then Dad lost job, got paper route, portion size = moot point.)

Have been sleepwalking through life, future reader. Can see that now. Scratch-Off win was like wake-up call. In rush to graduate college, win Pam, get job, make babies, move ahead in job, forgot former presentiment of special destiny I used to have when tiny, sitting in cedar-smelling bedroom closet, looking up at blowing trees through high windows, feeling I would someday do something great.

Hereby resolve to live life in new and more powerful way, starting THIS MOMENT (!).

September 23rd

Eva being a pain.

As I may have mentioned above, Eva = sensitive. This = good, Pam and I feel. This = sign of intelligence. But Eva seems to have somehow gotten idea that sensitivity = effective way to get attention, i.e., has developed tendency to set herself apart from others, possibly as way of distinguishing self, i.e., casting self as better, more refined than others? Has, in past, refused to eat meat, sit on leather seats, use plastic forks made in China. Is endearing enough in little kid. But Eva getting older now, this tendency to object on principle starting to feel a bit precious + becoming fundamental to how she views self?

Family life in our time sometimes seems like game of Whac-

A-Mole, future reader. Future generations still have? Plastic mole emerges, you whack with hammer, he dies, falls, another emerges, you whack, kill? Sometimes seems that, as soon as one kid happy, another kid "pops up," i.e., registers complaint, requiring parent to "whack" kid, i.e., address complaint.

Today Eva's teacher, Ms. Ross, sent home note: Eva acting out. Eva grouchy. Eva stamped foot. Eva threw fish-food container at John M. when John M. said it was his turn to feed fish. This not like Eva, Ms. R. says: Eva sweetest kid in class.

Also, Eva's artwork has recently gone odd. Sample odd artwork enclosed:

Typical house. (Can tell is meant to be our house by mock-cherry tree = swirl of pink.) In yard, SGs frowning. One (Betty) having thought in cartoon balloon: "OUCH! THIS SURE HERTS." Second (Gwen), pointing long bony finger at house: "THANKS LODES." Third (Lisa), tears rolling down cheeks: "WHAT IF I AM YOUR DAUHTER?"

Pam: Well. This doesn't seem to be going away.

Me: No, it does not.

Took Eva for drive. Drove through Eastridge, Lemon Hills. Pointed out houses w/SGs. Had Eva keep count. In end, of approx. fifty houses, thirty-nine had.

Eva: So, just because everyone is doing it, that makes it right.

This cute. Eva parroting me, Pam.

Stopped at Fritz's Chillhouse, had banana split. Eva had Snow-Melt. We sat on big wooden crocodile, watched sun go down.

Eva: I don't even—I don't even get it how they're not dead.

Suddenly occurred to me, w/little gust of relief: Eva resisting in part because she does not understand basic science of thing. Asked Eva if she even knew what Semplica Pathway was. Did not. Drew human head on napkin, explained: Lawrence Semplica = doctor + smart cookie. Found way to route microline through brain that does no damage, causes no pain. Technique uses lasers to make pilot route. Microline then threaded through w/silk leader. Microline goes in here (touched Eva's temple), comes out here (touched other). Is very gentle, does not hurt, SGs asleep during whole deal.

Then decided to level w/Eva.

Explained: Lilly at critical juncture. Next year, Lilly will start high school. Mommy and Daddy want Lilly to enter high school as confident young woman, feeling her family as good/affluent as any other family, her yard approx. in ballpark of yards of peers, i.e., not overt source of embarrassment.

This too much to ask?

Eva quiet.

Could see wheels turning.

Eva wild about Lilly, would walk in front of train for Lilly.

Then shared story w/Eva re summer job I had in high school, at Señor Tasty's (taco place). Was hot, was greasy, boss mean, boss always goosing us with tongs. By time I went home, hair + shirt always stank of grease. No way I could do that job now. But back then? Actually enjoyed: flirted with countergirls, participated in pranks with other employees (hid tongs of mean boss, slipped magazine down own pants so that, when mean boss tong-goosed me, did not hurt, mean boss = baffled).

Point is, I said, everything relative. SGs have lived very different lives from us. Their lives brutal, harsh, unpromising. What looks scary/unpleasant to us may not be so scary/unpleasant to them, i.e., they have seen worse.

Eva: You flirted with girls?

Me: I did. Don't tell Mom.

That got little smile.

Believe I somewhat broke through with Eva. Hope so.

Discussed situation w/Pam tonight. Pam, as usual, offered sound counsel: Go slow, be patient, Eva bright, savvy. In another month, Eva will have adjusted, forgotten, will once again be usual happy self.

Love Pam.

Pam my rock.

September 25th

Shit.

Fuck.

Family hit by absolute thunderclap, future reader.

Will explain.

This morning, kids sitting sleepily at table, Pam making eggs, Ferber under her feet, hoping scrap of food will drop. Thomas, eating bagel, drifts to window.

Thomas: Wow. What the heck. Dad? You better get over here.

Go to window.

SGs gone.

Totally gone (!).

Race out. Rack empty. Microline gone. Gate open. Take somewhat frantic run up block, to see if any sign of them.

Is not.

Race back inside. Call Greenway, call police. Cops arrive, scour yard. Cop shows me microline drag mark in mud near gate. Says this actually good news: with microline still in, will be easier to locate SGs, as microline limits how fast they can walk, since, fleeing in group, they are forced to take baby steps, so one does not get too far behind/ahead of others, hence causing yank on microline, yank that could damage brain of one yanked.

Other cop says yes, that would be case if SGs on foot. But come on, he says, SGs not on foot, SGs off in activist van somewhere, laughing butts off.

Me: Activists.

First cop: Yeah, you know: Women4Women, Citizens for Economic Parity, Semplica Rots in Hell.

Second cop: Fourth incident this month.

First cop: Those gals didn't get down by themselves.

Me: Why would they do that? They chose to be here. Why would they go off with some total—

Cops laugh.

First cop: Smelling that American dream, baby.

Kids beyond freaked. Kids huddled near fence.

School bus comes and goes.

Greenway field rep (Rob) arrives. Rob = tall, thin, bent. Looks like archery bow, if archery bow had pierced ear + long hair like pirate, was wearing short leather vest.

Rob immediately drops bombshell: says he is sorry to have to be more or less a hardass in our time of trial, but is legally obligated to inform us that, per our agreement w/Greenway, if SGs not located within three weeks, we will, at that time, become responsible for full payment of the required Replacement Debit.

Pam: Wait, the what?

Per Rob, Replacement Debit = $100/month, per individual, per each month still remaining on their Greenway contracts at time of loss (!). Betty (21 months remaining) = $2,100; Tami (13 months) = $1,300; Gwen (18 months) = $1,800; Lisa (34 months (!)) = $3,400.

Total: $2,100 + $1,300 + $1,800 + $3,400 = $8,600.

Pam: Fucksake.

Rob: Believe me, I know, that's a lot of money, right? But our take on it is—or, you know, their take on it, Greenway's take—is that we—or they—made an initial investment, and, I mean, obviously, that was not cheap, just in terms of like visas and airfares and all?

Pam: No one said anything to us about this.

Me: At all.

Rob: Huh. Who was on your account again?

Me: Melanie?

Rob: Right, yeah, I had a feeling. With Melanie, Melanie was sometimes rushing through things to close the deal. Especially with Package A folks, who were going chintzy in the first place? No offense. Anyway, which is why she's gone. If you want to yell at her, go to Home Depot. She's second in charge of Paint, probably lying her butt off about which color is which.

Feel angry, violated: someone came into our yard in dark of night, while kids sleeping nearby, stole? Stole from us? Stole $8,600, plus initial cost of SGs (approx. $7,400)?

Pam (to cop): How often do you find them?

First cop: Honestly? I'd have to say rarely.

Second cop: More like never.

First cop: Well, never yet.

Second cop: Right. There's always a first time.

Cops leave.

Pam (to Rob): So what happens if we don't pay?

Me: Can't pay.

Rob (uncomfortable, blushing): Well, that would be more of an issue for Legal.

Pam: You'd sue us?

Rob: I wouldn't. They would. I mean, that's what they do. They—what's that word? They garner your—

Pam (harshly): Garnish.

Rob: Sorry. Sorry about all this. Melanie, wow, I am going to snap your head back using that stupid braid of yours. Just kidding! I never even talk to her. But the thing is: all this is in your contract. You guys read your contract, right?

Silence.

Me: Well, we were kind of in a hurry. We were throwing a party.

Rob: Oh, sure, I remember that party. That was some party. We were all discussing that.

Rob leaves.

Pam (livid): You know what? Fuck 'em. Let 'em sue. I'm not paying. That's obscene. They can have the stupid house.

Lilly: Are we losing the house?

Me: We're not losing the—

Pam: You don't think? What do you think happens if you owe someone nine grand and can't pay?

Me: Look, let's calm down, no need to get all—

Eva's lower lip out in pre-crying way. Think, Oh, great, nice parenting, arguing + swearing + raising specter of loss of house in front of tightly wound kid already upset by troubling events of day.

Then Eva bursts into tears, starts mumbling, Sorry sorry sorry.

Pam: Oh, sweetie, I was just being silly. We're not going to lose the house. Mommy and Daddy would never let that—

Light goes on in my head.

Me: Eva. You didn't.

Look in Eva's eyes says, I did.

Pam: Did what?

Thomas: Eva did it?

Lilly: How could Eva do it? She's only eight. I couldn't even—

Eva leads us outside, shows us how she did: Dragged out stepladder, stood on stepladder at end of microline, released left-hand EzyReleese lever, then dragged stepladder to other end, released right-hand EzyReleese. At that point, microline completely loose, SGs standing on ground.

SGs briefly confer.

And off they go.

Am so mad. Eva has made huge mess here. Huge mess for us, yes, but also for SGs. Where are SGs now? In good place? Is it good when illegal fugitives in strange land have no money, no food, no water, are forced to hide in woods, swamp, etc., connected via microline, like chain gang?

Note to future generations: Sometimes, in our time, families get into dark place. Family feels: we are losers, everything we do is wrong. Parents fight at high volume, blaming each other for disastrous situation. Father kicks wall, puts hole in wall near fridge.

Family skips lunch. Tension too high for all to sit at same table. This unbearable. This makes person (Father) doubt value of whole enterprise, i.e., makes Father (me) wonder if humans would not be better off living alone, individually, in woods, minding own beeswax, not loving anyone.

Today like that for us.

Stormed out to garage. Stupid squirrel/mouse stain still there after all these weeks. Used bleach + hose to eradicate. In resulting calm, sat on wheelbarrow, had to laugh at situation. Won Scratch-Off, greatest luck of life, quickly converted greatest luck of life into greatest fiasco of life.

Laughter turned to tears.

Pam came out, asked had I been crying? I said no, just got dust in eyes from cleaning garage. Pam not buying. Pam gave me little side hug + hip nudge, to say, You were crying, is okay, is difficult time, I know.

Pam: Come on inside. Let's get things back to normal. We'll get through this. The kids are dying in there, they feel so bad.

Went inside.

Kids at kitchen table.

Opened arms. Thomas and Lilly rushed over.

Eva stayed sitting.

When Eva tiny, had big head of black curls. Would stand on couch, eating cereal from coffee mug, dancing to song in head, flicking around cord from window blinds.

Now this: Eva sitting w/head in hands like heartbroken old lady mourning loss of vigorous flower of youth, etc., etc.

Went over, scooped Eva up.

Poor thing shaking in my arms.

Eva (in whisper): I didn't know we would lose the house.

Me: We're not—we're not going to lose the house. Mommy and I are going to figure this out.

Sent kids off to watch TV.

Pam: So. You want me to call Dad?

Did not want Pam calling Pam's dad.

Pam's dad's first name = Rich. Actually calls self "Farmer Rich." Is funny because he is rich farmer. In terms of me, does not like me. Has said at various times that I (1) am not hard worker, and (2) had better watch self in terms of weight, and (3) had better watch self in terms of credit cards.

Farmer Rich in very good shape, with no credit cards.

Farmer Rich not fan of SGs. Feels having SGs = "showoffy move." Thinks anything fun = showoffy move. Even going to movie = showoffy move. Going to car wash, i.e., not doing self, in driveway = showoffy move. Once, when visiting, looked dubiously at me when I said I had to get root canal. What, I was thinking, root canal = showoffy move? But no: just disapproved of dentist I had chosen, due to he had seen dentist's TV ad, felt dentist having TV ad = showoffy move.

So did not want Pam calling Farmer Rich.

Told Pam we must try our best to handle this ourselves.

Got out bills, did mock payment exercise: If we pay mortgage, heat bill, AmEx, plus $200 in bills we deferred last time, would be down near zero ($12.78 remaining). If we defer AmEx + Visa, that would free up $880. If, in addition, we skip mortgage payment, heat bill, life-insurance premium, that would still only free up measly total of $3,100.

Me: Shit.

Pam: Maybe I'll e-mail him. You know. Just see what he says.

Pam upstairs e-mailing Farmer Rich as I write.

September 26th

When I got home, Pam standing in doorway w/e-mail from Farmer Rich.

Farmer Rich = bastard.

Will quote in part:

Let us now speak of what you intend to do with the requested money. Will you be putting it aside for a college fund? You will not. Investing in real estate? No. Given a chance to plant some seeds, you flushed those valuable seeds (dollars) away. And for what? A display some find pretty. Well, I do not find it pretty. Since when are people on display a desirable sight? Do-gooders in our church cite conditions of poverty. Okay, that is fine. But it appears you will soon have a situation of poverty within your own walls. And physician heal thyself is a motto I have oft remembered when tempted to put my oar in relative to some social cause or another. So am going to say no. You people have walked yourselves into some deep water and must now walk yourselves out, teaching your kids (and selves) a valuable lesson from which, in the long term, you and yours will benefit.

Long silence.

Pam: Jesus. Isn't this just like us?

Do not know what she means. Or, rather, do know but do not agree. Or, rather, agree but wish she would not say. Why say? Saying is negative, makes us feel bad about selves.

I say maybe we should just confess what Eva did, hope for mercy from Greenway.

Pam says no, no: Went online today. Releasing SGs = felony (!). Does not feel they would prosecute eight-year-old, but still. If we confess, this goes on Eva's record? Eva required to get counseling? Eva feels: I am bad kid? Starts erring on side of bad, hanging out with rough crowd, looking askance at whole notion of achievement? Fails to live up to full potential, all because of one mistake she made when little girl?

No.

Cannot take chance.

When kids born, Pam and I dropped everything (youthful dreams of travel, adventure, etc.) to be good parents. Has not been exciting life. Has been much drudgery. Many nights, tasks undone, have stayed up late, exhausted, doing tasks. On many occasions, disheveled + tired, baby poop and/or vomit on our shirt or blouse, one of us has stood smiling wearily/angrily at camera being held by other, hair shaggy because haircuts expensive, unfashionable glasses slipping down noses because never was time to get glasses tightened.

And now, after all that, our youngest to start out life w/potential black mark on record?

That not happening.

Pam and I discuss, agree: must be like sin-eaters who, in ancient times, ate sin. Or bodies of sinners? Ate meals off bodies of sinners who had died? Cannot exactly recall what sin-eaters did. But Pam and I agree: are going to be like sin-eaters in sense of, will err on side of protecting Eva, keep cops in dark at all cost, break law as req'd (!).

Just now went down hall to check on kids. Thomas sleeping w/ Ferber. This not allowed. Eva in bed w/Lilly. This not allowed. Eva, source of all mayhem, sleeping like baby.

Felt like waking Eva, giving Eva hug, telling Eva that, though we do not approve of what she did, she will always be our girl, will always be apple of our eye(s).

Did not do.

Eva needs rest.

On Lilly's desk: poster Lilly was working on for "Favorite Things Day" at school. Poster = photo of each SG, plus map of home country, plus stories Lilly apparently got during interview (!) with each. Gwen (Moldova) = very tough, due to Moldovan youth: used bloody sheets found in trash + duct tape to make soccer ball, then, after much practice with bloody-sheet ball, nearly made Olympic team (!). Betty (Philippines) has daughter, who, when swimming, will sometimes hitch ride on shell of sea turtle. Lisa (Somalia) once saw lion on roof of her uncle's "mini-lorry." Tami (Laos) had pet water buffalo, water buffalo stepped on her foot, now Tami must wear special shoe. "Fun Fact": their names (Betty, Tami, et al.) not their real names. These = SG names, given by Greenway at time of arrival. "Tami" = Januka = "happy ray of sun." "Betty" = Nenita = "blessed-beloved." "Gwen" = Evgenia. (Does not know what her name means.) "Lisa" = Ayan = "happy traveler."

SGs very much on my mind tonight, future reader.

Where are they now? Why did they leave?

Just do not get.

Letter comes, family celebrates, girl sheds tears, stoically packs bag, thinks, Must go, am family's only hope. Puts on brave face, promises she will return as soon as contract complete. Her mother feels, father feels: We cannot let her go. But they do. They must.

Whole town walks girl to train station/bus station/ferry stop? More tears, more vows. As train/bus/ferry pulls away, she takes last fond look at surrounding hills/river/quarry/shacks, whatever, i.e., all she has ever known of world, saying to self, Be not afraid, you will return, + return in victory, w/big bag of gifts, etc., etc.

And now?

No money, no papers. Who will remove microline? Who will give her job? When going for job, must fix hair so as to hide scars at Insertion Points. When will she ever see her home + family again? Why would she do this? Why would she ruin all, leave our yard? Could have had nice long run w/us. What in the world was she seeking? What could she want so much that would make her pull such desperate stunt?

Just now went to window.

Empty rack in yard, looking strange in moonlight.

Note to self: Call Greenway, have them take ugly thing away.

JIM SHEPARD

The World to Come

FROM *One Story*

Sunday 1 January

FAIR AND VERY cold. This morning, ice in our bedroom for the first time all winter, and in the kitchen, the water froze on the potatoes as soon as they were washed. Landscapes of frost on the windowpanes.

With little pride and less hope and only occasional and uncertain intervals of happiness, we begin the new year. Let me at least learn to be uncomplaining and unselfish. Let me feel gratitude for what I have: some strength, some sense of purpose, some capacity for progress. Some esteem, some respect, and some affection. Yet I cannot say I am improved in any manner, unless it be preferable to be wider in sensation and experience.

My husband has since our acquisition of this farm kept a diary to help him see the year whole, and plan and space his work. In his memorandum book he numbers each field and charges to each the manure, labor, seed &c and then credits each with each crop. This way he knows what each crop and field pays from year to year. He asked me as of last spring once we lost our Nellie to keep in addition a list in a notebook of matters that might otherwise go overlooked, from tools lent out to bills outstanding. But there is no record in these dull and simple pages of the most passionate circumstances of our seasons past, no record of our emotions or fears, our greatest joys or most piercing sorrows.

*

When I think of our old farm I think of rocks. My father hauled rocks for our driveway and rocks for our dooryard and rocks for the base on which our chimney was set. There were rock piles in every fence corner, miles of stone walls separating our fields, and stone bridges so that we might cross dry-shod over our numerous little water courses. Piles of rocks were always appearing and growing and every time we plowed we would have a new crop. As a toddler, my first tasks were filling the wood box and picking rocks out of new-plowed ground. My father before his day began would say to me, "While I'm gone, you can pick up the rocks on this or that piece, and when you get that done, you can play." And when he returned that sundown I'd still be in that field to which he'd pointed, on my hands and knees, in tears, the job always less than half done.

My sister's features were so fine that my mother liked to sketch them by lamplight, and her spirit was equally engaging, but when it came to others' affections, circumstances doomed me to striving and anxiety. I grew like a pot-bound root all curled in upon itself.

I resolve to strive even more fully for some of my former patience. And to remember that it was got at by practice. What most of us really need is simply to make habitual what we already know.

"Welcome, sweet day of rest" says the hymn and Sunday is most welcome for its few hours of quiet ease. A series of phaetons on the road despite the cold. Were it not for worship all of the ladies hereabouts would be in danger of becoming perfect recluses. As for me, I no longer attend. After the calamity of Nellie's loss, what calm I enjoy does not derive from the notion of a better world to come. In the far field, foxes at play on their hind legs, wrestling like boys. The wind heavy at intervals. The snow is falling from the trees about the house so that the liberated limbs straighten up like a man released from debt.

Old Mr. Manning who's been very low for several weeks died this morning.

The ink stopper has rolled on me and ruined a whole half-entry. Why is ink like a fire? Because it is a good servant and a hard master.

Sunday 8 January

A strong cold wind blowing all day from the west. Fried two chickens and made biscuits for breakfast. I want to purchase a dictionary. I have two dollars to spare and can't imagine I could expend it better to my own satisfaction. My self-education seems the only way to keep my unhappiness from overwhelming me. I will recommence as well with my long-neglected algebra. Some time not working during the week is always wise. The bow forever bent loses its power.

An hour spent this morning chopping and spreading old turnips on the snow for the sheep. Dyer has culled the wisest of the rams to be set aside for sale in the spring, to let someone else have the pleasure of matching wits with them.

Nothing stirring outside except Tallie's dog, who makes the rounds of the neighboring farms after woodchucks the way a doctor might visit his patients. Lurid clouds are rolling up against the wind. Dyer holds that the first twelve days of January portend the weather for the next twelve months. So that our fine day on the 4th promises good weather for the spring planting in April, the fourth month, and a storm tomorrow will guarantee trouble for the September harvest. He has spent the time I've been writing this reading an article in the *Rural New Yorker,* "The Inutility of Sporadic Reform." He seems pained at my skepticism as to his weather acumen and smiles at me every so often. My heart to him is like a pond to a crane: he wades round it, going in as far as he dares, and then attempts to snatch up what little fish come shoreward from the center.

He has a severe cut through the thumbnail.

Sunday 15 January

Deep snow. Cold. A shovel and broom necessary on the porch before light. Tallie called here after breakfast. She and Dyer chatted a few minutes in the sitting room before he left to see to the cows. Her husband is spending the day killing his hogs with a hired hand. She said after Dyer left that she hoped she wasn't intruding, and that it was the dullest of all things to have an ignorant neighbor come by and spoil an entire Sunday afternoon. I assured her that she was welcome and that I knew the feeling of which she spoke, and that during the widow Weldon's visits I always imagine I've been plunged up to my eyes in a vat of the prosaic. She took my hand as she laughed. She said she'd gotten the widow going on the county levy and that the woman's few ideas were like marbles on a level floor: they had no power to move themselves but rolled equally well in whichever direction you pushed them.

There seems to be something going on between us that I cannot unravel. Her manner is calm and mild and gracious, and yet her spirits seem to quicken at the prospect of further conversation with me. In the winter sun through the window, her skin had an underflush of rose and violet that disconcerted me until I looked away. I told her how pleasant it was finally to be getting to know her, and she responded that the first few times she had spied me she had kept to herself and thought, "Oh, I wish to get acquainted with her." And then, she said, she'd wondered what she would do if we were introduced.

She asked if Dyer was as sober when it came to the cows as he sounded and I told her that he deemed cows needed not only a uniform and plentiful diet but also perfect quiet, and warm and dry stabling in the winter. He was continually exhorting our neighbors to either enlarge their barns or diminish their stock. I admitted that at times if a cow was provokingly slow to drink I might push its head down into the bucket, and he would tell me that anyone who couldn't school herself to patience had no business with cows. Tallie said that her father had scolded her the same way, having assigned her work in the dairy barn at a very early age, which had become an ongoing vexation for him, since she had not been in favor of the idea. We compared childhood beds, mine in which the straw was always breaking up and matting together and hers that was as hard, she claimed, as the pharoah's heart. She asked if Dyer had also been raised Free Will Baptist and I told her he liked to say that he was indeed a member of the church but that he didn't work very hard at the trade. She said she felt the same.

She described how restlessness had been her lot for as far back as she could conceive, and I told her how when I was young I would think, "What a wasted day! I have accomplished nothing, and have neither learned anything nor grown in any way." She said her mother had always assured her that having children would resolve that dilemma, and I told her my mother had made the same claim. A short silence followed. Eventually we heard Dyer tromping about with his boots in the mudroom, and she exclaimed about the time, and said she must be getting on. I thanked her for coming and told her that I'd missed her. She answered that it was pleasant to be missed.

Sunday 22 January

Frigid night. Wintry morning. Dyer's third day with the fever. At sunup he had a spasm but he was restored by an enema of molasses, warm water, and lard. Also a drop of turpentine next to his nose. His feet are now soaking in a warm basin. After breakfast I was emptying the kitchen slops and heard, off by the canal, several discharges of guns or pistols.

Dyer brought me as his bride to his house five years after he had begun to farm. In the journal I kept for a few months back then, I noted the night to have been cloudy and cool. We had about thirty-six acres that was not muck swamp or bottomland. Of those thirty-six perhaps one-third was hillside covered with scattered timber from which all of the best woods had been culled. It was not the ideal situation, but we all wish we had land of none but the best quality and laid out just right in every respect for tillage.

My mother had married my father when she was very young, without much consideration and after a short acquaintance, and had had to learn in the bitter way of experience that there was no sympathy between them. She always felt that she had not the energy to avert an evil, but the fortitude to bear most that would be laid upon her. She always seemed possessed of a secret conviction that she had left much undone that she still ought to do.

Dyer, as the second son of my father's closest neighbor, helped out with numberless tasks around our farm for many years. He admired what he viewed as my practical good sense, my efficient habits, and my handy ways. As a suitor he was generous but not just, and affectionate but not constant. I was appreciative of his virtues and unconvinced of his suitability, but reminded by my family that more improvement might be in the offing. Because, as they say, it's a long lane that never turns. And so our hands were joined if our hearts not knitted together.

As a boy he made his own steam engines by fashioning boilers out of discarded tea kettles and sled shoes, and I have no doubt he would have been happier if allowed to follow the natural bent of his mind; but forces of circumstance compelled him to take up a business for which he had not the least love. He admitted this to me frankly during his courtship, but also maintained that with good health and push and a level head, there is always an excellent chance for a fellow willing to work. And if one's head went wrong, one could always level it up in good time, particularly if one was fortunate in one's choice of partner.

He believes that one should always live within one's income, misfortune excepted. He believes every farmer should talk over business matters with his wife; and then when he preaches thrift, she will know its necessity as well as he. Or she will be able to demonstrate to him why he worries too excessively. He feels he can never fully rid himself of his load. And I'm certain that because his mind is in such a bad state, it affects his whole system. He said to me this morning that contentment was like a friend he never gets to see.

Sunday 29 January

The night once again bitter cold. Despite an amaranthine fatigue, I'm unable to sleep. No sounds outside but the cracking and popping of the porch joints. Up in the dark to lay the kitchen fire, and through the window in the moonlight I could see one lean hare and not a creature stirring to chase it.

Snowpudding and corncakes for breakfast. Dyer up and about. He is much improved and has been given a dose of calomel and rhubarb. He intends running panels of new fence later this afternoon. Yesterday the timber was so hard-frozen the wedges wouldn't drive.

The previous night's unhappiness hangs between us like a veil. My reluctance seems to have become his shame. His nightly pleasures, which were never numerous, I have curtailed even more. He has been patient for what he believed to be a reasonable interval when it came to my grieving but has begun to pursue with more persistence the subject of another child. And in our bed, when he asks only for what is his right, I take his hand and lay it aside and tell him it is too soon, too soon, too soon. And so the one on whom all happiness should depend is the one who causes the discontent.

I can see that when I am unhappy his mind is in all ways out of turn, and so throughout the morning I made a greater effort at cheer. I shook out and stropped his coat while with a good deal of fuss he prepared himself for the long walk to the timberline. Inside his boots he wears his heavy woolen socks greased with a thick mixture of beeswax and tallow. Before leaving he suggested once again that perhaps the time had come for us to have our sleigh. He's laid aside in the barn's workroom some oak planks and a borrowed compass saw, which can make a cut following a curved line. He seemed to want only a smile and yet I was unable to provide it.

My mother told me more than once that when she prayed, her first object was to thank God that we'd been spared from harm throughout the day; her second was to ask forgiveness for all of her sins of omission and commission; and her third was to thank Him for not having dealt with her in a manner commensurate to all of the offenses for which she was responsible.

Sunday 5 February

Not too cold, though the moon this morning indicated foul weather. On the porch after sunup I could hear the low chirping of the sparrows in the snow-buried hedgerows. Breakfast of hot biscuit, sweet potatoes, oatmeal, and coffee. Dyer cutting timber for firewood.

A visit from Tallie yet again, and she came bearing gifts for my birthday! She arrayed on the table before us a horse chestnut, a pear—in February!—a needle case, and a pocket atlas. She brought as well for us to share a little pot of applesauce with an egg on top. While it was warming she reported that Mrs. Nottoway had had an accident; a horse fell on her, on the ice. Her leg by all accounts is crushed and Tallie is planning to pay a visit there later this afternoon. Tallie herself had an accident, she noted, on the way here, her foot having plunged into the brook through the thin ice in our field. I made her remove her boot and stocking and warmed her toes and ankle in my hands. For some few minutes we sat, just like that. The warmth of the stove and the smell of the applesauce filled our little room, and she closed her eyes and murmured as though speaking to herself how pleasant it was.

I asked after her health and she said she had generally been well, though she suffered chronically from painful tooth infections and the rash they call St. Anthony's Fire. I asked after her husband's health and she said that at times they seemed yoked in opposition to each other. I asked what had caused the latest disagreement and she said that he recorded the names of trespassers, whom he easily sighted across the open fields, in his journals, and that when she had asked what sort of retribution he planned, they had had an exchange that was so cheerless and unpleasant that they had agreed to shun the subject, since it was one on which they clearly had no common feeling. She had then resolved to come visit me, so that her day would not be given entirely over to such meanness.

I was still holding her foot and unsure how to express the fervor with which I wished her a greater share of happiness. I reminded myself: (1) Others first. (2) Correct and necessary speech only. And (3) don't waste a moment. I told her that Dyer thought Finney had many estimable qualities. She responded that her husband had a separate ledger, as well, in which he kept an accounting of whom she visited and how long she stayed. When I asked why, she said she was sure she had no idea. When I in my surprise had nothing to add to her response, she fell silent for some minutes, and then finally removed her foot from my hands' cradle and brought the subject to a close by remarking that she'd given up trying to fathom all the queer varieties of his little world. I was oddly moved, watching her try to wriggle her foot back into her stocking. We enjoyed the applesauce and I exclaimed again on the surprise of my gifts and we chatted for another three-quarters of an hour before she took her leave. As she stood on the porch, bundled against the cold, and stepped forward into the wind, I told her I thought she was quite the most pleasing and thoughtful person I knew. Because I remember how appreciation made me feel, when I was just a girl, and I had resolved way back then to praise those who took up important roles in my future life whenever they seemed worthy of it. Dyer returned with two wagonloads of timber minutes after she departed, and once it was fully unloaded and stacked and he was able to take his ease before the fire, he gave me his birthday gifts as well: a box of raisins, another needle case, and six tins of sardines.

Sunday 12 February

The blizzard that began this last Wednesday continues with a stupendous NE wind. The snow has drifted eight feet deep. The barn is holding up well and there is feed for the stock, but the henhouse has fallen in on one side. Half the chickens lost. We dug ice and snow from their dead open mouths in an attempt to revive them. I'm told the Friday newspaper reported a train of forty-two cars from the center of Vermont having arrived at the Albany depot with snow nearly two feet thick on its roofs. Of course there is no question of visiting or receiving anyone; we are in all ways weather-bound. I found myself vexed all afternoon by the realization that I might have taken a walk to Tallie's farm during a clear spell on Friday, but milk spilled on dry ground can't be gathered up. By the fire Dyer and I made ready to sketch out on some writing paper our plans for the sleigh, but soon laid them by, since as a project it was so ill-conceived and weakly begun. We retreated to separate corners, myself to darn and mend and my husband to his ledger books.

He finally looked so distraught that I asked how long the feed in the barn would sustain the stock, should the weather not improve. He estimated five days before he'd have to go to the mill, whatever the weather. He said the newspaper had quoted a prediction that the storm would let up by Tuesday, based on an expert's consultation of a goose bone. I let that prognostication sit between us while I repaired the heel of a sock, and he took his hair in both his hands and said with surprising vehemence that we offered and offered our hard work and God refused it by delivering brutal weather.

I joined him on the settee and reminded him that the best management always succeeds best, but in a real crisis of Nature, we are all at Another's mercy. He seemed unconsoled. We listened to the wind. We watched the fire. He recounted again the story of his poor mother's ordeal when just a child.

She had been seven and had awoken before dawn and gone to her window, and she told him that a flash of light that had seemed to run along the ground had preceded the earthquake. Her dogs when they saw it had given a sudden bark. A far-off murmur had floated to her on the still night air, followed by a slight ruffling wind. And then came the rumbling, and a sudden shock under which the house and barn had tottered and reeled. Latches leaped up and doors flew open. Timbers shook from mortises, hearthstones grated apart, pan lids sprang up and clattered back down in the kitchen, and pewter and glass pitched from their shelves. Their chimney tumbled down. The oxen and cows bellowed. She told him that she'd heard her mother calling for her, but she'd been unable to tear herself from her window, where she could see the birds even in the dark fluttering in the air as if fearing to again alight, and she could hear the river writhe and roil. She'd had to follow her brothers as they'd jumped down the collapsed staircase, and then the sun had risen and greeted with its complacent face her disconsolate and fearful family. And as soon as it set again that night, their fright had returned, a fright, his mother had told him, she had never again fully dispelled. For what was safe if the solid earth could do this? Before he finished his account, I stopped his lips with my fingers and led him to our bed, undressing him as I might a boy. We shared any number of caresses and he seized my hair in his fists and held my head to his own and passionately declared his love. Early this evening I rose while he slept and made us some beef tea and cornbread for dinner. For dessert, I cooked a very unsatisfactory rice pudding.

Sunday 19 February

Sleet, and ice, and a gloom so pervasive, all our lamps had to remain lit at midday. Both of us much borne down of mind all morning, and for the past five days. Dyer able to get to the mill.

Sunday 26 February

Bright sun. Biscuit and dried mackerel for breakfast. Tallie visiting her father in Oneonta. A lonesome and tedious week.

The Cobbs lost their son to pneumonia a few days ago. I think last week. Their only child. Dyer was loath to tell me, but the memories of Nellie came on only slowly after he had done so.

I never showed our daughter a face free of fatigue; the night I bore her I had just finished dipping twenty-four dozen candles, and she never seemed to lose her head colds and we had many hard nights. I never felt blessed with enough time for her when she was well and it was that much harder watching over her during her illnesses. I spent my days beyond distress, fearing the consequences of her sickliness, until when she was two years and five months on, she suffered an attack of the bilious fever, pleurisy, bowel problems, and croup. She was treated with bayberry and marsh rosemary to scour the stomach and bowels, and a tea of valerian and lady's slipper for the fever, and though she rallied for a day or two, when she gazed at me, she seemed to know that even if her condition were to be coaxed into a little clemency, it wouldn't spare her. The night came when she asked, "Mommy, take me up," and I lifted her from her bed while Dyer slept. She asked for my comb, and when I gave it to her she combed my hair and then smoothed it with her palm on my head and then asked me to lie down with her and put her arms around my neck and did not rise again.

Since the norms of polite society require that private woe be concealed from public view, I was allowed to sequester myself away for some months following. There I remained speechless. I was surrounded by objects that, if silent everywhere else, here had a voice that rang out with her presence. And I never forgot her face that final night, because there was something so affecting about mute and motionless grief in a child so young.

Sunday 4 March

Windy and very bright. Dined with the Hill family last evening. On our way there we saw hunters with ducks over their shoulders and boys skating on the river. A most excellent dinner of seven dishes of meat, four of vegetables, pickles and a pie, tarts and cheese, and wine and cider. This morning a breakfast of only oatmeal, jam, and coffee. Mr. Tarbell came and hung the bacon. Dyer is augmenting the padding in the cow stables with his hoardings of leaves and old straw, which he believes to increase the manure output.

It seemed Tallie would never appear, but time and the needle wear through the longest morning. When she arrived my heart was like a leaf borne over a rock by rapidly moving water. She said that a few days earlier their hired hand had pulled down a box of eggs and broke nearly two dozen, and that Finney had announced to him that he was unlucky to eggs and was no longer allowed to approach them. Her husband believed that he suffered a great deal from the carelessness of hired hands, she said. She claimed that old Mr. Holt was said to have swum his horse over the canal despite the cold, and that the widow Weldon's son had been contracted to carry the mail on skis, but that otherwise there was no news. She was much better in her health. She was overjoyed to see me.

She said she'd spent the previous two days rendering the lard from the hogs and making soap. She said her husband was even more out of sorts than usual, and that he had mentioned again the idea of migrating west. I told her that I considered migrating west a bad idea, since my uncle had moved to Ohio and had come to a desperate end. She asked if that wasn't where my sister had settled, and I said no, that my sister was out near Lackawanna, and that her husband was a manufacturer of horse cultivators. She asked me to tell her more about my sister and I told her how Rebecca had always loved legends of Indians and Quakers and county witches, and how our church had frowned on dancing but had allowed kissing games, and how she had been a champion at Copenhagen and Needle's Eye. She had met her future husband at an agricultural society fair in which she had been named Queen of the Livery. Tallie remarked with some wryness that it sounded very grand, and I wanted to embrace her for that kindness alone.

I asked about her brothers and she answered only about the one who had survived. She said that once he was old enough to stand, he'd gone round with a sling that he claimed was identical to the weapon with which David had slain Goliath. He never killed anyone but he did give his family some anxious moments. She said that when he was fourteen she'd caught him skinning baby rabbits alive and he'd told her that the rabbits were used to it. She said that a year later he'd knotted a rope on his wrist and their steer's horn, and had been dragged cross-country. When their mother had asked what made him do such a thing, he had said he hadn't gone a half-mile before he could see his mistake.

We talked of parents. I told her of remembering my father telling my mother that she shouldn't feel bad about me because sometimes the plain grew up to be enormously wise. She told me that only once in her life did her father say an encouraging word, though he said plenty of the other kind. She said that she refused to offer an excuse for her constant disobedience to him, but that she did believe now that her father had done her a far greater wrong. I said that I was sure she'd been as good as gold and she answered that she had been the kind of willful child that no frown would deny nor words restrain, and that because of that her father had often taken her in one hand and a strap in the other, and brought the two together until she had had enough.

By then we were in late afternoon light and Dyer had again returned to shed his outer clothing in the mudroom with maximum fidget and fuss. She stood and composed herself, and touched a finger to my shoulder. I felt, looking at her expression, as if she were in full sail on a flood tide while I bobbed along down backwaters. And yet I never saw on her countenance the indifference of the fortunate toward the less fortunate. At the mudroom door my husband greeted us before passing inside, and Tallie put her cheek to mine before leaving. I watched her ascend the snowy path toward her land, her dog running to greet her. While Dyer rubbed his lower extremities for warmth, I added to our hearth fire, contrary to my usual custom. It cheered the room a little but everything still looked desolate. That is me, I thought, taking my chair. One emotion succeeds another.

Sunday 11 March

A sloppy day. The wind chilly but with hints of a warmth. Up early. Ham and potatoes and coffee for breakfast. Scalded my wrist with boiling fat. Applied flour and hamamelis, since we have no plaster.

A bad week for burns. Dyer and Finney were summoned on Thursday to tend to Mrs. Manning's little girl, who had just been severely burned. They reported that they accomplished all that they could for the little sufferer until the doctor arrived. It's thought she didn't die of the burn but of pneumonia from taking a chill from the water thrown upon her. She complained of being cold from that moment until she died.

A cardinal pair has adopted the house. I've been laying out seed to sustain them, and sometimes when I forget they fly to the kitchen window to remind me. The female is the prettiest muted green.

The week spent sowing clover. What's needed are still mornings, ideally after frost heaves, when the sun has thawed the soil's surface just enough to fasten the seed in the mud. We sow with a Cahoon, which hangs on a pair of suspenders and throws out a continuous stream with a handle-crank. On Friday we had to finish in a headwind, which was hard on the eyes. I look as if I've been on a spree.

My mother's mother was born in 1780 in a log house right here in Schoharie County. I wonder now at the courage and the resourcefulness of those women who fared forth, not knowing where they were being led, to begin to chip into the wilderness the foundations of a civilization. Maybe they found love and kisses in their loved ones' regard, and a certain high hopefulness that we do not possess.

Astonishment and joy. Astonishment and joy. Astonishment and joy. I write with only the small hand lamp burning, as late as it is.

Dyer asked after breakfast apropos of nothing if my friend Tallie intended to visit us again today and when I informed him that I expected she would, he gave no further sign of having heard me, but went about the business of gathering his outer garments and eventually left the house.

Tallie arrived some minutes later with a handkerchief to her nose. When she heard I was well she claimed to be disappointed and said she'd hoped to compare colds. I showed her my burn.

When she had completed quizzing me on the various remedies I had applied, we talked of our admiration for each other. She said she had from her earliest childhood an instinct that shrank from selfishness or icy regard, and that she cherished the safety she felt when in my presence. She said she'd composed a poem titled "O Sick and Miserable Heart Be Still."

I told her how as a little girl I'd always imagined cultivating my intellect and doing something for the world, and she gazed at me as though I'd said the absolute perfect thing, and I thrilled at the possibility of having done so. And when I said nothing more she wrung both of my hands with hers, and said that that moment in which we were carried in triumph somewhere for having done something great and good, or we were received at home in a shower of tears of joy: was it really possible that such a moment had not yet come, for either of us? When I regained my voice, I said I thought that it had. Or it could. She asked what I imagined. And I said, astonishing myself with my own dauntlessness, that I loved how our encircling feelings left nothing out for us to miss or seek.

When her expression remained as it had been, I added that perhaps I presumed too much. The pyre in the hearth collapsed with a little show of sparks. We both gazed upon the flaming logs. Finally she murmured, so that I could just hear, that it was not those who showed the least who felt the least.

Her pacing dog's toenails were audible on the ice on the porch. She leaned forward and offered me her lips to kiss and then turned her cheek, which I then kissed instead. I asked why she hadn't done as she was going to do, and she had no reply. So I took her hands, and then her shoulders, and with our eyes fully open brought my mouth to hers.

She smelled of rosewater and an herb I couldn't identify. Her taste was suffusing and sweet and entirely full. Her mouth was at first diffident, and then feathery and tender, and then welcoming and immersive.

She worried I would catch her cold. She took in her breath at the passion of my response. We skidded our chairs closer and had no thought of peril nor satiety, listening to the wind's increase outside like an index of our exhilaration and starting up at every sound of her dog on the porch. There was a sweet biscuity smell to her hairline. Eventually she pulled free and bade me open my eyes and said she was leaving.

Dyer when he returned noted all that I still had not yet accomplished when it came to my evening's responsibilities, and asked with some irritation as I stood over the pump and sink if I required assistance. I came very near answering that I did, I felt so undone by my Tallie's departure. The moment she had left I was like a skiff pushed out to sea with neither hand nor helm to guide it.

Sunday 18 March

Falling weather soon, whether rain or snow. For three straight days my bowels have remained unmoved. A spell of dizziness and shortness of breath this morning, and no appetite, so Dyer made his own breakfast. He says that old Mr. Holt while returning from a sale in town was badly beaten by two strangers, so that he had to be hauled the rest of the way to his home in his own cart. Their intention had been to kill him but they were mistaken as to who he was.

Dyer also claims to have had many unpleasant dreams, owing to his mind. Otherwise he has been notably silent all day. I am happy to be left to my solitude. Thankful to my Maker for such blessings &c.

When still just a little girl I used to hope that God with a voice as loud as thunder would proclaim that all of my sins were forgiven. Now I know that I can wait until doomsday and I still will not hear any such thing. And yet the repentant sinner must actively seek God's forgiveness instead of waiting for Him to act.

Hard labor all week, sunup to sundown, helping Dyer in the outer fields with the smoothing harrow and the roller. Old Bill our horse has the heaves. Both of us fit to drop by Saturday eve. Both of us mournful this morning. Both of us seemed to have spent the day listening for footfalls on the porch. And yet when my thoughts turn to her I think with special heat, *Why* are we to be divided? Merciful Father turn the channel of events.

Still feeling poorly by nightfall, and so unable to cook. A dinner of tea, bread and butter, and cold ham.

Sunday 25 March

A wild mixture of wind and rain and clouds and sunshine. Muddy March has dragged on like a log through a wet field.

Downhearted and woebegone. A poor night. Fried corncakes and ham for breakfast. Poor Dyer suffering from a painful cough.

Opened the mudroom door this afternoon to Dyer having returned from the fields, and he said with some asperity that it was pleasant to be greeted by the smile one values above all others, only to see that smile vanish because it's been met by one's own presence, instead of someone else's.

He sat with me a while, then, still in his boots. I asked if he wanted more of the ham and he said no. I told him that when he next went to town we needed calico and muslin and buttons and shoe thread. He asked if he was troubling me, sitting with me like this, and when I assured him he was not, he remarked that he had learned consideration of others. And that he had learned the need of human sympathy by the unfulfilled want of it. I told him that I felt as though I had provided him with much sympathy throughout our years together, and he allowed as to how that had been so. We then waited again, sitting facing each other, and I thought with some pity how his life seems equal parts furious work and resignation. When Tallie arrived he greeted her and seemed in no hurry to take his leave. He remained sunk in his chair for nearly a half an hour while we exchanged pleasantries and news before he finally rose to his feet and left without announcing his business.

Once his figure was out of sight through the windows, I asked in a low voice after her spirits. She was content to repeat only that she was feeling doleful and unreasonable and unaware of what it was she wished. I asked what it was she then required of me, and she said, responding to my tone, that she wished me to be gentler. I asked again, chastened, what she desired, and she answered that she wanted to lay bare for me all of the hoardings of her imagination. I said nothing. Although I often speak before I think, I can keep still on occasion. She said our kisses had swept through her the way measles had the poor Indians, laying waste to everything. She said she had told herself to abolish all desire for comfort or any sort of happiness and then had immediately abandoned her resolution.

She asked that I speak. I almost cried out, How should I have known what was happening to me? There were no instruction booklets of which I was aware. I told her I could feel something rising in me as she approached, like hair on the back of a dog. I told her the thought of her during the week was my shelter, the way the chickadees took to the depths of the evergreens to keep the snow and ice and wind at bay. I told her that I believed that we were now encountering that species of education that proceeds from being forced to confront what we never before acknowledged.

She asked if we might share some tea and was silent until it was brewed. She said she believed that intimacy increased good will, and that if that were the case, then every moment we spent together would further tie happiness to utility. Wouldn't our farms benefit from our more joyful labor? Wouldn't our husbands' burdens be lightened?

We spent some additional interval thereafter consoling each other. We allowed ourselves some gentle excitement. And after she had departed I looked round the room and thought, "She's gone and it's as if she'd never been."

Sunday 1 April

Warm and windy with the appearance of rain. First day this spring we could go all afternoon without a fire. Fried chicken and potatoes for breakfast. The morning spent manuring the onions.

Dyer took the wagon after breakfast without explanation. My burn seems to be healing poorly. Tallie here earlier than her usual time, and we embraced in the mudroom as if rescued. She mentioned as if in passing that her dog would provide ample notice of arriving friends or strangers. Having done so she led me to our chairs and delivered herself over to our kissing as if it were the most urgent of errands. When I withdrew for breath she kept her face close, describing along my mouth delicate patterns with her tongue. During our longer kisses her breathing grew stronger.

When we separated, we took each other in. Myself, overquiet. Tallie, flushed and on the lookout. Together we made for a distressing pair.

I took her hands and she expressed pain at my sadness. She asked if I'd been to town during the week, and when I told her I hadn't, she reported that they were cleaning out the drain under the streets along the fork and that several people were down with the fever.

She added that her husband had told her that he didn't consider that he had a wife, and that he would not lie with a woman if it required a contention. She said that she had informed him that he shouldn't have anything to do with her; that she was opposed to it; that she was not willing. I was shocked and asked what his response had been. She said he had had no response. I asked if she believed he had given up on the notion of children. She said she had no insights to share on that question.

We were silent for some time, then, out of respect for our predicament. I asked her husband's age and she said he was nineteen years her senior and had been born in 1811, which would make him forty-five. I asked about his demeanor and she said that as mealtime conversation he had lately begun giving great credit to reports of men living far from town who had worked to poison and thereby kill their wives.

I asked if she really believed he would acquiesce to the notion of no sons. I asked if she believed he resented her visits here with any special fervor, and she said she thought not. We worked ourselves nonetheless into a state of alarm, which was then only assuaged by more embraces and two or three extended kisses of great sobriety.

She admitted to having been at work on another poem, which she had brought to show me, but she allowed me to see only the opening lines, which read: *I love to have gardens, I love to have plants / I love to have air but I don't love ants.* I told her I could not support the rhyme, which saddened her. She held the poem between us and together we studied it as if it were the incomplete map of our escape route. Finally she said she felt that when she drew near, I would retreat, and when she kept still, I would return but remain at a fixed distance, like those sparrows that will stay in the farmyard but not enter the house. I responded that in her presence I felt perpetually as if I were ready to take her by the hand and lead her to my garden gate and to say: everything in here is yours; come and go and gather as you like.

She also unwrapped from the same packet in which she had secreted the poem a sprig from her favorite cedar, which I told her I would plant where it would forever stay green.

After she left I took myself outside into the sunshine and spread some feed for the surviving chickens. Upon Dyer's return he found me taking my rest in the shade and kissed me, before withdrawing to refill the water buckets. After a dinner of duck and beets and sweet potatoes we enjoyed some little company together.

Sunday 8 April

Very damp, cloudy, and cool. Smoky. Perhaps the forest is somewhere on fire. A breakfast of hotcakes and custard and pickled peaches. Dyer seems now quite worn down at bedtime with grievance and care. We fear his cough is producing a decline. A syrup of old wine, flaxseed, and a medicinal called Balsom of Life seems to have helped. This morning he made me a trellis for the lima beans and shot a crow and filled it with salt to be hung in the shed over the corn to warn off others of its kind. The whole house seems both angry and repentant. God help us.

No word from Tallie. At midday I stood off the back porch in the sun, my face turned in her direction. Above me a circling hawk used a single cloud as his parasol.

Sunday 15 April

Rain in torrents nearly all night. The lane is flooded and the ditches brim full. This morning only a slight shower.

A breakfast of oatmeal alone. Prepared the pea sticks for the first crop of peas and drowned the barn cat's kittens. The new wheat because of the holes in our fencing is still exposed to the hogs, which we have driven out several times already. We keep identifying new holes, which we cannot adequately repair for lack of time. Thus we find our enterprise sinking, level by level.

A dispute with Dyer over the windows, open vs. shut. Unable to sit still afterward. Our quarrels always throw me out of harness. How many are there that have a happy fireside? Broad is the gate that leads to dissatisfaction and many wander through. Such is the effect of absence from what we love. But I have always been morose. My mother used to call me her rain crow, because she said time with me was like standing in an endless drizzle.

After Dyer retired I took his spyglass and crossed the fields in the darkness to Tallie's farm, approaching the front windows of her home as close as I dared and fixing through the kitchen glass, after some patient searching, her motionless figure in relief against the darkness within. Her features were still. By turning the lens-piece I drew her face nearer to mine and held it there until she turned away. Could I have been seen from the inside? I felt a giddiness like the violence of the impulse that sends a floating branch far out over a waterfall's precipice before it plummets. Her dog's barking drew her husband out onto the porch and I made my way back, plunging in over my boots in the mud.

At sunset, earlier, a good three minutes of the honking of mallards, winging their way northward. By what faith do they arrive at their destination? I imagine them alighting at some marshy pond, where one by one their scattered kind arrives in safety, there to be together.

A terribly bad spring so far but the clover has come up through it all and is all right.

Sunday 22 April

Finally a glimpse of her after three weeks of no word. She and her husband stopped their wagon outside our house to invite us to dinner this Saturday next. They were on their way again before Tallie and I could exchange much more than a look. The Nottoways report that our hogs have continued to stray into their fields, as well, and threaten increasingly harsh measures against them, including putting out their eyes and driving them into the river. The cardinals are enjoying the hornbeam and the catkins on the birches. The female seems to prefer feeding on the ground.

Cool, but warm enough for no fire in the sitting room.

Sunday 29 April

Rain all week long, so heavy that it broke down the mill. All of our ditches are running to overflow. The lower clover field is swamped.

Two of our hogs are still loose, since they are ailing and Dyer believes a hog is a good doctor and can cure himself if he can find the medicine he needs.

For dinner Saturday night Tallie served us ham, beef, duck, potatoes, beets, pickled cucumbers, biscuits, and cornbread. We commended her on her labor and her husband said that he recalled a day when every family was fed, clothed, shod, sheltered, and warmed from the products a wife gathered from within her own fence line. I said that it must have been two full days that Tallie had spent on this feast, and she responded that her mother had always said that the week's end was always the hardest part of the week.

Her husband while we ate offered up what news had lately occurred. We were all uneasy to find him so voluble. He mentioned that the Mannings' third daughter was now one week old. He said that old Mr. Holt had apparently by some means pitched himself forward out of his cart, which had then passed over his back with its load of five hundred pounds, and that because of the mud the doctor says he is not severely hurt. He said that he had heard, when examining the damage at the mill, of news from Middleburgh: that a man down there had of last week been admitted to jail for shooting his wife in the face.

There were silences. Tallie seemed to be keeping strict custody of her eyes. I remarked upon the duck and the men discussed for an interval the old shovel plow, which Dyer compared to dragging a cat by the tail. I marveled at the size and power of their hanging lamp, and Tallie answered that it was eighty candlepower and that she had induced her husband to purchase it so that everyone could read with equal ease all around the room. Finney said that he believed that even if he had been brought up not to read overmuch, he should give his children every chance to do so.

The rain came under discussion. Finney said that no matter what misfortunes arrived at his doorstep, he would seek improvement of his lot with his own industry; he would study his options closely and attend to everything to which he'd believed he had already adequately attended, but with more vehemence. Dyer commended him and reminded the table that when success comes, someone is working hard. Finney said as an example that when he'd first begun farming he'd been so vexed by his inability to stop his dog's barking one January that during a storm he'd held the animal around the corner of his barn in a gale until it had frozen to death.

I replied after a moment that I found that reprehensible, but he seemed not to hear. I felt sure I was white as a sheet. I could see from Tallie's face that she'd heard this story before. He held forth to Dyer about his hinged harrow, complaining that the spikes that caught the rocks and roots were forever breaking. He told Tallie, once he saw that we had finished eating, to bring the dessert, and

I said we were stuffed and she said that he insisted on his pastries and preserved fruits and creams, and rose to clear the table and fetch them. I excused myself to assist her, and in the kitchen I asked in a whisper about her situation and she shushed me with a shake of her head. I asked after a bruise on her neck and she said she'd taken a fall over the fence. I answered with some petulance and anxiety that I hadn't heard, and she responded that many things had happened to her about which I hadn't heard.

Back at table her husband's mood seemed to have darkened. He served the pastries and fruit and creams himself, leaving only her plate empty. "Is your wife being punished?" Dyer joked. And when Finney chose not to answer, Tallie finally said that it was not in her husband's temper either to give or to receive. He responded that he had lately been sick in the chest, but as she had expressed no feeling for him, he had been hardened.

The entire ride home my speculation was hectic with dread. I was finally able to ask if Dyer had felt anything amiss, but he shook his head while keeping his attention on Old Bill. Along the river he pointed out a flooding so extensive it had carried away the long wooden bridge at Washington; fragments of it, with the railing still erect, came floating down past us. Hard on its heels followed a tree of enormous length with uptorn roots and branches lashing the current. Once we reached our property he remarked with disgust on one of our line fences that he said hadn't been cleared in all the years I'd been here. I said that it looked perfectly serviceable to me and he said that it looked like a hedge.

Sunday 6 May

No word from Tallie. No visit. A mild and lonesome night. My anxieties cause me between tasks to pace the house like a prisoner. The windows open.

My mother told me once in a fury when I was just a girl that my father asked nothing of her except that she work the garden, harvest the vegetables, pick and preserve the fruit, supervise the poultry, milk the cows, do the dairy work, manage the cooking and cleaning and mending and doctoring, and help out in the fields when needed. She said she'd appeared in his ledger only when she'd purchased a dress. And how have things changed? Daughters are married off so young that everywhere you look a slender and unwilling girl is being forced to stem a sea of tribulations before she's even full grown in height.

Dyer keeping his distance seeing me in such a state. The night fair and warm with the appearance of a coming rain. A shower.

Sunday 13 May

My heart a maelstrom, my head a bedlam. Tallie gone. This morning the widow Weldon on the way to town reported their house and barn to be abandoned. Rushed over there myself, Dyer galloping along behind and calling to me. Their barn, which I passed first, had been emptied of stock and feed. Their front door was open. Some furniture &c was there but most was gone. A dishtowel lay on the kitchen floor. A spatter of blood spread up the wall above the sink. A handprint of the same marked the lintel above the door.

Furious colloquy with Dyer most of the night about the county sheriff's office. He promises tomorrow to make the rounds of the neighbors and if unsatisfied to take our fears there.

Monday 14 May

No work. The Nottoways report spotting their caravan on the county road in the late evening on Friday the 4th, heading NW. Dyer said Mrs. Nottoway believed she spied Tallie's figure alongside her husband's but was unsure. A hired hand, she thought, was driving the second wagon. The sheriff refuses to investigate. Dyer says if I refuse to calm myself he'll lash me to a chair and administer laudanum.

Sunday 20 May

I'm a library without books. I'm a sea of agitation and trepidation and grief. Dyer speaks every so often of how much we have for which to be grateful. The two of us sit violently conscious of the ticking of the clock while he continues to weep at what he imagines to be his poor forgotten self.

Sunday 3 June

A letter this Friday, delivered into my hands by the widow Weldon's son—! In it Tallie apologized for all it could not be. She said she understood that the best of letters were but fractions of fractions. She asked my pardon for having been prevented from offering a proper farewell and regretted that we'd traded one sort of anguish for another.

She said that houses deep in the backwoods always seem to feature something awful and unnatural in their loneliness, and were there only a ruined abbey, the view would be perfect. Their ramshackle roof shed water nicely in dry weather but they had to spread milk pans around the floor when it rained. Still, outside the kitchen there were already anemones and heart's ease and even lovelier flowers, which her ignorance prevented her from naming. She joked that when it came to her new situation, it was only the resilience of her nature that allowed her to overcome such a dismal start.

She said that during what little time she had to herself Finney read to her from the New Testament, but that when it came to the Bible, he was familiar with many passages that had neither entered his understanding nor touched his heart.

She said she had enjoyed herself less these last few weeks than any other female who had ever lived. She said she could not account for her husband's state of mind except her company being intensely disagreeable to him, and that if that were the case she was sorry for it.

She said that force alone would never have carried her to this spot but that she had been induced to act in support of the interest, happiness, and reputation of one she professed to love.

She said that as far as she might estimate we were now only eighty-five miles apart, but that she realized that poor people rarely visit.

She said she had always marveled that her name was so close to mine; didn't I think it strange? Though as with most things, she said, it probably gave her a greater pleasure to tell me than it did me to hear.

She said it was so difficult to write of gratitude, but that she had to begin. She said my companionship had been a spacious community. She said she felt for me a tenderness closer than that of sisters, since her passion had all the honor of election. She said the memory she most cherished was of my turning to her that smile I wore when I saw that I was loved. She said she wished to see me more than she had any chance of making me understand. She said she was unsure what was to come, but that our occasions of joy and trust and care and courage would shine on us and protect us. She said that though the future seemed to admit no relief she would hold me by her fire until we found a season of hope and the beginnings of mercy. She said she had always believed in me. She offered again her heart's thanks for all that I had given. She closed by pledging that any letter with which I responded would become her most closely guarded treasure, and would be preserved and returned to me in the event of her passing.

Cleaned out the shed, which was full of rusty and dusty rubbish. Washed windows and swept for the summer. Beneath it all, the irresistible current of the ongoing composition of my response. I will tell her that God caused this connection, and that what God has joined together let no man put asunder. I will tell her that I imagine the happiest of unions, of the sort in which two families previously at daggers-drawn are miraculously brought together on love's account. I will tell her that our cardinals have come to love the acacia, on which I today counted twelve full branches in flower. I'll describe for her our sudden wealth of fireflies, blown about in the evening breezes.

Fourteen dollars from the sale of our milk and butter.

Tuesday 5 June

A letter to Dyer from Finney informing him that Finney's wife died on Thursday the 24th of May in the full enjoyment of her Christian faith. She was taken on a Wednesday and gone on Thursday. Her husband said he wished all to know that her last prayers were to God to help her love His will even in her bitterness.

Thursday 7 June

Bleary and short of breath from the laudanum. I wake weeping, retire weeping, stand before my various duties weeping. Dyer takes the implements from my hands and finishes whatever tasks I've begun. I still move about the house as though performing in their appointed order my various offices.

He has conveyed my accusations to the sheriff, who was finally induced to visit. Despite some hours without the laudanum I was befogged and wild with anger and grief and the sheriff was left unsettled and wary at my state. Even so he claims to have satisfied himself in person after a two-day ride and interviews with both the bereaved husband and the sheriff of Oneida County that there has been an absence of foul play.

Monday 11 June

Took the wagon and rode to see Finney myself. Dyer refused to permit my departure and then refused to accompany me and then caught up to the cart just at the end of our property and climbed aboard. We were the very picture of anguish, rattling along side by side. A quiet but heavy rain persisted the entire second day.

The house even for that country had a wild and lonely situation. No one answered Dyer's knock or call but the door was ajar and when he pushed it to, Finney was sunk in a chair in the middle of the room, facing us. He seemed unsurprised at our appearance and asked us our business.

At Dyer's silence I gathered enough resolve to overcome my fear and said that we had come in order to learn what had happened to Tallie.

He said he thought that might have been our errand. He said he'd heard us arriving and had taken us for the tin knocker and had brought out all the pails and kettles that needed mending.

It was a hideously dark and dirty kitchen and it grieved me to think of Tallie among its spiders and yellow flies. I asked again for his account and he offered us nothing more than he had offered the sheriff. He remained in his chair and we remained in the doorway. He made no move to light a second lamp.

I said I had ridden three days for more particulars and that I would not leave without more particulars. He said he was not concerned with my desires. None of us said anything further and a mouse scuttled across the floor. He looked at Dyer with contempt. He related, finally, that Tallie had taken a chill and had continued ill for two days. He said he'd treated her with among other remedies a tea of soot and pine-tree roots, which had had some good effect, but that sickness always tests our willingness to bow before the greatest Authority.

He said nothing more after that. I was weeping such that I could barely see. I asked to view her grave and he said he had buried her up in the woods. I asked him to show me the location and he said that if he found us anywhere else on his land once we left his porch we would see what would happen. Dyer told him sharply that there was no cause for threats and that he should keep a civil tongue. He took my arm to lead me out and I pulled free and asked Finney how he lived with himself. He said he'd been sleeping well except for some rheumatism of the knees. He came onto the porch once we were seated on the wagon, and said that on the final day, Tallie had been able to sit up a little, with help, and that her expression at the very end had reminded him of the last afflictions of Mrs. Manning's little girl, who had suffered so with her burns. And I could see on his face that he could see on mine the effect he had desired.

Sunday 24 June

A cut on my hand from a paring knife. Dyer at work in the barn. Night after night we enact our separation. Anxiety is now his family, and discord his home. Dark spirits his company. Captious dignity and moonlit tears his two prevailing states. This love he seeks to win back he fails to apprehend would be only the hulk of a wrecked affection, fitted with new sails.

There is no more uphill business than farming. The most fortunate of us persist without prospering.

Carried off in the night by the immensity of what we promise ourselves and fail.

At one point during Tallie's last visit she expressed regret that I had never crossed the fields to visit her. I imagined telling her of my midnight expedition with the spyglass, but refrained. I joked instead about the need to preserve one's self-respect, and the way I sometimes seemed to believe the only safety to be within. She'd had to look away, as though sharing my shame. Finally she'd said she always feared that she called misfortune down onto those she loved because of her intemperance, and that that thought on occasion had terrorized her. After another silence she asked if I didn't think it eloquent that I had contributed nothing in response to her remark. I told her that I could not imagine what more we could do for each other, and she answered that the imagination could always be cultivated. And in the interval that followed, her fingers intertwined with mine but her silence was like the sight of a leafless tree in an arbor everywhere else blooming green.

Found Dyer in the late afternoon sitting beside Nellie's gravestone. Sat with him in the dry grass. As though it were someone else's I reread the poem I composed for her epitaph: *One sweet flower has bloomed and faded / One dear infant voice has fled / One sweet bud the grave has shaded / One sweet girl O now is dead.*

After dark across our upper fields I walked over the hills for the wide wide view. I stood there with my child's face and my selfish love. I imagined my Tallie in that home that had lived mostly in our thoughts. I imagined myself not governed by the fear that holds the wretch in order. I imagined my response to her crying, "What do I know about you at this moment? Nothing!" I imagined cherishing a life touched with such alchemy. I imagined the story of a girl made human. I imagined Tallie's grave, forsaken and remote. I imagined banishing forever those sentiments that she chastened and refined. I imagined everyone I knew sick to the point of death. I imagined a creature even more slow-hearted than myself. I imagined continuing to write in this ledger, here; as though that were life; as though life were not elsewhere.

ELIZABETH TALLENT

The Wilderness

FROM *Threepenny Review*

HER STUDENTS ARE the devotees and tenders of machines. Some of the machines are tiny and some of the machines are big. Nobody wrote down the law that students must have a machine with them at all times, yet this law is rarely broken, and when it is, the breaker suffers from deprivation and anxiety. Machines are sometimes lost, sometimes damaged, and this loss, this damage deranges existence until, mouseclick by mouseclick, chaos can be fended off with a new machine, existence regains confidence, harmony, interest, order, connectedness. Sleeping, certain machines display a dreamily pulsing heartbeat-like white light meaning *this machine is not dead.* Human voices, fragments of text: even in a silent room the machines are continually storing these up. The students never advance into a day or even an hour without the certainty of voices waiting for them, without the expectation of signals and signs. Rendered visible, the embrace of hyperconnectivity would float around their heads like gold-leaf halos. During class the machines grow restless and seek students' attention. Certain machines purr, certain machines tremble; certain machines imitate birdsong. Whoever invented the software that causes the machine to sing like a bird must have foreseen not only bewilderment like the professor's but also the pleasure her mistake, if visible (it is: flushed from her lecture notes, her gaze swerves around the room), gives to those in the know—that is, her students. For the fraction of an instant that either makes or breaks her authority (she would say she is not interested in *authority*)—the fraction when pure exhilarated hard-wired startlement tips into that very different laughter-inviting cognitive slough, bewilderment—the professor can't make the correct attribution. The realistic sequence of ascending trills is, for her and her alone among the two hundred and forty-three listeners in the lecture hall, "bird." To see the lift of her brows is to know that a bird flits through the wilderness of her brain, to understand that in the professor's life there have been far more instances of birdsong from birds than from machines. To her students this is endearing: she can't help letting it show that she belongs to the world that preceded theirs.

Her face gives her trouble as a teacher. Irony has inscribed certain lines—insincerity, others. The insincerity is estranging—estranging her from herself, that is, for she feels, inwardly, like the most honest person on the planet. Inwardly she is plain and kind—emotionally Amish. But outwardly, no. Outwardly she is a professor. With a mocking lift of her brows, she has more than once accidentally silenced a student and been stunned that it happened so fast. Now she strives, facially, for serenity. As a child in the depths of a great museum she was struck mute by the impersonally eloquent eyes painted onto the linen wrapped over the real face of the mummy—no detachment, no trace of aversion, rushed to defend her huge, vulnerable heart from the perfect painted face tenderly laid against the true hidden visage whose corruption seduced the imagination into graphic detail. That was going on right below an oval face whose uncanniness told her *I was alive,* whose individuality, almost completely submerged in stylization, was more poignant for having barely made it through. For the first time she understood death for what it was—once, a real person had spoken through those lips, *a person* had looked out from those eyes pointed at both ends. That was why they took children to museums—she had been meant to understand this great thing they all understood, whose inevitability they could somehow (she did not see how) bear, which they expected her to spend the rest of her life knowing: death, first recognized in the depths of the museum, would be alive for her now her whole life long, and could never be un-seen. Nothing had been offered in the way of preparation or protection, and this treachery of theirs, this cold willingness to let her see what she saw, could not be explained. Inconceivable, the demented precision of this blow aimed at her by forces pretending to be benign. Hours later, in the backseat of the station wagon trundling south on the highway leading away from the city, she had fallen asleep. When she woke, she was looking out of eyes pointed on each end.

Once another professor, a handsome old charmer and taunter, asked her by way of flirtation what she wanted on her gravestone. For years, long after losing touch with the other professor, who had left for a university on the opposite coast, she thought about this question. She wrote and rewrote her gravestone, always with him in mind, recalling that particular moment at the party when he had come up to her and with two fingers touched the inside of her wrist, exposed because of the way she was holding her glass, and then, as if his somewhat intrusive but tolerated touch required its counterweight in charm, he had smiled a beautiful male smile within a dark beard and asked what she wanted on her gravestone, and she has been answering him ever since, though he died years ago.

Her by now experienced soul (but her heart is no bigger than it was when she was a child) gazes out through pointed eyes at students whose great museum is all of literature. Her corner of the museum is in English, which she has always loved—which she will love to her dying breath. Here come students. Why do *they* love it? What do they want? Is the end of such love inevitable—will there be a last English major? Will he be eyebrow-pierced and tattooed, awkward as any culture's newest young hunter, a prowling, scanning searcher-boy invoking the name DeLillo; could she be that Raggedy Ann–haired anorexic cross-legged in the last chair in the line of four chairs in the hallway outside the professor's door, this girl with tattered paperback upheld? They come. They are enthralled. The professor likes how enthralled they are. It is an old thing, a deep thing, to be enthralled. While enthralled they are beautiful. She could swear that an enthralled reader nineteen years old is the most beautiful animal on earth—at least, she's seen one or two who were in their spellbound moment the incarnation of extremest human beauty. They were not themselves. Literature looked back at her from their eyes and told her certain things she was sure they ought not to have understood at their age. They had gotten it from books—books with their intricacies and the things they wanted you to know about love and death that you could have gone a long time not knowing if you had not been a reader, and which, even when you were a reader, you saw as universal truths that did not apply to *you*.

When the professor sees that a student loves a certain sentence, her heart lifts as if she's been told *great news! You will never die!* Why does it feel like this? That book in that student's hand has nothing to do with her. It's just luck she's in the same room.

In the center of a roundabout, a paved orbit around a central island whose pale gravel is set with concentric circles of a kind of agave she happens to know are called *foxtail* after the slender oblong upheld sleekness of their array of pointed leaves, the professor watches while bicycles skim and veer past within arm's reach, hundreds of bicycles. If she stands here long enough she could easily witness the whirling transit of a thousand bicycles with her as their still center. Either extinction or a drastic diminution of population worldwide is inevitable within their lifetimes, according to research well known by the students. Here we can make some really big, really simple connections—we can cease to care, for a moment, how it *looks* to make big simple connections instead of subtle small ones. So. The same world that warns them of extinction bestows toys for them to carry, to key, to rub with their thumbs in swift ovals, to insert into those aperatures called in *Hamlet* "the porch of the ear," natural distance between brain and music annihilated, the cacophony nudged deep, close, too close to the species' most exquisite bones, incalculably tiny, the miracle housed within each ridiculous naked human ear. That is the point of the ten thousand toys. They are not about strangeness and newness at all. They seek innateness, sensual invisibility, the body's quality of being not-there to itself. In their insinuated proximity they elude the soul's attempt to differentiate between soul and soulless. Which is basically all that literature has ever cared about, and why it will *never cease to be loved*. Sure, tell that to yourself, the professor tells herself. The strap of the professor's heavy leather messenger bag rests on her left shoulder, crosses her chest, and fits below her right armpit, an arrangement completed with inevitable creasing of her jacket, which is black or any of the dozen soft shades of gray in her closet; not much variation there, not much risk; the bag itself is revolved until it rests snugly against her back, a trick learned from students in the nick of time, just before her neck acquired a permanent ache from one-shouldered weight-carrying. Calculate it sometime: the weight of the books you have carried in your life, would it equal that of a horse, a boat, a house? Bicycles rush at her from nineteen directions. No one hits anyone. Just how this is accomplished—by what unerring divination of one another's intentions and how many hundreds of swift corrections—she wants to know, to see, or if she can't see it, if she's not quick enough to perceive the glance that averts disaster, and she's not, then she wants at least to be close to it, she needs to know it happens, it goes on and on happening.

Her heart has always been the same size as it was that long-ago Sunday when she first saw those eyes pointed at both ends, and she has always felt the same to herself. Secretly, because people are supposed to go through enormous changes and to mature, she wonders if there is something wrong with her, to feel such consistency between who she is now and who she was when she looked down into those alive-dead eyes. Is something wrong with still being who she was as a child, or is she fine? What book can answer that? A great number of them seem to the professor to intuit the existence of this question *from her,* however far away she is in time from the writer of the book, however remote, and in this context the right adverb to modify *remote* is *impossibly.* A great many of the books she loves most *hold* this question. It's in there somewhere, the question, if not the answers, and why is it enough, in reading, why is it beautiful simply to find your own questions?

Long ago, when she was a new professor with a new professor's keen motivation, she took the trouble to think of really good answers to certain questions students asked, and the trouble she took then has paid off ever since, because the answers can be revised according to the times, some needing more revision than others, but her original responses continue to strike her as sufficient, and form a sort of core around which revision can take place, and the questions haven't changed. Really there are only twelve or so, at least in her life. Twelve or so main ones. Around those, a haze or shimmer of worries and intimations that can't quite materialize into questions. Anxieties like droplets lacking the particles of dust or grit they need to coalesce into clouds. Things they fear. Questions she could not answer anyway.

In her mind she answers the professor who asked the question, who is no longer alive to hear what she wants on her gravestone, not that she plans to have a gravestone because she wants to be cremated and despite her fear of death is consoled by the notion of ending up as ashes—why, she's not sure: their lightness and vulnerability to dispersion suit her, as does their incorruptibility, the fact that nothing further can be done to ashes, that in their lack of ambition regarding immortality ashes are the opposite of those eyes she gazed into in the museum. In her mind he touches her wrist and asks his question, which for all she knows he's in the habit of asking as a disconcerting, cut-to-the-chase, *what are you really like?* refinement of flirtation, whose bad-boy contempt for the usual niceties at least some women would respond to. She had responded to the professor, not in the way he wanted, not with equal and opposite impudence, but with the awkwardness of needing to think before talking, an awkwardness despised at her university, which she mostly hid, but not that evening and not with him, and he hadn't liked that, and hadn't liked her answer, so they parted and not long after that lost touch and she was left answering him in her mind, saying yes, there was something she'd like, just one word, on her gravestone. *Reader.* And in her mind he loves this answer.

For instance, a student will ask whether reading critically and interpreting—by beginning to study *literature*—will cause the student to stop loving reading, because the student thinks there's a risk of this, and that is what the student never ever wants to happen, and what is the answer, is it right to reassure the student when after all the professor doesn't know how it will go for that student, she only knows how it went for her? Well, she says, in my experience, she says, the more someone learns about an intricate thing, like, say, the human heart—the more a surgeon knows about that heart, right?, the deeper *in,* the more beautiful the thing seems, and by thing I mean a heart or a book, either one. Then the student says thank you and goes away. But the professor does not know any heart surgeons and has never asked a heart surgeon if what is felt is wonder. She made that up.

Only when she is well away from that roundabout, safely settled into her favorite corner of the couch in her office—when a new student plunks down in that corner, it's a problem—only in this quiet, narrowing her pointed eyes in pleasure in an interval of aloneness she has no right to, because they should be here, the students, they've said they're going to come by and one of them will knock on the door at any second, meaning the value of this interval, the preface to losing oneself in a book, is heightened by her awareness of its likely end—only in the particular space created by unexpected liberty (in which thinking her own thoughts has a stolen or illegitimate savor, really fun) does she intuit the real reason for her love of standing absolutely still in the bicycle onslaught, in the student whirlwind. As usual the real reason has been expertly swaddled in and obscured by false, lesser reasons, very attractive in and of themselves. Oh yes there is pleasure in being unmoved in the midst of an every-which-way assault. But also, this is like her life. They come at her from every direction! They never touch her! No. That's not it, not the bottommost layer, not the meaning revealed only when other meanings are peeled away, whose existence you only ever discover if peeling is a habit, if you love this deft quiet work of lifting away length of gauze after length of gauze to find the true face. Down down down down down and down. They mean something, these almost-winged cyclists, in their seriousness and lightness, their concentration, in their searchingness that must discern every tiny signal *or else,* in their absorption. This is reading. No wonder she loves standing there: in the middle of a steady cascade of virtuoso reading on which everything depends.

It could be, the professor tells herself, that apart from your work and your teaching you do not have enough going for you, that you need to get out more, that due to your aloneness, which we're not going to call loneliness because it's not that—it's a deliberate, cultured, desirable, nonnegotiable state, absolutely necessary if you want to get work done, intelligent aloneness, *good* aloneness; it has a point!—because you are alone, conceivably your students matter too much. At least you have to ask yourself once in a while, you have to check in regarding whether or not it is wrong, what you feel for them, the students. Without fail you need to recognize that the easiest transition love ever makes is into coercion, and that your most useful trait as far as students are concerned is *dis*interestedness. You've said often enough that you love teaching, but you have never said the truer thing, which is that you love your students, because it would only worry everyone to hear it, it would worry even you, and it might not even be true, because there is, remember, the risk that aloneness has exaggerated what you feel for them. Which may not be love, but some minor, teacherly emotion that nobody ever bothered to give a name. Who were they, the people who figured out what the emotions were, and how many of them would be recognized and named, and which sad little shadings or gradations could safely be ignored—who were they, these feeling-namers and numberers, and what did they have against shades of gray?

The students rarely embark on a difficult or painful subject without some sort of rhetorical exit strategy. There is almost no sorrow they can't disown with an immediate laugh. In that case—in the case of a quick student laugh—the professor is not supposed to know that she has been permitted to glimpse serious emotion. After many years as a professor it still strikes her as unnatural that students, that *people* fear what she might think: who the fuck is she? But they watch her eyes for what she's thinking. Will she say something actually useful to them, or something they in their desperation (because sometimes it is desperation) can *twist* into usefulness, which will be more useful for seeming to have come from her, the professor? What can she tell them about what comes next?

In the corner of the couch with a light titanium-sheathed machine balanced partly on the arm of the couch and partly on one raised knee, the professor clicks through the forests and clearings of a few contested acres. Mild and unevocative except for being somewhat forlorn, these acres, sad in the way of woods that don't thrive, lacking the cannons, the plaques, the bronze generals on horseback that tell you blood was shed here. The Wilderness, this battlefield is called, capital T, capital W. Walmart wants this particular scrap of The Wilderness for a supercenter whose aisles will be lined with toys for the children of tourists drawn to other already-protected acres of battlefield. There is no telling from these unphotogenic scantily wooded fawn-colored hills that her great-great-grandfather almost died here. If he had died he would have been one among thirty thousand, and she, of course, would never have existed. He lived: the War Department records his new status as prisoner of war, sent by train to Camp Delaware, also known as Pea Patch Island. The professor both likes and hates the irony, the sunny *potager* promised by the name Pea Patch Island and the reality of filth and exposure and fever and starvation, tainted water and maggoty flour, befalling him at nineteen. Was he *as alive* to himself as she is to herself, did he feel *as real*—if he stretched out his hand and flexed its fingers and turned it to study the lines intersecting and diverging in the palm, did he marvel? The deepest despair, the blackest pitch of disillusion about humankind: those are what she imagines, imagining his emotions, but these conjectures could be wrong. He is remote in time and culture. He could have done improbably well, inwardly—could have come through with all his F-A-C-U-L-T-I-E-S intact. Consolations that seem to her the most childish lies and self-deceptions might have been his salvation. Not books, but Book. He might, if time were transcended and he could know her and what she thinks and what she teaches her students and her preference for ambiguity over conviction and her godlessness, turn his savage Civil War eyes on her, his billy-goat beard, his cavalryman's uprightness, his gaunt authority renouncing her, his distant child. A cousin sent the professor the only known photograph of him, a slouch-hatted elderly figure astride a sorrel horse, and even in this photo, no bigger than a matchbook, and even in extreme old age, he is clearly someone to reckon with. So, she thinks, love me. *Want* me to come into existence. From the year 2012 she gazes into the pixels that comprise his gaze. Back to the homepage of the historical trust fighting Walmart, and with several clicks of the mouse, she buys an acre of these woods where he lay wounded, and her inbox *dings* with instant thanks from a computer in the trust's distant offices. It's *his* thanks she wants to come dinging in. She is amused at herself, though there are tears in her eyes. Through mouseclicks she had hoped to connect to that long-ago, unknowable, very likely hostile old man. Who she's somehow as lonely for as if she had once been a child cradled in his arms, as if, leaning his head down so his mouth was close to her ear, he had said her name, and then said *listen,* and then told her the story that was the story within all the other stories of her life, the oldest and most beautiful and farthest back, the one that would elude death forever and ever and ever amen.

Me. Say you lived at least partly for *me.*

This is the story that must exist somewhere; this is what she can't find to read.

JOAN WICKERSHAM

The Tunnel, or The News from Spain

FROM *Glimmer Train*

THE NEWS FROM SPAIN is terrible. A bomb under a park bench in a small town near Madrid. Fifteen people have been killed and dozens injured. Harriet tells the aide, who crosses herself; the nurse, who says, "It makes you want to stay home and never leave the house—but that would just be giving in to terrorism"; and her daughter Rebecca, who says, "Why do you spend all day watching that stuff?"

Rebecca is tired. Harriet has been sick on and off for years, more than a decade. Rebecca has just driven four hours from Boston to get to the Connecticut nursing home where Harriet now lives. She is taking two days off from the small bookstore she owns, paying her part-time assistant extra to cover for her. She's brought a shopping bag full of things Harriet likes: rice pudding with raisins, shortbread, fresh figs, and a box of lamejuns from a Middle Eastern bakery. She has walked into the room, and Harriet has barely looked away from the TV to say hello.

What Harriet says is "They just interviewed a man whose granddaughter died in his arms."

Rebecca puts down the shopping bag and kisses the top of her mother's head. Someone has given Harriet a haircut, a surprisingly flattering one. Her head smells faintly of shampoo.

Harriet puts up a hand and feels for Rebecca's face, briefly cupping her chin. "They think it was a Basque separatist group."

Rebecca nods, and goes down the hall to the kitchen, to put the rice pudding and lamejuns in the fridge. The hallway is full of wheelchairs, a straggly becalmed flotilla of gray people just sitting there, some with their head lolling on their chest. On the way back to her mother's room, she runs into the social worker assigned to Harriet's case. Today is Halloween; the social worker is wearing a pirate hat and an eye patch. "How do you think your mom is doing?" she asks Rebecca.

"I think she's still angry about being here," Rebecca says. Harriet moved into the nursing home a month ago, after the rehab hospital said she had "plateaued" and the assisted-living place said they couldn't take her back.

"I know," the social worker says. "But they adjust."

When she goes back into her mother's room, Harriet is watching for her. The TV is off. "I'm so glad you came," Harriet says.

"I just ran into the social worker in the hall. She says you're adjusting."

"Bullshit," Harriet says. "Did you bring stuffed grape leaves?"

"I didn't remember that you liked them."

"I love them."

"Next time," Rebecca says. She pulls over a chair and sits facing her mother. Harriet is in a wheelchair, paralyzed again—it has happened before, she has some rare chronic spinal disease, but this time the neurologist says it is permanent. Rebecca had listened while he talked to Harriet about suffering and acceptance, about how what was happening to her was truly terrible, worse than what anyone should have to go through. Rebecca liked the doctor's humanity and thought it might be somewhat comforting to Harriet; certainly Harriet has always found it gratifying to be admired for her bravery. But Harriet was furious. "He's talking philosophy when what I really want to hear about is stem-cell research."

Rebecca feels guilty about not making it down to see her mother more often. Harriet is always mentioning something she needs—lavender talcum powder, or socks, or an afghan to put over her legs when they wheel her outside, or, she sighs, "Just a really good turkey club sandwich." Rebecca mails what she can, alternately touched by and annoyed by the many requests. (Are they wistful or reproachful? Both, she thinks.) (But they are also simply practical. These are the small things we live with, and Harriet now has no way to get hold of them.) She has talked to Harriet about moving to a nursing home in the Boston area. "It would be more convenient."

"For you, you mean," Harriet said. She is adamant about staying in this particular nursing home because the man she's in love with is in the assisted-living place next door, and comes over to visit her nearly every day. Rebecca thinks it's great that her mother has someone, though she could do without some of Harriet's more candid reports. ("Ralph called me this morning and said, 'I wish I could make love to you right now.'")

"How is Ralph?" Rebecca asks now.

Harriet shrugs. "He thinks I'm mad at him because he didn't give me a birthday present."

"Are you?"

"Yes." They laugh. They talk. Rebecca heats up some lamejuns in the kitchen microwave and makes Harriet a cup of tea. They hear the woman in the room next door say loudly, angrily, "Who washed my floor?" A low murmuring answer; then the angry woman again: "In the future I must ask that you not wash my floor without first giving me notice."

Rebecca looks at Harriet. Harriet says, "That's all she ever says, on and on, day and night, about the floor."

Some lamejun has fallen onto the front of Harriet's sweatshirt; when she finally notices and brushes it off, it leaves a spot. "Damn it." She wipes furiously away at it, but in the midst of the fury is also grinning ruefully at Rebecca—*Can you believe it? How does it happen every single time?* She's a very large woman, and she's been dropping food on her shirt for as long as Rebecca can remember. The last time Rebecca visited, on the day Harriet moved to the nursing home, the aide swathed Harriet's front in an enormous terrycloth bib before bringing in her dinner tray. Harriet allowed it, looking at Rebecca with a kind of stunned sadness; of all the enraging indignities of that day, this was the one that undid her. "She doesn't need that," Rebecca told the aide.

"We do it for everybody."

"Right, but my mother doesn't need it."

So that was one small battle that Rebecca was there to win for Harriet. Without Rebecca, Harriet could have won it just fine for herself. Both of them knew this—and yet, between them, love has always had to be proved. It is there; and it gets proved, over and over. Some of their worst fights, confusingly, seem to both prove and disprove it: two people who didn't love each other couldn't fight like that—certainly not repeatedly. Still, Rebecca has often wished for something quieter with Harriet. Are there mothers and daughters who can be happy together without saying much?

"You know," Harriet says now, frowning, clearly resuming an argument she's been conducting in her own head, "you jump on me about watching the news all the time, but it's not because I'm just some morbid tragedy hound, it's—"

"I know why it is," Rebecca says.

Rebecca's younger sister, Cath, disapproves of the relationship between Rebecca and Harriet. She thinks it's unhealthily close. She says she is tired of giving Harriet inches and having her take miles. (Rebecca, who has never seen Cath give Harriet an inch, finds this declaration both funny and infuriating.) Cath is a sculptor who lives in Denver. She thinks Harriet is a monster. She thinks—and here Rebecca agrees with her—that their father, a quiet, scholarly, self-deprecating man who drank, had ended up drinking more and walling himself up more and dying lonely because Harriet took up so much room. Harriet always had another man, single, recently divorced, or widowed. "She had affairs," Cath said. "She broke Daddy's heart."

"You think those were affairs?" Rebecca asked, remembering all those wistful, mostly handsome, young men who had always seemed to her to be intruding—What were they doing at the Thanksgiving table? Why were they hanging around on Christmas Eve?—eagerly passing the cranberry sauce and trying brightly and unsuccessfully to engage her father in conversation.

"Not *consummated* affairs," Cath said, with exasperated authority. "Mom was never brave enough, or radical enough, to actually sleep with anyone else. Those affairs were all about noble renunciation of actual sex. They were all about deprivation and suffering."

She has said, more recently, to Rebecca over the phone: "She's going to live to be a hundred, you know. People like that, who only care about themselves, live forever, because every ounce of energy they have goes into preserving the organism."

Rebecca and her mother had begun to get close only when, nearly fifteen years ago, Harriet seemed to be dying.

She was diagnosed with stage four colon cancer just when the revelations broke about the rotten marriage of the Prince and Princess of Wales. Rebecca was going through her own fierce divorce at the time (it had started amicably, with a mediator, and then escalated to the point where the lawyers' bills had become so horrifying, so disproportionate to whatever it was that she and Steve had been fighting over, that the two of them had met for a drink one night and agreed to do everything the mediator had suggested in the first place).

But when Harriet got sick, Rebecca picked up the phone and called her soon-to-be-ex-father-in-law, who was on the board of a famous cancer hospital. She believed that Steve's father, who had never liked her much and never done much to conceal it, was nonetheless fundamentally ethical and would do what he could to help. (Another belief, both bitter and accurate, was that he liked to remind himself of his own power by pulling strings and making things happen.) He got Harriet admitted to the hospital, and the surgeon who was supposed to be brilliant lived up to his billing.

The doctor came and spoke to Rebecca after Harriet's surgery, which took an entire day. "I got it all," he said, and went on to list all the places where he'd found it: pretty much everywhere, as far as Rebecca could tell.

"So what's her prognosis?" Rebecca made herself ask, though she felt she already knew.

The surgeon looked seriously at her. "I have no idea," he said.

Rebecca wanted to hug him for that, and would have hugged Steve's father, if he had been there. She did hug Steve, who had showed up unexpectedly at the hospital and sat in the waiting room with her all day. They had spent most of the time hunched over a book of Sunday *New York Times* crossword puzzles; they screwed up each one irreparably, in ink, and then they would make a big blue *X* on it before moving on to the next one.

During that day, and right afterward, Rebecca thought that maybe the divorce was a mistake, and that she and Steve would get back together. But it turned out to be like the illness of Anna Karenina: a kind of temporary exalted goodwill, a glimpse of how lovely things might have been if everybody hadn't felt the way they actually did feel.

She went out and bought *People* magazine, and a copy of *Diana:*

Her True Story. Every day she read to Harriet, who lay in bed with tubes coming out of her nose, and puffy boots automatically inflating and deflating around her legs at intervals, to prevent blood clots. "She tried to kill herself with a *lemon slicer*?" Harriet said. "What's a lemon slicer? Do they mean a peeler? She tried to peel herself to death?" The two of them sat there in the dark hospital room, laughing. Whenever the surgeon came in, Rebecca hid the book and the magazine in the nightstand, because Harriet didn't want him to think she was the kind of woman who read trash.

Harriet would later say of that time, "It was a nightmare." Rebecca, who, partly in reaction to her mother's hyperbolic way of putting things, tends toward understatement, would say, "It was tough." But while it was going on, it was, in some bizarre way, also wonderful. They liked being together, for the first time in years. One afternoon, a couple of days after the surgery, Harriet needed a blood transfusion. The drip was still running when someone, mistakenly, brought in a dinner tray. Harriet was not allowed to have anything by mouth, and so Rebecca told the aide: "We don't need that."

"Oh, you've eaten already?" the aide said.

Harriet, lying on her back with the blood still dripping into her arm, raised her hands and curved them into little bat claws and said, in what Rebecca somehow understood was meant to be a Transylvanian accent, "I'm still eating."

Rebecca laughed, and her eyes filled with tears at the valiancy of it, the surprise of that sudden little flash of wit.

It was before Rebecca started the bookstore; she was teaching high school English then, so she had the summer off. She went to the hospital every day and stayed there all day.

Then Harriet went through her year of chemotherapy. Rebecca was teaching again, but she went down to Connecticut on a lot of weekends. The pope got colon cancer. They watched the networks grappling with the delicate challenge of reporting on a pontiff's gastrointestinal system: lots of disembodied scientific diagrams juxtaposed with footage of worried-looking nuns praying in St. Peter's Square.

"What do you think the nurses are saying to him right now?" Harriet said, lying on the couch and looking at a shot of the outside of the hospital where the pope had been operated on earlier that week.

"Okay, Your Holiness, scoot your hiney over to the edge of the bed," Rebecca said.

Harriet laughed and laughed. Then she threw up.

So here's the glib psychological explanation: Harriet had always craved attention and now, made vulnerable by illness, needed more; Rebecca had failed at her marriage and needed to feel like a hero.

All of which was true. But it was more that they both discovered, almost shyly, that they liked each other. That they were having, in the middle of all this dire stuff, a good time together.

It was also, Rebecca knew, that her mother was dying. She sometimes lay in bed at night and cried, alone, or with Peter Bigelow, who taught architectural history at Harvard and whose two children—he was divorced—went to the school where Rebecca taught. He held her and listened while she talked about how hard it was to be finding her mother and losing her at the same time.

But, Peter said, it sounds like the knowledge that you're losing her has been part of what allowed you to find her.

Oh, he was a nice man, Peter. Back then, her romance with him felt too new, too green and slight to bear the weight of everything Rebecca was feeling, about her divorce, about Harriet. Poor guy, she had thought, looking at Peter's kind, earnest face, his sandy rumpled hair, his open trusting bare chest, his hand resting on the sleeve of her flannel nightgown.

Are you sure you don't mind, if we don't, tonight?

Of course not.

I'm sorry, I thought I wanted to, but—

Rebecca. Don't worry. It's fine.

She might have been suspicious of his tenderness, seen it as his own need for heroism, or as a ploy to hook her before revealing his true selfish self (remember, she was just wrapping up a divorce). But she'd seen him for years with his kids. He was nice, period. He took her out to dinner and to concerts, talked to her about his work enthusiastically and not at all pompously (he was writing a book on H. H. Richardson), listened while she talked about wanting to quit teaching to open a bookstore, and was frank and relaxed in bed.

He advised her to pace herself, with Harriet. Her friends were saying the same thing, especially the ones who'd had sick parents. Go easy, take time for yourself, don't let this take over your whole life. But her mother was dying, and Rebecca wanted to cram in as much as she could. In some unexpected way she and Harriet had fallen in love.

Incredibly, Harriet didn't die. Her cancer never came back. She kept having more surgeries: to insert a catheter for the chemo drugs under her chest wall, to remove it again because of recurrent infections, to remove scar tissue in her abdomen, to remove more scar tissue. Rebecca kept driving down and spending time with her mother.

The glow wore off.

What a disconcerting thing to feel, to acknowledge! It wasn't that she was sorry Harriet was still alive. It was more that she couldn't keep it up: the attention, the rapport, the camaraderie, the aimless joy of just hanging around with her mother, watching the news. She had burned herself out, just as Peter and her friends had warned she might; but looking back at the time when Harriet had seemed to be dying, she couldn't imagine having managed it any other way.

Harriet started feeling that Rebecca wasn't visiting often enough. It was true, she was coming down less often. But oh, that "enough." That tricky guilt-laden word that doesn't even need to be spoken between a mother and daughter because both of them can see it lying there between them, injured and whimpering, a big throbbing violent-colored bruise of a word.

"What about Easter?" Harriet asked—plaintively? coldly? in a resolutely plucky way that emphasized how admirably she was refraining from trying to make Rebecca feel guilty? It could have been any of those ways of asking, or any of a number of others, all of which did make Rebecca feel guilty, and angry, and confused. The burnout took the form of an almost frantic protectiveness of her own time whenever Harriet wasn't sick. If her mother needed her, she dropped everything and went; but if her mother didn't need her, she wanted to feel free to say no.

Harriet, on the other hand, seemed to feel that the time Rebecca spent caring for her didn't count. Hurting, drugged, frightened, throwing up—that's not what Harriet called spending time with her daughter. (The watching-the-news part was engrossing, and sometimes fun, but it was more like a jailhouse party, a desperate entertainment concocted by people who have very little to work with.) Harriet wanted to travel with Rebecca—to go on a cruise to Alaska or the Panama Canal. Or see Moscow and St. Petersburg, for heaven's sake—all those mythical places that you could now, suddenly, actually go to.

Rebecca had no desire to travel with Harriet, and she was getting ready to start her bookstore, looking for space, making a business plan, applying for loans. "A *bookstore?*" Harriet said. "With your education you want to start a store, and one that doesn't even have a hope of making money?"

"It's what I care about," Rebecca said.

"I worry about you," Harriet said. "What is your life adding up to?"

Rebecca was hurt, furious. What did a life, anyone's life, add up to? Why did Harriet feel she had a right to say things like that? (In her head, Rebecca wrote the script for what a mother should say in this situation: "That's wonderful.") They had one of their old fights, made worse by the fact that Rebecca hadn't realized these old fights were still possible. The recent long entente around Harriet's illness had lulled Rebecca into a false sense of safety. She felt ambushed.

Then Harriet sent Rebecca a check, for quite a lot of money. *To help with the bookstore,* she wrote on the card.

"You can't afford this," Rebecca said.

"It's what I want to do," Harriet said.

Then she got sick again.

Pneumonia—not life-threatening, but it took a long time to get over. Rebecca drove down and made Harriet chicken soup and vanilla custard, and lay across the foot of Harriet's bed, watching the vigil outside the Fifth Avenue apartment building where Jacqueline Onassis was dying. They watched while John Kennedy Jr. came out and told the reporters that his mother was dead.

"Poor Jackie," Rebecca said.

She was remembering how much her mother had admired and pitied Jackie, in the years after JFK's assassination, when Rebecca was growing up.

But "What's poor about her?" Harriet said. "She's been living with another woman's husband."

So this has been going on for years. Harriet ailing and rallying. Rebecca showing up and withdrawing. Living her life between interruptions—which, she herself knows, is not really a fair or accurate way to characterize it. Harriet has been sick a lot, needed her a lot; but most of the time she has not been sick or needy. Most of the time, Rebecca is relatively free. Maybe, then, it's that Rebecca doesn't feel that she's done much with her freedom. That each interruption points up how little has happened since the last one.

She runs her bookstore quite successfully. She tried opening a second store in a nearby suburb, which did not do well; the experiment was stressful, but not disastrous; after a year she closed the new store, paid back the loans, and felt relieved.

She's been seeing Peter for a long time. They enjoy each other. They trust each other. They spend a few nights together most weeks, but both of them like having their own apartments. His kids went away to college; his ex-wife remarried, and so did Steve.

Early on—a couple of years into their relationship—Peter asked Rebecca how she would feel about getting married. That was how he did it: not a proposal, but an introduction of a topic for discussion. She said she wasn't sure. The truth was that when he said it, she got a cold, sick feeling in her stomach. This lovely, good, thoughtful man: what was the matter with her? She was nervous, and also miffed that he seemed so equable about the whole thing, that he wasn't made desperate by her ambivalence, that he wasn't knocking her over with forceful demands that she belong to him. On the other hand, she wasn't knocking him over either.

Then his book on Richardson was finished, and published. He brought over a copy one night, and she had a bottle of champagne waiting. "Peter, I'm so happy for you," and she kissed him, and they smiled at each other and drank, and she kept touching the cover of the book, a very beautiful photograph of the Stoughton House on Brattle Street. *"Peter,"* she said, and he smiled at her. Then he went into her kitchen to carve the chicken, and she began to flip through the book. She turned to the acknowledgments page, and her own name jumped out at her: ". . . and to Rebecca Hunt, who has given me so many pleasant hours."

It was understatement, wasn't it? The kind of understatement that can exist between two people who understand each other? (The kind she was always wishing for, and never getting, from Harriet.)

What did she want: a dedication that said, "For Rebecca, whom I adore and would die for"?

Here was something she suddenly saw and deplored in herself, something she seemed to have in common with Harriet: a raw belief that love had to be declared and proved, baldly, loudly, explicitly.

She saw the danger, the wrongness, of this; yet when Peter came in from the kitchen, carrying the chicken over to the table Rebecca had set in front of the fireplace, she said, "Pleasant? Is that what I've given you—many pleasant hours?"

"Some unpleasant ones too," he said, humorously, nervously—he saw, suddenly, what was coming, and he was trying to head it off.

What came, though, that night, turned out to be not so bad. Rebecca was able to rein it in; she didn't need to harangue him, or freeze him, although they talked less at dinner than usual. Peter said, "You know, I'm not sure what made me choose that word, but it was probably not the right one."

"That's okay," Rebecca said, and it was, really. What they had together *was* pleasant.

But still the word continued to bother her whenever she thought of it. The fact that it appeared to be lauding, but the thing that it praised was a limitation. Thanks for not getting too close to me. Thanks for not getting too deeply under my skin. Peter had disowned it somewhat, said it might not have been the right word—but Rebecca thought that it was probably not so much an aberration as it was a revelation: one of those sudden, sometimes accidental instances when everything is brightly lit and you see where you are. Long ago, Rebecca had had a friend named Mary; they'd been close for a couple of years when they'd both been trying to keep sinking marriages afloat. One night they had sat on the front steps of Rebecca's apartment building, talking about their husbands, and Mary had said, "You know those things in the beginning of the relationship—the things that bother you and you tell yourself, 'Oh, that doesn't matter'? I'm realizing now: all of it matters."

Rebecca and Peter, of course, aren't at the beginning of their relationship. They're more than ten years in. And isn't that the problem really—that they are so far in, and yet not far in at all?

"Where do things stand these days with Peter?" Harriet is always asking. She means: Why don't you marry him? Or, if you don't love him enough to marry him, why don't you move on and find someone else? (Both questions are unspoken; but the second, nevertheless, carries all the buried force of an ultimatum: if you're too stupid to appreciate Peter, give him up, and *then* you'll be sorry.)

She asks again on the Halloween when Rebecca visits her at the nursing home: the day of the bombing in Spain, the lamejuns, when Harriet is supposedly "adjusting." It's about a month after Peter's book has been published; he has sent down an inscribed copy for Harriet, which she holds in her lap, stroking the picture of the Stoughton House.

"Things don't stand anywhere," Rebecca tells her. "Things stand where they always stand."

She goes down again a month later, for Thanksgiving. She would like to take Harriet out for dinner, but this is impossible, because Harriet can't go anywhere except in an ambulance or a wheelchair van, either of which would cost several hundred dollars. So they sit in Harriet's room and eat nursing-home turkey with very wet stuffing. Then there is pumpkin pie—not too bad—and dark chocolate pastilles that Rebecca has brought because Harriet loves them.

"I had a very strange conversation with Cath," Harriet says. "She called me, and she asked me why, when you girls were little and I would take you to a Broadway musical, why wouldn't I ever buy you the original cast album when they were selling it in the lobby."

"What did you tell her?"

"I said I didn't remember. Which is the truth." Harriet looked at Rebecca, puzzled. "Do you think she's in therapy?"

This makes Rebecca laugh, and after a moment Harriet snorts too, and the two of them end up wiping away tears, trying to collect themselves.

The legs of Harriet's stretch pants have ridden up, and Rebecca notices a bandage on her calf.

"It's infected," Harriet tells her when she asks. "It got bumped on the wheelchair, and I asked them to put some antibiotic ointment on it, but they never got around to it."

They play Scrabble; Harriet is still pretty good. From somewhere down the hall, a woman begins to moan. The same words over and over: Take me home. Please, please take me home.

"She does that all the time," Harriet says, her hand hovering over the box of tiles. "I don't know if she thinks her children are in the room with her, or if she's talking to God."

"Either way," Rebecca says, somber, not even sure what she means by "Either way."

But Harriet makes it explicit. "Either way, she's not crazy to want it; and either way, it isn't happening."

A man has been coming into Rebecca's bookstore every couple of weeks. He buys a lot—no specific category, he just seems generally ravenous—novels, poetry, history. He is short, probably in his late fifties, with silver-rimmed glasses, a large shaggy graying head, and a big square jaw that reminds Rebecca of a lion. He grins at Rebecca when he pays. They don't talk. Their not talking, which might at first have been shyness or reserve, has begun to feel deliberate, erotic. His name, on the credit slips, is Benjamin Ehrman.

Already Rebecca can tell the story two different ways. One ends with them getting married. The other ends with her looking back over a cratered battlefield of a love affair and wondering: What were you *thinking?*

Harriet calls late one morning, practically in tears.

"What is it?" Rebecca asks.

"I'm still in bed. They haven't—when I woke up I said I needed the bedpan. And the aide told me it was too much trouble, I should just . . . go, and they'd come clean me up. So I did, but that was a couple of hours ago—"

Rebecca looks at the clock hanging on the wall of the bookstore. It's eleven-thirty. "I'll call you right back." She hangs up, and then calls the nursing home and asks to speak to Harriet's caseworker. She describes what Harriet has just told her and ends by saying, "That is not okay."

"No, it's not," the caseworker agrees smoothly. "You're right. But sometimes they can make it sound worse than it really is; there may be a little more to the story. Let me go look into it."

Rebecca's hands are shaking. "I don't think my mother is confused about what's going on." She keeps picturing the caseworker in her Halloween costume: her eye patch, her blackened tooth, her little plastic dagger. And she says again, "This is not okay."

She hangs up and calls Harriet back. "The social worker is sending someone to help you."

"I'm sorry."

"Mom. *I'm* sorry." They stay on the phone until Harriet has to hang up because, she says, "Here everybody is, all of a sudden."

Benjamin Ehrman comes in and buys the *Oresteia* and the complete Ecco Press set of Chekhov stories. Is he taking some sort of middle-aged Great Books course? Is he courting her, trying (successfully) to slay her with his taste?

He pays. He smiles. He doesn't say anything, not even thank you. At the point when any other customer would have said, "Thank you," he smiles at her again.

Oh, Rebecca, you tired, confused woman. You are so ripe for this kind of thing.

She goes down to visit Harriet at Christmas. (She and Peter have never spent the holiday together; she always goes to Harriet, and he is either with his kids or off skiing in Utah. This year, the separation bothers her. Not in itself—she hates skiing—but the fact that there is no expectation that they will make a plan together. How could there not be, after all this time? On the other hand, doesn't the ease with which they go their separate ways—the pleasantness of it—confirm that she is free?)

She brings Harriet a beef tenderloin she has cooked, and she reheats au gratin potatoes and green beans in the kitchen microwave. The gray people in their straggly hallway flotilla watch, or don't watch, as she walks by, holding dishes aloft. One woman looks at her and raises a forefinger, like someone timidly hailing a cab. "Excuse me," the woman says, "but is this Washington Square?"

"No, it isn't," Rebecca says.

"Do you know how to get there from here?"

Rebecca shakes her head, and the woman smiles and shrugs.

Harriet says of the dinner, "You can't imagine what a treat this is."

"Yes, I can," Rebecca says. "That's why I brought it."

Ralph's children have taken him out for dinner—they all live nearby—but later that evening he comes to see Harriet. Rebecca likes him: he is blunt and loyal, and quick, like Harriet.

Rebecca sits trying to straighten out a piece of knitting (a red scarf, Harriet's Christmas present to her, which, Harriet says, "should have been done ages ago but I keep screwing it up—you know I'm not domestic"), while Ralph and Harriet play anagrams on a table rolled up against Harriet's wheelchair. They take turns flipping over a new letter and seeing if they can steal a word the other person has already made.

Rebecca, ripping out rows of Harriet's impatient, thwarted knitting, is nearly in tears watching them: the speed, the sureness with which they play. Ralph steals *risked* from Harriet, adds his own *T,* and makes *skirted.* She steals *donuts* and makes *astound.*

One Sunday afternoon, in the middle of January, Rebecca goes to the movies by herself. She stands in line—a long one—not thinking of much. The smell of popcorn, and how sickening it is. The fact that the hole in the right-hand pocket of her orange wool coat has now become big enough that she ought to start carrying her loose change in the left one. Ahead of her in line a man is waving, beckoning, smiling. Benjamin Ehrman. She turns around to see if he means someone behind her; he grins, and points at her, and beckons again. So she goes to him.

"What movie are you seeing?" he asks, and she tells him, and he says, "Me too."

She says, "So, you do know how to talk after all." She feels like a jerk as soon as it's out of her mouth.

But, "I know," he says. "One of us was going to have to break that silence." That sounds meaningful, erotic again; he defuses it by adding, "It was getting to be like those staring contests you have when you're a kid."

So they go in together, sit together, are deferential about the armrest, are aware of exactly where each other's hands are in the darkness. The movie is a "little" one that has received doting reviews. The audience is enraptured with it, laughing, sighing. Rebecca hates it. She looks over at him and he looks back and rolls his eyes at her. They don't know each other well enough to agree to walk out—they don't know each other at all, so walking out would mean going their separate ways. They stay, sitting there through the whole thing grimacing at each other, sinking down in their seats, their shoulders growing conspiratorially closer as their silent agreement that the thing just stinks grows more and more intense. At the end they throw themselves out into the street, laughing. They go for coffee, but order wine instead.

A list of what shocks Rebecca, over the next weeks and months:

Bed. That something she's done a lot of, and enjoyed in the past, could feel so fiercely new.

Underwear. He likes it, so he buys it for her, and she starts buying it for herself. Tarty, expensive stuff. And nothing in her objects—not the feminist part, not the shy part, not the part that is aware of weighing fifteen pounds more than she did in college.

Her hair. It's long, it nearly reaches her waist; she's always worn it up, or in a braid. He wants it down. She sits on the bed between his thighs with her back to him, and he brushes her hair, crooning to her. And she loves it—she, who has always disliked having anyone touch her hair since childhood, when Harriet used to yank a brush through it and say impatiently, when Rebecca flinched, "You have such a tender *scalp*."

Pet names for each other. We won't even put them in here, because the ones they make up are so incredibly silly.

German chocolate eggs with toys inside. He hands her one after dinner on one of the first nights he cooks for her. She thinks, Oh, how nice, a chocolate egg. When she unwraps it and breaks off a piece, she discovers a small plastic capsule inside; when she opens that, she finds six plastic pieces; when she puts the pieces together, they make a tiny pterodactyl holding a jackhammer. Oh, he says, the pterodactyl-road-crew ones are the best.

Jealousy. He is separated, but not divorced. Rebecca sees the wife around Cambridge, a narrow pretty greyhound of a woman, with a face that is at once anxious and arrogant. She looks rich. She is rich, because Ben is rich. Five years ago he sold his dot-com company and made the kind of money that can scatter people all over an expensive city in big houses: one for himself, one for his parents, one for a son and daughter-in-law, and then another one for himself when he moved out of the first one and left his wife alone there. That had happened a year before Rebecca met him. Rebecca hates seeing this woman—Dorinda. After a sighting she always has a sense of belated, alert panic, the kind you feel when you narrowly miss having a traffic accident. She sees Dorinda in the supermarket, and Dorinda's eyes hold hers for an instant and then sweep coldly away. Is this just one person registering the presence of another, unknown one? Or is it the snubbing of a rival?

She asks Ben if Dorinda knows about her. Ben says he's mentioned to Dorinda that he's seeing someone, but that they've never discussed whom. Implying that they do still discuss some things. What things? What do they talk about? How often? How married are they? There is also another, much earlier wife: Carol, the mother of Ben's three grown children. She lives on Martha's Vineyard. Rebecca doesn't know what she looks like and is not bothered by her as she is by Dorinda, though it does worry her that there are two of them, two of Ben's former loves cast adrift in the world. Does it mean she will one day be a third? Is he a serial discarder? No, she tells herself: he is fifty-seven, he's had a life. Rebecca is forty-five, and has a past of her own. Her quantity is equal to Ben's: two. Steve, who had grown less and less interested in sex, and eventually told her that it would be okay with him if she wanted to go out and have an affair; and then Peter.

She has of course by now broken up with Peter, who, she thinks, barely seemed to notice. In fact, it's Rebecca who has failed to notice. She is so far gone, so deeply drunk on love, that she doesn't notice how surprised and hurt he is; how aware he has been over the years of his own caution and reticence; how miserably, suddenly certain he is that their long civilized mildness was fatal and largely his fault; how far from mild he is feeling now. He's angry at her, but angrier at himself.

"We could still see each other sometimes," she said vaguely, cravenly, at the end. (She was thinking that it had been so friendly all along, maybe it could just keep being friendly.) "I'll miss you."

"No. Don't call me. Don't call me again unless you mean it," Peter said; and then he amended it to: "Don't call me."

It was very clear and clean, Rebecca thought at the time. They had met for a cup of coffee in Harvard Square, and they were done and she was walking home within fifteen minutes. She was relieved that there hadn't been a scene, but also not surprised. She did feel sad: she *would* miss him. She passed the store that sold the chocolate eggs and went in and bought one to hide somewhere—Ben's slipper, the piano bench. They've taken to stashing them all over his house for each other to find.

What does Harriet make of all this? Nothing. Rebecca hasn't told her. She doesn't know what Harriet would say, but she knows she doesn't want to hear it. She doesn't want to hear anything from anybody.

She wants to be utterly alone with Ben: she wants to drink him, eat him, climb inside him, run away with him. She's never felt this way about anyone.

What she has always thought, watching friends of hers disappear into similar love affairs in the past, is, "Uh-oh."

But who is ever able to apply to her own current love affair a word like *similar*?

She gets calls from the nursing home. "I'm just calling to report that your mother fell this morning. She slid down out of her wheelchair. She wasn't hurt."

"We're calling to let you know that your mother is in the emergency room. She has a pretty high fever, and the doctor was worried she might be dehydrated."

She calls Harriet. "Mom?"

Harriet says she's okay, or she's tired, or she's mad that they didn't take action sooner, or she knows they're short-staffed and that it's not their fault, or that they're a bunch of stupid uncaring assholes who just want her money. Rebecca murmurs and soothes, gets indignant, calls the nursing home to complain, suggests to Harriet yet again that they hire a private aide to keep a closer eye on her (which Harriet has always refused to do, because the nursing home is already gobbling up her money and once it's gone she'll have to go on Medicaid and have a roommate, the idea of which she finds abhorrent).

Rebecca has always been competent whenever there's a crisis—but it's different now, more automatic, because she has Ben. When something happens with Harriet, she does what needs to be done, but it feels more like Honor Thy Mother than it does like running into a burning building to save someone you love who is trapped inside.

"And you're sure you don't want me to look for a place near Boston?" Rebecca asks.

No, Harriet always says, because of Ralph.

She talks to Cath occasionally, and Cath says, from the safe distance of Denver, "It's time for her to live closer to one of us."

(Rebecca is tempted sometimes to say, Okay, Cath, I've arranged to have Mom med-flighted out to you.)

Harriet gets a urinary tract infection, another leg infection, bronchitis.

She has been sick now for so long, this has all been going on forever. Rebecca wishes it would all just stop—but the only thing that will stop it is Harriet's death, and she doesn't want that.

She asks Harriet one afternoon—it's when Harriet is in the hospital with bronchitis, and Rebecca has driven down to Connecticut to spend the afternoon with her (just the afternoon: she wants to be back in Cambridge again by bedtime)—"Aren't you tired of all this?"

"Yes," Harriet says. "But I don't want it to be over, because I want to know the end of the story."

"What story?" Rebecca asks.

"All the stories," Harriet says.

"You're so sad," Ben says, rubbing the backs of his fingers against her cheek when she gets home from the bookstore one evening.

"My mother's in the hospital again. Septic shock. Another urinary tract infection, which I guess they didn't catch fast enough. I'm going to drive down there tomorrow."

"I'll make you a drink," he says, and then he calls her one of the incredibly silly pet names, which for the first time fails to delight her. It seems irritating and ill-timed. "And then I'll run you a bath," he says.

"A bath sounds good."

"And I'll come watch you take it."

"Come talk to me, you mean?"

"No. Watch you."

That's an aberration, not a revelation, she thinks. Being objectified, when she just wants to be accompanied.

"You're so sad," he keeps saying. It starts as sympathy. A week or two later it's cool, a diagnosis. Then it becomes a criticism.

He starts wanting the underwear to be kinkier. And he wants her to wear it every time.

He used to talk a lot about divorcing Dorinda. But it's been months now since he mentioned it.

Rebecca asks him about it one night, as they are lying in bed, happy, she thinks, naked, with scraps of underwear scattered all around them.

"I would love to marry you," she says, with a boldness that is new and luxurious for her. She's echoing something he has said to her many times by now. "I hate it that you're still married to someone else."

He is silent. Then he says: "You knew I was married when we started this."

She tries to get out of it without too much self-abasement. She knows the uselessness of asking questions. She manages to sound less desperate than she is—but still, it's more desperate than she would like to sound.

Women ask for explanations, over and over, when love goes. There is no explanation. The explanation is: It's gone.

The whole thing, from the time they met at the little movie to the end, took sixteen months.

Back in her apartment, she's cold. It's a cold spring, wet, dark. She doesn't cook, she doesn't sleep well, she doesn't read, she doesn't see many friends. She gets her hair cut to just below her jawline, knowing it's an angry, masochistic thing to do, but hoping that it will somehow make her feel better. (And also because she can't bear now to attend to it: shampooing, brushing.) She talks to two people, her assistant from the bookstore who has had something of a front-row seat for all this—she used to raise her eyebrows at Rebecca all those months ago when Ben would come in, buy books, and leave without saying anything—and an old friend from the school where she used to teach. Both of them are kind, but both seem to be saying, without saying it, "What did you expect?" (In fact, they're not saying this. They've been watching Rebecca all this time with some concern because she has seemed so engulfed in Ben and remote from everything else, but they have also been rooting for her, wanting it to work. The "What did you expect?" is coming straight from Rebecca herself, spoken in a voice not unlike Harriet's.)

Summer comes, then fall. Rebecca still can't walk by the store that sells the chocolate eggs.

"What's wrong?" Harriet asks over the phone. Her voice is feebler these days, hoarse.

"Nothing," Rebecca says. "I'm just tired."

"You want to hear something shitty?" Harriet asks.

"What?"

"They've stopped giving me physical therapy. They say I'm not making any progress. I said, 'Well, how the hell am I supposed to make progress if you stop giving me physical therapy?' But you want to hear something wonderful?"

"What?"

"When Ralph comes over, he moves my legs for me. And he makes me do arm exercises. So I don't atrophy."

The nursing home calls.

"We're calling to let you know your mother is in the hospital again—she had a fever, and so we sent her over to the ER."

The hospital calls. Harriet once again has a urinary tract infection that has gone undiagnosed—she can't feel any pain, because of the paralysis—and once again she's in severe septic shock. They're putting her on antibiotics.

Harriet calls. Her voice is weak and shivery, but animated, excited. "Oh, my God—did you hear about the tunnel?"

"What tunnel?"

"It collapsed. Turn on the TV. It just happened, at the height of the morning commute, they said."

"Where was this? What city?"

"I don't know. It was my roommate's TV, so I couldn't hear very well, and then the nurse or someone came in and shut it off. But it sounded awful. People were killed, they think some people may still be trapped in their cars. You need to turn it on."

"Mom, we don't even know where it's happening."

"It's in a commuter tunnel. The main one that leads to the city, they said. Or maybe it was the bridge that collapsed, the bridge that leads to the tunnel. But *everybody* goes through the tunnel."

That night the hospital calls. Harriet's fever isn't coming down. They're going to try a different antibiotic.

Early the next morning, Rebecca is trying to decide what to do—call in the assistant, or close the store for the day, so she can go to Connecticut? Stay here and keep in touch with the hospital and Harriet by phone?—when the hospital calls again and someone tells her in a clear, soft voice that Harriet is dead.

She sits there.

She needs to call Cath. (Who will say, "Do you think we need to do a funeral?")

She needs to call Ralph. (Who will cry. Who will be heartbroken. Who will now begin to decline very fast.)

She wants to call Harriet.

It has all gone on for so long without Harriet dying that Rebecca lost track of the fact that Harriet was going to die.

Guilt: if she hadn't gotten tired and distracted—if she hadn't let herself be so easily dazzled—if she had not relaxed her vigilance, this would not have happened.

Even in the moment, she recognizes this guilt as irrational, bogus; but it pierces anyway.

Harriet died when Rebecca wasn't looking.

She sits there.

She wants to call Harriet, more passionately than she would have believed, an hour ago, that it was possible to want that, or to want anything.

The only other person she finds she wants to call—and of course she can't—is Peter.

She will, though. Not now. Not until almost a year from now.

She will wrestle during that time with questions having to do with forgiveness. Can she forgive herself for what she did to him?

(For the most part, yes. The two of them made their polite, inhibited, explosive mess together, she believes; it ended the way it might have been expected to end, although the particular trigger could not have been predicted.)

(But oh, the folly of that particular trigger.)

Can he forgive her? No way to know. She puts off the phone call for so long partly because she is afraid to find out.

She keeps pitting his final "Don't call me" against his penultimate, "Don't call me unless you mean it," trying to figure out which one carries more weight.

And she gets tangled in that "unless you mean it." Which she didn't even really hear when he said it; which she has discovered in her memory since then. Unless she means what? She can't define it explicitly, the thing that Peter insisted she had better mean—but she does feel she understands what *he* meant by that insistence, and it gives her hope.

By the time she finally does call him, she will know that she means it, even though it will be a scary phone call to make, and even if she still won't be capable of saying clearly what exactly it is she does mean.

Harriet would have been quick to tell her, accurately or inaccurately. To guess, to analyze, to explain, to make predictions. Harriet was always the one who wanted to talk about the news, from Spain, or from the Vatican, or from some uncertain city where something had collapsed—from any place, really, where anything of interest might be going on.

CALLAN WINK

Breatharians

FROM *The New Yorker*

THERE WERE CATS in the barn. Litters begetting litters begetting litters—some thin or misshapen with the afflictions of blood too many times remixed.

"Get rid of the damn things," August's father said. "The haymow smells like piss. Take a tire iron or a shovel or whatever tool suits you. You've been after me for school money? I'll give you a dollar a tail. You have your jackknife sharp? You take their tails and pound them to a board, and then after a few days we'll have a settling up. Small tails worth as much as large tails, it's all the same."

The cats—calicos, tabbies, dirty white, gray, jet black, and tawny—sat among the hay bales, scratching and yawning like indolent apes inhabiting the remains of a ruined temple. August had never actually killed a cat before, but, like most farm boys, he had engaged in plenty of casual acts of torture. Cats, as a species, retained a feral edge, and as a result were not subject to the rules of husbandry that governed man's relation with horses or cows or dogs. August figured that somewhere along the line cats had struck a bargain—they knew they could expect to feel a man's boot if they came too close; in return, they kept their freedom and nothing much was expected of them.

A dollar a tail. August thought of the severed appendages, pressed and dried, stacking up like currency in the teller drawer of some strange Martian bank. He could earn fifty dollars at least, maybe seventy-five, possibly even a hundred if he was able to track down the newborn litters.

He went to the equipment shed to look for weapons. It was a

massive structure, large enough to fit a full-sized diesel combine, made of metal posts skinned with corrugated sheet metal. August often went there when it rained. He thought it was like being a small creature trapped inside a percussion instrument. The fat drops of rain would hit the thin metal skin in an infinite drumroll, punctuated by the clash of lightning cymbals and the hollow booming of space.

In the shed there was a long, low workbench covered in the tangled intestine of machinery: the looping coils of compressor hoses, hydraulic arms leaking viscous fluid, batteries squat and heavy, baling twine like ligaments stitching the whole crazy mess together, tongue-and-ball trailer knobs, Mason jars of rusting bolts and nuts and screws, a medieval-looking welder's mask, and, interspersed among the other wreckage like crumpled birds, soiled leather gloves in varying stages of decomposition. August picked up a short length of rusted, heavy-linked logging chain and swung it a few times experimentally before discarding it. He put on a pair of too-large gloves and hefted a mower blade the size of a broadsword, slicing slow patterns in the air, before discarding it too. Then he uncovered a three-foot-long torque wrench with a slim stainless-steel handle that swelled at the end into a glistening and deadly crescent head. He brought the head down into his glove several times to hear the satisfying whack. He practiced a few horrendous death-dealing swing techniques—the sidearm golf follow-through, the overhead back-crushing ax chop, the short, quick, line-drive baseball checked swing—the wrench head making ragged divots in the hard-packed dirt floor. He worked up a light sweat and then shouldered his weapon, put the gloves in his back pocket, and went to see his mother.

The old house was set back against a low, rock-plated hill. A year-round spring wept from the face of the rock, and the dampness of it filled the house with the smell of wet leaves and impending rain. The house was a single-level ranch, low-slung, like a dog crouching to avoid a kick. August's mother's parents had built the house with their own hands and lived in it until they died. The old house looked up at the new house, the one August's father had finished the year August turned one. The new house was tall, with a sharp-peaked roof. It had white shutters, a full wraparound porch. August's grandparents had both died shortly before he was born, and the first thing his father had done when the farm became his was sell fifty acres of fallow pasture and build the new house.

"He feels like it's his own," August's mother had said to him once, while smoking at the dining room table of the new house. "His people didn't have much. Everything we got came from my side, you know. He would never admit it in a hundred years, but it bothers him." She coughed. "It's too big. That was my complaint from the get-go. It's hard to heat too, exposed up on the hill like this; the wind gets in everywhere. My father would never have done it like that. He built the best possible house for himself and my mother. That's the type of man he was."

August tapped on the front door a few times with the wrench, then went inside. The old house had been built by folks interested in efficiency, not landscape, and its windows were few and small. The kitchen was dimly lit by a single shaft of light that came through the window above the sink. The room smelled like frying bacon, and the radio was on. Paul Harvey was extolling the virtues of a Firmness Control Sleep System. *At my age there are few things I appreciate more than a night of restful sleep. Get this mattress. It was dreamed up by a team of scientists. It's infinitely adjustable. Your dreams will thank you.*

"Augie, my fair son, how does the day find you?"

His mother was at the kitchen table playing solitaire. A pan of sliced potatoes fried with pieces of bacon and onion sat next to her ashtray. She smoked Swisher Sweet cigarillos, and a thin layer of smoke undulated above her head like a flying carpet waiting for a charge to transport.

"I made lunch, and it smelled so good while it was cooking, but then I found myself suddenly not hungry. I don't know, I may have finally broken through."

August pulled out a chair and sat across from his mother at the small table. "Broken through to what?" he said.

"Oh, I didn't tell you? I've been devoting myself to a new teaching." She stubbed out the cigarillo and shook another from the pack sitting on the table, a fine network of lines appearing around her mouth as she pursed her lips to light it. Her nails were long and gray, her fingertips jaundiced with tobacco stain. "Yeah," she continued, "I've become an inediate."

"A what?"

"An inediate—you know, a breatharian?"

"I don't know what that is."

"Air eaters? Sky swallowers? Ether ingesters?"

"Nope."

"You can attune your mind and your body, Augie. Perfectly attune them by healthy living and meditation, so that you completely lose the food requirement. I mean, it's not just that you're not hungry. That's not too hard. I'm talking about getting to the point where all you have to do is breathe the air and you're satisfied. You get full and you never have to eat. And you can survive that way, happy as a clam." She took a sip of coffee, smoke dribbling from her nose after she swallowed. "That's what I've been working on."

She pushed the pan of potatoes and bacon toward him, and August ate some even though Lisa had told him she would make him a sandwich when she got up from the barn. The potatoes were greasy and good, the bacon little pieces of semi-charred saltiness, the onions soft, translucent, and sweet. August ate, then wiped his hands on his jeans and put his wrench on the table for his mother to see.

"Dad gave me a job," he said. "For money."

"Oh, well, I'm proud to hear it. Did you negotiate a contract? Set a salary-review option pending exemplary performance?"

"No, I'm just killing the cats in the barn."

"I see. And this is your Excalibur?" She tinked the chrome-handled wrench with her fingernail.

"Yeah. It's a torque wrench."

She made a low whistle and coughed softly into the back of her hand. "It's a big job, Augie. Is he paying you upon completion or piecemeal?"

"I'm taking the tails. We're going to settle up at the end of the week."

"Grisly work, son. That's the kind of work you stand a chance of bringing home with you, if you know what I mean."

"The haymow smells like piss. It's getting real bad."

"This is gruesome, even for your father. Jesus." She looked down blankly at the cards in front of her. "I keep forgetting where I'm at with this." She gathered up her game, her nails scrabbling to pick the cards up off the Formica. "I can go only so far with solitaire before I get stumped. You ever win?"

"I never play."

"I suppose it's a game for old women."

"You're not old."

"If I'm not, then I don't want to feel what old is like."

"Are you ever going to come back to the new house?"

"You can tell him no, if you want. About the cats—you don't have to do it."

"She's been staying over."

"I found all Grandma's old quilts. They were in a trunk in the back closet. Beautiful things. She made them all; some of them took her months. All of them hand-stitched. I never had the patience. She used to make me sit there with her for hours, learning the stitches. I'll show them to you if you want."

"Sure. I should get to work now, though."

"Next time, then."

August ate a few more potatoes and stood up.

"I wish you Godspeed," his mother said, coaxing another cigarillo from the pack with her lips. "May your arrows fly true."

"I don't have any arrows."

"I know. It's just an old Indian saying." She blew smoke at him. "I don't care about the cats," she said, smiling in such a way that her mouth didn't move and it was all in her eyes. "I look at you and it's clear as day to me that he hasn't won."

The barn was empty. His dad and Lisa were out rounding up the cows for milking. August put on his gloves and wedged the wrench down under his belt and climbed the wooden ladder up to the haymow.

Half-blind in the murk, wrinkling his nose at the burning ammonia stench of cat piss, he crushed the skull of the first pale form that came sidling up to him. He got two more in quick succession, and then there was nothing but hissing from the rafters, green-gold eyes glowing and shifting among the hulking stacks of baled hay. August tried to give chase. He clambered over the bales, scratching his bare arms and filling his eyes and ears and nose with the dusty chaff of old hay. But the cats were always out of reach, darting and leaping from one stack to the next, climbing the joists to the rafters, where they faded into the gloom. August imagined them up there, a seething furry mass, a foul clan of fanged wingless bats clinging to a cave roof. This was going to be harder than he had thought.

August inspected his kills. A full-sized calico and two grays, thin and in bad shape, patches of bare skin showing through their matted fur. He pitched them down the hay chute and climbed after them. On ground level, he took a deep breath of the comparatively sweet manure-scented air and fished his knife from his pocket. He picked up the first cat by the tail and severed it at the base, dropping the carcass on the cement with a wet thud. He dealt similarly with the other two cats, pitched them all in the conveyor trough, and went looking for a hammer. By the time he returned to the barn, his father and Lisa had the cows driven in and stanchioned in their stalls. The radio was on, loud enough that Paul Harvey's disembodied voice could be heard above the muttering of the cows and the drone of the compressor. *I don't know about you-all, but I have never seen a monument erected to a pessimist.*

August nailed his three tails on a long pine board and propped it up in the corner of the barn, where it wouldn't get knocked over by cows milling in and out. He could hear his father doing something in the milk room. He passed Lisa on his way out of the barn. She was leaning on a shovel and spitting sunflower seeds into the dirt. She had on blue overalls and muck boots, and her frizzy blond hair was tamed into a ponytail that burst through the hole in the rear of her seed co-op cap.

"Hi, August," she said, scooping seeds out of her lower lip and thwacking them into the dirt at her feet. "You didn't come up to the house for lunch."

"Yeah. I ate at the old house with my mom."

"Oh, okay. I'm going to stick around tonight. I think I'll make some tacos for you guys for dinner. Sound good?"

August looked at her face, her round, constantly red cheeks. She called it rosacea, a skin condition. It made her seem to exist in a state of perpetual embarrassment. He wondered if she'd been teased about it at school.

She was only seven years older than he was and had graduated from the high school last year. August's father had hired her in her senior year to help him with the milking. She'd worked before school and after school and on weekends. August's father had said that she worked harder than any hired man he'd ever had. Now that she was done with school, she put in full days. She could drive a tractor with a harrow, she could muck out the barn, she could give antibiotic shots to the cows, and when the calving season came she could plunge her hands in up to her wrists to help a difficult calf come bawling into the world.

"Crunchy shells or soft shells?" August said, knocking at the toes of his boots with the wrench.

"Soft?"

"I like crunchy."

"Well, I'll see what you guys have in the cupboards, but I bought some soft ones already."

"Flour or corn?"

"Flour, I think."

"I like corn." August spat at his feet, but his mouth was dry, so the spit trailed out on his chin and he wiped at it with the back of his sleeve.

"I asked your dad what kind he wanted and he said it didn't matter."

"He likes the crunchy shells too. Trust me. Do you make them with beans or without?"

Lisa hesitated for a moment and tugged at the brim of her cap. "Which do you prefer?" she said.

"Well, that depends."

"I bought some black beans. I usually put some of those in. But I don't have to."

"I like beans. But I don't eat black beans. I think they look like rabbit turds. My dad thinks that too."

"Okay, I'll leave those out, then. Sound good?" The red on Lisa's cheeks had spread. A crimson blush was leaching down her neck all the way to the collar of her barn overalls.

"All right, August, see you at dinner. Your dad's probably wondering where I got off to. We have to get these cows taken care of." Lisa headed into the barn, and August wandered out to the back pasture, swinging his wrench at stalks of burdock and thistle, stepping around the thick plots of fresh manure.

He climbed the low hill before the tree line on the property's boundary and sat next to the pile of rocks that marked Skyler's grave. There was a slightly bent sassafras stick, with the bark whittled off, jutting up from the rocks. It was all that was left of a cross August had fashioned from two such sticks lashed together with a piece of old shoelace. This was a gesture August had seen performed in all the old Westerns he watched with his father. Whenever a gunslinger went down, his buddies erected a cross just like that. During the course of the past year, the sun had rotted August's old shoelace so that the crosspiece had fallen off, leaving just the vertical stick pointing up at the sky like a crooked, accusatory finger.

Skyler had been his birth dog. His father had brought the tiny six-week-old pup home when August had been out of the hospital less than a week. It was something that August's father said his own father had done for him. He thought that it was good for a boy to have a dog to grow up with. And, against August's mother's objections, he'd put the soft, pug-faced shepherd mix in the crib with August—"to get acquainted," he said. "A boy with a dog is healthier, more active." And it seemed true. August had been a particularly sturdy baby, a bright, energetic boy who grew up with a shaggy, tongue-lolling, good-natured four-legged shadow.

At twelve, Skyler had been in remarkably good shape, a little stiff in the mornings but by noon harassing the barn cats like a dog half his age. But then, one day after school, August didn't see him anywhere in the barn or the yard. He went to the equipment shed and found him stretched out on his side with a greenish-blue froth discoloring his grayed muzzle. He'd chewed through a gallon jug of antifreeze that August's father kept under the workbench.

August and his father had carted the body up to the hill and taken turns with the pickax and shovel. When they'd finished they stood and regarded the cairn of rocks they'd stacked over the raw earth to keep the skunks out.

"I guess twelve is as good an age as any," his father had said. At the time, August thought he was talking about the dog. Later, he thought maybe his father had meant that twelve was as good an age as any for a boy to lose a thing he loved for the first time.

August watched the sky in the west become washed in dusky, pink-tinged clouds. Unbidden came the thought of Lisa, the crimson in her cheeks that spread like a hot infection down her neck and shoulders and back and arms, all the way to her legs. That this was the case wasn't mere supposition. He'd seen it.

It had been an early-dismissal day the previous fall. August, off the bus and out of his school clothes, eating a piece of cake from the new house, wandered down to the barn, the air sharp with the acrid tang of the oak leaves his father had been burning in the front yard. The pile smoldered; there was no one around. Skyler slept in the shade of a stock tank. The cows were yoked up in their stanchions. The whole barn was full of the low rumble of suction, the automatic milkers chugging away.

And then, through the open doorway of the grain room, there was his father, thrusting behind Lisa, who was bent over a hay bale, her cheek and forearms pressed down into the cut ends of the hay. Their overalls were around their legs like shed exoskeletons, as if they were insects emerging, their conjoined bodies larval, soft and mottled. August saw the flush of Lisa then, the creeping red that extended all the way down her back to her thick thighs and her spread calves. She had her underwear pulled down around her knees, and its brilliant lacy pinkness was a glaring insult to the honest, flyspecked gray and manure-brown of the barn.

On his way out, August turned the barn radio up as loud as it would go. *Golf,* Paul Harvey was saying, *is a game in which you yell "Fore," shoot six, and write down five.*

At the dinner table, Lisa and August's father each had a beer. Lisa cut a lime wedge and jammed it down the neck of her bottle, and August's father said, what the hell, he might try it like that too. They smiled at each other and clinked their bottles together and drank, and August watched the lime wedges bobbing in the bottles like floats in a level held on a surface that was out of true. When they'd finished eating, August's father leaned back in his chair and belched mightily, his rough, callused fingers shredding the paper napkin as he wiped taco juice from his hands.

"Best meal I've had in a while. Thanks, Lisa."

Lisa smiled and said, "You're welcome, Darwin. I'm glad you liked it."

"I got three cats today," August said to break up their stupid smiling competition. "I did it with a wrench. Right in the head. They never knew what happened." Out of the corner of his eye he could see Lisa wrinkle her nose slightly.

His father finished his beer and piled his fork and knife and napkin on his plate. He was a large man; all his joints seemed too big—hard, knobby wrists and knuckles, his hands darkened from the sun up to the point where his shirt cuffs lay. He was forty-five years old and still had a full head of hair, dark brown, just starting to gray at the temples. In the cold months, he liked to wear a bright silk cowboy scarf knotted around his neck. He smiled at women often, and, August noticed, women often smiled back. His mother used to say that for a guy with manure on his boots he could be fairly charming.

"Come on, now, Augie. I gave you a job and I appreciate you getting right down to it. But there's barn talk and there's house talk. I'm sure Lisa wouldn't mind a little house talk now. How about you clear the table and clean up the dishes. And why don't you thank Lisa for making that delicious meal? She worked all day and then came up to do that for us."

"Thanks," August said, and scooted his chair back loudly. He stacked the dishes into a precarious pile and carried them off to the kitchen. He ran the water until steam rose and squirted in soap until the bubbles grew in great tumorous mounds, and then he did the dishes. Clanking plate against plate, banging pot against pot, running the water unnecessarily, making as much noise as possible to cover the low murmur of Lisa and his father talking in the next room.

Through the kitchen window he could see the murky green cast of the yard light, the hulking form of the barn, and, farther out, the long, low shape of the old house, completely dark. When his father came in to get two more beers, August didn't turn around to look at him. He stood next to August at the sink and took the tops off the bottles. He nudged August with an elbow, and August scrubbed at a pan, ignoring him.

"How's your mother?"

August shrugged.

"I'm not going to run her down, Augie, but she's not a woman that will ever give you her true mind. You know what I mean?"

August shrugged.

"She's been disappointed her whole life, probably came out of the womb that way. You don't disappoint her, I know that, but everything else does—me included, always have, always will. She never learned to hold herself accountable. That's the way her parents allowed her to grow up. She's very smart and she thinks she sees things I don't see, but she's wrong, I'll tell you that. I see plenty. You hear me?"

August swirled a cup in the dishwater and didn't say anything. His father slapped him on the back of the head.

"I said, you hear me?"

"Yeah. I hear you." August looked straight ahead out the window.

"Okay, then." He reached into the dishwater, came up with a handful of suds, and smeared them on August's cheek. "You're all right," he said. "When you think it's time, you let me know and we'll go find you a pup."

In the morning, the smells of toast and coffee and bacon pulled August from his bed before the sun had even hit the east-facing window. He clumped down the stairs into the kitchen and sat at the table, rubbing his eyes. Lisa stood at the stove, making eggs. Her feet were bare and she had on the gray long underwear she wore under her barn overalls. They were made for men and were tight around her hips, and when she bent over to get the butter out of the refrigerator August could see the faint lines of her panties curving across her full rear.

"Would you like coffee, August?" August nodded, and she put a steaming mug in front of him. "I figure you like it black, like your dad does?"

"Sure," he said, taking a sip, trying not to grimace. "Black and strong."

His mother mixed his coffee with hot whole milk, dumping in heaping spoonfuls of sugar. She told him that was how she'd learned to make coffee when she lived in New Orleans, in another lifetime, before she married his father. August knew that Lisa would never go to New Orleans in a million lifetimes.

His father came from the bedroom. He had a dab of shaving foam under one earlobe. He put his hand on Lisa's waist as he got a coffee mug from the cupboard, and she turned and wiped off the shaving foam with her sleeve.

"How long before the eggs are done?" August asked, tapping his fingers on the tabletop.

"A few minutes. The bacon is almost ready."

August sighed, downed his coffee, and took a piece of toast from the plate on the counter. "Well," he said, "some of us can't sit around. I have to get to work."

He got his wrench from the mudroom and slid on his boots, leaving them unlaced, and walked across the lawn with his boot tongues flapping like dogs breathing in the heat. The cows were milling in the pasture, gathered up close to the gate. They rolled their dumb baleful eyes at him and lowed, their udders straining and heavy with milk.

"Shut up, you idiots," August said. He picked a small handful of pebbles and continued to walk, pelting any cow within reach.

The trees that lined the back pasture were old oaks and maples and a few massive beech trees, the ground around them covered with the scattered, spiny shells of their nuts. There was a barbed-wire fence strung across the trees. It was rusted and had been mended many times, so old that it had become embedded in the trunks. August walked down the line and ran his fingers over the rough oaks and maples and the gray crêpe of the beeches, with their bark that looked like smooth, hairless hide stretched over muscle. He let his fingers linger on the places where the wire cut into the trunks, and then he knelt and sighted all the way down the fence, squinting into the strengthening light, and imagined that he was looking at a row of gnarled old people, the soft skin of their necks garroted by barbed wire, the twisted branches like arms raised, fingers splayed, trembling and clutching for air.

Until last year, August had assisted with the milking every morning before school and every evening after school, and then his mother forbade it.

"Do you like helping your father with the milking?" she asked one evening as they cleaned up the dinner dishes. His father was on the porch listening to a baseball game, and the sound of the play-by-play came through the screen door, garbled and frantic. The announcer spat hoarsely, *A hard line drive—he's going, he's going, he's going.*

"I don't mind it too much," August said, wiping a plate dry. "Most of the time I like it."

"Huh, well, that's a problem," his mother said. She had a cigarette tucked into the corner of her mouth and ash drifted into the dishwater as she spoke. "You'll be in high school soon, you know. And then there'll be girls. They're going to find you so handsome. And then there'll be college, and then there'll be any life you want after that. This is just a small piece, Augie, and if you hate it, you should know that soon you'll be making your own way."

"But I said I don't hate it, Mom."

"Jesus. I really hope you don't mean that. Getting up early, the shitty cows, the dullness?"

"What about it?"

"My God, Augie, look at me and tell me you don't hate it." She turned to him and held his chin with her soapy hand and her cigarette trembled, and August tried but couldn't tell if she was serious and about to cry or joking and about to laugh.

"I don't hate anything. It's fine. I like everything fine."

"You're serious?"

"Yes."

"Then I'm disappointed in you," she said, turning back to the dishes. "But I suppose it's my fault, for letting it go on. I'm going to talk to your father. Your barn days are coming to an end. I'll finish up here. Go and listen to the game with your dad."

On the porch, his father was in the rocker, his legs stretched out long in front of him. He nodded at August as he sat on the step.

We're going into extra innings. Hang on as we pause for station identification. You're not going to want to miss this. The radio crackled and an ad for a used-car lot came on. Bats flew from the eaves, and August threw pebbles to make them dive, and then the game came back on and Cecil Fielder won it all for the Tigers on a long sacrifice fly to center field. August looked at his father. He was slumped in the chair with his eyes closed and his hands clasped together over his chest.

"Night," August said, getting up to go inside.

His father yawned and stretched. "Night," he said.

Later, his parents' arguing had kept him awake, and the next morning his father didn't roust him for the day's milking, and soon after that Lisa was always around, and not long after that his mother started spending time at the old house. At first, just a few nights a week, and then one morning she didn't come back to make breakfast, and his father burned the toast and slammed the door on his way to the barn.

August tied his boots. He climbed up to the haymow and surprised two cats that had been intently pawing at a dead sparrow on the hay-littered floor. He broke one's back with a quick chop of the wrench and stunned the other with a jab to the head. The cats were indistinct as they writhed, blurred in the gloom. August silenced their yowling with two more sharp blows from the wrench, and then gave chase to a few more slinking forms that eluded him by leaping to join their wailing, spitting clan in the rafters.

August didn't curse much. His father always said that no one took a man who cursed too much seriously and it was better to be the type of man who, when he did curse, made everyone else sit up and take notice.

Now, however, in the dark barn with the hay dander swirling around his face and the cats twitching and bristling out of reach above him, he cursed.

"Motherfucker," he said. "Motherfucking, cocksucking, shit-faced, goddam, fucking cats."

It was the most curse words he'd ever strung together, and he hoped the cats were sitting up to take notice, trembling in fear at the rain of fire that was about to be visited upon their mangy heads.

At the old house, his mother had the blinds drawn. She had cut a ragged hole in a quilt, pulled it over her head, and belted it around her waist, poncho style. Her arms stuck out, bare, and the quilt ends trailed across the floor when she got up to let him in. With the shades drawn it was dark, and she had lit an old kerosene lamp. The flame guttered, sending up tendrils of black smoke. She had been playing solitaire. There was a fried pork chop steaming in a pan on the table.

"You want some lunch?" she said, after she had settled in her chair, smoothing the quilt down under her and over her bare legs. "I'm finished. You can have the rest." She slid the pork chop over to August. It hadn't been touched.

He took a bite. It was seared crispy on the outside and juicy and tender on the inside, quick-fried in butter and finished in the oven. That was how she always made pork chops. Lisa wouldn't know how to do this, he thought. Perhaps his father would get so fed up with Lisa's tough, dried-out pork chops that he would send her away and his mother would come back to the new house and he'd start helping his dad with the barn chores again.

"Are you still not eating?" He picked up the pork chop to gnaw at the bone, where the best-tasting meat was.

"Augie, that's a common misconception about us breatharians.

I eat. Good Lord, I eat all the time. Here, actually, let me have one more bite of that." She leaned over and wafted her hand around his pork chop, bringing the smell toward her, and then took a quick hiccuping breath and smiled and leaned back in her seat. "Meat from an animal you know always has the best flavor," she said, lighting one of her little cigars. "That's something city people probably don't understand. You remember taking kitchen scraps out to that hog every night after dinner? You fed that animal, and now it feeds you. That lends a certain something to the savor—I'm sure there's a word for it in another language."

She pulled the quilt tighter around her shoulders. "Did you know that, Augie? That there are all sorts of words for things in other languages that we don't have in English? It's like your soul is tongue-tied when that happens, when you have a feeling or experience that you can't explain, because there isn't a specific word for it. If you knew all the languages in the world, you could express yourself perfectly, and all experiences would be understandable to you because you would have a word, a perfect word, to attach to any possible occasion. See what I mean?"

August was fairly certain that his mother was naked under her quilt. He wondered if there was a word for that in another language. A word to classify the feeling you get sitting across from your mother, eating a pork chop, with your mother naked under a quilt.

"I don't know," he said. "Just because you have a word to put on something doesn't mean you understand it any better. Does it?"

"Oh, I think so. Definitely. I don't think things really exist until we can name them. Without names, the world is just populated by spooks and monsters."

"Giving something a name doesn't change what it is. It's still the same thing."

"You couldn't be more wrong, Augie dear. How about death?"

"What about it?"

"What if instead of death everyone called it being born and looked forward to it as the great reward at the end of seventy or so years of slow rot on earth?"

"That doesn't make any sense. Why would anyone look forward to death?"

"Maybe you're too young for this conversation," she said, coughing into the back of her hand. "That's an interesting thought. I bet in some language there is a word for the state you exist in now—the state of being incapable of formulating a concept of, or discussing abstractly, death in all its various forms, owing to a lack of experience. You need to have someone you love die, and then you get it. All the understanding of the world comes rushing in on you like a vacuum seal was broken somewhere. I'm not saying you'll ever understand why the world works the way it does, but you'll surely come to the conclusion that it does work, and that, as a result, it will someday come to a grinding halt, because nothing can work forever. See what I mean?"

"No."

"Huh. Well, in time you will. I'm sure."

She picked up her solitaire game and shuffled the cards, splitting the deck, riffling the ends together with a brisk splat and then condensing the deck back together by making the cards bow and bridge and *shush* into one. August sat listening, enjoying the sound of the cards and thinking, knowing that she was wrong. He had loved someone who had died.

"How's the job coming?"

"Not great."

"Motivational issues?"

"No. They're just fast. I've been thinking about a change of tactics."

"Oh, yeah?"

"I don't know if it will work. Can I borrow some bowls?"

Lisa stayed for dinner again. August sensed that his life was now split into two distinct pieces. There was the part where Skyler was alive, where his father and mother and he had all lived in the new house, and now there was this new part, where things were foggy and indistinct. August twirled Lisa's spaghetti around on his fork and realized, for the very first time, that all of his life up to this very point existed only in the past, which meant that it didn't exist at all, not really. It might as well have been buried right there in the pasture, next to Skyler.

It was dark and cool in the barn, and August switched on the radio for company. He hadn't been able to sleep, so he'd risen early, before Lisa, even, and he hadn't had breakfast and his stomach rumbled as he climbed the wooden ladder up to the haymow. He could see the faint pinpricks of stars through the knotholes and chinks of the barn planks, and then his groping fingers found the pull chain and the haymow was flooded with fluorescent light.

The floor was carpeted with twisted feline forms—tabbies, calicos, some night-black, some pure white, intermingled and lumpy and irrevocably dead. They lay like pieces of dirty laundry where they'd fallen from their perches after the tainted milk had taken its hold on their guts. August coughed and spat, slightly awed, thinking about the night before and the way the antifreeze had turned the bluish-white milk a sickly rotten green. He nudged a few of the still forms with his boot and looked toward the rafters, where there was a calico, its dead claws stuck in the joist, so that it dangled there like a shabby, moth-eaten piñata.

He pulled his shirt cuffs into his gloves against the fleas jumping everywhere and began pitching the cats down the hay chute. As he worked, the voice of Paul Harvey found its way up from the radio on the ground floor.

Just think about it. All things considered, is there any time in history in which you'd rather live than now? I'll leave you with that thought. I'm Paul Harvey, and now you know the rest of the story.

August climbed down the ladder and stepped shin deep into a pile of cats. He got out his jackknife and stropped it a few times against the side of his boot and set to work separating the cats from their tails. As he worked he pushed the cats into the conveyor trough, and when he was done he flipped the wall switch to set the belt moving. August watched the cats ride the conveyor until all of them went out of sight under the back wall of the barn. Outside, they were falling from the track to the cart on the back of the manure spreader. He didn't go out to look, but he imagined them piling up, covering the dirty straw and cow slop, a stack of forms as lifeless and soft as old fruit, furred with mold. Tomorrow, or the next day, his father would hook the cart up to the tractor and drive it to the back pasture to spread its strange load across the cow-pocked grass.

It took him a long time to nail the tails to the board and, as he pounded, the last one was already stiffening. Dawn struck as August carried the board up to the new house. In the mudroom, he stopped and listened. There was no sound coming from the kitchen, but he knew that his father and Lisa would be up soon.

He leaned the board against the coat rack, directly over his father's barn boots, and regarded his work as it was, totem and trophy, altogether alien against a backdrop of lilac-patterned wallpaper.

August tried to whistle as he walked across the lawn and down the hill to the old house. He'd never got the hang of whistling. The best he could muster was a spit-laced warble. On the porch, he wiped his lips with the back of his sleeve and looked in the window. His mother was at the kitchen table. She held a card in her hand, raised, as if she were deciding her next move, but August could see that the cards in front of her were scattered across the table in disarray, a jumbled mess, as if they'd been thrown there.

Contributors' Notes

DANIEL ALARCÓN is the author of two story collections, a graphic novel, and *Lost City Radio,* which won the 2009 International Literature Prize. He was named one of *The New Yorker*'s 20 Under 40 in 2010, and his new novel, *At Night We Walk in Circles,* will be published in October 2013.

• I've spent the last seven or so years working on a novel, so most every story I've published in that time began the same way: it was meant to be part of the bigger book, but somehow outgrew its confines.

I think of these as sketches for the novel, and in the case of "The Provincials," there's quite a lot of overlap: this piece and the novel share a protagonist (Nelson), an obsession (acting), a troubled relationship, a father, an absent brother, a dreary coastal town. When the play began I knew it wouldn't be part of the book, but I wanted to follow the story and see where it went.

CHARLES BAXTER is the author of five novels and five books of short stories, most recently *Gryphon: New and Selected Stories.* He has also written two books of literary essays, *Burning Down the House* and *The Art of Subtext,* published by Graywolf. He was the editor for the Library of America edition of Sherwood Anderson's stories. He teaches at the University of Minnesota and lives in Minneapolis.

• The city of Prague is haunted by the armies that have invaded it, by Catholicism, and by Franz Kafka, among other presences. I visited the city three years ago and in one of its chapels had a jolting experience that led directly to this story. That memory found itself grafted onto a scene I had already witnessed in downtown Palo Alto, where some teenage girls riding in a car were taunting some boys standing together at a street corner. But the core of the story grew out of a quarrel I had thirty-four years ago with my wife about who would feed the baby. I never forgot that quarrel because it seemed telling to me. Everything else in the story is the essential brick-and-mortar of invention, the imaginary, and the possible.

MICHAEL BYERS is the author of a book of stories, *The Coast of Good Intentions,* and two novels, *Long for This World* and *Percival's Planet.* He directs the MFA program at the University of Michigan.

• As tends to be the way with my stories, I set out to write one thing and ended up with something seriously unrelated, which may be why "Malaria" didn't quite come together for a long time. I had most of it in hand, including the ending, but was stymied by what should happen after George went crazy and before Orlando and Nora went back to visit him again. I tried a dozen avenues, none that went anywhere.

Sometimes when I'm late in a story that's dead-ended like this, I'll poke around in the story's bag of emotions to see what I've got along with me—joy, envy, sorrow? Sometimes I can actually burrow under to the originating impulse of the material—the Platonic thing the story was before it got linted-up with particulars of character, setting, and so on—and tug something useful out into the light. In this case, I finally flashed that the story wasn't about Orlando and Nora as a couple but about Orlando himself. Once I got him alone, then put him on the tennis court with a bunch of strangers, I knew I had it right. Like most simple things the fix seems stupidly obvious in retrospect, but it took forever to discover.

JUNOT DÍAZ was born in the Dominican Republic and raised in New Jersey. He is the author of *Drown, The Brief Wondrous Life of Oscar Wao*—which won the John Sargent Sr. First Novel Prize, the National Book Critics Circle Award, the Anisfield-Wolf Book Award, and the 2008 Pulitzer Prize—and *This Is How You Lose Her,* which was a finalist for the National Book Award. Díaz is a recipient of the Eugene McDermott Award, a fellowship from the Guggenheim Foundation, the Lila Acheson Wallace Reader's Digest Award, the 2002 PEN/Malamud Award, the 2003 U.S./Japan Creative Artist Fellowship from the National Endowment for the Arts, a fellowship at the Radcliffe Institute for Advanced Study at Harvard University, the Rome Prize from the American Academy of Arts and Letters, a fellowship from the MacArthur Foundation, and the Sunday Times Short Story Prize. A Rutgers University graduate, he is the fiction editor at the *Boston Review* and a founding member of the Voices Writers Workshop (http://voicesatvona.org/Home.html). The Rudge and Nancy Allen Professor at the Massachusetts Institute of Technology, he splits his time between Cambridge and New York City.

• I'd been trying to write "Miss Lora" for nearly seven years. As is usually the case with me, the story just wouldn't come together. I tried it in first person and in third person, as a journal, a series of letters, a confession, but nada. Nevertheless I stayed on it, producing lame draft after lame draft. What made the difference finally was a trip that I took with some of my boys, and one night in a club in Bayahibe some of them started opening up about how their first sexual relationships were with these older women in the neighborhood and that just broke the last pinion, gave me the permission I needed to get it done.

KARL TARO GREENFELD has written six books, including the novel *Triburbia.* His fiction has appeared in *Harper's Magazine,* the *Paris Review, Ploughshares, Playboy, Commentary,* the *Southern Review, One Story,* PEN/*O. Henry Prize Stories,* and a previous edition of *The Best American Short Stories.* His nonfiction is widely published and anthologized. Follow him @karltaro or visit karltarogreenfeld.com.

▪ When I was a freshman in college, our dormitory was what had once been a mansion, now subdivided into doubles. My roommate was digging around in the back of our closet one day, and in a narrow alcove behind a stud he found a small devil's head sculpted from clay. We didn't know what to make of this and after studying it, we left it where it had been. I don't recall being frightened by it. We assumed it was something planted by previous students. But I obviously remembered the little totem and found it noteworthy.

I wrote "Horned Men" in the fall of 2009 and submitted it to about fifty journals over the next two years. It was turned down by every single journal you've ever heard of—including *Zyzzyva*—and many that you haven't. Finally, hearing that *Zyzzyva* had changed editors, I re-sent it and this time it was accepted.

GISH JEN's new book, based on a series of lectures she gave about writing and culture, is titled *Tiger Writing: Art, Culture, and the Interdependent Self.* She is also the author of four novels—*World and Town, Typical American, Mona in the Promised Land,* and *The Love Wife*—as well as a collection of stories, *Who's Irish?* Her short fiction has appeared in *The New Yorker, The Atlantic,* the *Paris Review, Granta,* and numerous anthologies, including *The Best American Short Stories of the Century,* edited by John Updike; she has also written nonfiction for the *New Republic,* the *New York Times* op-ed page, and other publications. Grant support has come from the Guggenheim Foundation, the Fulbright Foundation, the National Endowment for the Arts, and the Radcliffe Institute for Advanced Study, among other sources. She received a Lannan Award for Fiction in 1999 and a Harold and Mildred Strauss Living from the American Academy of Arts and Letters in 2003. In 2009, she was elected to the American Academy of Arts and Sciences.

▪ The origins of stories are always murky for me. No doubt my own parents were on my mind when I wrote "The Third Dumpster." They never viewed assisted living as an option for a million reasons, starting with the food; and it's true that I felt that the older they got, the more clearly you could see how difficult it was to have come to America—what an opportunity it was, but what a price they had paid in terms of connection and community. How, though, did this feeling—a feeling that I'd had for at least a decade—suddenly become story material? How did it suddenly become funny? Painfully funny, of course, but nonetheless funny. Liberatingly funny.

I don't know for sure. As it happens, though, I wrote a little about the writing of this story in my recent book, *Tiger Writing: Art, Culture, and the Interdependent Self,* speculating that one day at my computer, I simply found myself in a more Asian frame of mind. There is evidence to support this idea. For example, the Chinese author Lin Yutang observed in his 1935 classic, *My Country and My People,* how the Chinese are given to a farcical view of life, with "Chinese humor . . . consist[ing] in compliance with outward form . . . and the total disregard of the substance in actuality," and certainly this describes Morehouse's approach to the problems he and his brother face. It is an approach Goodwin adopts too, from time to time, cloaking his desire for independence so transparently—"And the elevators! Didn't they just make you want go up?"—that he, and we, find it funny. But probably the story behind the story was that I myself had hit some tipping point in dealing with my own real aging parents, where I needed to "throw off the too heavy burden imposed . . . by life," as Freud puts it, "and win the high yield of pleasure afforded by humour." That's to say that I wrote this story because I myself needed to laugh and had somehow found a way to do that.

BRET ANTHONY JOHNSTON is the author of *Corpus Christi: Stories* and the editor of *Naming the World and Other Exercises for the Creative Writer.* His work has appeared in *The Atlantic, Esquire,* the *Paris Review, Glimmer Train,* and anthologies such as *The Best American Short Stories, The Best American Sports Writing,* and *The Pushcart Prize: Best of the Small Presses.* He wrote the documentary film *Waiting for Lightning,* and his novel, *Remember Me Like This,* is forthcoming in 2014. He teaches in the Bennington Writing Seminars and at Harvard University, where he is director of creative writing. His website is www.bretanthonyjohnston.com.

• This story was born from the image of teenagers playing on an abandoned golf course, and although there's only a passing mention of that here, I think of it as indispensible. The tattoo and animal stuff has been batting around in my head for years, and I've tried to get the phrase "a trickle of water tracking through pebbles" into just about everything I've ever written. I should also say that I thought the father's plan would work. I thought he was trying to do right by his boy, and until things went wrong, I thought he'd say his piece, deliver the girl home, and the night would end quietly. I'm grateful it didn't.

And I'm grateful, immeasurably so, to Heidi Pitlor for the kindness she's shown my work. That Elizabeth Strout, a writer whom you read again and again to greater reward, would like this story is beyond humbling. I'm also indebted to Tyler Cabot at *Esquire* for his keen edits and the home he gave the story, and to Amy Hempel for her generous and unsurprisingly spot-on suggestions on how to make the story its best self.

Finally, this story is dedicated to the memory of Mike Anzaldúa. Without him, the story wouldn't exist. None of mine would.

SHEILA KOHLER is the author of three volumes of short stories and ten novels, including *Cracks, Becoming Jane Eyre,* and most recently, *The Bay of Foxes* (2012). *Dreaming for Freud* will be published in 2014. Her short stories have appeared in *The O. Henry Prize Stories* and the *Best American* series. Her work has been published in twelve countries. *Cracks* has been filmed with Jordan Scott as director and Ridley Scott as executive producer and Eva Green playing Miss G.

• There are elements of my life in the story. I do come from South Africa and I did lose a beloved sister in violent domestic circumstances. However, the story also has echoes from literature. I was thinking of the German myth in which a child is led to death by a supernatural being, which Goethe uses in his great poem "Erlkönig."

DAVID MEANS was born and raised in Michigan. His second collection of short stories, *Assorted Fire Events,* earned the Los Angeles Times Book Prize for fiction and has recently been reissued by Faber. His third collection, *The Secret Goldfish,* was a finalist for the Frank O'Connor International Short Story Prize. His most recent book, *The Spot,* was a New York Times Notable Book. He lives in Nyack, New York.

• "The Chair" came out of my experiences as a father and drew on a particular feeling of isolation that comes from being alone at home with your kids, trying to instruct, to guide, to find a way to persuade and protect. There's an aspect of crime and punishment in so much parental interaction—along with a strange, dangerous dynamic that involves living vicariously through your kids (sometimes for just a few seconds) even as you're paradoxically aware that you really can't. This dynamic is hugely problematic, and I've thought about it a lot over the years until, finally, I started writing "The Chair," which began as a much longer story—a man and a woman in bed discussing their son, analyzing his recent behavior, asking themselves how they might better parent him—and then, in revisions, began to zero in on the incident in the yard. A breakthrough came when the father said to the son, "You'll get the chair." Then I understood that the story wanted to be about potential punishment, and it was being fueled by the fact that I've always detested the term "time out." You're going to get a "time out" sounded, and still sounds, linguistically crazy. If you don't do what I say you should do, I'm going to remove you from time? As a parenting technique, it was popular a few years ago—maybe it still is.

STEVEN MILLHAUSER's most recent book is *We Others: New and Selected Stories.* Other works include *Edwin Mullhouse: The Life and Death of an American Writer* and *Martin Dressler: The Tale of an American Dreamer.* His stories have appeared in *The New Yorker, Harper's Magazine, McSweeney's,* and *Tin House.* He was born in Brooklyn, grew up in Connecticut, and now lives in Saratoga Springs, New York.

• I've always been fascinated by the story of Saul. Last year I reread the two books of Samuel, with the vague idea of writing about Saul and David. I quickly abandoned the idea, but my reading awoke a childhood memory of first hearing the story of Samuel, the boy whose name was called in the night. That memory gave rise to my story.

LORRIE MOORE is the Gertrude Conaway Vanderbilt Professor of English in the creative writing program at Vanderbilt University.

• Nabokov's famous story "Signs and Symbols" is one of those perfect narrative objects that reveals different things when read at different times, even as it itself remains unchanging. A rereading of this story last year left me in a somewhat new referential condition (though shattered; one is always shattered), and whether it was good inspiration or misbegotten, I was led to try to compose a kind of narrative dance with the story—though I am the hat rack and Nabokov is Fred Astaire. Good idea or bad?—I felt possessed and did not decide nor resist. It was less a "revisioning" and more of a "wandering toward then away then back again." But it was an honoring exercise, perhaps also an exorcism. "Amateurs imitate, artists steal": a variation on an old saw I was reminded of recently in a nifty book called *Steal Like an Artist,* which is full of things said by other people—natch. But "Referential" is not an actual theft nor trying to slink about as if committing one but is intended as—what? A tribute—and like most tributes it contains both debts and detours, shadowings and separatenesses, the collaging of other narratives, and even a joke or two.

ALICE MUNRO grew up in Wingham, Ontario, and attended the University of Western Ontario. She has published many books, including *Dance of the Happy Shades; Lives of Girls and Women; Something I've Been Meaning to Tell You; Who Do You Think You Are?; The Moons of Jupiter; The Progress of Love; Friend of My Youth; Open Secrets; The Love of a Good Woman; Hateship, Friendship, Courtship, Loveship, Marriage; The View from Castle Rock; Too Much Happiness;* and *Dear Life.*

During her distinguished career, Munro has been the recipient of many awards and prizes, including the W. H. Smith Award in the United

Kingdom and the National Book Critics Circle Award, the PEN/Malamud Award for Excellence in Short Fiction, the Lannan Literary Award, and the Rea Award for the Short Story in the United States. *Away from Her,* the film version of Munro's "The Bear Came over the Mountain," won seven Genie Awards and was nominated for two Academy Awards.

In Canada, her prize-winning record is extraordinary: three Governor General's Awards, two Giller Prizes, the Trillium Book Award, the Jubilee Prize, and the Libris Award. Abroad, acclaim continues to pour in. *Runaway* and *Hateship, Friendship, Courtship, Loveship, Marriage* won the Commonwealth Writer's Prize Best Book Award, Caribbean and Canada region, and were chosen as Books of the Year by the *New York Times.* In 2005, Munro was included in *Time* magazine's list of the world's one hundred most influential people. In 2009, she was awarded the prestigious Man Booker International Prize for "a body of work that has contributed to an achievement in fiction on the world stage."

Alice Munro's stories appear regularly in *The New Yorker,* as well as in *The Atlantic* and the *Paris Review.* She and her husband divide their time between Clinton, Ontario, and Comox, British Columbia.

▪ "Train" examines a man's desire to avoid his past mistakes by essentially becoming someone new, someone in whom others can place trust and belief and even memories of loved ones now gone. To atone is so often to assume a new, cleaner identity. To attempt, of course, to begin again. I don't know whether this is an effective strategy, but the desire to escape and rebuild is something I find interesting.

ANTONYA NELSON is the author, most recently, of *Bound* (a novel) and *Nothing Right* (stories). She teaches in the creative writing programs at the University of Houston and Warren Wilson College. Her favorite color is green, and she loves babies and corgi dogs and earrings and standup comedy and cocktail hour.

▪ "Chapter Two" was in my head for years before it was on the page. Based loosely on an actual person, the proximity of high-hilarity hijinks and sudden sobering utter mortal demise was a story I couldn't seem to tell, although I knew I wanted to somehow capture that exact sensation. How to frame a story? It's my main question, right after Is it happy hour yet?

KIRSTIN VALDEZ QUADE was a Wallace Stegner and Truman Capote Fellow at Stanford University, where she is now a Jones Lecturer. She holds degrees from Stanford and the University of Oregon and has received fellowships from Yaddo, Bread Loaf, and the MacDowell Colony, as well as a grant from the Elizabeth George Foundation. Her work has appeared in *The New Yorker, Narrative Magazine, The Best of the West 2010,* and elsewhere.

▪ The violent backstory of "Nemecia" is based loosely on true events.

As a small child, my godmother watched as her father brutally beat her mother and murdered her grandfather. Her father fled to the mountains but was eventually caught by a posse of neighbors. When he was released from prison, my great-grandmother said, he wasn't the same man. "He was innocent, like a child." Her phrasing struck me, and suddenly I saw him vividly: reduced, broken, vacant.

I peopled the incident with invented characters and gave them needs and motivations entirely their own. Nemecia is not my godmother, who was generous and deeply loyal to her family and friends. As I wrote I discovered that I was less interested in the murder itself than in its reverberations and in the way trauma can become a kind of treasure, a currency to be hoarded or envied or spent.

SUZANNE RIVECCA is the author of *Death Is Not an Option* (2010), a finalist for the Story Prize, the New York Public Library Young Lions Award, the Frank O'Connor International Short Story Award, and the PEN/Hemingway Award. The recipient of a Rome Prize in Literature from the American Academy of Arts and Letters, she lives in San Francisco and works at an organization that serves the homeless.

• I work as a grant writer for a nonprofit that serves homeless runaways in San Francisco. "Philanthropy" had its genesis in my frustration with the sometimes sanitized and simplified way in which I have to portray our clients' lives, circumstances, and trajectories for the benefit of potential funders. When you're scrounging for money from rich faceless entities, a penitential quality infuses the prose by default; it's like you revert back to some hard-wired feudal mindset, hat in hand. There's no bigger sin in America than having the temerity to make others bear witness to destitution, and I atone for that sin by grafting an implicitly flattering aspirational arc onto each request: if you give us money, rich people, you'll be helping these poor boys and girls become more like you. Normal. Relatable. Sympathetic.

There's an expectation that once "recovery" happens, all past hedonism and experimentation must be renounced and rendered an utter waste. Whenever I interview a former client for a newsletter article or grant proposal, she'll invariably say something like, "I don't regret all the drugs I did and all the insane experiences I had, because I wouldn't be the person I am without them, and that's what I needed to be doing at the time." And I think to myself, "Well, shit, I can't put that in there." But I should be able to. You shouldn't have to disown and amputate your past in order to forge a future.

When I wrote a first draft of this story, I showed it to a few people at an artists' residency. One woman, who may or may not have been the female incarnation of Mitt Romney, approached me to give me a lecture about my unfair portrayal of the downtrodden rich. She said, "Look, my family has a lot of money, and I have a LOT of rich friends. And they're good people from Brookline, Massachusetts! Just because someone's rich doesn't mean they're bad and foolish. After all, they're the ones who are putting up the money! They put up all the money but they still have to take all the ridicule. It's just not fair!"

Well, lady, this is for you. If any residents of Brookline want to redeem their town's image, I invite them to go to homelessyouthalliance.org and chip in a dollar.

Above all, this story is essentially a love letter to my boss, who does an impossible job every day with tenacity, ingenuity, and humor.

GEORGE SAUNDERS is the author of four story collections, the most recent being *Tenth of December.* In 2006 he was awarded fellowships from the Guggenheim Foundation and the MacArthur Foundation. He was awarded the 2013 PEN/Malamud Award for excellence in the art of short fiction. He teaches at Syracuse University.

• "The Semplica-Girl Diaries" came directly out of a dream: in the dream, I got out of bed, went to a (nonexistent) window in our house, looked out, and saw four women suspended between two A-shaped frames on a tiny wire that ran in one side of the head and out the other. The women—who, in my dream-logic, I understood to be poor women from Third World countries—wore matching white smocks, had beautiful long black hair, were alive, and were not in any pain—they were talking happily in the moonlight. And—the kicker—my reaction (that is, the reaction of the guy I was in the dream) was not "Holy shit, what's going on here?" but "Oh wow, we are so lucky to finally be able to get these for our kids." That is: pure gratitude. The story then took twelve years to finish.

JIM SHEPARD is the author of six novels, including, most recently, *Project X,* and four story collections, including *Like You'd Understand, Anyway,* which was a finalist for the National Book Award and won the Story Prize, and *You Think That's Bad,* released in 2011. He teaches at Williams College.

• My mother, who lived through the Great Depression, and my brother are two of the more frugal people you could ever meet, so frugal, in fact, that they enjoy browsing at their local Goodwill, and sometimes I'll go along, both to spend some time with them and because I occasionally nurse the fantasy that I'll stumble across some unexpected find when sorting through the dollar books. Ninety-five percent of those book piles are exactly the sort of battered and dispiriting bestsellers and self-help books you'd expect, but the other 5 percent can feature the truly arcane and strange. Out of one such pile, for example, I pulled Sidney Perley's fantastically bizarre *Historic Storms of New England,* a chronological compendium of eyewitness accounts of the most destructive storms to hit the region, from the first settlements to the late nineteenth century. Nearly all of those accounts, unsurprisingly, were from the point of view of farmers whose entire livelihoods had been threatened by what they'd experienced. The inability to predict such catastrophes—and the sense that you might work hard yet never know what was rolling toward you over the next set of hills—stuck in my imagination for years. I started thinking about writing a story about such a life.

That led to books on nineteenth-century farming, the sort of texts that almost no one in their right mind would check out of a library: things like Jared Van Wagenen Jr.'s *The Golden Age of Homespun* or T. B. Terry's *Our Farming*. And it was in one of those texts that I came across a forlorn little emotional moment that spawned "The World to Come" in its entirety: a notation in a farm wife's daily journal that the one friend that she had had in the entire valley, to whom she had been utterly devoted, had been forced to move away. And suddenly a whole vista of desolation and loneliness and foreclosed options seemed to peep forth.

ELIZABETH TALLENT teaches in Stanford University's creative writing program.

• While I was working on this little essay I called the Word document Wilderness_Explanation, and that was a mistake—I kept opening it, thinking I can't explain, and closing it. My mistake, but one of those mistakes that reflect flatteringly on the mistaker, since each time the doc winked shut, I felt I had honored some essential obscurity in my relation to the story. I don't want to take an authoritative stance toward something inexplicable, partly out of fear that if I do, nothing inexplicable will happen to me again as a writer.

So, my none-too-sure guess is that this story began with bewilderment, and that the source of the bewilderment was one of those ordinary, small-scale, recurrent rifts between what you know you feel and what you are willing for others to see. It was this: even with teaching colleagues I know and trust, I'd rather keep my mouth shut than confess to the absorption, connection, and intimacy it's possible to feel while teaching. Delight regularly figures in my dealings with students, but that delight couldn't be declared, or it would reflect badly on me. Only, where did that notion come from? I picked it up somewhere. I picked it up everywhere. Teaching is not supposed to be about delight any more than the books on the syllabus are there for delight. I was dissembling about pleasure and whenever there's dissembling about pleasure, there's the hint of a story.

Once there was that hint, I began watching for any bits or pieces belonging to the story, for details or phrases or any experience of incongruity that would belong with the other pieces. I liked this because it was a collagelike, collecting way of working whose progression was less like carpentry than like browsing, with browsing's readiness to like. I might as well have been on a beach looking around for stones that struck me as individuals. That sounds—simple! When I teach, what I want to encourage in young writers is some internalizable Winnicottian/Keatsian willingness to tolerate uncertainties, errors, etc., while they're working, but my own unwillingness is a problem for me. With this story, for whatever reason, a door opened in perfectionism's wall. There was also the weird, refracted pleasure of being in the process of writing this story when I'd run into some fresh bewilderment in teaching because I could think, Ah, this is my real life giving me a piece of my fictional life. Which it (my real life) suddenly seemed very happy to do.

Maybe it mattered less, but there was also the grain-of-sand/oyster vexation of fictional professors' almost always being assholes, with Pnin as the fantastically lovable exception to the rule. In fiction, professor is predatory, student is prey. This ironclad dyad goes to bed without caring much about the intricacy, anxiety, and comedy of teaching. So there's room.

JOAN WICKERSHAM's most recent book of fiction is *The News from Spain: Seven Variations on a Love Story*. Her memoir *The Suicide Index* was a National Book Award finalist. Her short fiction has appeared in many magazines as well as in *The Best American Short Stories* and *The Best American Nonrequired Reading*. She also writes a regular op-ed column for the *Boston Globe,* and her pieces often run in the *International Herald Tribune*. She lives with her husband and their two sons in Cambridge, Massachusetts.

• A few years ago I got an idea for a story called "The News from Spain." I never got a chance to write it, and the next time I thought of it, I realized I'd forgotten everything except the title. The loss was maddening but also somehow evocative. And suddenly I imagined a book: a suite of asymmetrical, thwarted love stories, each of which would be called "The News from Spain." I wanted the title to feel central to each story and to mean something different in each, but to acquire more resonance—an accrued sense of something deeply felt and elusive, impossible to put into words—as the book went along.

So this is one of those stories. (In the book it, like all the others, is called simply "The News from Spain," but in order to publish different stories in different magazines I had to differentiate them somehow—hence "The Tunnel.") I wrote it soon after my mother had gone to live in a nursing home; her physical condition was dire but her mind was still sharp. And our relationship was prickly but close.

Rebecca's romantic history has nothing to do with mine. But the central love story here, between the mother and the daughter, was pretty much a straightforward example of "Write what you know," which I always amend to read, "Write what matters to you."

CALLAN WINK's stories have appeared in *Granta, The New Yorker, Ecotone,* and others. He lives in Livingston, Montana.

• This story, especially the setting, stems largely from the farm of one of my childhood friends. I would go there on the weekends and we would just run wild around the place—play in the barns, climb the hay, etc.

Once, I saw a cat, a small calico, dead on a pile of manure that was going to be spread on the fields. I think, in large part, this story developed as some sort of justification for this image, one that twenty years later I still can picture very clearly.

Other Distinguished Stories of 2012

ALMOND, STEVE
Gondwana. *Ploughshares,* vol. 38, no. 1.

APPEL, JACOB M.
The Price of Storks. *Western Humanities Review,* vol. 66, no. 2.

BAKER, MATTHEW
Everything That Somehow Found Us Here. *New England Review,* vol. 33, no. 2.

BARRETT, ANDREA
The Particles. *Tin House,* no. 51.

BEAMS, CLARE
World's End. *One Story,* no. 166.

BEATTIE, ANN
The Astonished Woodchopper. *Paris Review,* no. 201.

BERGMAN, MEGAN MAYHEW
Phoenix. *Ploughshares Pshares Singles,* no. 3.

BLACK, ALETHEA
You, on a Good Day. *One Story,* no. 163.

BOSWELL, ROBERT
American Epiphany. *American Short Fiction,* vol. 15, no. 54.

BOYLE, T. CORAGHESSAN
Birnam Wood. *The New Yorker,* September 3.

BRADLEY, DAVID
You Remember the Pin Mill. *Narrative Magazine,* Spring.

BROWN, KAREN
Stillborn. *Epoch,* vol. 61, no. 2.

CARLSON, RON
Line from a Movie. *Zyzzyva,* no. 96.

CELONA, MARJORIE
The Everpresent Hell of Other People. *Harvard Review,* no. 42.

CHABON, MICHAEL
Citizen Conn. *The New Yorker,* February 13 & 20.

CLARK, GEORGE MAKANA
The Incomplete Priest. *Ecotone,* no. 114.

COOPER, RAND RICHARDS
Tunneling. *Commonweal,* July.

CORE, LEOPOLDINE
The Underside of Charm. *Joyland,* vol. 1, no. 2.

CREWS, HARRY
You'll Like My Mother's Grave. *Georgia Review,* vol. 66, no. 3.

DAHLIE, MICHAEL
The Pharmacist from Jena. *Harper's Magazine,* January.

DARK, ALICE ELLIOT
Rumm Road. *The Literarian,* no. 7.
DE JARNATT, STEVE
Mulligan. *Cincinnati Review,* vol. 8, no. 2.
DEWILLE, JAMES
Last Days on Rossmore. *American Short Fiction,* vol. 15, no. 55.
DÍAZ, JUNOT
The Cheater's Guide to Love. *The New Yorker,* July 23.
DONOGHUE, EMMA
Onward. *The Atlantic,* September.
DUVAL, PETE
Orchard Tender. *Meridian,* no. 28.

EDOCHIE, CHIDELIA
The King of Hispaniola. *Michigan Quarterly Review,* vol. 51, no. 1.
EGAN, JENNIFER
Black Box. *The New Yorker,* June 4 & 11.
ELLIOTT, JULIA
LIMBs. *Tin House,* no. 51.
ERDRICH, LOUISE
Nero. *The New Yorker,* May 7.

FRISCH, SARAH
Housebreaking. *Paris Review,* no. 203.

GALCHEN, RIVKA
Appreciation. *The New Yorker,* March 19.
GENI, ABBY
Dharma at the Gate. *Glimmer Train,* no. 83.
GILSON, WILLIAM
At the Dark End of the Street. *New England Review,* vol. 33, no. 1.
GROFF, LAUREN
Abundance. *Ecotone,* no. 13.
A Season by the Shore. *Glimmer Train,* no. 82.

HAIGH, JENNIFER
A Place in the Sun. *The Common,* no. 4.
HARDY, EDWARD
Hole in the Sand. *Glimmer Train,* no. 85.
HEMPEL, AMY
A Full-Service Shelter. *Tin House,* vol. 13, no. 4.

JAMES, TANIA
Lion and Panther in London. *Granta,* no. 119.
The Scriptological Review. *A Public Space,* no. 15.

KADETSKY, ELIZABETH
An Incident at the Plaza. *Antioch Review,* vol. 70, no. 1.
KING, STEPHEN
Batman and Robin Have an Altercation. *Harper's Magazine,* September.
KRAUSS, NICOLE
An Arrangement of Light. *Byliner,* August.

LA FARGE, PAUL
Another Life. *The New Yorker,* July 2.
LANCELOTTA, VICTORIA
So Happy. *Hayden's Ferry Review,* no. 50.
LERNER, BEN
The Golden Vanity. *The New Yorker,* June 18.
LIPSYTE, SAM
The Republic of Empathy. *The New Yorker,* June 4 & 11.
LODATO, VICTOR
P.E. *The New Yorker,* April 2.

MARTIN, JEFF
When the Water Rises. *Greensboro Review,* no. 92.
MCCANN, COLUM
Transatlantic. *The New Yorker,* April 16.
MCCRACKEN, ELIZABETH
A Dream of Being Sufficient. *Zoetrope: All-Story,* vol. 13, no. 3.
MCDERMOTT, ALICE
Someone. *The New Yorker,* January 30.

McGraw, Erin
Step. *Image,* no. 73.
McGuane, Thomas
The Casserole. *The New Yorker,* September 10.
A Prairie Girl. *The New Yorker,* February 27.
Meloy, Maile
The Proxy Marriage. *The New Yorker,* May 21.
Moore, Lorrie
Wings. *Paris Review,* no. 20.
Morrissey, Colleen
Good Faith. *Cincinnati Review,* vol. 9, no. 2.
Munro, Alice
Amundsen. *The New Yorker,* August 27.
Haven. *The New Yorker,* March 5.

Naiditch, Dovber
The Angel in the House. *Prairie Schooner,* vol. 86, no. 4.
Nelson, Kent
La Mer de L'Ouest. *Georgia Review,* vol. 66, no. 2.
Null, Matthew Neill
Telemetry. *Ploughshares,* vol. 38, no. 4.

Okparanta, Chinelo
America. *Granta,* no. 118.
Orner, Peter
The Hole. *Ecotone,* no. 13.

Parameswaran, Rajesh
On the Banks of Table River (Planet Lucina, Andromeda Galaxy, A.D. 2319). *Zoetrope: All-Story,* vol. 16, no. 1.
Parry, Leslie
New Heaven. *Missouri Review,* vol. 35, no. 2.
Pearlman, Edith
Life Lessons. *Cincinnati Review,* vol. 8, no. 2.
Stone. *Agni,* no. 75.
Podos, Rebecca
The Fourth. *Glimmer Train,* no. 84.
Poole, Nathan
Stretch Out Your Hand. *Narrative Magazine,* Winter.
Powers, Richard
Genie. *Byliner,* November.

Ratcliffe, Jane
You Can't Be Too Careful. *New England Review,* vol. 33, no. 1.
Rawlings, Wendy
Tics. *Agni,* no. 76.
Row, Jess
Summer Song. *Tin House,* vol. 13, no. 4.
Ruskovich, Emily
An Impending Change of Heart. *Zoetrope: All-Story,* vol. 16, no. 4.
Russell, Karen
Reeling for the Empire. *Tin House,* vol. 14, no. 2.

Schaffert, Timothy
Lady of the Burlesque Ballet. *Ploughshares Pshares Singles,* no. 1.
Schutz, Greg
The Sweet Nothings. *Carolina Quarterly,* vol. 62, no. 2.
Shapiro, Gerald
A Drunkard's Walk. *Michigan Quarterly Review,* vol. 51, no. 2.
Shipstead, Maggie
The Great Central Pacific Guano Company. *American Short Fiction,* vol. 15, no. 54.
In the Olympic Village. *Subtropics,* no. 13.
Siegel, Robert Anthony
The Right Imaginary Person. *Tin House,* vol. 14, no. 2.
Slouka, Mark
Russian Mammoths. *Orion,* March/April.
Sneed, Christine
The Finest Medical Attention. *New England Review,* vol. 33, no. 1.

SPENCER, DARRELL
Squeeze Me, I Sing. *Georgia Review,* vol. 66, no. 1.
SPENCER, ELIZABETH
Blackie. *Epoch,* vol. 61, no. 1.

TAYLOR, JUSTIN
After Ellen. *The New Yorker,* August 13 & 20.
THEROUX, PAUL
Our Raccoon Year. *Harper's Magazine,* May.
TOUTONGHI, PAULS
The Limit of the World. *Epoch,* vol. 61, no. 3.
TROY, JUDY
My Buried Life. *Kenyon Review,* vol. 34, no. 3.

VAN DEN BERG, LAURA
Lessons. *American Short Fiction,* vol. 15, no. 54.
Opa Locka. *Southern Review,* vol. 48, no. 3.
VAPNYAR, LARA
Fischer vs. Spassky. *The New Yorker,* October 8.
VIERGUYTZ, DINA NAYARI
A Teaspoon of Earth and Sea. *Southern Review,* vol. 48, no. 2.
VOLLMER, MATTHEW
Advanced Placement Question 3, Free Response. *The Normal School,* vol. 5, no. 2.

WALTER, JESS
Thief. *Harper's Magazine,* March.
WATERS, DON
Full of Days. *Southwest Review,* vol. 97, no. 1.
WATKINS, CLAIRE VAYE
The Archivist. *Glimmer Train,* no. 83.

Editorial Addresses of American and Canadian Magazines Publishing Short Stories

Able Muse Review
467 Saratoga Avenue, #602
San Jose, CA 95129
$24, Nina Schyler

African American Review
http://aar.expressacademic.org
$40, Nathan Grant

Agni
Boston University Writing Program
Boston University
236 Bay State Road
Boston, MA 02115
$20, Sven Birkerts

Alaska Quarterly Review
University of Alaska, Anchorage
3211 Providence Drive
Anchorage, AK 99508
$18, Ronald Spatz

Alimentum
www.alimentumjournal.com
$18, Paulette Licitra

Alligator Juniper
http://www.prescott.edu/alligator_juniper/
$15, Melanie Bishop

American Letters and Commentary
Department of English
University of Texas at San Antonio
One UTSA Boulevard
San Antonio, TX 78249
$10, David Ray Vance, Catherine Kasper

American Short Fiction
P.O. Box 302678
Austin, TX 78703
$30, Stacey Swann

Amoskeag
Southern New Hampshire University
2500 N. River Road
Manchester, NH 03106
$7, Michael J. Brien

Anderbo.com
anderbo.com
Rick Rofihe

Annalemma
annalemma.net
Chris Heavener

Antioch Review
Antioch University
P.O. Box 148
Yellow Springs, OH 45387
$40, Robert S. Fogerty

Apalachee Review
P.O. Box 10469
Tallahassee, FL 32302
$15, Michael Trammell

Apple Valley Review
88 S. 3rd Street, Suite 336
San Jose, CA 95113

Arkansas Review
P.O. Box 1890
Arkansas State University
State University, AR 72467
$20, Janelle Collins

Armchair/Shotgun
377 Flatbush Avenue, #3
Brooklyn, NY 11238

Arroyo
Department of English
California State University, East Bay
25800 Carlos Bee Boulevard
Hayward, CA 94542

Arts and Letters
Campus Box 89
Georgia College and State University
Milledgeville, GA 31061
$15, Martin Lammon

Ascent
English Department
Concordia College
readthebestwriting.com
W. Scott Olsen

Assisi
http://www.sfc.edu/acadmics/publications/assisi#issue
Wendy Galgan

The Atlantic
600 NH Avenue NW
Washington, DC 20037
$39.95, C. Michael Curtis

Baltimore Review
P.O. Box 36418
Towson, MD 21286

Bayou
Department of English
University of New Orleans
2000 Lakeshore Drive
New Orleans, LA 70148
$15, Joanna Leake

Bear Deluxe
810 SE Belmont, Studio 5
Portland, OR 97214
$20, Tom Webb

The Believer
849 Valencia Street

San Francisco, CA 94110
Heidi Julavits

Bellevue Literary Review
Department of Medicine
New York University School of Medicine
550 First Avenue
New York, NY 10016
$15, Danielle Ofri

Bellingham Review
MS-9053
Western Washington University
Bellingham, WA 98225
$12, Brenda Miller

Bellowing Ark
P.O. Box 55564
Shoreline, WA 98155
$20, Robert Ward

Blackbird
Department of English
Virginia Commonwealth University
P.O. Box 843082
Richmond, VA 23284-3082
Gregory Donovan, Mary Flinn

Black Clock
California Institute of the Arts
24700 McBean Parkway
Valencia, CA 91355
Steve Erickson

Black Warrior Review
P.O. Box 862936
Tuscaloosa, AL 35486-0027
$16, Farren Stanley

Blue Mesa Review
The Creative Writing Program
University of New Mexico
MSC03-2170
Albuquerque, NM 87131
Samantha Tetangco

Bomb
New Art Publications
80 Hanson Place
Brooklyn, NY 11217
$22, Betsy Sussler

Bosque
http://www.abqwriterscoop.com/bosque.html
Lisa Lenard-Cook

Boston Review
P.O. Box 425
Cambridge, MA 02142
$25, Joshua Cohen, Deborah Chasman

Boulevard
PMB 325
6614 Clayton Road
Richmond Heights, MO 63117
$20, Richard Burgin

Brain, Child: The Magazine for Thinking Mothers
P.O. Box 714
Lexington, VA 24450-0714
$22, Jennifer Niesslein, Stephanie Wilkinson

Briar Cliff Review
3303 Rebecca Street
P.O. Box 2100
Sioux City, IA 51104-2100
$10, Tricia Currans-Sheehan

Bull: Men's Fiction
343 Parkorash Avenue

South Bend, IN 46617
Janett Haley

Byliner
hello@byliner.com
Mark Bryant

Callaloo
Callalloo.tamu.edu
$50, Charles H. Rowell

Calyx
P.O. Box B
Corvallis, OR 097339
$23, the collective

Camera Obscura
obscurajournal.com
M. E. Parker

Canteen
96 Pierrepont Street, #4
Brooklyn, NY 11201
$35, Stephen Pierson

Carolina Quarterly
Greenlaw Hall
CB #3520
University of North Carolina
Chapel Hill, NC 27599
$24, editors

Carve Magazine
Carvezine.com
$39.95, Matthew Limpede

Chariton Review
Truman State University
100 E. Normal Avenue
Kinesville, MO 63501
$20, James D'Agostino

Chattahoochee Review
www.chattahoochee-review.org
Anna Schachner

Chautauqua
Department of Creative Writing
University of North Carolina, Wilmington
601 S. College Road
Wilmington, NC 28403
$14.95, Jill and Philip Gerard

Chicago Quarterly Review
www.chicagoquaterlyreview.com
$17, S. Afzal Haider

Chicago Review
5801 South Kenwood
University of Chicago
Chicago, IL 60637
$25, Ben Merriman

Cimarron Review
205 Morrill Hall
Oklahoma State University
Stillwater, OK 74078-4069
$32, Toni Graham

Cincinnati Review
Department of English
McMicken Hall, Room 369
P.O. Box 210069
Cincinnati, OH 45221
$15, Michael Griffith

Coffin Factory
Thecoffinfactory.com
Laura Isaacman

Colorado Review
Department of English

Colorado State University
Fort Collins, CO 80523
$24, Stephanie G'Schwind

Columbia
Columbia University Alumni Center
622 W. 113th Street
MC4521
New York, NY 10025
$50, Michael B. Sharleson

Commentary
165 East 56th Street
New York, NY 10022
$45, Neal Kozody

The Common
Thecommononline.org/submit
$30, Jennifer Acker

Confrontation
English Department
C. W. Post College of Long Island University
Brookville, NY 11548
$15, Jenna G. Semeiks

Conjunctions
21 East 10th Street, Suite 3E
New York, NY 10003
$18, Bradford Morrow

Crab Orchard Review
Department of English
Faner Hall 2380
Southern Illinois University at Carbondale
1000 Faner Drive
Carbondale, IL 62901
$20, Carolyn Alessio

Crazyhorse
Department of English
College of Charleston
66 George Street
Charleston, SC 29424
$20, Anthony Varallo

Cream City Review
Department of English
University of Wisconsin, Milwaukee
Box 413
Milwaukee, WI 53201
$22, Ann McBree

Crucible
Barton Collge
P.O. Box 5000
Wilson, NC 27893
$16, Terrence L. Grimes

Cutbank
Department of English
University of Montana
Missoula, MT 59812
$15, Josh Fomon

Daedalus
136 Irving Street, Suite 100
Cambridge, MA 02138
$41, James Miller

Denver Quarterly
University of Denver
Denver, CO 80208
$20, Bin Ramke

Descant
P.O. Box 314
Station P
Toronto, Ontario M5S 2S8
$28, Karen Mulhallen

descant
Department of English
Texas Christian University
TCU Box 297270
Fort Worth, TX 76129
$12, Dave Kuhne

Dogwood
Department of English
Fairfield University
1073 N. Benson Road
Fairfield, CT 06824
Pete Duval

Drash
2632 NE 80th Street
Temple Beth Am
Seattle, WA 98115
$11, Wendy Marcus

Ecotone
Department of Creative Writing
University of North Carolina, Wilmington
601 South College Road
Wilmington, NC 28403
$16.95, David Gessner

Electric Literature
electricliterature.com
Andy Hunter, Scott Lindenbaum

Eleven Eleven
California College of the Arts
1111 Eighth Street
San Francisco, CA 94107
Hugh Behm-Steinberg

Epiphany
www.epiphanyzine.com
$20, Willard Cook

Epoch
251 Goldwin Smith Hall
Cornell University
Ithaca, NY 14853-3201
$11, Michael Koch

Esquire
300 West 57th Street, 21st Floor
New York, NY 10019
$17.94, Fiction Editor

Event
Douglas College
P.O. Box 2503
New Westminster,
British Columbia V3L 5B2
$29.95, Christine Dewar

Fantasy and Science Fiction
P.O. Box 3447
Hoboken, NJ 07030
$39, Gordon Van Gelder

Farallon Review
1017 L Street, #348
Sacramento, CA 95814
$10, The Editors

Fiction
Department of English
The City College of New York
Convent Avenue at 138th Street
New York, NY 10031
$38, Mark Jay Mirsky

Fiction International
Department of English and Comparative Literature
5500 Campanile Drive
San Diego State University
San Diego, CA 92182
$18, Harold Jaffe

The Fiddlehead
Campus House
11 Garland Court

UNB P.O. Box 4400
Fredericton,
New Brunswick E3B 5A3
$30, Mark Anthony Jarman

Fifth Wednesday
www.fifthwednesdayjournal.org
$20, Vern Miller

Five Points
Georgia State University
P.O. Box 3999
Atlanta, GA 30302
$21, David Bottoms and Megan Sexton

Fjords Review
www.fjordsreview.com
$12, John Gosslee

Florida Review
Department of English
P.O. Box 161346
University of Central Florida
Orlando, FL 32816
$15, Jocelyn Bartkevicius

Flyway
206 Ross Hall
Department of English
Iowa State University
Ames, IA 50011
$24, Genevieve DuBois

Fourteen Hills
Department of Creative Writing
San Francisco State University
1600 Halloway Avenue
San Francisco, CA 94132-1722
$15, Stephanie Doeing

Fugue
uidaho.edu/fugue
$18, Warren Bromley-Vogel

Gargoyle
3819 North 13th Street
Arlington, VA 22201
$30, Lucinda Ebersole, Richard Peabody

Gemini
P.O. Box 1485
Onset, MA 02558
David Bright

Georgetown Review
400 E. College Street
Box 227
Georgetown, KY 40324
$5, Steven Carter

Georgia Review
Gilbert Hall
University of Georgia
Athens, GA 30602
$35, Stephen Corey

Gettysburg Review
Gettysburg College
300 N. Washington Street
Gettysburg, PA 17325
$28, Peter Stitt

Ghost Town/The Pacific Review
Department of English
California State University, San Bernadino
5500 University Parkway
San Bernadino, CA 92407
Tim Manifesta

Glimmer Train
1211 NW Glisan Street, Suite 207
Portland, OR 97209
$38, Susan Burmeister-Brown, Linda Swanson-Davies

Good Housekeeping
300 West 57th Street
New York, NY 10019
Laura Matthews

Grain
Box 67
Saskatoon, Saskatchewan 57K 3K9
$35, Rilla Friesen

Granta
841 Broadway, 4th Floor
New York, NY 10019-3780
$48, John Freeman

Grasslands Review
Creative Writing Program
Department of English
Indiana State University
Terre Haute, IN 47809
$8, Brenda Corcoran

Gray's Sporting Journal
P.O. Box 1207
Augusta, GA 30903
$36.95, James R. Rabb

Green Mountains Review
Box A58
Johnson State College
Johnson, VT 05656
$15, Leslie Daniels

Greensboro Review
3302 Hall for Humanities
and Research Administration
University of North Carolina
Greensboro, NC 27402
$14, Jim Clark

Grey Sparrow
P.O. Box 211664
Saint Paul, MN 55121
Diane Smith

Guernica
P.O. Box 219 Cooper Station
New York, NY 10276
Meakin Armstrong

Gulf Coast
Department of English
University of Houston
Houston, TX 77204-3012
$16, Nick Flynn

Hanging Loose
231 Wyckoff Street
Brooklyn, NY 11217
$27, group

Harper's Magazine
666 Broadway
New York, NY 10012
$16.79, Ben Metcalf

Harpur Palate
Department of English
Binghamton University
P.O. Box 6000
Binghamton, NY 13902
$16, Barrett Bowlin

Harvard Review
Lamont Library
Harvard University
Cambridge, MA 02138
$20, Christina Thompson

Hawaii Review
Department of English
University of Hawaii at Manoa
P.O. Box 11674
Honolulu, HI 96828
$10, Stephanie Mizushima

Hayden's Ferry Review
Box 807302
Arizona State University
Tempe, AZ 85287
$25, Angie Dell

High Desert Journal
P.O. Box 7647
Bend, OR 97708
$16, Elizabeth Quinn

Hobart
P.O. Box 11658
Ann Arbor, MI 48106
$18, Aaron Burch

Hotel Amerika
Columbia College
English Department
600 S. Michigan Avenue
Chicago, IL 60657
$18, David Lazar

Hudson Review
684 Park Avenue
New York, NY 10065
$36, Paula Deitz

Hunger Mountain
www.hungermtn.org
$12, Miciah Boy Gault

Idaho Review
Boise State University
1910 University Drive
Boise, ID 83725
$10, Mitch Wieland

Image
Center for Religious Humanism
3307 Third Avenue West
Seattle, WA 98119
$39.95, Gregory Wolfe

Indiana Review
Ballantine Hall 465
1020 East Kirkwood Avenue
Bloomington, IN 47405-7103
$20, Jennifer Luebbers

Inkwell
Manhattanville College
2900 Purchase Street
Purchase, NY 10577
$10, Todd Bowes

Iowa Review
Department of English
University of Iowa
308 EPB
Iowa City, IA 52242
$25, Russell Scott Valentino

Iron Horse Literary Review
Department of English
Texas Tech University
Box 43091
Lubbock, TX 79409-3091
$15, Leslie Jill Patterson

Isotope
Utah State University
3200 Old Main Hill
Logan, UT 84322
$15, the editors

Italian Americana
University of Rhode Island
Providence Campus
80 Washington Street
Providence, RI 02903
$20, Carol Bonomo Albright

Jabberwock Review
Department of English
Drawer E
Mississippi State University

Mississippi State, MS 39762
$15, Michael P. Kardos

Jelly Bucket
www.jellybucket.org
Lindsey S. Flantz

Jewish Currents
45 East 33rd Street
New York, NY 10016-5335
$25, editorial board

The Journal
The Ohio State University
Department of English
164 W. 17th Avenue
Columbus, OH 43210
$15, Kathy Fagon

Joyland
joylandmagazine.com
Emily Schultz

Juked
220 Atkinson Drive, #B
Tallahassee, FL 32304
$10, J. W. Wang

Kenyon Review
www.kenyonreview.org
$30, the editors

Kugelmass
http://firewheel-editions.org/
kugelmass
$26, David Holub

Lady Churchill's Rosebud Wristlet
Small Beer Press
150 Pleasant Street
Easthampton, MA 01027
$20, Kelly Link

Lake Effect
Penn State Erie
4951 College Drive
Erie, PA 16563-1501
$6, George Looney

Lalitamba
P.O. Box 131
Planetarium Station
New York, NY 10024
$12, Florence Homolka

The Literarian
www.centerforfiction.org
Dawn Raffel

Literary Review
Fairleigh Dickinson University
285 Madison Avenue
Madison, NJ 07940
$24, Minna Proctor

Little Patuxent Review
6012 Jamina Downs
Columbia, MD 21045
Laura Shovan

Los Angeles Review
redhen.org/losangelesreview
$20, Kate Gale

Louisiana Literature
SLU-10792
Southeastern Louisiana University
Hammond, LA 70402
$12, Jack B. Bedell

Louisville Review
Spalding University
851 South Fourth Street
Louisville, KY 40203
$14, Sena Jeter Naslund

Lumina
Sarah Lawrence College
Slonim House
One Mead Way
Bronxville, NY 10708
Lillian Ho

Madison Review
University of Wisconsin
Department of English
H. C. White Hall
600 North Park Street
Madison, WI 53706
$25, Elzbieta Beck

Make
www.makemag.com
Sarah Dodson

Mānoa
English Department
University of Hawaii
Honolulu, HI 96822
$30, Frank Stewart

Massachusetts Review
South College
University of Massachusetts
Amherst, MA 01003
$29, Ellen Doré Watson

McSweeney's
826 Valencia Street
San Francisco, CA 94110
$55, Dave Eggers

Memorious
521 Winston Drive
Vestal, NY 13850
Rebecca Morgan Frank

Meridian
Department of English
P.O. Box 400145
University of Virginia
Charlottesville, VA 22904-4145
$12, Julianna Daugherty

Michigan Quarterly Review
0576 Rackham Building
915 East Washington Street
University of Michigan
Ann Arbor, MI 48109
$25, Jonathan Freedman

Mid-American Review
Department of English
Bowling Green State University
Bowling Green, OH 43403
$12, Michael Czyzniejewski

Minnesota Review
ASPECT Virginia Tech
202 Major Williams Hall (0192)
Blacksburg, VA 24061
$30, Jeffrey Williams

Mississippi Review
University of Southern
Mississippi
118 College Drive #5144
Hattiesburg, MS 39406-5144
$15, Julia Johnson

Missouri Review
357 McReynolds Hall
University of Missouri
Columbia, MO 65211
$24, Speer Morgan

Montana Quarterly
2820 W. College Street
Bozeman, MT 59771
Megan Ault Regnerus

Mount Hope
www.mounthopemagazine.com
$20, Edward J. Delaney

n + 1
68 Jay Street, #405
Brooklyn, NY 11201
$30, Keith Gessen, Mark Greif

Narrative Magazine
narrativemagazine.com
the editors

Nashville Review
331 Benson Hall
Vanderbilt University
Nashville, TN 37203
Matthew Maker

Natural Bridge
Department of English
University of Missouri, St. Louis
St. Louis, MO 63121
$10, Mary Troy

New England Review
Middlebury College
Middlebury, VT 05753
$30, Carolyn Kuebler

New Letters
University of Missouri
5101 Rockhill Road
Kansas City, MO 64110
$22, Robert Stewart

New Madrid
www.newmadridjournal.org
$15, Ann Neelon

New Millennium Writings
www.newmillenniumwritings.com
$12, Don Williams

New Ohio Review
English Department
360 Ellis Hall
Ohio University
Athens, OH 45701
$20, John Bullock

New Orphic Review
706 Mill Street
Nelson, British Columbia V1L 4S5
$30, Ernest Hekkanen

New Quarterly
Saint Jerome's University
290 Westmount Road
N. Waterloo, Ontario N2L 3G3
$36, Kim Jernigan

New South
www.reivew.gsu.edu
$8, Matt Sailor

The New Yorker
4 Times Square
New York, NY 10036
$46, Deborah Treisman

New York Tyrant
676A Ninth Avenue, #153
New York, NY 10036
Giancarlo Di'Trapano

Nimrod International Journal
Arts and Humanities Council of Tulsa
600 South College Avenue
Tulsa, OK 74104
$17.50, Francine Ringold

Ninth Letter
Department of English
University of Illinois
608 South Wright Street
Urbana, IL 61801
$21.95, Jodee Rubins

Noon
1324 Lexington Avenue

PMB 298
New York, NY 10128
$12, Diane Williams

The Normal School
5245 North Backer Avenue
M/S PB 98
California State University
Fresno, CA 93470
$5, Sophie Beck

North American Review
University of Northern Iowa
1222 West 27th Street
Cedar Falls, IA 50614
$22, Grant Tracey

North Carolina Literary Review
Department of English
Mailstop 555 English
East Carolina University
Greenville, NC 27858-4353
$25, Margaret Bauer

North Dakota Quarterly
University of North Dakota
Merrifield Hall, Room 110
276 Centennial Drive, Stop 27209
Grand Forks, ND 58202
$25, Robert Lewis

Northern New England Review
Humanities Department
Franklin Pierce University
Rindge, NH 03461
$5, Edie Clark

Northwest Review
5243 University of Oregon
Eugene, OR 97403
$20, Ehud Havazelet

Notre Dame Review
840 Flanner Hall
Department of English
University of Notre Dame
Notre Dame, IN 46556
$15, John Matthias, William O'Rourke

One Story
232 Third Street, #A111
Brooklyn, NY 11215
$21, Maribeth Batcha, Hannah Tinti

Open City
270 Lafayette Street, Suite 1412
New York, NY 10012
$30, Thomas Beller, Joanna Yas

Orion
187 Main Street
Great Barrington, MA 01230
$35, the editors

Oxford American
201 Donaghey Avenue, Main 107
Conway, AR 72035
$24.95, Marc Smirnoff

Pak N Treger
National Yiddish Book Center
Harry and Jeanette Weinberg Bldg.
1021 West Street
Amherst, MA 01002
$36, Aaron Lansky

Paris Review
62 White Street
New York, NY 10013
$34, Lorin Stein

Pearl
3030 East Second Street
Long Beach, CA 90803
$21, Joan Jobe Smith

PEN America
PEN America Center

588 Broadway, Suite 303
New York, NY 10012
$10, M Mark

Per Contra
250 S. 13th Street, #10B
Philadelphia, PA 19107
Miriam N. Kotzin

Persimmon Tree
www.persimmontree.org
Sue Leonard

Phoebe
MSN 2C5
George Mason University
4400 University Drive
Fairax, VA 22030
$12, Brian Koen

The Pinch
Department of English
University of Memphis
Memphis, TN 38152
$28, Kristen Iverson

Playboy
730 Fifth Avenue
New York, NY 10019

Pleiades
Department of English and Philosophy
University of Central Missouri
Warrensburg, MO 64093
$18, Wayne Miller

Ploughshares
Emerson College
120 Boylston Street
Boston, MA 02116
$30, Ladette Randolph

PoemMemoirStory
HB 217
1530 Third Avenue South
Birmingham, AL 35294
$7, Kerry Madden

Post Road
postroadmag.com
$18, Rebecca Boyd

Potomac Review
Montgomery College
51 Mannakee Street
Rockville, MD 20850
$20, Julie Wakeman-Linn

Prairie Fire
423-100 Arthur Street
Winnipeg, Manitoba
R3B 1H3
$30, Andris Taskans

Prairie Schooner
201 Andrews Hall
University of Nebraska
Lincoln, NE 68588-0334
$28, Kwame Dawes

Prism International
Department of Creative Writing
University of British Columbia
Buchanan E-462
Vancouver, British Columbia
V6T 1Z1
$28, Cara Woodruff

A Public Space
323 Dean Street
Brooklyn, NY 11217
$36, Brigid Hughes

Puerto del Sol
MSC 3E

New Mexico State University
P.O. Box 30001
Las Cruces, NM 88003
$20, Evan Lavender-Smith

Redivider
Emerson College
120 Boylston Street
Boston, MA 02116
$10, Matt Salesses

Red Rock Review
English Department, J2A
Community College of Southern Nevada
3200 East Cheyenne Avenue
North Las Vegas, NV 89030
$9.50, Richard Logsdon

Reed
One Washington Square
San Jose, CA 95192
Nick Taylor

River Oak Review
Elmhurst College
190 Prospect Avenue
Box 2633
Elmhurst, IL 60126
$12, Ron Wiginton

River Styx
3547 Olive Street,
Suite 107
St. Louis, MO 63103-1014
$20, Richard Newman

Roanoke Review
221 College Lane
Salem, VA 24153
$5, Paul Hanstedt

Room Magazine
P.O. Box 46160
Station D
Vancouver, British Columbia
V6J 5G5
$10, Clélie Rich

Ruminate
140 N. Roosevelt Avenue
Ft. Collins, CO 80521
$28, Brianna Van Dyke

Salamander
Suffolk University
English Department
41 Temple Street
Boston, MA 02114
$23, Jennifer Barber

Salmagundi
Skidmore College
Saratoga Springs, NY 12866
$20, Robert Boyers

Salt Hill
salthilljournal.com
$15, Kayla Blatchley

Santa Clara Review
Santa Clara University
500 El Camino Road,
Box 3212
Santa Clara, CA 95053
$16, Nick Sanchez

Santa Monica Review
1900 Pico Boulevard
Santa Monica, CA 90405
$12, Andrew Tonkovich

Seattle Review
P.O. Box 354330
University of Washington
Seattle, WA 98195
$20, Andrew Feld

Sewanee Review
735 University Avenue
Sewanee, TN 37383
$25, George Core

Shenandoah
Mattingly House
2 Lee Avenue
Washington and Lee University
Lexington, VA 24450-2116
$25, R. T. Smith, Lynn Leech

Slake
P.O. Box 385
2658 Griffith Park Boulevard
Los Angeles, CA 90039
$60, Joe Donnelly

Slice
www.slicemagazine.org
Elizabeth Blachman

Sonora Review
Department of English
University of Arizona
Tucson, AZ 85721
$16, Astrid Duffy

So To Speak
George Mason University
4400 University Drive
MSN 2C5
Fairfax, VA 22030

South Carolina Review
Center for Electronic and Digital Publishing
Clemson University
Strode Tower
Box 340522
Clemson, SC 29634
$28, Wayne Chapman

South Dakota Review
University of South Dakota
414 E. Clark Street
Vermilion, SD 57069
$30, Lee Ann Roripaugh

Southeast Review
Department of English
Florida State University
Tallahassee, FL 32306
$15, Katie Cortese

Southern Humanities Review
9088 Haley Center
Auburn University
Auburn, AL 36849
$18, Chantal Acevedo

Southern Indiana Review
College of Liberal Arts
University of Southern Indiana
8600 University Boulevard
Evansville, IN 47712
$20, Ron Mitchell

Southern Review
3990 W. Lakeshore Drive
Louisiana State University
Baton Rouge, LA 70808
$40, Cora Blue Adams

Southwest Review
Southern Methodist University
P.O. Box 750374
Dallas, TX 75275
$30, Willard Spiegelman

Sou'wester
Department of English
Box 1438
Southern Illinois University
Edwardsville, IL 62026
Adrian Matejka

Subtropics
Department of English
University of Florida
P.O. Box 112075
Gainesville, FL 32611-2075
$21, David Leavitt

The Sun
107 North Roberson Street
Chapel Hill, NC 27516
$39, Sy Safransky

Sycamore Review
Department of English
500 Oval Drive
Purdue University
West Lafayette, IN 47907
$16, Jessica Jacobs

Tampa Review
The University of Tampa
401 W. Kennedy Boulevard
Tampa, FL 33606
$22, Richard Mathews

Third Coast
Department of English
Western Michigan University
Kalamazoo, MI 49008
$16, Emily J. Stinson

Threepenny Review
2163 Vine Street
Berkeley, CA 94709
$25, Wendy Lesser

Timber Creek Review
8969 UNCG Station
Greensboro, NC 27413
$17, John Freiermuth

Tin House
P.O. Box 10500
Portland, OR 97296-0500
$50, Rob Spillman

TriQuarterly
629 Noyes Street
Evanston, IL 60208
$24, Susan Firestone Hahn

Unstuck
unstuckbooks.submittable.com
Matt Williamson

Upstreet
P.O. Box 105
Richmond, MA 01254
$10, Vivian Dorsel

Vermont Literary Review
Department of English
Castleton State College
Castleton, VT 05735
Flo Keyes

Virginia Quarterly Review
One West Range
P.O. Box 400223
Charlottesville, VA 22903
$32, Ted Genoways

Wake: Great Lakes Thought and Culture
www.wakegreatlakes.org
Chris Haven

War, Literature, and the Arts
Department of English
and Fine Arts
2354 Fairchild Drive, Suite 6D45
USAF Academy, CO 80840-6242
$10, Donald Anderson

Water-Stone Review
Graduate School of Liberal Studies

Hamline University, MS-A1730
1536 Hewitt Avenue
Saint Paul, MN 55104
$32, the editors

Weber Studies
Weber State University
1405 University Circle
Ogden, UT 84408-1214
$20, Michael Wutz

West Branch
Bucknell Hall
Bucknell University
Lewisburg, PA 17837
$10, G. C. Waldrep

Westchester Review
P.O. Box 246H
Scarsdale, NY 10583
$10, JoAnn Duncan Terdiman

Western Humanities Review
University of Utah
255 South Central Campus Drive
Room 3500
Salt Lake City, UT 84112
$21, Barry Weller

Willow Springs
Eastern Washington University
501 N. Riverpoint Boulevard
Spokane, WA 99201
$18, Samuel Ligon

Witness
Black Mountain Institute
University of Nevada
Las Vegas, NV 89154
$10, Amber Withycombe

World Literature Today
The University of Oklahoma
630 Parrington Oval, Suite 110
Norman, OK 73019
Michelle Johnson

Yale Review
P.O. Box 208243
New Haven, CT 06520-8243
$36, J. D. McClatchy

Zoetrope: All-Story
The Sentinel Building
916 Kearney Street
San Francisco, CA 94133
$24, Michael Ray

Zone 3
APSU
Box 4565
Clarksville, TN 37044
$10, Barry Kitterman

ZYZZYVA
466 Geary Street, #401
San Francisco, CA 94102
$40, Laura Cogan